Unequaled praise from everywhere for a unique bestseller—

Harper Lee's To Kill A Mockingbird

The New York Times: "Marvelous . . . Miss Lee's original characters are people to cherish in this winning first novel."

Harper's Magazine: "A novel of great sweetness, humor, compassion, and of mystery carefully sustained."

Boston Herald: "Has pace and power . . . overflowing with life."

The New Yorker: "Skilled, unpretentious and totally ingenuous . . . tough, melodramatic, acute, funny."

San Francisco Examiner: "Miss Lee wonderfully builds the tranquil atmosphere of her Southern town, and as adroitly causes it to erupt a shocking lava of emotions."

(continued on next page)

TO KILL A MOCKINGBIRD

By HARPER LEE

WARNER BOOKS

A Warner Communications Company

WARNER BOOKS EDITION

Copyright © 1960 by Harper Lee
All rights reserved.

Published by arrangement with J. B. Lippincott Company, Subsidiary of
Harper & Row Publishers, Inc., East Washington Square, Philadelphia,
Pennsylvania 19105.

Warner Books, Inc.
666 Fifth Avenue
New York, N.Y. 10103

 A Warner Communications Company

Printed in the United States of America

First Warner Books Printing: December, 1982

25   24   23   22   21

Lawyers, I suppose, were children once.
CHARLES LAMB

PART ONE

1.

When he was nearly thirteen, my brother Jem got his arm badly broken at the elbow. When it healed, and Jem's fears of never being able to play football were assuaged, he was seldom self-conscious about his injury. His left arm was somewhat shorter than his right; when he stood or walked, the back of his hand was at right angles to his body, his thumb parallel to his thigh. He couldn't have cared less, so long as he could pass and punt.

When enough years had gone by to enable us to look back on them, we sometimes discussed the events leading to his accident. I maintain that the Ewells started it all, but Jem, who was four years my senior, said it started long before that. He said it began the summer Dill came to us, when Dill first gave us the idea of making Boo Radley come out.

I said if he wanted to take a broad view of the thing, it really began with Andrew Jackson. If General Jackson hadn't run the Creeks up the creek, Simon Finch would never have paddled up the Alabama, and where would we be if he hadn't? We were far too old to settle an argument with a fist-fight, so we consulted Atticus. Our father said we were both right.

Being Southerners, it was a source of shame to some members of the family that we had no recorded ancestors on either side of the Battle of Hastings. All we had was Simon Finch, a fur-trapping apothecary from Cornwall whose piety was exceeded only by his stinginess. In England, Simon was irritated by the persecution of those who called themselves Methodists at the hands of their more liberal brethren, and as Simon called himself a Methodist, he worked his way across the Atlantic to Philadelphia, thence to Jamaica, thence to Mobile, and up the Saint Stephens. Mindful of John Wesley's strictures on the use of many words in buying and selling, Simon made a pile practicing medicine, but in this pursuit he was unhappy lest he be tempted into doing what he knew was not for the glory of God, as the putting on of gold and costly apparel. So Simon, having forgotten his teacher's dictum on the possession of human chattels, bought three slaves and with their aid established a homestead on the banks of the Alabama River some forty miles above Saint Stephens. He returned to Saint Stephens only once, to find a wife, and with her established a line that ran high to daughters. Simon lived to an impressive age and died rich.

It was customary for the men in the family to remain on Simon's homestead, Finch's Landing, and make their living from cotton. The place was self-sufficient: modest in comparison with the empires around it, the Landing nevertheless produced everything required to sustain life except ice, wheat flour, and articles of clothing, supplied by river-boats from Mobile.

Simon would have regarded with impotent fury the disturbance between the North and the South, as it left his descendants stripped of everything but their land, yet the tradition of living on the land remained unbroken until well into the twentieth century, when my father, Atticus Finch, went to Montgomery to read law, and his younger brother went to Boston to study medicine. Their sister Alexandra was the Finch who remained at the Landing: she married a taciturn man who spent most of his time lying in a hammock by the river wondering if his trot-lines were full.

When my father was admitted to the bar, he returned to Maycomb and began his practice. Maycomb, some twenty miles east of Finch's Landing, was the county seat of Maycomb County. Atticus's office in the courthouse contained little more than a hat rack, a spittoon, a checkerboard and an unsullied Code of Alabama. His first two clients were the last two persons hanged in the Maycomb County jail. Atticus had urged them to accept the state's generosity in allowing them to plead Guilty to second-degree murder and escape with their lives, but they were Haverfords, in Maycomb County a name synonymous with jackass. The Haverfords had dispatched Maycomb's leading blacksmith in a misunderstanding arising from the alleged wrongful detention of a mare, were imprudent enough to do it in the presence of three witnesses, and insisted that the-son-of-a-bitch-had-it-coming-to-him was a good enough defense for anybody. They persisted in pleading Not Guilty to first-degree murder, so there was nothing much Atticus could do for his clients except be present at their departure, an occasion that was probably the beginning of my father's profound distaste for the practice of criminal law.

During his first five years in Maycomb, Atticus practiced economy more than anything; for several years thereafter he invested his earnings in his brother's education. John Hale Finch was ten years younger than my father, and chose to study medicine at a time when cotton was not worth growing; but after getting Uncle Jack started, Atticus derived a reasonable income from the law. He liked Maycomb, he was Maycomb County born and bred; he knew his people, they knew him, and because of Simon Finch's industry, Atticus was related by blood or marriage to nearly every family in the town.

Maycomb was an old town, but it was a tired old town when I first knew it. In rainy weather the streets turned to red slop; grass grew on the sidewalks, the courthouse sagged in the square. Somehow, it was hotter then:

a black dog suffered on a summer's day; bony mules hitched to Hoover carts flicked flies in the sweltering shade of the live oaks on the square. Men's stiff collars wilted by nine in the morning. Ladies bathed before noon, after their three-o'clock naps, and by nightfall were like soft teacakes with frostings of sweat and sweet talcum.

People moved slowly then. They ambled across the square, shuffled in and out of the stores around it, took their time about everything. A day was twenty-four hours long but seemed longer. There was no hurry, for there was nowhere to go, nothing to buy and no money to buy it with, nothing to see outside the boundaries of Maycomb County. But it was a time of vague optimism for some of the people: Maycomb County had recently been told that it had nothing to fear but fear itself.

We lived on the main residential street in town—Atticus, Jem and I, plus Calpurnia our cook. Jem and I found our father satisfactory: he played with us, read to us, and treated us with courteous detachment.

Calpurnia was something else again. She was all angles and bones; she was nearsighted; she squinted; her hand was wide as a bed slat and twice as hard. She was always ordering me out of the kitchen, asking me why I couldn't behave as well as Jem when she knew he was older, and calling me home when I wasn't ready to come. Our battles were epic and one-sided. Calpurnia always won, mainly because Atticus always took her side. She had been with us ever since Jem was born, and I had felt her tyrannical presence as long as I could remember.

Our mother died when I was two, so I never felt her absence. She was a Graham from Montgomery; Atticus met her when he was first elected to the state legislature. He was middle-aged then, she was fifteen years his junior. Jem was the product of their first year of marriage; four years later I was born, and two years later our mother died from a sudden heart attack. They said it ran in her family. I did not miss her, but I think Jem did. He remembered her clearly, and sometimes in the middle of a game he would sigh at length, then go off and play by himself behind the car-house. When he was like that, I knew better than to bother him.

When I was almost six and Jem was nearly ten, our

summertime boundaries (within calling distance of Calpurnia) were Mrs. Henry Lafayette Dubose's house two doors to the north of us, and the Radley Place three doors to the south. We were never tempted to break them. The Radley Place was inhabited by an unknown entity the mere description of whom was enough to make us behave for days on end; Mrs. Dubose was plain hell.

That was the summer Dill came to us.

Early one morning as we were beginning our day's play in the back yard, Jem and I heard something next door in Miss Rachel Haverford's collard patch. We went to the wire fence to see if there was a puppy—Miss Rachel's rat terrier was expecting—instead we found someone sitting looking at us. Sitting down, he wasn't much higher than the collards. We stared at him until he spoke:

"Hey."

"Hey yourself," said Jem pleasantly.

"I'm Charles Baker Harris," he said. "I can read."

"So what?" I said.

"I just thought you'd like to know I can read. You got anything needs readin' I can do it. . . ."

"How old are you," asked Jem, "four-and-a-half?"

"Goin' on seven."

"Shoot no wonder, then," said Jem, jerking his thumb at me. "Scout yonder's been readin' ever since she was born, and she ain't even started to school yet. You look right puny for goin' on seven."

"I'm little but I'm old," he said.

Jem brushed his hair back to get a better look. "Why don't you come over, Charles Baker Harris?" he said. "Lord, what a name."

"'s not any funnier'n yours. Aunt Rachel says your name's Jeremy Atticus Finch."

Jem scowled. "I'm big enough to fit mine," he said. "Your name's longer'n you are. Bet it's a foot longer."

"Folks call me Dill," said Dill, struggling under the fence.

"Do better if you go over it instead of under it," I said. "Where'd you come from?"

Dill was from Meridian, Mississippi, was spending the summer with his aunt, Miss Rachel, and would be spending every summer in Maycomb from now on. His family was from Maycomb County originally, his mother worked for a photographer in Meridian, had entered his picture in a Beautiful Child contest and won five dollars. She gave the money to Dill, who went to the picture show twenty times on it.

"Don't have any picture shows here, except Jesus ones in the courthouse sometimes," said Jem. "Ever see anything good?"

Dill had seen *Dracula*, a revelation that moved Jem to eye him with the beginning of respect. "Tell it to us," he said.

Dill was a curiosity. He wore blue linen shorts that buttoned to his shirt, his hair was snow white and stuck to his head like duckfluff; he was a year my senior but I towered over him. As he told us the old tale his blue eyes would lighten and darken; his laugh was sudden and happy; he habitually pulled at a cowlick in the center of his forehead.

When Dill reduced Dracula to dust, and Jem said the show sounded better than the book, I asked Dill where his father was: "You ain't said anything about him."

"I haven't got one."

"Is he dead?"

"No . . ."

"Then if he's not dead you've got one, haven't you?"

Dill blushed and Jem told me to hush, a sure sign that Dill had been studied and found acceptable. Thereafter the summer passed in routine contentment. Routine contentment was: improving our treehouse that rested between giant twin chinaberry trees in the back yard, fussing, running through our list of dramas based on the works of Oliver Optic, Victor Appleton, and Edgar Rice Burroughs. In this matter we were lucky to have Dill. He played the character parts formerly thrust upon me—the ape in *Tarzan*, Mr. Crabtree in *The Rover Boys*, Mr. Damon in *Tom Swift*. Thus we came to know Dill as a pocket Merlin, whose head teemed with eccentric plans, strange longings, and quaint fancies.

But by the end of August our repertoire was vapid from countless reproductions, and it was then that Dill gave us the idea of making Boo Radley come out.

The Radley Place fascinated Dill. In spite of our warnings and explanations it drew him as the moon draws water, but drew him no nearer than the light-pole on the corner, a safe distance from the Radley gate. There he would stand, his arm around the fat pole, staring and wondering.

The Radley Place jutted into a sharp curve beyond our house. Walking south, one faced its porch; the sidewalk turned and ran beside the lot. The house was low, was once white with a deep front porch and green shutters, but had long ago darkened to the color of the slate-gray yard around it. Rain-rotted shingles drooped over the eaves of the veranda; oak trees kept the sun away. The remains of a picket drunkenly guarded the front yard— a "swept" yard that was never swept—where johnson grass and rabbit-tobacco grew in abundance.

Inside the house lived a malevolent phantom. People said he existed, but Jem and I had never seen him. People said he went out at night when the moon was down, and peeped in windows. When people's azaleas froze in a cold snap, it was because he had breathed on them. Any stealthy small crimes committed in Maycomb were his work. Once the town was terrorized by a series of morbid nocturnal events: people's chickens and household pets were found mutilated; although the culprit was Crazy Addie, who eventually drowned himself in Barker's Eddy, people still looked at the Radley Place, unwilling to discard their initial suspicions. A Negro would not pass the Radley Place at night, he would cut across to the sidewalk opposite and whistle as he walked. The Maycomb school grounds adjoined the back of the Radley lot; from the Radley chickenyard tall pecan trees shook their fruit into the schoolyard, but the nuts lay untouched by the children: Radley pecans would kill you. A baseball hit into the Radley yard was a lost ball and no questions asked.

The misery of that house began many years before Jem and I were born. The Radleys, welcome anywhere in town, kept to themselves, a predilection unforgivable in Maycomb. They did not go to church, Maycomb's principal recreation, but worshiped at home; Mrs. Radley seldom if ever crossed the street for a mid-morning coffee break with her neighbors, and certainly never joined a missionary circle. Mr. Radley walked to town at eleven-thirty every morning and came back promptly at twelve,

13

sometimes carrying a brown paper bag that the neighborhood assumed contained the family groceries. I never knew how old Mr. Radley made his living—Jem said he "bought cotton," a polite term for doing nothing—but Mr. Radley and his wife had lived there with their two sons as long as anybody could remember.

The shutters and doors of the Radley house were closed on Sundays, another thing alien to Maycomb's ways: closed doors meant illness and cold weather only. Of all days Sunday was the day for formal afternoon visiting: ladies wore corsets, men wore coats, children wore shoes. But to climb the Radley front steps and call, "He-y," of a Sunday afternoon was something their neighbors never did. The Radley house had no screen doors. I once asked Atticus if it ever had any; Atticus said yes, but before I was born.

According to neighborhood legend, when the younger Radley boy was in his teens he became acquainted with some of the Cunninghams from Old Sarum, an enormous and confusing tribe domiciled in the northern part of the county, and they formed the nearest thing to a gang ever seen in Maycomb. They did little, but enough to be discussed by the town and publicly warned from three pulpits: they hung around the barbershop; they rode the bus to Abbottsville on Sundays and went to the picture show; they attended dances at the county's riverside gambling hell, the Dew-Drop Inn & Fishing Camp; they experimented with stumphole whiskey. Nobody in Maycomb had nerve enough to tell Mr. Radley that his boy was in with the wrong crowd.

One night, in an excessive spurt of high spirits, the boys backed around the square in a borrowed flivver, resisted arrest by Maycomb's ancient beadle, Mr. Conner, and locked him in the courthouse outhouse. The town decided something had to be done; Mr. Conner said he knew who each and every one of them was, and he was bound and determined they wouldn't get away with it, so the boys came before the probate judge on charges of disorderly conduct, disturbing the peace, assault and battery, and using abusive and profane language in the presence and hearing of a female. The judge asked Mr. Conner why he included the last charge; Mr. Conner said they cussed so loud he was sure every lady in Maycomb heard them. The judge decided to send the boys to the state industrial school, where boys were sometimes sent for no other reason than to provide them with food and decent shelter: it was no prison and it was no disgrace. Mr. Radley thought it was. If the judge released Arthur, Mr. Radley would see to it that Arthur gave no further trouble. Knowing that Mr. Radley's word was his bond, the judge was glad to do so.

The other boys attended the industrial school and received the best secondary education to be had in the state; one of them eventually worked his way through engineering school at Auburn. The doors of the Radley house were closed on weekdays as well as Sundays, and Mr. Radley's boy was not seen again for fifteen years.

But there came a day, barely within Jem's memory, when Boo Radley was heard from and was seen by several people, but not by Jem. He said Atticus never talked much about the Radleys: when Jem would question him Atticus's only answer was for him to mind his own business and let the Radleys mind theirs, they had a right to; but when it happened Jem said Atticus shook his head and said, "Mm, mm, mm."

So Jem received most of his information from Miss Stephanie Crawford, a neighborhood scold, who said she knew the whole thing. According to Miss Stephanie, Boo was sitting in the livingroom cutting some items from *The Maycomb Tribune* to paste in his scrapbook. His father entered the room. As Mr. Radley passed by, Boo drove the scissors into his parent's leg, pulled them out, wiped them on his pants, and resumed his activities.

Mrs. Radley ran screaming into the street that Arthur was killing them all, but when the sheriff arrived he found Boo still sitting in the livingroom, cutting up the *Tribune*. He was thirty-three years old then.

Miss Stephanie said old Mr. Radley said no Radley was going to any asylum, when it was suggested that a season in Tuscaloosa might be helpful to Boo. Boo wasn't crazy, he was high-strung at times. It was all right to shut him up, Mr. Radley conceded, but insisted that Boo not be charged with anything: he was not a criminal. The sheriff hadn't the heart to put him in jail alongside Negroes, so Boo was locked in the courthouse basement.

Boo's transition from the basement to back home

15

was nebulous in Jem's memory. Miss Stephanie Crawford said some of the town council told Mr. Radley that if he didn't take Boo back, Boo would die of mold from the damp. Besides, Boo could not live forever on the bounty of the county.

Nobody knew what form of intimidation Mr. Radley employed to keep Boo out of sight, but Jem figured that Mr. Radley kept him chained to the bed most of the time. Atticus said no, it wasn't that sort of thing, that there were other ways of making people into ghosts.

My memory came alive to see Mrs. Radley occasionally open the front door, walk to the edge of the porch, and pour water on her cannas. But every day Jem and I would see Mr. Radley walking to and from town. He was a thin leathery man with colorless eyes, so colorless they did not reflect light. His cheekbones were sharp and his mouth was wide, with a thin upper lip and a full lower lip. Miss Stephanie Crawford said he was so upright he took the word of God as his only law, and we believed her, because Mr. Radley's posture was ramrod straight.

He never spoke to us. When he passed we would look at the ground and say, "Good morning, sir," and he would cough in reply. Mr. Radley's elder son lived in Pensacola; he came home at Christmas, and he was one of the few persons we ever saw enter or leave the place. From the day Mr. Radley took Arthur home, people said the house died.

But there came a day when Atticus told us he'd wear us out if we made any noise in the yard and commissioned Calpurnia to serve in his absence if she heard a sound out of us. Mr. Radley was dying.

He took his time about it. Wooden sawhorses blocked the road at each end of the Radley lot, straw was put down on the sidewalk, traffic was diverted to the back street. Dr. Reynolds parked his car in front of our house and walked to the Radleys' every time he called. Jem and I crept around the yard for days. At last the sawhorses were taken away, and we stood watching from the front porch when Mr. Radley made his final journey past our house.

"There goes the meanest man ever God blew breath into," murmured Calpurnia, and she spat meditatively into the yard. We looked at her in surprise, for Calpurnia rarely commented on the ways of white people.

The neighborhood thought when Mr. Radley went under Boo would come out, but it had another think coming: Boo's elder brother returned from Pensacola and took Mr. Radley's place. The only difference between him and his father was their ages. Jem said Mr. Nathan Radley "bought cotton," too. Mr. Nathan would speak to us, however, when we said good morning, and sometimes we saw him coming from town with a magazine in his hand.

The more we told Dill about the Radleys, the more he wanted to know, the longer he would stand hugging the light-pole on the corner, the more he would wonder.

"Wonder what he does in there," he would murmur. "Looks like he'd just stick his head out the door."

Jem said, "He goes out, all right, when it's pitch dark. Miss Stephanie Crawford said she woke up in the middle of the night one time and saw him looking straight through the window at her . . . said his head was like a skull lookin' at her. Ain't you ever waked up at night and heard him, Dill? He walks like this—" Jem slid his feet through the gravel. "Why do you think Miss Rachel locks up so tight at night? I've seen his tracks in our back yard many a mornin', and one night I heard him scratching on the back screen, but he was gone time Atticus got there."

"Wonder what he looks like?" said Dill.

Jem gave a reasonable description of Boo: Boo was about six-and-a-half feet tall, judging from his tracks; he dined on raw squirrels and any cats he could catch, that's why his hands were bloodstained—if you ate an animal raw, you could never wash the blood off. There was a long jagged scar that ran across his face; what teeth he had were yellow and rotten; his eyes popped, and he drooled most of the time.

"Let's try to make him come out," said Dill. "I'd like to see what he looks like."

Jem said if Dill wanted to get himself killed, all he had to do was go up and knock on the front door.

Our first raid came to pass only because Dill bet Jem *The Gray Ghost* against two Tom Swifts that Jem wouldn't get any farther than the Radley gate. In all his life, Jem had never declined a dare.

Jem thought about it for three days. I suppose he

loved honor more than his head, for Dill wore him down easily: "You're scared," Dill said, the first day. "Ain't scared, just respectful," Jem said. The next day Dill said, "You're too scared even to put your big toe in the front yard." Jem said he reckoned he wasn't, he'd passed the Radley Place every school day of his life.

"Always runnin'," I said.

But Dill got him the third day, when he told Jem that folks in Meridian certainly weren't as afraid as the folks in Maycomb, that he'd never seen such scary folks as the ones in Maycomb.

This was enough to make Jem march to the corner, where he stopped and leaned against the light-pole, watching the gate hanging crazily on its homemade hinge.

"I hope you've got it through your head that he'll kill us each and every one, Dill Harris," said Jem, when we joined him. "Don't blame me when he gouges your eyes out. You started it, remember."

"You're still scared," murmured Dill patiently.

Jem wanted Dill to know once and for all that he wasn't scared of anything: "It's just that I can't think of a way to make him come out without him gettin' us." Besides, Jem had his little sister to think of.

When he said that, I knew he was afraid. Jem had his little sister to think of the time I dared him to jump off the top of the house: "If I got killed, what'd become of you?" he asked. Then he jumped, landed unhurt, and his sense of responsibility left him until confronted by the Radley Place.

"You gonna run out on a dare?" asked Dill. "If you are, then—"

"Dill, you have to think about these things," Jem said. "Lemme think a minute . . . it's sort of like making a turtle come out . . ."

"How's that?" asked Dill.

"Strike a match under him."

I told Jem if he set fire to the Radley house I was going to tell Atticus on him.

Dill said striking a match under a turtle was hateful.

"Ain't hateful, just persuades him—'s not like you'd chunk him in the fire," Jem growled.

"How do you know a match don't hurt him?"

"Turtles can't feel, stupid," said Jem.

"Were you ever a turtle, huh?"

"My stars, Dill! Now lemme think . . . reckon we can rock him. . . ."

Jem stood in thought so long that Dill made a mild concession: "I won't say you ran out on a dare an' I'll swap you *The Gray Ghost* if you just go up and touch the house."

Jem brightened. "Touch the house, that all?"

Dill nodded.

"Sure that's all, now? I don't want you hollerin' something different the minute I get back."

"Yeah, that's all," said Dill. "He'll probably come out after you when he sees you in the yard, then Scout'n' me'll jump on him and hold him down till we can tell him we ain't gonna hurt him."

We left the corner, crossed the side street that ran in front of the Radley house, and stopped at the gate.

"Well go on," said Dill, "Scout and me's right behind you."

"I'm going," said Jem, "don't hurry me."

He walked to the corner of the lot, then back again, studying the simple terrain as if deciding how best to effect an entry, frowning and scratching his head.

Then I sneered at him.

Jem threw open the gate and sped to the side of the house, slapped it with his palm and ran back past us, not waiting to see if his foray was successful. Dill and I followed on his heels. Safely on our porch, panting and out of breath, we looked back.

The old house was the same, droopy and sick, but as we stared down the street we thought we saw an inside shutter move. Flick. A tiny, almost invisible movement, and the house was still.

2.

Dill left us early in September, to return to Meridian. We saw him off on the five o'clock bus and I was miserable without him until it occurred to me that I would be starting to school in a week. I never looked forward more to anything in my life. Hours of wintertime had found me in the treehouse, looking over at the schoolyard, spying on multitudes of children through a two-power telescope Jem had given me, learning their games, following Jem's red jacket through wriggling circles of blind man's bluff, secretly sharing their misfortunes and minor victories. I longed to join them.

Jem condescended to take me to school the first day, a job usually done by one's parents, but Atticus had said Jem would be delighted to show me where my room was. I think some money changed hands in this transaction, for as we trotted around the corner past the Radley Place I heard an unfamiliar jingle in Jem's pockets. When we slowed to a walk at the edge of the schoolyard, Jem was careful to explain that during school hours I was not to bother him, I was not to approach him with requests to enact a chapter of *Tarzan and the Ant Men*, to embarrass him with references to his private life, or tag along behind him at recess and noon. I was to stick with the first grade and he would stick with the fifth. In short, I was to leave him alone.

"You mean we can't play any more?" I asked.

"We'll do like we always do at home," he said, "but you'll see—school's different."

It certainly was. Before the first morning was over, Miss Caroline Fisher, our teacher, hauled me up to the front of the room and patted the palm of my hand with a ruler, then made me stand in the corner until noon.

Miss Caroline was no more than twenty-one. She had bright auburn hair, pink cheeks, and wore crimson fingernail polish. She also wore high-heeled pumps and a red-

and-white-striped dress. She looked and smelled like a peppermint drop. She boarded across the street one door down from us in Miss Maudie Atkinson's upstairs front room, and when Miss Maudie introduced us to her, Jem was in a haze for days.

Miss Caroline printed her name on the blackboard and said, "This says I am Miss Caroline Fisher. I am from North Alabama, from Winston County." The class murmured apprehensively, should she prove to harbor her share of the peculiarities indigenous to that region. (When Alabama seceded from the Union on January 11, 1861, Winston County seceded from Alabama, and every child in Maycomb County knew it.) North Alabama was full of Liquor Interests, Big Mules, steel companies, Republicans, professors, and other persons of no background.

Miss Caroline began the day by reading us a story about cats. The cats had long conversations with one another, they wore cunning little clothes and lived in a warm house beneath a kitchen stove. By the time Mrs. Cat called the drugstore for an order of chocolate malted mice the class was wriggling like a bucketful of catawba worms. Miss Caroline seemed unaware that the ragged, denim-shirted and floursack-skirted first grade, most of whom had chopped cotton and fed hogs from the time they were able to walk, were immune to imaginative literature. Miss Caroline came to the end of the story and said, *"Oh, my, wasn't that nice?"*

Then she went to the blackboard and printed the alphabet in enormous square capitals, turned to the class and asked, "Does anybody know what these are?"

Everybody did; most of the first grade had failed it last year.

I suppose she chose me because she knew my name; as I read the alphabet a faint line appeared between her eyebrows, and after making me read most of *My First Reader* and the stock-market quotations from *The Mobile Register* aloud, she discovered that I was literate and looked at me with more than faint distaste. Miss Caroline told me to tell my father not to teach me any more, it would interfere with my reading.

"Teach me?" I said in surprise. "He hasn't taught me anything, Miss Caroline. Atticus ain't got time to teach me anything," I added, when Miss Caroline smiled and shook her head. "Why, he's so tired at night he just sits in the livingroom and reads."

"If he didn't teach you, who did?" Miss Caroline asked good-naturedly. "Somebody did. You weren't born reading *The Mobile Register*."

"Jem says I was. He read in a book where I was a Bullfinch instead of a Finch. Jem says my name's really Jean Louise Bullfinch, that I got swapped when I was born and I'm really a—"

Miss Caroline apparently thought I was lying. "Let's not let our imaginations run away with us, dear," she said. "Now you tell your father not to teach you any more. It's best to begin reading with a fresh mind. You tell him I'll take over from here and try to undo the damage—"

"Ma'am?"

"Your father does not know how to teach. You can have a seat now."

I mumbled that I was sorry and retired meditating upon my crime. I never deliberately learned to read, but somehow I had been wallowing illicitly in the daily papers. In the long hours of church—was it then I learned? I could not remember not being able to read hymns. Now that I was compelled to think about it, reading was something that just came to me, as learning to fasten the seat of my union suit without looking around, or achieving two bows from a snarl of shoelaces. I could not remember when the lines above Atticus's moving finger separated into words, but I had stared at them all the evenings in my memory, listening to the news of the day, Bills To Be Enacted into Laws, the diaries of Lorenzo Dow—anything Atticus happened to be reading when I crawled into his lap every night. Until I feared I would lose it, I never loved to read. One does not love breathing.

I knew I had annoyed Miss Caroline, so I let well enough alone and stared out the window until recess when Jem cut me from the covey of first-graders in the schoolyard. He asked how I was getting along. I told him.

"If I didn't have to stay I'd leave. Jem, that damn lady says Atticus's been teaching me to read and for him to stop it—"

"Don't worry, Scout," Jem comforted me. "Our teacher

says Miss Caroline's introducing a new way of teaching. She learned about it in college. It'll be in all the grades soon. You don't have to learn much out of books that way —it's like if you wanta learn about cows, you go milk one, see?"

"Yeah Jem, but I don't wanta study cows, I—"

"Sure you do. You hafta know about cows, they're a big part of life in Maycomb County."

I contented myself with asking Jem if he'd lost his mind.

"I'm just trying to tell you the new way they're teachin' the first grade, stubborn. It's the Dewey Decimal System."

Having never questioned Jem's pronouncements, I saw no reason to begin now. The Dewey Decimal System consisted, in part, of Miss Caroline waving cards at us on which were printed "the," "cat," "rat," "man," and "you." No comment seemed to be expected of us, and the class received these impressionistic revelations in silence. I was bored, so I began a letter to Dill. Miss Caroline caught me writing and told me to tell my father to stop teaching me. "Besides," she said. "We don't write in the first grade, we print. You won't learn to write until you're in the third grade."

Calpurnia was to blame for this. It kept me from driving her crazy on rainy days, I guess. She would set me a writing task by scrawling the alphabet firmly across the top of a tablet, then copying out a chapter of the Bible beneath. If I reproduced her penmanship satisfactorily, she rewarded me with an open-faced sandwich of bread and butter and sugar. In Calpurnia's teaching, there was no sentimentality: I seldom pleased her and she seldom rewarded me.

"Everybody who goes home to lunch hold up your hands," said Miss Caroline, breaking into my new grudge against Calpurnia.

The town children did so, and she looked us over.

"Everybody who brings his lunch put it on top of his desk."

Molasses buckets appeared from nowhere, and the ceiling danced with metallic light. Miss Caroline walked up and down the rows peering and poking into lunch containers, nodding if the contents pleased her, frowning a little at others. She stopped at Walter Cunningham's desk. "Where's yours?" she asked.

Walter Cunningham's face told everybody in the first grade he had hookworms. His absence of shoes told us how he got them. People caught hookworms going barefooted in barnyards and hog wallows. If Walter had owned any shoes he would have worn them the first day of school and then discarded them until mid-winter. He did have on a clean shirt and neatly mended overalls.

"Did you forget your lunch this morning?" asked Miss Caroline.

Walter looked straight ahead. I saw a muscle jump in his skinny jaw.

"Did you forget it this morning?" asked Miss Caroline. Walter's jaw twitched again.

"Yeb'm," he finally mumbled.

Miss Caroline went to her desk and opened her purse. "Here's a quarter," she said to Walter. "Go and eat downtown today. You can pay me back tomorrow."

Walter shook his head. "Nome thank you ma'am," he drawled softly.

Impatience crept into Miss Caroline's voice: "Here Walter, come get it."

Walter shook his head again.

When Walter shook his head a third time someone whispered, "Go on and tell her, Scout."

I turned around and saw most of the town people and the entire bus delegation looking at me. Miss Caroline and I had conferred twice already, and they were looking at me in the innocent assurance that familiarity breeds understanding.

I rose graciously on Walter's behalf: "Ah—Miss Caroline?"

"What is it, Jean Louise?"

"Miss Caroline, he's a Cunningham."

I sat back down.

"What, Jean Louise?"

I thought I had made things sufficiently clear. It was clear enough to the rest of us: Walter Cunningham was sitting there lying his head off. He didn't forget his lunch, he didn't have any. He had none today nor would he have any tomorrow or the next day. He had probably never seen three quarters together at the same time in his life.

I tried again: "Walter's one of the Cunninghams, Miss Caroline."

"I beg your pardon, Jean Louise?"

"That's okay, ma'am, you'll get to know all the county folks after a while. The Cunninghams never took anything they can't pay back—no church baskets and no scrip stamps. They never took anything off of anybody, they get along on what they have. They don't have much, but they get along on it."

My special knowledge of the Cunningham tribe—one branch, that is—was gained from events of last winter. Walter's father was one of Atticus's clients. After a dreary conversation in our livingroom one night about his entailment, before Mr. Cunningham left he said, "Mr. Finch, I don't know when I'll ever be able to pay you."

"Let that be the least of your worries, Walter," Atticus said.

When I asked Jem what entailment was, and Jem described it as a condition of having your tail in a crack, I asked Atticus if Mr. Cunningham would ever pay us.

"Not in money," Atticus said, "but before the year's out I'll have been paid. You watch."

We watched. One morning Jem and I found a load of stovewood in the back yard. Later, a sack of hickory nuts appeared on the back steps. With Christmas came a crate of smilax and holly. That spring when we found a croker-sack full of turnip greens, Atticus said Mr. Cunningham had more than paid him.

"Why does he pay you like that?" I asked.

"Because that's the only way he can pay me. He has no money."

"Are we poor, Atticus?"

Atticus nodded. "We are indeed."

Jem's nose wrinkled. "Are we as poor as the Cunninghams?"

"Not exactly. The Cunninghams are country folks, farmers, and the crash hit them hardest."

Atticus said professional people were poor because the farmers were poor. As Maycomb County was farm country, nickels and dimes were hard to come by for doctors and dentists and lawyers. Entailment was only a part of Mr. Cunningham's vexations. The acres not entailed were mortgaged to the hilt, and the little cash he made went to interest. If he held his mouth right, Mr. Cunningham could get a WPA job, but his land would go to ruin if he left it, and he was willing to go hungry to keep his land and vote as he pleased. Mr. Cunningham, said Atticus, came from a set breed of men.

As the Cunninghams had no money to pay a lawyer, they simply paid us with what they had. "Did you know," said Atticus, "that Dr. Reynolds works the same way? He charges some folks a bushel of potatoes for delivery of a baby. Miss Scout, if you give me your attention I'll tell you what entailment is. Jem's definitions are very nearly accurate sometimes."

If I could have explained these things to Miss Caroline, I would have saved myself some inconvenience and Miss Caroline subsequent mortification, but it was beyond my ability to explain things as well as Atticus, so I said, "You're shamin' him, Miss Caroline. Walter hasn't got a quarter at home to bring you, and you can't use any stovewood."

Miss Caroline stood stock still, then grabbed me by the collar and hauled me back to her desk. "Jean Louise, I've had about enough of you this morning," she said. "You're starting off on the wrong foot in every way, my dear. Hold out your hand."

I thought she was going to spit in it, which was the only reason anybody in Maycomb held out his hand: it was a time-honored method of sealing oral contracts. Wondering what bargain we had made, I turned to the class for an answer, but the class looked back at me in puzzlement. Miss Caroline picked up her ruler, gave me half a dozen quick little pats, then told me to stand in the corner. A storm of laughter broke loose when it finally occurred to the class that Miss Caroline had whipped me.

When Miss Caroline threatened it with a similar fate the first grade exploded again, becoming cold sober only when the shadow of Miss Blount fell over them. Miss Blount, a native Maycombian as yet uninitiated in the mysteries of the Decimal System, appeared at the door hands on hips and announced: "If I hear another sound from this room I'll burn up everybody in it. Miss Caroline, the sixth grade cannot concentrate on the pyramids for all this racket!"

My sojourn in the corner was a short one. Saved by the

26

bell, Miss Caroline watched the class file out for lunch. As I was the last to leave, I saw her sink down into her chair and bury her head in her arms. Had her conduct been more friendly toward me, I would have felt sorry for her. She was a pretty little thing.

3.

Catching Walter Cunningham in the schoolyard gave me some pleasure, but when I was rubbing his nose in the dirt Jem came by and told me to stop. "You're bigger'n he is," he said.

"He's as old as you, nearly," I said. "He made me start off on the wrong foot."

"Let him go, Scout. Why?"

"He didn't have any lunch," I said, and explained my involvement in Walter's dietary affairs.

Walter had picked himself up and was standing quietly listening to Jem and me. His fists were half cocked, as if expecting an onslaught from both of us. I stomped at him to chase him away, but Jem put out his hand and stopped me. He examined Walter with an air of speculation. "Your daddy Mr. Walter Cunningham from Old Sarum?" he asked, and Walter nodded.

Walter looked as if he had been raised on fish food: his eyes, as blue as Dill Harris's, were red-rimmed and watery. There was no color in his face except at the tip of his nose, which was moistly pink. He fingered the straps of his overalls, nervously picking at the metal hooks.

Jem suddenly grinned at him. "Come on home to dinner with us, Walter," he said. "We'd be glad to have you."

Walter's face brightened, then darkened.

Jem said, "Our daddy's a friend of your daddy's. Scout here, she's crazy—she won't fight you any more."

"I wouldn't be too certain of that," I said. Jem's free dispensation of my pledge irked me, but precious noon-time minutes were ticking away. "Yeah Walter, I won't

27

jump on you again. Don't you like butterbeans? Our Cal's a real good cook."

Walter stood where he was, biting his lip. Jem and I gave up, and we were nearly to the Radley Place when Walter called, "Hey, I'm comin'!"

When Walter caught up with us, Jem made pleasant conversation with him. "A hain't lives there," he said cordially, pointing to the Radley house. "Ever hear about him, Walter?"

"Reckon I have," said Walter. "Almost died first year I come to school and et them pecans—folks say he pizened 'em and put 'em over on the school side of the fence."

Jem seemed to have little fear of Boo Radley now that Walter and I walked beside him. Indeed, Jem grew boastful: "I went all the way up to the house once," he said to Walter.

"Anybody who went up to the house once oughta not to still run every time he passes it," I said to the clouds above.

"And who's runnin', Miss Priss?"

"You are, when ain't anybody with you."

By the time we reached our front steps Walter had forgotten he was a Cunningham. Jem ran to the kitchen and asked Calpurnia to set an extra plate, we had company. Atticus greeted Walter and began a discussion about crops neither Jem nor I could follow.

"Reason I can't pass the first grade, Mr. Finch, is I've had to stay out ever' spring an' help Papa with the choppin', but there's another'n at the house now that's field size."

"Did you pay a bushel of potatoes for him?" I asked, but Atticus shook his head at me.

While Walter piled food on his plate, he and Atticus talked together like two men, to the wonderment of Jem and me. Atticus was expounding upon farm problems when Walter interrupted to ask if there was any molasses in the house. Atticus summoned Calpurnia, who returned bearing the syrup pitcher. She stood waiting for Walter to help himself. Walter poured syrup on his vegetables and meat with a generous hand. He would probably have poured it into his milk glass had I not asked what the sam hill he was doing.

28

The silver saucer clattered when he replaced the pitcher, and he quickly put his hands in his lap. Then he ducked his head.

Atticus shook his head at me again. "But he's gone and drowned his dinner in syrup," I protested. "He's poured it all over—"

It was then that Calpurnia requested my presence in the kitchen.

She was furious, and when she was furious Calpurnia's grammar became erratic. When in tranquility, her grammar was as good as anybody's in Maycomb. Atticus said Calpurnia had more education than most colored folks.

When she squinted down at me the tiny lines around her eyes deepened. "There's some folks who don't eat like us," she whispered fiercely, "but you ain't called on to contradict 'em at the table when they don't. That boy's yo' comp'ny and if he wants to eat up the table cloth you let him, you hear?"

"He ain't company, Cal, he's just a Cunningham—"

"Hush your mouth! Don't matter who they are, anybody sets foot in this house's yo' comp'ny, and don't you let me catch you remarkin' on their ways like you was so high and mighty! Yo' folks might be better'n the Cunninghams but it don't count for nothin' the way you're disgracin' 'em—if you can't act fit to eat at the table you can just set here and eat in the kitchen!"

Calpurnia sent me through the swinging door to the diningroom with a stinging smack. I retrieved my plate and finished dinner in the kitchen, thankful, though, that I was spared the humiliation of facing them again. I told Calpurnia to just wait, I'd fix her: one of these days when she wasn't looking I'd go off and drown myself in Barker's Eddy and then she'd be sorry. Besides, I added, she'd already gotten me in trouble once today: she had taught me to write and it was all her fault. "Hush your fussin'," she said.

Jem and Walter returned to school ahead of me: staying behind to advise Atticus of Calpurnia's iniquities was worth a solitary sprint past the Radley Place. "She likes Jem better'n she likes me, anyway," I concluded, and suggested that Atticus lose no time in packing her off.

"Have you ever considered that Jem doesn't worry her half as much?" Atticus's voice was flinty. "I've no intention of getting rid of her, now or ever. We couldn't operate a single day without Cal, have you ever thought of that? You think about how much Cal does for you, and you mind her, you hear?"

I returned to school and hated Calpurnia steadily until a sudden shriek shattered my resentments. I looked up to see Miss Caroline standing in the middle of the room, sheer horror flooding her face. Apparently she had revived enough to persevere in her profession.

"It's alive!" she screamed.

The male population of the class rushed as one to her assistance. Lord, I thought, she's scared of a mouse. Little Chuck Little, whose patience with all living things was phenomenal, said, "Which way did he go, Miss Caroline? Tell us where he went, quick! D.C.—" he turned to a boy behind him—"D.C., shut the door and we'll catch him. Quick, ma'am, where'd he go?"

Miss Caroline pointed a shaking finger not at the floor nor at a desk, but to a hulking individual unknown to me. Little Chuck's face contracted and he said gently, "You mean him, ma'am? Yessum, he's alive. Did he scare you some way?"

Miss Caroline said desperately, "I was just walking by when it crawled out of his hair . . . just crawled out of his hair—"

Little Chuck grinned broadly. "There ain't no need to fear a cootie, ma'am. Ain't you ever seen one? Now don't you be afraid, you just go back to your desk and teach us some more."

Little Chuck Little was another member of the population who didn't know where his next meal was coming from, but he was a born gentleman. He put his hand under her elbow and led Miss Caroline to the front of the room. "Now don't you fret, ma'am," he said. "There ain't no need to fear a cootie. I'll just fetch you some cool water."

The cootie's host showed not the faintest interest in the furor he had wrought. He searched the scalp above his forehead, located his guest and pinched it between his thumb and forefinger.

Miss Caroline watched the process in horrid fascination. Little Chuck brought water in a paper cup, and she drank it gratefully. Finally she found her voice. "What is your name, son?" she asked softly.

The boy blinked. "Who, me?" Miss Caroline nodded.

"Burris Ewell."

Miss Caroline inspected her roll-book. "I have a Ewell here, but I don't have a first name . . . would you spell your first name for me?"

"Don't know how. They call me Burris't home."

"Well, Burris," said Miss Caroline, "I think we'd better excuse you for the rest of the afternoon. I want you to go home and wash your hair."

From her desk she produced a thick volume, leafed through its pages and read for a moment. "A good home remedy for—Burris, I want you to go home and wash your hair with lye soap. When you've done that, treat your scalp with kerosene."

"What fer, missus?"

"To get rid of the—er, cooties. You see, Burris, the other children might catch them, and you wouldn't want that, would you?"

The boy stood up. He was the filthiest human I had ever seen. His neck was dark gray, the backs of his hands were rusty, and his fingernails were black deep into the quick. He peered at Miss Caroline from a fist-sized clean space on his face. No one had noticed him, probably, because Miss Caroline and I had entertained the class most of the morning.

"And Burris," said Miss Caroline, "please bathe yourself before you come back tomorrow."

The boy laughed rudely. "You ain't sendin' me home, missus. I was on the verge of leavin'—I done done my time for this year."

Miss Caroline looked puzzled. "What do you mean by that?"

The boy did not answer. He gave a short contemptuous snort.

One of the elderly members of the class answered her: "He's one of the Ewells, ma'am," and I wondered if this explanation would be as unsuccessful as my attempt. But Miss Caroline seemed willing to listen. "Whole school's full of 'em. They come first day every year and then leave. The truant lady gets 'em here 'cause she threatens

31

'em with the sheriff, but she's give up tryin' to hold 'em. She reckons she's carried out the law just gettin' their names on the roll and runnin' 'em here the first day. You're supposed to mark 'em absent the rest of the year . . ."

"But what about their parents?" asked Miss Caroline, in genuine concern.

"Ain't got no mother," was the answer, "and their paw's right contentious."

Burris Ewell was flattered by the recital. "Been comin' to the first day o' the first grade fer three year now," he said expansively. "Reckon if I'm smart this year they'll promote me to the second. . . ."

Miss Caroline said, "Sit back down, please, Burris," and the moment she said it I knew she had made a serious mistake. The boy's condescension flashed to anger.

"You try and make me, missus."

Little Chuck Little got to his feet. "Let him go, ma'am," he said. "He's a mean one, a hard-down mean one. He's liable to start somethin', and there's some little folks here."

He was among the most diminutive of men, but when Burris Ewell turned toward him, Little Chuck's right hand went to his pocket. "Watch your step, Burris," he said. "I'd soon's kill you as look at you. Now go home."

Burris seemed to be afraid of a child half his height, and Miss Caroline took advantage of his indecision: "Burris, go home. If you don't I'll call the principal," she said. "I'll have to report this, anyway."

The boy snorted and slouched leisurely to the door.

Safely out of range, he turned and shouted: "Report and be damned to ye! Ain't no snot-nosed slut of a schoolteacher ever born c'n make me do nothin'! You ain't makin' me go nowhere, missus. You just remember that, you ain't makin' me go nowhere!"

He waited until he was sure she was crying, then he shuffled out of the building.

Soon we were clustered around her desk, trying in our various ways to comfort her. He was a real mean one . . . below the belt . . . you ain't called on to teach folks like that . . . them ain't Maycomb's ways, Miss Caroline, not really . . . now don't you fret, ma'am. Miss Caroline, why don't you read us a story? That cat thing was real fine this mornin'. . . .

Miss Caroline smiled, blew her nose, said, "Thank you, darlings," dispersed us, opened a book and mystified the first grade with a long narrative about a toadfrog that lived in a hall.

When I passed the Radley Place for the fourth time that day—twice at a full gallop—my gloom had deepened to match the house. If the remainder of the school year were as fraught with drama as the first day, perhaps it would be mildly entertaining, but the prospect of spending nine months refraining from reading and writing made me think of running away.

By late afternoon most of my traveling plans were complete; when Jem and I raced each other up the sidewalk to meet Atticus coming home from work, I didn't give him much of a race. It was our habit to run meet Atticus the moment we saw him round the post office corner in the distance. Atticus seemed to have forgotten my noontime fall from grace; he was full of questions about school. My replies were monosyllabic and he did not press me.

Perhaps Calpurnia sensed that my day had been a grim one: she let me watch her fix supper. "Shut your eyes and open your mouth and I'll give you a surprise," she said.

It was not often that she made crackling bread, she said she never had time, but with both of us at school today had been an easy one for her. She knew I loved crackling bread.

"I missed you today," she said. "The house got so lonesome 'long about two o'clock I had to turn on the radio."

"Why? Jem'n me ain't ever in the house unless it's rainin'."

"I know," she said, "But one of you's always in callin' distance. I wonder how much of the day I spend just callin' after you. Well," she said, getting up from the kitchen chair, "it's enough time to make a pan of cracklin' bread, I reckon. You run along now and let me get supper on the table."

Calpurnia bent down and kissed me. I ran along, wondering what had come over her. She had wanted to make up with me, that was it. She had always been too hard on me, she had at last seen the error of her fractious ways, she was sorry and too stubborn to say so. I was weary from the day's crimes.

After supper, Atticus sat down with the paper and called, "Scout, ready to read?" The Lord sent me more than I could bear, and I went to the front porch. Atticus followed me.

"Something wrong, Scout?"

I told Atticus I didn't feel very well and didn't think I'd go to school any more if it was all right with him.

Atticus sat down in the swing and crossed his legs. His fingers wandered to his watchpocket; he said that was the only way he could think. He waited in amiable silence, and I sought to reinforce my position: "You never went to school and you do all right, so I'll just stay home too. You can teach me like Granddaddy taught you 'n' Uncle Jack."

"No I can't," said Atticus. "I have to make a living. Besides, they'd put me in jail if I kept you at home—dose of magnesia for you tonight and school tomorrow."

"I'm feeling all right, really."

"Thought so. Now what's the matter?"

Bit by bit, I told him the day's misfortunes. "—and she said you taught me all wrong, so we can't ever read any more, ever. Please don't send me back, please sir."

Atticus stood up and walked to the end of the porch. When he completed his examination of the wisteria vine he strolled back to me.

"First of all," he said, "if you can learn a simple trick, Scout, you'll get along a lot better with all kinds of folks. You never really understand a person until you consider things from his point of view—"

"Sir?"

"—until you climb into his skin and walk around in it."

Atticus said I had learned many things today, and Miss Caroline had learned several things herself. She had learned not to hand something to a Cunningham, for one thing, but if Walter and I had put ourselves in her shoes we'd have seen it was an honest mistake on her part. We could not expect her to learn all Maycomb's ways in one day, and we could not hold her responsible when she knew no better.

"I'll be dogged," I said. "I didn't know no better than

not to read to her, and she held me responsible—listen Atticus, I don't have to go to school!" I was bursting with a sudden thought. "Burris Ewell, remember? He just goes to school the first day. The truant lady reckons she's carried out the law when she gets his name on the roll—"

"You can't do that, Scout," Atticus said. "Sometimes it's better to bend the law a little in special cases. In your case, the law remains rigid. So to school you must go."

"I don't see why I have to when he doesn't."

"Then listen."

Atticus said the Ewells had been the disgrace of Maycomb for three generations. None of them had done an honest day's work in his recollection. He said that some Christmas, when he was getting rid of the tree, he would take me with him and show me where and how they lived. They were people, but they lived like animals. "They can go to school any time they want to, when they show the faintest symptom of wanting an education," said Atticus. "There are ways of keeping them in school by force, but it's silly to force people like the Ewells into a new environment—"

"If I didn't go to school tomorrow, you'd force me to."

"Let us leave it at this," said Atticus dryly. "You, Miss Scout Finch, are of the common folk. You must obey the law." He said that the Ewells were members of an exclusive society made up of Ewells. In certain circumstances the common folk judiciously allowed them certain privileges by the simple method of becoming blind to some of the Ewells' activities. They didn't have to go to school, for one thing. Another thing, Mr. Bob Ewell, Burris's father, was permitted to hunt and trap out of season.

"Atticus, that's bad," I said. In Maycomb County, hunting out of season was a misdemeanor at law, a capital felony in the eyes of the populace.

"It's against the law, all right," said my father, "and it's certainly bad, but when a man spends his relief checks on green whiskey his children have a way of crying from hunger pains. I don't know of any landowner around here who begrudges those children any game their father can hit."

"Mr. Ewell shouldn't do that—"

"Of course he shouldn't, but he'll never change his

ways. Are you going to take out your disapproval on his children?"

"No sir," I murmured, and made a final stand: "But if I keep on goin' to school, we can't ever read any more. . . ."

"That's really bothering you, isn't it?"

"Yes sir."

When Atticus looked down at me I saw the expression on his face that always made me expect something. "Do you know what a compromise is?" he asked.

"Bending the law?"

"No, an agreement reached by mutual concessions. It works this way," he said. "If you'll concede the necessity of going to school, we'll go on reading every night just as we always have. Is it a bargain?"

"Yes sir!"

"We'll consider it sealed without the usual formality," Atticus said, when he saw me preparing to spit.

As I opened the front screen door Atticus said, "By the way, Scout, you'd better not say anything at school about our agreement."

"Why not?"

"I'm afraid our activities would be received with considerable disapprobation by the more learned authorities."

Jem and I were accustomed to our father's last-will-and-testament diction, and we were at all times free to interrupt Atticus for a translation when it was beyond our understanding.

"Huh, sir?"

"I never went to school," he said, "but I have a feeling that if you tell Miss Caroline we read every night she'll get after me, and I wouldn't want her after *me*."

Atticus kept us in fits that evening, gravely reading columns of print about a man who sat on a flagpole for no discernible reason, which was reason enough for Jem to spend the following Saturday aloft in the treehouse. Jem sat from after breakfast until sunset and would have remained overnight had not Atticus severed his supply lines. I had spent most of the day climbing up and down, running errands for him, providing him with literature, nourishment and water, and was carrying him blankets for the night when Atticus said if I paid no attention to him, Jem would come down. Atticus was right.

4.

The remainder of my schooldays were no more auspicious than the first. Indeed, they were an endless Project that slowly evolved into a Unit, in which miles of construction paper and wax crayon were expended by the State of Alabama in its well-meaning but fruitless efforts to teach me Group Dynamics. What Jem called the Dewey Decimal System was school-wide by the end of my first year, so I had no chance to compare it with other teaching techniques. I could only look around me: Atticus and my uncle, who went to school at home, knew everything—at least, what one didn't know the other did. Furthermore, I couldn't help noticing that my father had served for years in the state legislature, elected each time without opposition, innocent of the adjustments my teachers thought essential to the development of Good Citizenship. Jem, educated on a half-Decimal half-Dunce-cap basis, seemed to function effectively alone or in a group, but Jem was a poor example: no tutorial system devised by man could have stopped him from getting at books. As for me, I knew nothing except what I gathered from *Time* magazine and reading everything I could lay hands on at home, but as I inched sluggishly along the treadmill of the Maycomb County school system, I could not help receiving the impression that I was being cheated out of something. Out of what I knew not, yet I did not believe that twelve years of unrelieved boredom was exactly what the state had in mind for me.

As the year passed, released from school thirty minutes before Jem, who had to stay until three o'clock, I ran by the Radley Place as fast as I could, not stopping until I reached the safety of our front porch. One afternoon as I raced by, something caught my eye and caught it in such a way that I took a deep breath, a long look around, and went back.

Two live oaks stood at the edge of the Radley lot; their

roots reached out into the side-road and made it bumpy. Something about one of the trees attracted my attention.

Some tinfoil was sticking in a knot-hole just above my eye level, winking at me in the afternoon sun. I stood on tiptoe, hastily looked around once more, reached into the hole, and withdrew two pieces of chewing gum minus their outer wrappers.

My first impulse was to get it into my mouth as quickly as possible, but I remembered where I was. I ran home, and on our front porch I examined my loot. The gum looked fresh. I sniffed it and it smelled all right. I licked it and waited for a while. When I did not die I crammed it into my mouth: Wrigley's Double-Mint.

When Jem came home he asked me where I got such a wad. I told him I found it.

"Don't eat things you find, Scout."

"This wasn't on the ground, it was in a tree."

Jem growled.

"Well it was," I said. "It was sticking in that tree yonder, the one comin' from school."

"Spit it out right now!"

I spat it out. The tang was fading, anyway. "I've been chewin' it all afternoon and I ain't dead yet, not even sick."

Jem stamped his foot. "Don't you know you're not supposed to even touch the trees over there? You'll get killed if you do!"

"You touched the house once!"

"That was different! You go gargle—right now, you hear me?"

"Ain't neither, it'll take the taste outa my mouth."

"You don't 'n' I'll tell Calpurnia on you!"

Rather than risk a tangle with Calpurnia, I did as Jem told me. For some reason, my first year of school had wrought a great change in our relationship: Calpurnia's tyranny, unfairness, and meddling in my business had faded to gentle grumblings of general disapproval. On my part, I went to much trouble, sometimes, not to provoke her.

Summer was on the way; Jem and I awaited it with impatience. Summer was our best season: it was sleeping on the back screened porch in cots, or trying to sleep in the treehouse; summer was everything good to eat; it was a thousand colors in a parched landscape; but most of all, summer was Dill.

The authorities released us early the last day of school, and Jem and I walked home together. "Reckon old Dill'll be coming home tomorrow," I said.

"Probably day after," said Jem. "Mis'sippi turns 'em loose a day later."

As we came to the live oaks at the Radley Place I raised my finger to point for the hundredth time to the knot-hole where I had found the chewing gum, trying to make Jem believe I had found it there, and found myself pointing at another piece of tinfoil.

"I see it, Scout! I see it—"

Jem looked around, reached up, and gingerly pocketed a tiny shiny package. We ran home, and on the front porch we looked at a small box patchworked with bits of tinfoil collected from chewing-gum wrappers. It was the kind of box wedding rings came in, purple velvet with a minute catch. Jem flicked open the tiny catch. Inside were two scrubbed and polished pennies, one on top of the other. Jem examined them.

"Indian-heads," he said. "Nineteen-six and Scout, one of 'em's nineteen-hundred. These are real old."

"Nineteen-hundred," I echoed. "Say—"

"Hush a minute, I'm thinkin'."

"Jem, you reckon that's somebody's hidin' place?"

"Naw, don't anybody much but us pass by there, unless it's some grown person's—"

"Grown folks don't have hidin' places. You reckon we ought to keep 'em, Jem?"

"I don't know what we could do, Scout. Who'd we give 'em back to? I know for a fact don't anybody go by there —Cecil goes by the back street an' all the way around by town to get home."

Cecil Jacobs, who lived at the far end of our street next door to the post office, walked a total of one mile per school day to avoid the Radley Place and old Mrs. Henry Lafayette Dubose. Mrs. Dubose lived two doors up the street from us; neighborhood opinion was unanimous that Mrs. Dubose was the meanest old woman who ever lived. Jem wouldn't go by her place without Atticus beside him.

"What you reckon we oughta do, Jem?"

Finders were keepers unless title was proven. Plucking an occasional camellia, getting a squirt of hot milk from Miss Maudie Atkinson's cow on a summer day, helping ourselves to someone's scuppernongs was part of our ethical culture, but money was different.

"Tell you what," said Jem. "We'll keep 'em till school starts, then go around and ask everybody if they're theirs. They're some bus child's, maybe—he was too taken up with gettin' outa school today an' forgot 'em. These are somebody's, I know that. See how they've been slicked up? They've been saved."

"Yeah, but why should somebody wanta put away chewing gum like that? You know it doesn't last."

"I don't know, Scout. But these are important to somebody. . . ."

"How's that, Jem . . . ?"

"Well, Indian-heads—well, they come from the Indians. They're real strong magic, they make you have good luck. Not like fried chicken when you're not lookin' for it, but things like long life 'n' good health, 'n' passin' six-weeks tests . . . these are real valuable to somebody. I'm gonna put 'em in my trunk."

Before Jem went to his room, he looked for a long time at the Radley Place. He seemed to be thinking again.

Two days later Dill arrived in a blaze of glory: he had ridden the train by himself from Meridian to Maycomb Junction (a courtesy title—Maycomb Junction was in Abbott County) where he had been met by Miss Rachel in Maycomb's one taxi; he had eaten dinner in the diner, he had seen two twins hitched together get off the train in Bay St. Louis and stuck to his story regardless of threats. He had discarded the abominable blue shorts that were buttoned to his shirts and wore real short pants with a belt; he was somewhat heavier, no taller, and said he had seen his father. Dill's father was taller than ours, he had a black beard (pointed), and was president of the L & N Railroad.

"I helped the engineer for a while," said Dill, yawning.

"In a pig's ear you did, Dill. Hush," said Jem. "What'll we play today?"

"Tom and Sam and Dick," said Dill. "Let's go in the front yard." Dill wanted the Rover Boys because there were three respectable parts. He was clearly tired of being our character man.

"I'm tired of those," I said. I was tired of playing Tom Rover, who suddenly lost his memory in the middle of a picture show and was out of the script until the end, when he was found in Alaska.

"Make us up one, Jem," I said.

"I'm tired of makin' 'em up."

Our first days of freedom, and we were tired. I wondered what the summer would bring.

We had strolled to the front yard, where Dill stood looking down the street at the dreary face of the Radley Place. "I—smell—death," he said. "I do, I mean it," he said, when I told him to shut up.

"You mean when somebody's dyin' you can smell it?"

"No, I mean I can smell somebody an' tell if they're gonna die. An old lady taught me how." Dill leaned over and sniffed me. "Jean—Louise—Finch, you are going to die in three days."

"Dill if you don't hush I'll knock you bowlegged. I mean it, now—"

"Yawl hush," growled Jem, "you act like you believe in Hot Steams."

"You act like you don't," I said.

"What's a Hot Steam?" asked Dill.

"Haven't you ever walked along a lonesome road at night and passed by a hot place?" Jem asked Dill. "A Hot Steam's somebody who can't get to heaven, just wallows around on lonesome roads an' if you walk through him, when you die you'll be one too, an' you'll go around at night suckin' people's breath—"

"How can you keep from passing through one?"

"You can't," said Jem. "Sometimes they stretch all the way across the road, but if you hafta go through one you say, 'Angel-bright, life-in-death; get off the road, don't suck my breath.' That keeps 'em from wrapping around you—"

"Don't you believe a word he says, Dill," I said. "Calpurnia says that's nigger-talk."

Jem scowled darkly at me, but said, "Well, are we gonna play anything or not?"

"Let's roll in the tire," I suggested.

Jem sighed. "You know I'm too big."

"You c'n push."

41

I ran to the back yard and pulled an old car tire from under the house. I slapped it up to the front yard. "I'm first," I said.

Dill said he ought to be first, he just got here.

Jem arbitrated, awarded me first push with an extra time for Dill, and I folded myself inside the tire.

Until it happened I did not realize that Jem was offended by my contradicting him on Hot Steams, and that he was patiently awaiting an opportunity to reward me. He did, by pushing the tire down the sidewalk with all the force in his body. Ground, sky and houses melted into a mad palette, my ears throbbed, I was suffocating. I could not put out my hands to stop, they were wedged between my chest and knees. I could only hope that Jem would outrun the tire and me, or that I would be stopped by a bump in the sidewalk. I heard him behind me, chasing and shouting.

The tire bumped on gravel, skeetered across the road, crashed into a barrier and popped me like a cork onto pavement. Dizzy and nauseated, I lay on the cement and shook my head still, pounded my ears to silence, and heard Jem's voice: "Scout, get away from there, come on!"

I raised my head and stared at the Radley Place steps in front of me. I froze.

"Come on, Scout, don't just lie there!" Jem was screaming. "Get up, can'tcha?"

I got to my feet, trembling as I thawed.

"Get the tire!" Jem hollered. "Bring it with you! Ain't you got any sense at all?"

When I was able to navigate, I ran back to them as fast as my shaking knees would carry me.

"Why didn't you bring it?" Jem yelled.

"Why don't *you* get it?" I screamed.

Jem was silent.

"Go on, it ain't far inside the gate. Why, you even touched the house once, remember?"

Jem looked at me furiously, could not decline, ran down the sidewalk, treaded water at the gate, then dashed in and retrieved the tire.

"See there?" Jem was scowling triumphantly. "Nothin' to it. I swear, Scout, sometimes you act so much like a girl it's mortifyin'."

There was more to it than he knew, but I decided not to tell him.

Calpurnia appeared in the front door and yelled, "Lemonade time! You all get in outa that hot sun 'fore you fry alive!" Lemonade in the middle of the morning was a summertime ritual. Calpurnia set a pitcher and three glasses on the porch, then went about her business. Being out of Jem's good graces did not worry me especially. Lemonade would restore his good humor.

Jem gulped down his second glassful and slapped his chest. "I know what we are going to play," he announced. "Something new, something different."

"What?" asked Dill.

"Boo Radley."

Jem's head at times was transparent: he had thought that up to make me understand he wasn't afraid of Radleys in any shape or form, to contrast his own fearless heroism with my cowardice.

"Boo Radley? How?" asked Dill.

Jem said, "Scout, you can be Mrs. Radley—"

"I declare if I will. I don't think—"

"'Smatter?" said Dill. "Still scared?"

"He can get out at night when we're all asleep. . . ." I said.

Jem hissed. "Scout, how's he gonna know what we're doin'? Besides, I don't think he's still there. He died years ago and they stuffed him up the chimney."

Dill said, "Jem, you and me can play and Scout can watch if she's scared."

I was fairly sure Boo Radley was inside that house, but I couldn't prove it, and felt it best to keep my mouth shut or I would be accused of believing in Hot Steams, phenomena I was immune to in the daytime.

Jem parceled out our roles: I was Mrs. Radley, and all I had to do was come out and sweep the porch. Dill was old Mr. Radley: he walked up and down the sidewalk and coughed when Jem spoke to him. Jem, naturally, was Boo: he went under the front steps and shrieked and howled from time to time.

As the summer progressed, so did our game. We polished and perfected it, added dialogue and plot until we had manufactured a small play upon which we rang changes every day.

43

Dill was a villain's villain: he could get into any character part assigned him, and appear tall if height was part of the devilry required. He was as good as his worst performance; his worst performance was Gothic. I reluctantly played assorted ladies who entered the script. I never thought it as much fun as Tarzan, and I played that summer with more than vague anxiety despite Jem's assurances that Boo Radley was dead and nothing would get me, with him and Calpurnia there in the daytime and Atticus home at night.

Jem was a born hero.

It was a melancholy little drama, woven from bits and scraps of gossip and neighborhood legend: Mrs. Radley had been beautiful until she married Mr. Radley and lost all her money. She also lost most of her teeth, her hair, and her right forefinger (Dill's contribution. Boo bit it off one night when he couldn't find any cats and squirrels to eat.); she sat in the livingroom and cried most of the time, while Boo slowly whittled away all the furniture in the house.

The three of us were the boys who got into trouble; I was the probate judge, for a change; Dill led Jem away and crammed him beneath the steps, poking him with the brushbroom. Jem would reappear as needed in the shapes of the sheriff, assorted townsfolk, and Miss Stephanie Crawford, who had more to say about the Radleys than anybody in Maycomb.

When it was time to play Boo's big scene, Jem would sneak into the house, steal the scissors from the sewing-machine drawer when Calpurnia's back was turned, then sit in the swing and cut up newspapers. Dill would walk by, cough at Jem, and Jem would fake a plunge into Dill's thigh. From where I stood it looked real.

When Mr. Nathan Radley passed us on his daily trip to town, we would stand still and silent until he was out of sight, then wonder what he would do to us if he suspected. Our activities halted when any of the neighbors appeared, and once I saw Miss Maudie Atkinson staring across the street at us, her hedge clippers poised in mid-air.

One day we were so busily playing Chapter XXV, Book II of One Man's Family, we did not see Atticus standing on the sidewalk looking at us, slapping a rolled magazine against his knee. The sun said twelve noon.

"What are you all playing?" he asked.

"Nothing," said Jem.

Jem's evasion told me our game was a secret, so I kept quiet.

"What are you doing with those scissors, then? Why are you tearing up that newspaper? If it's today's I'll tan you."

"Nothing."

"Nothing what?" said Atticus.

"Nothing, sir."

"Give me those scissors," Atticus said. "They're no things to play with. Does this by any chance have anything to do with the Radleys?"

"No sir," said Jem, reddening.

"I hope it doesn't," he said shortly, and went inside the house.

"Je-m . . ."

"Shut up! He's gone in the livingroom, he can hear us in there."

Safely in the yard, Dill asked Jem if we could play any more.

"I don't know. Atticus didn't say we couldn't—"

"Jem," I said, "I think Atticus knows it anyway."

"No he don't. If he did he'd say he did."

I was not so sure, but Jem told me I was being a girl, that girls always imagined things, that's why other people hated them so, and if I started behaving like one I could just go off and find some to play with.

"All right, you just keep it up then," I said. "You'll find out."

Atticus's arrival was the second reason I wanted to quit the game. The first reason happened the day I rolled into the Radley front yard. Through all the head-shaking, quelling of nausea and Jem-yelling, I had heard another sound, so low I could not have heard it from the sidewalk. Someone inside the house was laughing.

5.

My nagging got the better of Jem
eventually, as I knew it would, and to my relief we slowed
down the game for a while. He still maintained, however,
that Atticus hadn't said we couldn't, therefore we could;
and if Atticus ever said we couldn't, Jem had thought of
a way around it: he would simply change the names of
the characters and then we couldn't be accused of playing
anything.

Dill was in hearty agreement with this plan of action.
Dill was becoming something of a trial anyway, following Jem about. He had asked me earlier in the summer to
marry him, then he promptly forgot about it. He staked
me out, marked as his property, said I was the only girl
he would ever love, then he neglected me. I beat him up
twice but it did no good, he only grew closer to Jem.
They spent days together in the treehouse plotting and
planning, calling me only when they needed a third party.
But I kept aloof from their more foolhardy schemes for a
while, and on pain of being called a g-irl, I spent most of
the remaining twilights that summer sitting with Miss
Maudie Atkinson on her front porch.

Jem and I had always enjoyed the free run of Miss
Maudie's yard if we kept out of her azaleas, but our contact with her was not clearly defined. Until Jem and Dill
excluded me from their plans, she was only another lady
in the neighborhood, but a relatively benign presence.

Our tacit treaty with Miss Maudie was that we could
play on her lawn, eat her scuppernongs if we didn't jump
on the arbor, and explore her vast back lot, terms so generous we seldom spoke to her, so careful were we to
preserve the delicate balance of our relationship, but Jem
and Dill drove me closer to her with their behavior.

Miss Maudie hated her house: time spent indoors was
time wasted. She was a widow, a chameleon lady who
worked in her flower beds in an old straw hat and men's
coveralls, but after her five o'clock bath she would ap-

46

pear on the porch and reign over the street in magisterial beauty.

She loved everything that grew in God's earth, even the weeds. With one exception. If she found a blade of nut grass in her yard it was like the Second Battle of the Marne: she swooped down upon it with a tin tub and subjected it to blasts from beneath with a poisonous substance she said was so powerful it'd kill us all if we didn't stand out of the way.

"Why can't you just pull it up?" I asked, after witnessing a prolonged campaign against a blade not three inches high.

"Pull it up, child, pull it up?" She picked up the limp sprout and squeezed her thumb up its tiny stalk. Microscopic grains oozed out. "Why, one sprig of nut grass can ruin a whole yard. Look here. When it comes fall this dries up and the wind blows it all over Maycomb County!" Miss Maudie's face likened such an occurrence unto an Old Testament pestilence.

Her speech was crisp for a Maycomb County inhabitant. She called us by all our names, and when she grinned she revealed two minute gold prongs clipped to her eyeteeth. When I admired them and hoped I would have some eventually, she said, "Look here." With a click of her tongue she thrust out her bridgework, a gesture of cordiality that cemented our friendship.

Miss Maudie's benevolence extended to Jem and Dill, whenever they paused in their pursuits: we reaped the benefits of a talent Miss Maudie had hitherto kept hidden from us. She made the best cakes in the neighborhood. When she was admitted into our confidence, every time she baked she made a big cake and three little ones, and she would call across the street: "Jem Finch, Scout Finch, Charles Baker Harris, come here!" Our promptness was always rewarded.

In summertime, twilights are long and peaceful. Often as not, Miss Maudie and I would sit silently on her porch, watching the sky go from yellow to pink as the sun went down, watching flights of martins sweep low over the neighborhood and disappear behind the schoolhouse rooftops.

"Miss Maudie," I said one evening, "do you think Boo Radley's still alive?"

"His name's Arthur and he's alive," she said. She was rocking slowly in her big oak chair. "Do you smell my mimosa? It's like angels' breath this evening."

"Yessum. How do you know?"

"Know what, child?"

"That B—Mr. Arthur's still alive?"

"What a morbid question. But I suppose it's a morbid subject. I know he's alive, Jean Louise, because I haven't seen him carried out yet."

"Maybe he died and they stuffed him up the chimney."

"Where did you get such a notion?"

"That's what Jem said he thought they did."

"S-ss-ss. He gets more like Jack Finch every day."

Miss Maudie had known Uncle Jack Finch, Atticus's brother, since they were children. Nearly the same age, they had grown up together at Finch's Landing. Miss Maudie was the daughter of a neighboring landowner, Dr. Frank Buford. Dr. Buford's profession was medicine and his obsession was anything that grew in the ground, so he stayed poor. Uncle Jack Finch confined his passion for digging to his window boxes in Nashville and stayed rich. We saw Uncle Jack every Christmas, and every Christmas he yelled across the street for Miss Maudie to come marry him. Miss Maudie would yell back, "Call a little louder, Jack Finch, and they'll hear you at the post office, I haven't heard you yet!" Jem and I thought this a strange way to ask for a lady's hand in marriage, but then Uncle Jack was rather strange. He said he was trying to get Miss Maudie's goat, that he had been trying unsuccessfully for forty years, that he was the last person in the world Miss Maudie would think about marrying but the first person she thought about teasing, and the best defense to her was spirited offense, all of which we understood clearly.

"Arthur Radley just stays in the house, that's all," said Miss Maudie. "Wouldn't you stay in the house if you didn't want to come out?"

"Yessum, but I'd wanta come out. Why doesn't he?"

Miss Maudie's eyes narrowed. "You know that story as well as I do."

"I never heard why, though. Nobody ever told me why."

Miss Maudie settled her bridgework. "You know old

Mr. Radley was a foot-washing Baptist—"

"That's what you are, ain't it?"

"My shell's not that hard, child. I'm just a Baptist."

"Don't you all believe in foot-washing?"

"We do. At home in the bathtub."

"But we can't have communion with you all—"

Apparently deciding that it was easier to define primitive baptistry than closed communion, Miss Maudie said: "Foot-washers believe anything that's pleasure is a sin. Did you know some of 'em came out of the woods one Saturday and passed by this place and told me me and my flowers were going to hell?"

"Your flowers, too?"

"Yes ma'am. They'd burn right with me. They thought I spent too much time in God's outdoors and not enough time inside the house reading the Bible."

My confidence in pulpit Gospel lessened at the vision of Miss Maudie stewing forever in various Protestant hells. True enough, she had an acid tongue in her head, and she did not go about the neighborhood doing good, as did Miss Stephanie Crawford. But while no one with a grain of sense trusted Miss Stephanie, Jem and I had considerable faith in Miss Maudie. She had never told on us, had never played cat-and-mouse with us, she was not at all interested in our private lives. She was our friend. How so reasonable a creature could live in peril of everlasting torment was incomprehensible.

"That ain't right, Miss Maudie. You're the best lady I know."

Miss Maudie grinned. "Thank you ma'am. Thing is, foot-washers think women are a sin by definition. They take the Bible literally, you know."

"Is that why Mr. Arthur stays in the house, to keep away from women?"

"I've no idea."

"It doesn't make sense to me. Looks like if Mr. Arthur was hankerin' after heaven he'd come out on the porch at least. Atticus says God's loving folks like you love yourself—"

Miss Maudie stopped rocking, and her voice hardened. "You are too young to understand it," she said, "but sometimes the Bible in the hand of one man is worse than a whiskey bottle in the hand of—oh, of your father."

I was shocked. "Atticus doesn't drink whiskey," I said. "He never drunk a drop in his life—nome, yes he did. He said he drank some one time and didn't like it."

Miss Maudie laughed. "Wasn't talking about your father," she said. "What I meant was, if Atticus Finch drank until he was drunk he wouldn't be as hard as some men are at their best. There are just some kind of men who—who're so busy worrying about the next world they've never learned to live in this one, and you can look down the street and see the results."

"Do you think they're true, all those things they say about B—Mr. Arthur?"

"What things?"

I told her.

"That is three-fourths colored folks and one-fourth Stephanie Crawford," said Miss Maudie grimly. "Stephanie Crawford even told me once she woke up in the middle of the night and found him looking in the window at her. I said what did you do, Stephanie, move over in the bed and make room for him? That shut her up a while."

I was sure it did. Miss Maudie's voice was enough to shut anybody up.

"No, child," she said, "that is a sad house. I remember Arthur Radley when he was a boy. He always spoke nicely to me, no matter what folks said he did. Spoke as nicely as he knew how."

"You reckon he's crazy?"

Miss Maudie shook her head. "If he's not he should be by now. The things that happen to people we never really know. What happens in houses behind closed doors, what secrets—"

"Atticus don't ever do anything to Jem and me in the house that he don't do in the yard," I said, feeling it my duty to defend my parent.

"Gracious child, I was raveling a thread, wasn't even thinking about your father, but now that I am I'll say this: Atticus Finch is the same in his house as he is on the public streets. How'd you like some fresh poundcake to take home?"

I liked it very much.

Next morning when I awakened I found Jem and Dill in the back yard deep in conversation. When I joined them, as usual they said go away.

"Will not. This yard's as much mine as it is yours, Jem Finch. I got just as much right to play in it as you have."

Dill and Jem emerged from a brief huddle: "If you stay you've got to do what we tell you," Dill warned.

"We-ll," I said, "who's so high and mighty all of a sudden?"

"If you don't say you'll do what we tell you, we ain't gonna tell you anything," Dill continued.

"You act like you grew ten inches in the night! All right, what is it?"

Jem said placidly, "We are going to give a note to Boo Radley."

"Just how?" I was trying to fight down the automatic terror rising in me. It was all right for Miss Maudie to talk—she was old and snug on her porch. It was different for us.

Jem was merely going to put the note on the end of a fishing pole and stick it through the shutters. If anyone came along, Dill would ring the bell.

Dill raised his right hand. In it was my mother's silver dinner-bell.

"I'm goin' around to the side of the house," said Jem. "We looked yesterday from across the street, and there's a shutter loose. Think maybe I can make it stick on the window sill, at least."

"Jem—"

"Now you're in it and you can't get out of it, you'll just stay in it, Miss Priss!"

"Okay, okay, but I don't wanta watch. Jem, somebody was—"

"Yes you will, you'll watch the back end of the lot and Dill's gonna watch the front of the house an' up the street, an' if anybody comes he'll ring the bell. That clear?"

"All right then. What'd you write him?"

Dill said, "We're askin' him real politely to come out sometimes, and tell us what he does in there—we said we wouldn't hurt him and we'd buy him an ice cream."

"You all've gone crazy, he'll kill us!"

Dill said, "It's my idea. I figure if he'd come out and sit a spell with us he might feel better."

"How do you know he don't feel good?"

"Well how'd you feel if you'd been shut up for a hundred years with nothin' but cats to eat? I bet he's got a beard down to here—"

"Like your daddy's?"

"He ain't got a beard, he—" Dill stopped, as if trying to remember.

"Uh huh, caughtcha," I said. "You said 'fore you were off the train good your daddy had a black beard—"

"If it's all the same to you he shaved it off last summer! Yeah, an' I've got the letter to prove it—he sent me two dollars, too!"

"Keep on—I reckon he even sent you a mounted police uniform! That'n never showed up, did it? You just keep on tellin' 'em, son—"

Dill Harris could tell the biggest ones I ever heard. Among other things, he had been up in a mail plane seventeen times, he had been to Nova Scotia, he had seen an elephant, and his granddaddy was Brigadier General Joe Wheeler and left him his sword.

"You all hush," said Jem. He scuttled beneath the house and came out with a yellow bamboo pole. "Reckon this is long enough to reach from the sidewalk?"

"Anybody who's brave enough to go up and touch the house hadn't oughta use a fishin' pole," I said. "Why don't you just knock the front door down?"

"This—is—different," said Jem, "how many times do I have to tell you that?"

Dill took a piece of paper from his pocket and gave it to Jem. The three of us walked cautiously toward the old house. Dill remained at the light-pole on the front corner of the lot, and Jem and I edged down the sidewalk parallel to the side of the house. I walked beyond Jem and stood where I could see around the curve.

"All clear," I said. "Not a soul in sight."

Jem looked up the sidewalk to Dill, who nodded.

Jem attached the note to the end of the fishing pole, let the pole out across the yard and pushed it toward the window he had selected. The pole lacked several inches of being long enough, and Jem leaned over as far as he could. I watched him making jabbing motions for so long, I abandoned my post and went to him.

"Can't get it off the pole," he muttered, "or if I get it off I can't make it stay. G'on back down the street, Scout."

I returned and gazed around the curve at the empty road. Occasionally I looked back at Jem, who was patiently trying to place the note on the window sill. It would flutter to the ground and Jem would jab it up, until I thought if Boo Radley ever received it he wouldn't be able to read it. I was looking down the street when the dinner-bell rang.

Shoulder up, I reeled around to face Boo Radley and his bloody fangs; instead, I saw Dill ringing the bell with all his might in Atticus's face.

Jem looked so awful I didn't have the heart to tell him I told him so. He trudged along, dragging the pole behind him on the sidewalk.

Atticus said, "Stop ringing that bell."

Dill grabbed the clapper; in the silence that followed, I wished he'd start ringing it again. Atticus pushed his hat to the back of his head and put his hands on his hips. "Jem," he said, "what were you doing?"

"Nothin', sir."

"I don't want any of that. Tell me."

"I was—we were just tryin' to give somethin' to Mr. Radley."

"What were you trying to give him?"

"Just a letter."

"Let me see it."

Jem held out a filthy piece of paper. Atticus took it and tried to read it. "Why do you want Mr. Radley to come out?"

Dill said, "We thought he might enjoy us . . ." and dried up when Atticus looked at him.

"Son," he said to Jem, "I'm going to tell you something and tell you one time: stop tormenting that man. That goes for the other two of you."

What Mr. Radley did was his own business. If he wanted to come out, he would. If he wanted to stay inside his own house he had the right to stay inside free from the attentions of inquisitive children, which was a mild term for the likes of us. How would we like it if Atticus barged in on us without knocking, when we were in our rooms at night? We were, in effect, doing the same thing to Mr. Radley. What Mr. Radley did might seem peculiar to us, but it did not seem peculiar to him. Furthermore, had it never occurred to us that the civil way to communicate with another being was by the front door instead of a side window? Lastly, we were to stay away from that house until we were invited there, we were not to play an asinine game he had seen us playing or make fun of anybody on this street or in this town—

"We weren't makin' fun of him, we weren't laughin' at him," said Jem, "we were just—"

"So that was what you were doing, wasn't it?"

"Makin' fun of him?"

"No," said Atticus, "putting his life's history on display for the edification of the neighborhood."

Jem seemed to swell a little. "I didn't say we were doin' that, I didn't say it!"

Atticus grinned dryly. "You just told me," he said. "You stop this nonsense right now, every one of you."

Jem gaped at him.

"You want to be a lawyer, don't you?" Our father's mouth was suspiciously firm, as if he were trying to hold it in line.

Jem decided there was no point in quibbling, and was silent. When Atticus went inside the house to retrieve a file he had forgotten to take to work that morning, Jem finally realized that he had been done in by the oldest lawyer's trick on record. He waited a respectful distance from the front steps, watched Atticus leave the house and walk toward town. When Atticus was out of earshot Jem yelled after him: "I thought I wanted to be a lawyer but I ain't so sure now!"

6.

Yes," said our father, when Jem asked him if we could go over and sit by Miss Rachel's fishpool with Dill, as this was his last night in Maycomb. "Tell him so long for me, and we'll see him next summer."

We leaped over the low wall that separated Miss Rachel's yard from our driveway. Jem whistled bob-white and Dill answered in the darkness.

"Not a breath blowing," said Jem. "Looka yonder."

He pointed to the east. A gigantic moon was rising behind Miss Maudie's pecan trees. "That makes it seem hotter," he said.

"Cross in it tonight?" asked Dill, not looking up. He was constructing a cigarette from newspaper and string.

"No, just the lady. Don't light that thing, Dill, you'll stink up this whole end of town."

There was a lady in the moon in Maycomb. She sat at a dresser combing her hair.

"We're gonna miss you, boy," I said. "Reckon we better watch for Mr. Avery?"

Mr. Avery boarded across the street from Mrs. Henry Lafayette Dubose's house. Besides making change in the collection plate every Sunday, Mr. Avery sat on the porch every night until nine o'clock and sneezed. One evening we were privileged to witness a performance by him which seemed to have been his positively last, for he never did it again so long as we watched. Jem and I were leaving Miss Rachel's front steps one night when Dill stopped us: "Golly, looka yonder." He pointed across the street. At first we saw nothing but a kudzu-covered front porch, but a closer inspection revealed an arc of water descending from the leaves and splashing in the yellow circle of the street light, some ten feet from source to earth, it seemed to us. Jem said Mr. Avery misfigured, Dill said he must drink a gallon a day, and the ensuing contest to determine relative distances and respective prowess only made me feel left out again, as I was untalented in this area.

Dill stretched, yawned, and said altogether too casually, "I know what, let's go for a walk."

He sounded fishy to me. Nobody in Maycomb just went for a walk. "Where to, Dill?"

Dill jerked his head in a southerly direction.

Jem said, "Okay." When I protested, he said sweetly, "You don't have to come along, Angel May."

"You don't have to go. Remember—"

Jem was not one to dwell on past defeats: it seemed the only message he got from Atticus was insight into the art of cross examination. "Scout, we ain't gonna do anything, we're just goin' to the street light and back."

We strolled silently down the sidewalk, listening to porch swings creaking with the weight of the neighborhood, listening to the soft night-murmurs of the grown people on our street. Occasionally we heard Miss Stephanie Crawford laugh.

"Well?" said Dill.

"Okay," said Jem. "Why don't you go on home, Scout?"

"What are you gonna do?"

Dill and Jem were simply going to peep in the window with the loose shutter to see if they could get a look at Boo Radley, and if I didn't want to go with them I could go straight home and keep my fat flopping mouth shut, that was all.

"But what in the sam holy hill did you wait till tonight?"

Because nobody could see them at night, because Atticus would be so deep in a book he wouldn't hear the Kingdom coming, because if Boo Radley killed them they'd miss school instead of vacation, and because it was easier to see inside a dark house in the dark than in the daytime, did I understand?

"Jem, *please*—"

"Scout, I'm tellin' you for the last time, shut your trap or go home—I declare to the Lord you're gettin' more like a girl every day!"

With that, I had no option but to join them. We thought it was better to go under the high wire fence at the rear of the Radley lot, we stood less chance of being seen. The fence enclosed a large garden and a narrow wooden outhouse.

Jem held up the bottom wire and motioned Dill under it. I followed, and held up the wire for Jem. It was a tight squeeze for him. "Don't make a sound," he whispered. "Don't get in a row of collards whatever you do, they'll wake the dead."

With this thought in mind, I made perhaps one step per minute. I moved faster when I saw Jem far ahead beckoning in the moonlight. We came to the gate that divided the garden from the back yard. Jem touched it. The gate squeaked.

"Spit on it," whispered Dill.

"You've got us in a box, Jem," I muttered. "We can't

get out of here so easy."

"Sh-h. Spit on it, Scout."

We spat ourselves dry, and Jem opened the gate slowly, lifting it aside and resting it on the fence. We were in the back yard.

The back of the Radley house was less inviting than the front: a ramshackle porch ran the width of the house; there were two doors and two dark windows between the doors. Instead of a column, a rough two-by-four supported one end of the roof. An old Franklin stove sat in a corner of the porch; above it a hat-rack mirror caught the moon and shone eerily.

"Ar-r," said Jem softly, lifting his foot.

"'Smatter?"

"Chickens," he breathed.

That we would be obliged to dodge the unseen from all directions was confirmed when Dill ahead of us spelled G-o-d in a whisper. We crept to the side of the house, around to the window with the hanging shutter. The sill was several inches taller than Jem.

"Give you a hand up," he muttered to Dill. "Wait, though." Jem grabbed his left wrist and my right wrist, I grabbed my left wrist and Jem's right wrist, we crouched, and Dill sat on our saddle. We raised him and he caught the window sill.

"Hurry," Jem whispered, "we can't last much longer."

Dill punched my shoulder, and we lowered him to the ground.

"What'd you see?"

"Nothing. Curtains. There's a little teeny light way off somewhere, though."

"Let's get away from here," breathed Jem. "Let's go 'round in back again. Sh-h," he warned me, as I was about to protest.

"Let's try the back window."

"Dill, *no*," I said.

Dill stopped and let Jem go ahead. When Jem put his foot on the bottom step, the step squeaked. He stood still, then tried his weight by degrees. The step was silent. Jem skipped two steps, put his foot on the porch, heaved himself to it, and teetered a long moment. He regained his balance and dropped to his knees. He crawled to the window, raised his head and looked in.

Then I saw the shadow. It was the shadow of a man with a hat on. At first I thought it was a tree, but there was no wind blowing, and tree-trunks never walked. The back porch was bathed in moonlight, and the shadow, crisp as toast, moved across the porch toward Jem.

Dill saw it next. He put his hands to his face.

When it crossed Jem, Jem saw it. He put his arms over his head and went rigid.

The shadow stopped about a foot beyond Jem. Its arm came out from its side, dropped, and was still. Then it turned and moved back across Jem, walked along the porch and off the side of the house, returning as it had come.

Jem leaped off the porch and galloped toward us. He flung open the gate, danced Dill and me through, and shooed us between two rows of swishing collards. Halfway through the collards I tripped; as I tripped the roar of a shotgun shattered the neighborhood.

Dill and Jem dived beside me. Jem's breath came in sobs: "Fence by the schoolyard!—hurry, Scout!"

Jem held the bottom wire; Dill and I rolled through and were halfway to the shelter of the schoolyard's solitary oak when we sensed that Jem was not with us. We ran back and found him struggling in the fence, kicking his pants off to get loose. He ran to the oak tree in his shorts.

Safely behind it, we gave way to numbness, but Jem's mind was racing: "We gotta get home, they'll miss us."

We ran across the schoolyard, crawled under the fence to Deer's Pasture behind our house, climbed our back fence and were at the back steps before Jem would let us pause to rest.

Respiration normal, the three of us strolled as casually as we could to the front yard. We looked down the street and saw a circle of neighbors at the Radley front gate.

"We better go down there," said Jem. "They'll think it's funny if we don't show up."

Mr. Nathan Radley was standing inside his gate, a shotgun broken across his arm. Atticus was standing beside Miss Maudie and Miss Stephanie Crawford. Miss Rachel and Mr. Avery were near by. None of them saw us come up.

We eased in beside Miss Maudie, who looked around.

"Where were you all, didn't you hear the commotion?"

"What happened?" asked Jem.

"Mr. Radley shot at a Negro in his collard patch."

"Oh. Did he hit him?"

"No," said Miss Stephanie. "Shot in the air. Scared him pale, though. Says if anybody sees a white nigger around, that's the one. Says he's got the other barrel waitin' for the next sound he hears in that patch, an' next time he won't aim high, be it dog, nigger, or—Jem *Finch!*"

"Ma'am?" asked Jem.

Atticus spoke. "Where're your pants, son?"

"Pants, sir?"

"Pants."

It was no use. In his shorts before God and everybody. I sighed.

"Ah—Mr. Finch?"

In the glare from the streetlight, I could see Dill hatching one: his eyes widened, his fat cherub face grew rounder.

"What is it, Dill?" asked Atticus.

"Ah—I won 'em from him," he said vaguely.

"Won them? How?"

Dill's hand sought the back of his head. He brought it forward and across his forehead. "We were playin' strip poker up yonder by the fishpool," he said.

Jem and I relaxed. The neighbors seemed satisfied: they all stiffened. But what was strip poker?

We had no chance to find out: Miss Rachel went off like the town fire siren: "Do-o-o Jee-sus, Dill Harris! Gamblin' by my fishpool? I'll strip-poker you, sir!"

Atticus saved Dill from immediate dismemberment. "Just a minute, Miss Rachel," he said. "I've never heard of 'em doing that before. Were you all playing cards?"

Jem fielded Dill's fly with his eyes shut: "No sir, just with matches."

I admired my brother. Matches were dangerous, but cards were fatal.

"Jem, Scout," said Atticus, "I don't want to hear of poker in any form again. Go by Dill's and get your pants, Jem. Settle it yourselves."

"Don't worry, Dill," said Jem, as we trotted up the sidewalk, "she ain't gonna get you. He'll talk her out of it. That was fast thinkin', son. Listen . . . you hear?"

We stopped, and heard Atticus's voice: ". . . not serious . . . they all go through it, Miss Rachel. . . ."

Dill was comforted, but Jem and I weren't. There was the problem of Jem showing up some pants in the morning.

"'d give you some of mine," said Dill, as we came to Miss Rachel's steps. Jem said he couldn't get in them, but thanks anyway. We said good-bye, and Dill went inside the house. He evidently remembered he was engaged to me, for he ran back out and kissed me swiftly in front of Jem. "Yawl write, hear?" he bawled after us.

Had Jem's pants been safely on him, we would not have slept much anyway. Every night-sound I heard from my cot on the back porch was magnified three-fold; every scratch of feet on gravel was Boo Radley seeking revenge, every passing Negro laughing in the night was Boo Radley loose and after us; insects splashing against the screen were Boo Radley's insane fingers picking the wire to pieces; the chinaberry trees were malignant, hovering, alive. I lingered between sleep and wakefulness until I heard Jem murmur.

"Sleep, Little Three-Eyes?"

"Are you crazy?"

"Sh-h. Atticus's light's out."

In the waning moonlight I saw Jem swing his feet to the floor.

"I'm goin' after 'em," he said.

I sat upright. "You can't. I won't let you."

He was struggling into his shirt. "I've got to."

"You do an' I'll wake up Atticus."

"You do and I'll kill you."

I pulled him down beside me on the cot. I tried to reason with him. "Mr. Nathan's gonna find 'em in the morning, Jem. He knows you lost 'em. When he shows 'em to Atticus it'll be pretty bad, that's all there is to it. Go'n back to bed."

"That's what I know," said Jem. "That's why I'm goin' after 'em."

I began to feel sick. Going back to that place by himself—I remembered Miss Stephanie: Mr. Nathan had the other barrel waiting for the next sound he heard, be it nigger, dog . . . Jem knew that better than I.

I was desperate: "Look, it ain't worth it, Jem. A lickin' hurts but it doesn't last. You'll get your head shot off, Jem. Please . . ."

He blew out his breath patiently. "I—it's like this, Scout," he muttered. "Atticus ain't ever whipped me since I can remember. I wanta keep it that way."

This was a thought. It seemed that Atticus threatened us every other day. "You mean he's never caught you at anything."

"Maybe so, but—I just wanta keep it that way, Scout. We shouldn'a done that tonight, Scout."

It was then, I suppose, that Jem and I first began to part company. Sometimes I did not understand him, but my periods of bewilderment were short-lived. This was beyond me. "Please," I pleaded, "can'tcha just think about it for a minute—by yourself on that place—"

"Shut up!"

"It's not like he'd never speak to you again or some-thin' . . . I'm gonna wake him up, Jem, I swear I am—"

Jem grabbed my pajama collar and wrenched it tight. "Then I'm goin' with you—" I choked.

"No you ain't, you'll just make noise."

It was no use. I unlatched the back door and held it while he crept down the steps. It must have been two o'clock. The moon was setting and the lattice-work shadows were fading into fuzzy nothingness. Jem's white shirt-tail dipped and bobbed like a small ghost dancing away to escape the coming morning. A faint breeze stirred and cooled the sweat running down my sides.

He went the back way, through Deer's Pasture, across the school-yard and around to the fence, I thought—at least that was the way he was headed. It would take longer, so it was not time to worry yet. I waited until it was time to worry and listened for Mr. Radley's shotgun. Then I thought I heard the back fence squeak. It was wishful thinking.

Then I heard Atticus cough. I held my breath. Sometimes when we made a midnight pilgrimage to the bathroom we would find him reading. He said he often woke up during the night, checked on us, and read himself back to sleep. I waited for his light to go on, straining my eyes to see it flood the hall. It stayed off, and I breathed again.

The night-crawlers had retired, but ripe chinaberries drummed on the roof when the wind stirred, and the darkness was desolate with the barking of distant dogs.

There he was, returning to me. His white shirt bobbed over the back fence and slowly grew larger. He came up the back steps, latched the door behind him, and sat on his cot. Wordlessly, he held up his pants. He lay down, and for a while I heard his cot trembling. Soon he was still. I did not hear him stir again.

7.

Jem stayed moody and silent for a week. As Atticus had once advised me to do, I tried to climb into Jem's skin and walk around in it: if I had gone alone to the Radley Place at two in the morning, my funeral would have been held the next afternoon. So I left Jem alone and tried not to bother him.

School started. The second grade was as bad as the first, only worse—they still flashed cards at you and wouldn't let you read or write. Miss Caroline's progress next door could be estimated by the frequency of laughter; however, the usual crew had flunked the first grade again, and were helpful in keeping order. The only thing good about the second grade was that this year I had to stay as late as Jem, and we usually walked home together at three o'clock.

One afternoon when we were crossing the schoolyard toward home, Jem suddenly said: "There's something I didn't tell you."

As this was his first complete sentence in several days, I encouraged him: "About what?"

"About that night."

"You've never told me anything about that night," I said.

Jem waved my words away as if fanning gnats. He

was silent for a while, then he said, "When I went back for my breeches—they were all in a tangle when I was gettin' out of 'em, I couldn't get 'em loose. When I went back—" Jem took a deep breath. "When I went back, they were folded across the fence . . . like they were expectin' me."

"Across—"

"And something else—" Jem's voice was flat. "Show you when we get home. They'd been sewed up. Not like a lady sewed 'em, like somethin' I'd try to do. All crooked. It's almost like—"

"—somebody knew you were comin' back for 'em."

Jem shuddered. "Like somebody was readin' my mind . . . like somebody could tell what I was gonna do. Can't anybody tell what I'm gonna do lest they know me, can they, Scout?"

Jem's question was an appeal. I reassured him: "Can't anybody tell what you're gonna do lest they live in the house with you, and even I can't tell sometimes."

We were walking past our tree. In its knot-hole rested a ball of gray twine.

"Don't take it, Jem," I said. "This is somebody's hidin' place."

"I don't think so, Scout."

"Yes it is. Somebody like Walter Cunningham comes down here every recess and hides his things—and we come along and take 'em away from him. Listen, let's leave it and wait a couple of days. If it ain't gone then, we'll take it, okay?"

"Okay, you might be right," said Jem. "It must be some little kid's place—hides his things from the bigger folks. You know it's only when school's in that we've found things."

"Yeah," I said, "but we never go by here in the summertime."

We went home. Next morning the twine was where we had left it. When it was still there on the third day, Jem pocketed it. From then on, we considered everything we found in the knot-hole our property.

The second grade was grim, but Jem assured me that the older I got the better school would be, that he started off the same way, and it was not until one reached the sixth grade that one learned anything of value. The sixth grade seemed to please him from the beginning: he went through a brief Egyptian Period that baffled me—he tried to walk flat a great deal, sticking one arm in front of him and one in back of him, putting one foot behind the other. He declared Egyptians walked that way; I said if they did I didn't see how they got anything done, but Jem said they accomplished more than the Americans ever did, they invented toilet paper and perpetual embalming, and asked where would we be today if they hadn't? Atticus told me to delete the adjectives and I'd have the facts.

There are no clearly defined seasons in South Alabama; summer drifts into autumn, and autumn is sometimes never followed by winter, but turns to a days-old spring that melts into summer again. That fall was a long one, hardly cool enough for a light jacket. Jem and I were trotting in our orbit one mild October afternoon when our knot-hole stopped us again. Something white was inside this time.

Jem let me do the honors: I pulled out two small images carved in soap. One was the figure of a boy, the other wore a crude dress.

Before I remembered that there was no such thing as hoo-dooing, I shrieked and threw them down.

Jem snatched them up. "What's the matter with you?" he yelled. He rubbed the figures free of red dust. "These are good," he said. "I've never seen any these good."

He held them down to me. They were almost perfect miniatures of two children. The boy had on shorts, and a shock of soapy hair fell to his eyebrows. I looked up at Jem. A point of straight brown hair kicked downwards from his part. I had never noticed it before.

Jem looked from the girl-doll to me. The girl-doll wore bangs. So did I.

"These are us," he said.

"Who did 'em, you reckon?"

"Who do we know around here who whittles?" he asked.

"Mr. Avery."

"Mr. Avery just does like this. I mean carves."

64

Mr. Avery averaged a stick of stovewood per week; he honed it down to a toothpick and chewed it.

"There's old Miss Stephanie Crawford's sweetheart," I said.

"He carves all right, but he lives down the country. When would he ever pay any attention to us?"

"Maybe he sits on the porch and looks at us instead of Miss Stephanie. If I was him, I would."

Jem stared at me so long I asked what was the matter, but got Nothing, Scout for an answer. When we went home, Jem put the dolls in his trunk.

Less than two weeks later we found a whole package of chewing gum, which we enjoyed, the fact that everything on the Radley Place was poison having slipped Jem's memory.

The following week the knot-hole yielded a tarnished medal. Jem showed it to Atticus, who said it was a spelling medal, that before we were born the Maycomb County schools had spelling contests and awarded medals to the winners. Atticus said someone must have lost it, and had we asked around? Jem camel-kicked me when I tried to say where we had found it. Jem asked Atticus if he remembered anybody who ever won one, and Atticus said no.

Our biggest prize appeared four days later. It was a pocket watch that wouldn't run, on a chain with an aluminum knife.

"You reckon it's white gold, Jem?"

"Don't know. I'll show it to Atticus."

Atticus said it would probably be worth ten dollars, knife, chain and all, if it were new. "Did you swap with somebody at school?" he asked.

"Oh, no sir!" Jem pulled out his grandfather's watch that Atticus let him carry once a week if Jem were careful with it. On the days he carried the watch, Jem walked on eggs. "Atticus, if it's all right with you, I'd rather have this one instead. Maybe I can fix it."

When the new wore off his grandfather's watch, and carrying it became a day's burdensome task, Jem no longer felt the necessity of ascertaining the hour every five minutes.

He did a fair job, only one spring and two tiny pieces left over, but the watch would not run. "Oh-h," he sighed, "it'll never go. Scout—?"

"Huh?"

"You reckon we oughta write a letter to whoever's leaving us these things?"

"That'd be right nice, Jem, we can thank 'em—what's wrong?"

Jem was holding his ears, shaking his head from side to side. "I don't get it, I just don't get it—I don't know why, Scout . . ." He looked toward the livingroom. "I've gotta good mind to tell Atticus—no, I reckon not."

"I'll tell him for you."

"No, don't do that, Scout. Scout?"

"Wha-t?"

He had been on the verge of telling me something all evening; his face would brighten and he would lean toward me, then he would change his mind. He changed it again. "Oh, nothin'."

"Here, let's write a letter." I pushed a tablet and pencil under his nose.

"Okay. Dear Mister . . ."

"How do you know it's a man? I bet it's Miss Maudie—been bettin' that for a long time."

"Ar-r, Miss Maudie can't chew gum—" Jem broke into a grin. "You know, she can talk real pretty sometimes. One time I asked her to have a chew and she said no thanks, that—chewing gum cleaved to her palate and rendered her speechless," said Jem carefully. "Doesn't that sound nice?"

"Yeah, she can say nice things sometimes. She wouldn't have a watch and chain anyway."

"Dear sir," said Jem. "We appreciate the—no, we appreciate everything which you have put into the tree for us. Yours very truly, Jeremy Atticus Finch."

"He won't know who you are if you sign it like that, Jem."

Jem erased his name and wrote, "Jem Finch." I signed, "Jean Louise Finch (Scout)," beneath it. Jem put the note in an envelope.

Next morning on the way to school he ran ahead of me and stopped at the tree. Jem was facing me when he looked up, and I saw him go stark white.

"Scout!"

I ran to him.

Someone had filled our knot-hole with cement.

"Don't you cry, now, Scout . . . don't cry now, don't you worry—" he muttered at me all the way to school.

When we went home for dinner Jem bolted his food, ran to the porch and stood on the steps. I followed him. "Hasn't passed by yet," he said.

Next day Jem repeated his vigil and was rewarded.

"Hidy do, Mr. Nathan," he said.

"Morning Jem, Scout," said Mr. Radley, as he went by.

"Mr. Radley," said Jem.

Mr. Radley turned around.

"Mr. Radley, ah—did you put cement in that hole in that tree down yonder?"

"Yes," he said. "I filled it up."

"Why'd you do it, sir?"

"Tree's dying. You plug 'em with cement when they're sick. You ought to know that, Jem."

Jem said nothing more about it until late afternoon. When we passed our tree he gave it a meditative pat on its cement, and remained deep in thought. He seemed to be working himself into a bad humor, so I kept my distance.

As usual, we met Atticus coming home from work that evening. When we were at our steps Jem said, "Atticus, look down yonder at that tree, please sir."

"What tree, son?"

"The one on the corner of the Radley lot comin' from school."

"Yes?"

"Is that tree dyin'?"

"Why no, son, I don't think so. Look at the leaves, they're all green and full, no brown patches anywhere—"

"It ain't even sick?"

"That tree's as healthy as you are, Jem. Why?"

"Mr. Nathan Radley said it was dyin'."

"Well maybe it is. I'm sure Mr. Radley knows more about his trees than we do."

Atticus left us on the porch. Jem leaned on a pillar, rubbing his shoulders against it.

"Do you itch, Jem?" I asked as politely as I could. He did not answer. "Come on in, Jem," I said.

"After while."

He stood there until nightfall, and I waited for him.

67

When we went in the house I saw he had been crying; his face was dirty in the right places, but I thought it odd that I had not heard him.

8.

For reasons unfathomable to the most experienced prophets in Maycomb County, autumn turned to winter that year. We had two weeks of the coldest weather since 1885, Atticus said. Mr. Avery said it was written on the Rosetta Stone that when children disobeyed their parents, smoked cigarettes and made war on each other, the seasons would change: Jem and I were burdened with the guilt of contributing to the aberrations of nature, thereby causing unhappiness to our neighbors and discomfort to ourselves.

Old Mrs. Radley died that winter, but her death caused hardly a ripple—the neighborhood seldom saw her, except when she watered her cannas. Jem and I decided that Boo had got her at last, but when Atticus returned from the Radley house he said she died of natural causes, to our disappointment.

"Ask him," Jem whispered.

"You ask him, you're the oldest."

"That's why you oughta ask him."

"Atticus," I said, "did you see Mr. Arthur?"

Atticus looked sternly around his newspaper at me: "I did not."

Jem restrained me from further questions. He said Atticus was still touchous about us and the Radleys and it wouldn't do to push him any. Jem had a notion that Atticus thought our activities that night last summer were not solely confined to strip poker. Jem had no firm basis for his ideas, he said it was merely a twitch.

Next morning I awoke, looked out the window and nearly died of fright. My screams brought Atticus from his bathroom half-shaven.

"The world's endin', Atticus! Please do something—!"

I dragged him to the window and pointed.

"No it's not," he said. "It's snowing."

Jem asked Atticus would it keep up. Jem had never seen snow either, but he knew what it was. Atticus said he didn't know any more about snow than Jem did. "I think, though, if it's watery like that, it'll turn to rain."

The telephone rang and Atticus left the breakfast table to answer it. "That was Eula May," he said when he returned. "I quote—'As it has not snowed in Maycomb County since 1885, there will be no school today.'"

Eula May was Maycomb's leading telephone operator. She was entrusted with issuing public announcements, wedding invitations, setting off the fire siren, and giving first-aid instructions when Dr. Reynolds was away.

When Atticus finally called us to order and bade us look at our plates instead of out the windows, Jem asked, "How do you make a snowman?"

"I haven't the slightest idea," said Atticus. "I don't want you all to be disappointed, but I doubt if there'll be enough snow for a snowball, even."

Calpurnia came in and said she thought it was sticking. When we ran to the back yard, it was covered with a feeble layer of soggy snow.

"We shouldn't walk about in it," said Jem. "Look, every step you take's wasting it."

I looked back at my mushy footprints. Jem said if we waited until it snowed some more we could scrape it all up for a snowman. I stuck out my tongue and caught a fat flake. It burned.

"Jem, it's hot!"

"No it ain't, it's so cold it burns. Now don't eat it, Scout, you're wasting it. Let it come down."

"But I want to walk in it."

"I know what, we can go walk over at Miss Maudie's."

Jem hopped across the front yard. I followed in his tracks. When we were on the sidewalk in front of Miss Maudie's, Mr. Avery accosted us. He had a pink face and a big stomach below his belt.

"See what you've done?" he said. "Hasn't snowed in Maycomb since Appomattox. It's bad children like you makes the seasons change."

I wondered if Mr. Avery knew how hopefully we had watched last summer for him to repeat his performance, and reflected that if this was our reward, there was something to say for sin. I did not wonder where Mr. Avery gathered his meteorological statistics: they came straight from the Rosetta Stone.

"Jem Finch, you Jem Finch!"

"Miss Maudie's callin' you, Jem."

"You all stay in the middle of the yard. There's some thrift buried under the snow near the porch. Don't step on it!"

"Yessum!" called Jem. "It's beautiful, ain't it, Miss Maudie?"

"Beautiful my hind foot! If it freezes tonight it'll carry off all my azaleas!"

Miss Maudie's old sunhat glistened with snow crystals. She was bending over some small bushes, wrapping them in burlap bags. Jem asked her what she was doing that for.

"Keep 'em warm," she said.

"How can flowers keep warm? They don't circulate."

"I cannot answer that question, Jem Finch. All I know is if it freezes tonight these plants'll freeze, so you cover 'em up. Is that clear?"

"Yessum. Miss Maudie?"

"What, sir?"

"Could Scout and me borrow some of your snow?"

"Heavens alive, take it all! There's an old peach basket under the house, haul it off in that." Miss Maudie's eyes narrowed. "Jem Finch, what are you going to do with my snow?"

"You'll see," said Jem, and we transferred as much snow as we could from Miss Maudie's yard to ours, a slushy operation.

"What are we gonna do, Jem?" I asked.

"You'll see," he said. "Now get the basket and haul all the snow you can rake up from the back yard to the front. Walk back in your tracks, though," he cautioned.

"Are we gonna have a snow baby, Jem?"

"No, a real snowman. Gotta work hard, now."

Jem ran to the back yard, produced the garden hoe and began digging quickly behind the woodpile, placing any worms he found to one side. He went in the house,

70

returned with the laundry hamper, filled it with earth and carried it to the front yard:

When we had five baskets of earth and two baskets of snow, Jem said we were ready to begin.

"Don't you think this is kind of a mess?" I asked.

"Looks messy now, but it won't later," he said.

Jem scooped up an armful of dirt, patted it into a mound on which he added another load, and another until he had constructed a torso.

"Jem, I ain't ever heard of a nigger snowman," I said.

"He won't be black long," he grunted.

Jem procured some peachtree switches from the back yard, plaited them, and bent them into bones to be covered with dirt.

"He looks like Stephanie Crawford with her hands on her hips," I said. "Fat in the middle and little-bitty arms."

"I'll make 'em bigger." Jem sloshed water over the mud man and added more dirt. He looked thoughtfully at it for a moment, then he molded a big stomach below the figure's waistline. Jem glanced at me, his eyes twinkling: "Mr. Avery's sort of shaped like a snowman, ain't he?"

Jem scooped up some snow and began plastering it on. He permitted me to cover only the back, saving the public parts for himself. Gradually Mr. Avery turned white.

Using bits of wood for eyes, nose, mouth, and buttons, Jem succeeded in making Mr. Avery look cross. A stick of stovewood completed the picture. Jem stepped back and viewed his creation.

"It's lovely, Jem," I said. "Looks almost like he'd talk to you."

"It is, ain't it?" he said shyly.

We could not wait for Atticus to come home for dinner, but called and said we had a big surprise for him. He seemed surprised when he saw most of the back yard in the front yard, but he said we had done a jim-dandy job. "I didn't know how you were going to do it," he said to Jem, "but from now on I'll never worry about what'll become of you, son, you'll always have an idea."

Jem's ears reddened from Atticus's compliment, but he looked up sharply when he saw Atticus stepping back. Atticus squinted at the snowman a while. He grinned, then laughed. "Son, I can't tell what you're going to be—an engineer, a lawyer, or a portrait painter. You've perpetrated a near libel here in the front yard. We've got to disguise this fellow."

Atticus suggested that Jem hone down his creation's front a little, swap a broom for the stovewood, and put an apron on him.

Jem explained that if he did, the snowman would become muddy and cease to be a snowman.

"I don't care what you do, so long as you do something," said Atticus. "You can't go around making caricatures of the neighbors."

"Ain't a characterture," said Jem. "It looks just like him."

"Mr. Avery might not think so."

"I know what!" said Jem. He raced across the street, disappeared into Miss Maudie's back yard and returned triumphant. He stuck her sunhat on the snowman's head and jammed her hedge-clippers into the crook of his arm. Atticus said that would be fine.

Miss Maudie opened her front door and came out on the porch. She looked across the street at us. Suddenly she grinned. "Jem Finch," she called. "You devil, bring me back my hat, sir!"

Jem looked up at Atticus, who shook his head. "She's just fussing," he said. "She's really impressed with your —accomplishments."

Atticus strolled over to Miss Maudie's sidewalk, where they engaged in an arm-waving conversation, the only phrase of which I caught was ". . . erected an absolute morphodite in that yard! Atticus, you'll never raise 'em!"

The snow stopped in the afternoon, the temperature dropped, and by nightfall Mr. Avery's direst predictions came true: Calpurnia kept every fireplace in the house blazing, but we were cold. When Atticus came home that evening he said we were in for it, and asked Calpurnia if she wanted to stay with us for the night. Calpurnia glanced up at the high ceilings and long windows and said she thought she'd be warmer at her house. Atticus drove her home in the car.

Before I went to sleep Atticus put more coal on the fire in my room. He said the thermometer registered sixteen, that it was the coldest night in his memory, and that our snowman outside was frozen solid.

Minutes later, it seemed, I was awakened by someone shaking me. Atticus's overcoat was spread across me. "Is it morning already?"

"Baby, get up."

Atticus was holding out my bathrobe and coat. "Put your robe on first," he said.

Jem was standing beside Atticus, groggy and tousled. He was holding his overcoat closed at the neck, his other hand was jammed into his pocket. He looked strangely overweight.

"Hurry, hon," said Atticus. "Here're your shoes and socks."

Stupidly, I put them on. "Is it morning?"

"No, it's a little after one. Hurry now."

That something was wrong finally got through to me. "What's the matter?"

By then he did not have to tell me. Just as the birds know where to go when it rains, I knew when there was trouble in our street. Soft taffeta-like sounds and muffled scurrying sounds filled me with helpless dread.

"Whose is it?"

"Miss Maudie's, hon," said Atticus gently.

At the front door, we saw fire spewing from Miss Maudie's diningroom windows. As if to confirm what we saw, the town fire siren wailed up the scale to a treble pitch and remained there, screaming.

"It's gone, ain't it?" moaned Jem.

"I expect so," said Atticus. "Now listen, both of you. Go down and stand in front of the Radley Place. Keep out of the way, do you hear? See which way the wind's blowing?"

"Oh," said Jem. "Atticus, reckon we oughta start moving the furniture out?"

"Not yet, son. Do as I tell you. Run now. Take care of Scout, you hear? Don't let her out of your sight."

With a push, Atticus started us toward the Radley front gate. We stood watching the street fill with men and cars while fire silently devoured Miss Maudie's house. "Why don't they hurry, why don't they hurry . . ." muttered Jem.

We saw why. The old fire truck, killed by the cold, was being pushed from town by a crowd of men. When the men attached its hose to a hydrant, the hose burst and water shot up, tinkling down on the pavement.

"Oh-h Lord, Jem . . ."

Jem put his arm around me. "Hush, Scout," he said. "It ain't time to worry yet. I'll let you know when."

The men of Maycomb, in all degrees of dress and undress, took furniture from Miss Maudie's house to a yard across the street. I saw Atticus carrying Miss Maudie's heavy oak rocking chair, and thought it sensible of him to save what she valued most.

Sometimes we heard shouts. Then Mr. Avery's face appeared in an upstairs window. He pushed a mattress out the window into the street and threw down furniture until men shouted, "Come down from there, Dick! The stairs are going! Get outta there, Mr. Avery!"

Mr. Avery began climbing through the window.

"Scout, he's stuck . . ." breathed Jem. "Oh God . . ."

Mr. Avery was wedged tightly. I buried my head under Jem's arm and didn't look again until Jem cried, "He's got loose, Scout! He's all right!"

I looked up to see Mr. Avery cross the upstairs porch. He swung his legs over the railing and was sliding down a pillar when he slipped. He fell, yelled, and hit Miss Maudie's shrubbery.

Suddenly I noticed that the men were backing away from Miss Maudie's house, moving down the street toward us. They were no longer carrying furniture. The fire was well into the second floor and had eaten its way to the roof: window frames were black against a vivid orange center.

"Jem, it looks like a pumpkin—"

"Scout, look!"

Smoke was rolling off our house and Miss Rachel's house like fog off a riverbank, and men were pulling hoses toward them. Behind us, the fire truck from Abbottsville screamed around the curve and stopped in front of our house.

"That book . . ." I said.

"What?" said Jem.

"That Tom Swift book, it ain't mine, it's Dill's . . ."

"Don't worry, Scout, it ain't time to worry yet," said Jem. He pointed. "Looka yonder."

In a group of neighbors, Atticus was standing with his

hands in his overcoat pockets. He might have been watching a football game. Miss Maudie was beside him.

"See there, he's not worried yet," said Jem.

"Why ain't he on top of one of the houses?"

"He's too old, he'd break his neck."

"You think we oughta make him get our stuff out?"

"Let's don't pester him, he'll know when it's time," said Jem.

The Abbottsville fire truck began pumping water on our house; a man on the roof pointed to places that needed it most. I watched our Absolute Morphodite go black and crumble; Miss Maudie's sunhat settled on top of the heap. I could not see her hedge-clippers. In the heat between our house, Miss Rachel's and Miss Maudie's, the men had long ago shed coats and bathrobes. They worked in pajama tops and nightshirts stuffed into their pants, but I became aware that I was slowly freezing where I stood. Jem tried to keep me warm, but his arm was not enough. I pulled free of it and clutched my shoulders. By dancing a little, I could feel my feet.

Another fire truck appeared and stopped in front of Miss Stephanie Crawford's. There was no hydrant for another hose, and the men tried to soak her house with hand extinguishers.

Miss Maudie's tin roof quelled the flames. Roaring, the house collapsed; fire gushed everywhere, followed by a flurry of blankets from men on top of the adjacent houses, beating out sparks and burning chunks of wood.

It was dawn before the men began to leave, first one by one, then in groups. They pushed the Maycomb fire truck back to town, the Abbottsville truck departed, the third one remained. We found out next day it had come from Clark's Ferry, sixty miles away.

Jem and I slid across the street. Miss Maudie was staring at the smoking black hole in her yard, and Atticus shook his head to tell us she did not want to talk. He led us home, holding onto our shoulders to cross the icy street. He said Miss Maudie would stay with Miss Stephanie for the time being.

"Anybody want some hot chocolate?" he asked. I shuddered when Atticus started a fire in the kitchen stove.

As we drank our cocoa I noticed Atticus looking at me,

first with curiosity, then with sternness. "I thought I told you and Jem to stay put," he said.

"Why, we did. We stayed—"

"Then whose blanket is that?"

"Blanket?"

"Yes ma'am, blanket. It isn't ours."

I looked down and found myself clutching a brown woolen blanket I was wearing around my shoulders, squaw-fashion.

"Atticus, I don't know, sir . . . I—"

I turned to Jem for an answer, but Jem was even more bewildered than I. He said he didn't know how it got there, we did exactly as Atticus had told us, we stood down by the Radley gate away from everybody, we didn't move an inch—Jem stopped.

"Mr. Nathan was at the fire," he babbled, "I saw him, I saw him, he was tuggin' that mattress—Atticus, I swear . . ."

"That's all right, son." Atticus grinned slowly. "Looks like all of Maycomb was out tonight, in one way or another. Jem, there's some wrapping paper in the pantry, I think. Go get it and we'll—"

"Atticus, no sir!"

Jem seemed to have lost his mind. He began pouring out our secrets right and left in total disregard for my safety if not for his own, omitting nothing, knot-hole, pants and all.

". . . Mr. Nathan put cement in that tree, Atticus, an' he did it to stop us findin' things—he's crazy, I reckon, like they say, but Atticus, I swear to God he ain't ever harmed us, he ain't ever hurt us, he coulda cut my throat from ear to ear that night but he tried to mend my pants instead . . . he ain't ever hurt us, Atticus—"

Atticus said, "Whoa, son," so gently that I was greatly heartened. It was obvious that he had not followed a word Jem said, for all Atticus said was, "You're right. We'd better keep this and the blanket to ourselves. Someday, maybe, Scout can thank him for covering her up."

"Thank who?" I asked.

"Boo Radley. You were so busy looking at the fire you didn't know it when he put the blanket around you."

My stomach turned to water and I nearly threw up when Jem held out the blanket and crept toward me. "He sneaked out of the house—turn 'round—sneaked up, an' went like this!"

Atticus said dryly, "Do not let this inspire you to further glory, Jeremy."

Jem scowled, "I ain't gonna do anything to him," but I watched the spark of fresh adventure leave his eyes. "Just think, Scout," he said, "if you'd just turned around, you'da seen him."

Calpurnia woke us at noon. Atticus had said we need not go to school that day, we'd learn nothing after no sleep. Calpurnia said for us to try and clean up the front yard.

Miss Maudie's sunhat was suspended in a thin layer of ice, like a fly in amber, and we had to dig under the dirt for her hedge-clippers. We found her in her back yard, gazing at her frozen charred azaleas.

"We're bringing back your things, Miss Maudie," said Jem. "We're awful sorry."

Miss Maudie looked around, and the shadow of her old grin crossed her face. "Always wanted a smaller house, Jem Finch. Gives me more yard. Just think, I'll have more room for my azaleas now!"

"You ain't grievin', Miss Maudie?" I asked, surprised. Atticus said her house was nearly all she had.

"Grieving, child? Why, I hated that old cow barn. Thought of settin' fire to it a hundred times myself, except they'd lock me up."

"But—"

"Don't you worry about me, Jean Louise Finch. There are ways of doing things you don't know about. Why, I'll build me a little house and take me a couple of roomers and—gracious, I'll have the finest yard in Alabama. Those Bellingraths'll look plain puny when I get started!"

Jem and I looked at each other. "How'd it catch, Miss Maudie?" he asked.

"I don't know, Jem. Probably the flue in the kitchen. I kept a fire in there last night for my potted plants. Hear you had some unexpected company last night, Miss Jean Louise."

"How'd you know?"

"Atticus told me on his way to town this morning. Tell you the truth, I'd like to've been with you. And I'd've had sense enough to turn around, too."

Miss Maudie puzzled me. With most of her possessions gone and her beloved yard a shambles, she still took a lively and cordial interest in Jem's and my affairs.

She must have seen my perplexity. She said, "Only thing I worried about last night was all the danger and commotion it caused. This whole neighborhood could have gone up. Mr. Avery'll be in bed for a week—he's right stove up. He's too old to do things like that and I told him so. Soon as I can get my hands clean and when Stephanie Crawford's not looking, I'll make him a Lane cake. That Stephanie's been after my recipe for thirty years, and if she thinks I'll give it to her just because I'm staying with her she's got another think coming."

I reflected that if Miss Maudie broke down and gave it to her, Miss Stephanie couldn't follow it anyway. Miss Maudie had once let me see it: among other things, the recipe called for one large cup of sugar.

It was a still day. The air was so cold and clear we heard the courthouse clock clank, rattle and strain before it struck the hour. Miss Maudie's nose was a color I had never seen before, and I inquired about it.

"I've been out here since six o'clock," she said. "Should be frozen by now." She held up her hands. A network of tiny lines crisscrossed her palms, brown with dirt and dried blood.

"You've ruined 'em," said Jem. "Why don't you get a colored man?" There was no note of sacrifice in his voice when he added. "Or Scout'n'me, we can help you."

Miss Maudie said, "Thank you sir, but you've got a job of your own over there." She pointed to our yard.

"You mean the Morphodite?" I asked. "Shoot, we can rake him up in a jiffy."

Miss Maudie stared down at me, her lips moving silently. Suddenly she put her hands to her head and whooped. When we left her, she was still chuckling.

Jem said he didn't know what was the matter with her —that was just Miss Maudie.

9.

You can just take that back, boy!"

This order, given by me to Cecil Jacobs, was the beginning of a rather thin time for Jem and me. My fists were clenched and I was ready to let fly. Atticus had promised me he would wear me out if he ever heard of me fighting any more; I was far too old and too big for such childish things, and the sooner I learned to hold in, the better off everybody would be. I soon forgot.

Cecil Jacobs made me forget. He had announced in the schoolyard the day before that Scout Finch's daddy defended niggers. I denied it, but told Jem.

"What'd he mean sayin' that?" I asked.

"Nothing," Jem said. "Ask Atticus, he'll tell you."

"Do you defend niggers, Atticus?" I asked him that evening.

"Of course I do. Don't say nigger, Scout. That's common."

"'s what everybody at school says."

"From now on it'll be everybody less one—"

"Well if you don't want me to grow up talkin' that way, why do you send me to school?"

My father looked at me mildly, amusement in his eyes. Despite our compromise, my campaign to avoid school had continued in one form or another since my first day's dose of it: the beginning of last September had brought on sinking spells, dizziness, and mild gastric complaints. I went so far as to pay a nickel for the privilege of rubbing my head against the head of Miss Rachel's cook's son, who was afflicted with a tremendous ringworm. It didn't take.

But I was worrying another bone. "Do all lawyers defend n-Negroes, Atticus?"

"Of course they do, Scout."

"Then why did Cecil say you defended niggers? He made it sound like you were runnin' a still."

Atticus sighed. "I'm simply defending a Negro—his name's Tom Robinson. He lives in that little settlement beyond the town dump. He's a member of Calpurnia's church, and Cal knows his family well. She says they're clean-living folks. Scout, you aren't old enough to understand some things yet, but there's been some high talk around town to the effect that I shouldn't do much about defending this man. It's a peculiar case—it won't come to trial until summer session. John Taylor was kind enough to give us a postponement . . ."

"If you shouldn't be defendin' him, then why are you doin' it?"

"For a number of reasons," said Atticus. "The main one is, if I didn't I couldn't hold up my head in town, I couldn't represent this county in the legislature, I couldn't even tell you or Jem not to do something again."

"You mean if you didn't defend that man, Jem and me wouldn't have to mind you any more?"

"That's about right."

"Why?"

"Because I could never ask you to mind me again. Scout, simply by the nature of the work, every lawyer gets at least one case in his lifetime that affects him personally. This one's mine, I guess. You might hear some ugly talk about it at school, but do one thing for me if you will: you just hold your head high and keep those fists down. No matter what anybody says to you, don't you let 'em get your goat. Try fighting with your head for a change . . . it's a good one, even if it does resist learning."

"Atticus, are we going to win it?"

"No, honey."

"Then why—"

"Simply because we were licked a hundred years before we started is no reason for us not to try to win," Atticus said.

"You sound like Cousin Ike Finch," I said. Cousin Ike Finch was Maycomb County's sole surviving Confederate veteran. He wore a General Hood type beard of which he was inordinately vain. At least once a year Atticus, Jem and I called on him, and I would have to kiss him. It was horrible. Jem and I would listen respectfully to Atticus and Cousin Ike rehash the war. "Tell you, Atticus,"

Cousin Ike would say, "the Missouri Compromise was what licked us, but if I had to go through it agin I'd walk every step of the way there an' every step back jist like I did before an' furthermore we'd whip 'em this time . . . now in 1864, when Stonewall Jackson came around by—I beg your pardon, young folks. Ol' Blue Light was in heaven then, God rest his saintly brow. . . ."

"Come here, Scout," said Atticus. I crawled into his lap and tucked my head under his chin. He put his arms around me and rocked me gently. "It's different this time," he said. "This time we aren't fighting the Yankees, we're fighting our friends. But remember this, no matter how bitter things get, they're still our friends and this is still our home."

With this in mind, I faced Cecil Jacobs in the schoolyard next day: "You gonna take that back, boy?"

"You gotta make me first!" he yelled. "My folks said your daddy was a disgrace an' that nigger oughta hang from the water-tank!"

I drew a bead on him, remembered what Atticus had said, then dropped my fists and walked away, "Scout's a cow—ward!" ringing in my ears. It was the first time I ever walked away from a fight.

Somehow, if I fought Cecil I would let Atticus down. Atticus so rarely asked Jem and me to do something for him, I could take being called a coward for him. I felt extremely noble for having remembered, and remained noble for three weeks. Then Christmas came and disaster struck.

Jem and I viewed Christmas with mixed feelings. The good side was the tree and Uncle Jack Finch. Every Christmas Eve day we met Uncle Jack at Maycomb Junction, and he would spend a week with us.

A flip of the coin revealed the uncompromising lineaments of Aunt Alexandra and Francis.

I suppose I should include Uncle Jimmy, Aunt Alexandra's husband, but as he never spoke a word to me in my life except to say, "Get off the fence," once, I never saw any reason to take notice of him. Neither did Aunt Alexandra. Long ago, in a burst of friendliness, Aunty and Uncle Jimmy produced a son named Henry, who left home as soon as was humanly possible, married, and produced Francis. Henry and his wife deposited Francis at his grandparents' every Christmas, then pursued their own pleasures.

No amount of sighing could induce Atticus to let us spend Christmas day at home. We went to Finch's Landing every Christmas in my memory. The fact that Aunty was a good cook was some compensation for being forced to spend a religious holiday with Francis Hancock. He was a year older than I, and I avoided him on principle: he enjoyed everything I disapproved of, and disliked my ingenuous diversions.

Aunt Alexandra was Atticus's sister, but when Jem told me about changelings and siblings, I decided that she had been swapped at birth, that my grandparents had perhaps received a Crawford instead of a Finch. Had I ever harbored the mystical notions about mountains that seem to obsess lawyers and judges, Aunt Alexandra would have been analogous to Mount Everest: throughout my early life, she was cold and there.

When Uncle Jack jumped down from the train Christmas Eve day, we had to wait for the porter to hand him two long packages. Jem and I always thought it funny when Uncle Jack pecked Atticus on the cheek; they were the only two men we ever saw kiss each other. Uncle Jack shook hands with Jem and swung me high, but not high enough: Uncle Jack was a head shorter than Atticus; the baby of the family, he was younger than Aunt Alexandra. He and Aunty looked alike, but Uncle Jack made better use of his face: we were never wary of his sharp nose and chin.

He was one of the few men of science who never terrified me, probably because he never behaved like a doctor. Whenever he performed a minor service for Jem and me, as removing a splinter from a foot, he would tell us exactly what he was going to do, give us an estimation of how much it would hurt, and explain the use of any tongs he employed. One Christmas I lurked in corners nursing a twisted splinter in my foot, permitting no one to come near me. When Uncle Jack caught me, he kept me laughing about a preacher who hated going to church so much that every day he stood at his gate in his dressing-gown, smoking a hookah and delivering five-minute sermons to any passers-by who desired spiritual comfort. I interrupted to make Uncle Jack let me know when he would pull it out, but he held up a bloody splinter in a pair of tweezers and said he yanked it while I was laughing, that was what was known as relativity.

"What's in those packages?" I asked him, pointing to the long thin parcels the porter had given him.

"None of your business," he said.

Jem said, "How's Rose Aylmer?"

Rose Aylmer was Uncle Jack's cat. She was a beautiful yellow female Uncle Jack said was one of the few women he could stand permanently. He reached into his coat pocket and brought out some snapshots. We admired them.

"She's gettin' fat," I said.

"I should think so. She eats all the leftover fingers and ears from the hospital."

"Aw, that's a damn story," I said.

"I beg your pardon?"

Atticus said, "Don't pay any attention to her, Jack. She's trying you out. Cal says she's been cussing fluently for a week, now."

Uncle Jack raised his eyebrows and said nothing. I was proceeding on the dim theory, aside from the innate attractiveness of such words, that if Atticus discovered I had picked them up at school he wouldn't make me go.

But at supper that evening when I asked him to pass the damn ham, please, Uncle Jack pointed at me. "See me afterwards, young lady," he said.

When supper was over, Uncle Jack went to the livingroom and sat down. He slapped his thighs for me to come sit on his lap. I liked to smell him: he was like a bottle of alcohol and something pleasantly sweet. He pushed back my bangs and looked at me. "You're more like Atticus than your mother," he said. "You're also growing out of your pants a little."

"I reckon they fit all right."

"You like words like damn and hell now, don't you?"

I said I reckoned so.

"Well I don't," said Uncle Jack, "not unless there's extreme provocation connected with 'em. I'll be here a week, and I don't want to hear any words like that while I'm here. Scout, you'll get in trouble if you go around saying things like that. You want to grow up to be a lady, don't you?"

I said not particularly.

"Of course you do. Now let's get to the tree."

We decorated the tree until bedtime, and that night I dreamed of the two long packages for Jem and me. Next morning Jem and I dived for them: they were from Atticus, who had written Uncle Jack to get them for us, and they were what we had asked for.

"Don't point them in the house," said Atticus, when Jem aimed at a picture on the wall.

"You'll have to teach 'em to shoot," said Uncle Jack.

"That's your job," said Atticus. "I merely bowed to the inevitable."

It took Atticus's courtroom voice to drag us away from the tree. He declined to let us take our air rifles to the Landing (I had already begun to think of shooting Francis) and said if we made one false move he'd take them away from us for good.

Finch's Landing consisted of three hundred and sixty-six steps down a high bluff and ending in a jetty. Farther down stream, beyond the bluff, were traces of an old cotton landing, where Finch Negroes had loaded bales and produce, unloaded blocks of ice, flour and sugar, farm equipment, and feminine apparel. A two-rut road ran from the riverside and vanished among dark trees. At the end of the road was a two-storied white house with porches circling it upstairs and downstairs. In his old age, our ancestor Simon Finch had built it to please his nagging wife; but with the porches all resemblance to ordinary houses of its era ended. The internal arrangements of the Finch house were indicative of Simon's guilelessness and the absolute trust with which he regarded his offspring.

There were six bedrooms upstairs, four for the eight female children, one for Welcome Finch, the sole son, and one for visiting relatives. Simple enough; but the daughters' rooms could be reached only by one staircase, Welcome's room and the guestroom only by another. The Daughters' Staircase was in the ground-floor bedroom of their parents, so Simon always knew the hours of his daughters' nocturnal comings and goings.

There was a kitchen separate from the rest of the

house, tacked onto it by a wooden catwalk; in the back yard was a rusty bell on a pole, used to summon field hands or as a distress signal; a widow's walk was on the roof, but no widows walked there—from it, Simon oversaw his overseer, watched the river-boats, and gazed into the lives of surrounding landholders.

There went with the house the usual legend about the Yankees: one Finch female, recently engaged, donned her complete trousseau to save it from raiders in the neighborhood; she became stuck in the door to the Daughters' Staircase but was doused with water and finally pushed through. When we arrived at the Landing, Aunt Alexandra kissed Uncle Jack, Francis kissed Uncle Jack, Uncle Jimmy shook hands silently with Uncle Jack, Jem and I gave our presents to Francis, who gave us a present. Jem felt his age and gravitated to the adults, leaving me to entertain our cousin. Francis was eight and slicked back his hair.

"What'd you get for Christmas?" I asked politely.

"Just what I asked for," he said. Francis had requested a pair of knee-pants, a red leather booksack, five shirts and an untied bow tie.

"That's nice," I lied. "Jem and me got air rifles, and Jem got a chemistry set—"

"A toy one, I reckon."

"No, a real one. He's gonna make me some invisible ink, and I'm gonna write to Dill in it."

Francis asked what was the use of that.

"Well, can't you just see his face when he gets a letter from me with nothing in it? It'll drive him nuts."

Talking to Francis gave me the sensation of settling slowly to the bottom of the ocean. He was the most boring child I ever met. As he lived in Mobile, he could not inform on me to school authorities, but he managed to tell everything he knew to Aunt Alexandra, who in turn unburdened herself to Atticus, who either forgot it or gave me hell, whichever struck his fancy. But the only time I ever heard Atticus speak sharply to anyone was when I once heard him say, "Sister, I do the best I can with them!" It had something to do with my going around in overalls.

Aunt Alexandra was fanatical on the subject of my attire. I could not possibly hope to be a lady if I wore breeches; when I said I could do nothing in a dress, she said I wasn't supposed to be doing things that required pants. Aunt Alexandra's vision of my deportment involved playing with small stoves, tea sets, and wearing the Add-A-Pearl necklace she gave me when I was born; furthermore, I should be a ray of sunshine in my father's lonely life. I suggested that one could be a ray of sunshine in pants just as well, but Aunty said that one had to behave like a sunbeam, that I was born good but had grown progressively worse every year. She hurt my feelings and set my teeth permanently on edge, but when I asked Atticus about it, he said there were already enough sunbeams in the family and to go on about my business, he didn't mind me much the way I was.

At Christmas dinner, I sat at the little table in the diningroom; Jem and Francis sat with the adults at the dining table. Aunty had continued to isolate me long after Jem and Francis graduated to the big table. I often wondered what she thought I'd do, get up and throw something? I sometimes thought of asking her if she would let me sit at the big table with the rest of them just once, I would prove to her how civilized I could be; after all, I ate at home every day with no major mishaps. When I begged Atticus to use his influence, he said he had none —we were guests, and we sat where she told us to sit. He also said Aunt Alexandra didn't understand girls much, she'd never had one.

But her cooking made up for everything: three kinds of meat, summer vegetables from her pantry shelves; peach pickles, two kinds of cake and ambrosia constituted a modest Christmas dinner. Afterwards, the adults made for the livingroom and sat around in a dazed condition. Jem lay on the floor, and I went to the back yard. "Put on your coat," said Atticus dreamily, so I didn't hear him.

Francis sat beside me on the back steps. "That was the best yet," I said.

"Grandma's a wonderful cook," said Francis. "She's gonna teach me how."

"Boys don't cook." I giggled at the thought of Jem in an apron.

"Grandma says all men should learn to cook, that men oughta be careful with their wives and wait on 'em when they don't feel good," said my cousin.

"I don't want Dill waitin' on me," I said. "I'd rather wait on him."

"Dill?"

"Yeah. Don't say anything about it yet, but we're gonna get married as soon as we're big enough. He asked me last summer."

Francis hooted.

"What's the matter with him?" I asked. "Ain't anything the matter with him."

"You mean that little runt Grandma says stays with Miss Rachel every summer?"

"That's exactly who I mean."

"I know all about him," said Francis.

"What about him?"

"Grandma says he hasn't got a home—"

"Has too, he lives in Meridian."

"—he just gets passed around from relative to relative, and Miss Rachel keeps him every summer."

"Francis, that's not so!"

Francis grinned at me. "You're mighty dumb sometimes, Jean Louise. Guess you don't know any better, though."

"What do you mean?"

"If Uncle Atticus lets you run around with stray dogs, that's his own business, like Grandma says, so it ain't your fault. I guess it ain't your fault if Uncle Atticus is a nigger-lover besides, but I'm here to tell you it certainly does mortify the rest of the family—"

"Francis, what the hell do you mean?"

"Just what I said. Grandma says it's bad enough he lets you all run wild, but now he's turned out a nigger-lover we'll never be able to walk the streets of Maycomb agin. He's ruinin' the family, that's what he's doin'."

Francis rose and sprinted down the catwalk to the old kitchen. At a safe distance he called, "He's nothin' but a nigger-lover!"

"He is not!" I roared. "I don't know what you're talkin' about, but you better cut it out this red hot minute!"

I leaped off the steps and ran down the catwalk. It was easy to collar Francis. I said take it back quick.

Francis jerked loose and sped into the old kitchen. "Nigger-lover!" he yelled.

When stalking one's prey, it is best to take one's time. Say nothing, and as sure as eggs he will become curious and emerge. Francis appeared at the kitchen door. "You still mad, Jean Louise?" he asked tentatively.

"Nothing to speak of," I said.

Francis came out on the catwalk.

"You gonna take it back, Fra—ancis?" But I was too quick on the draw. Francis shot back into the kitchen, so I retired to the steps. I could wait patiently. I had sat there perhaps five minutes when I heard Aunt Alexandra speak: "Where's Francis?"

"He's out yonder in the kitchen."

"He knows he's not supposed to play in there."

Francis came to the door and yelled, "Grandma, she's got me in here and she won't let me out!"

"What is all this, Jean Louise?"

I looked up at Aunt Alexandra. "I haven't got him in there, Aunty, I ain't holdin' him."

"Yes she is," shouted Francis, "she won't let me out!"

"Have you all been fussing?"

"Jean Louise got mad at me, Grandma," called Francis.

"Francis, come out of there! Jean Louise, if I hear another word out of you I'll tell your father. Did I hear you say hell a while ago?"

"Nome."

"I thought I did. I'd better not hear it again."

Aunt Alexandra was a back-porch listener. The moment she was out of sight Francis came out head up and grinning. "Don't you fool with me," he said.

He jumped into the yard and kept his distance, kicking tufts of grass, turning around occasionally to smile at me. Jem appeared on the porch, looked at us, and went away. Francis climbed the mimosa tree, came down, put his hands in his pockets and strolled around the yard. "Hah!" he said. I asked him who he thought he was, Uncle Jack? Francis said he reckoned I got told, for me to just sit there and leave him alone.

"I ain't botherin' you," I said.

Francis looked at me carefully, concluded that I had been sufficiently subdued, and crooned softly, "Nigger-lover . . ."

This time, I split my knuckle to the bone on his front teeth. My left impaired, I sailed in with my right, but

88

not for long. Uncle Jack pinned my arms to my sides and said, "Stand still!"

Aunt Alexandra ministered to Francis, wiping his tears away with her handkerchief, rubbing his hair, patting his cheek. Atticus, Jem, and Uncle Jimmy had come to the back porch when Francis started yelling.

"Who started this?" said Uncle Jack.

Francis and I pointed at each other. "Grandma," he bawled, "she called me a whore-lady and jumped on me!"

"Is that true, Scout?" said Uncle Jack.

"I reckon so."

When Uncle Jack looked down at me, his features were like Aunt Alexandra's. "You know I told you you'd get in trouble if you used words like that? I told you, didn't I?"

"Yes sir, but—"

"Well, you're in trouble now. Stay there."

I was debating whether to stand there or run, and tarried in indecision a moment too long: I turned to flee but Uncle Jack was quicker. I found myself suddenly looking at a tiny ant struggling with a bread crumb in the grass.

"I'll never speak to you again as long as I live! I hate you an' despise you an' hope you die tomorrow!" A statement that seemed to encourage Uncle Jack, more than anything. I ran to Atticus for comfort, but he said I had it coming and it was high time we went home. I climbed into the back seat of the car without saying good-bye to anyone, and at home I ran to my room and slammed the door. Jem tried to say something nice, but I wouldn't let him.

When I surveyed the damage there were only seven or eight red marks, and I was reflecting upon relativity when someone knocked on the door. I asked who it was; Uncle Jack answered.

"Go away!"

Uncle Jack said if I talked like that he'd lick me again, so I was quiet. When he entered the room I retreated to a corner and turned my back on him. "Scout," he said, "do you still hate me?"

"Go on, please sir."

"Why, I didn't think you'd hold it against me," he said. "I'm disappointed in you—you had that coming and you know it."

"Didn't either."

"Honey, you can't go around calling people—"

"You ain't fair," I said, "you ain't fair."

Uncle Jack's eyebrows went up. "Not fair? How not?"

"You're real nice, Uncle Jack, an' I reckon I love you even after what you did, but you don't understand children much."

Uncle Jack put his hands on his hips and looked down at me. "And why do I not understand children, Miss Jean Louise? Such conduct as yours required little understanding. It was obstreperous, disorderly and abusive—"

"You gonna give me a chance to tell you? I don't mean to sass you, I'm just tryin' to tell you."

Uncle Jack sat down on the bed. His eyebrows came together, and he peered up at me from under them. "Proceed," he said.

I took a deep breath. "Well, in the first place you never stopped to gimme a chance to tell you my side of it—you just lit right into me. When Jem an' I fuss Atticus doesn't ever just listen to Jem's side of it, he hears mine too, an' in the second place you told me never to use words like that except in ex-extreme provocation, and Francis provocated me enough to knock his block off—"

Uncle Jack scratched his head. "What was your side of it, Scout?"

"Francis called Atticus somethin', an' I wasn't about to take it off him."

"What did Francis call him?"

"A nigger-lover. I ain't very sure what it means, but the way Francis said it—tell you one thing right now, Uncle Jack, I'll be—I swear before God if I'll sit there and let him say somethin' about Atticus."

"He called Atticus that?"

"Yes sir, he did, an' a lot more. Said Atticus'd be the ruination of the family an' he let Jem an me run wild. . . ."

From the look on Uncle Jack's face, I thought I was in for it again. When he said, "We'll see about this," I knew Francis was in for it. "I've a good mind to go out there tonight."

"Please sir, just let it go. Please."

"I've no intention of letting it go," he said. "Alexandra should know about this. The idea of—wait'll I get my hands on that boy. . . ."

"Uncle Jack, please promise me somethin', please sir. Promise you won't tell Atticus about this. He—he asked me one time not to let anything I heard about him make me mad, an' I'd ruther him think we were fightin' about somethin' else instead. Please promise . . ."

"But I don't like Francis getting away with something like that—"

"He didn't. You reckon you could tie up my hand? It's still bleedin' some."

"Of course I will, baby. I know of no hand I would be more delighted to tie up. Will you come this way?"

Uncle Jack gallantly bowed me to the bathroom. While he cleaned and bandaged my knuckles, he entertained me with a tale about a funny nearsighted old gentleman who had a cat named Hodge, and who counted all the cracks in the sidewalk when he went to town. "There now," he said. "You'll have a very unladylike scar on your wedding-ring finger."

"Thank you sir. Uncle Jack?"

"Ma'am?"

"What's a whore-lady?"

Uncle Jack plunged into another long tale about an old Prime Minister who sat in the House of Commons and blew feathers in the air and tried to keep them there when all about him men were losing their heads. I guess he was trying to answer my question, but he made no sense whatsoever.

Later, when I was supposed to be in bed, I went down the hall for a drink of water and heard Atticus and Uncle Jack in the livingroom:

"I shall never marry, Atticus."

"Why?"

"I might have children."

Atticus said, "You've a lot to learn, Jack."

"I know. Your daughter gave me my first lessons this afternoon. She said I didn't understand children much and told me why. She was quite right. Atticus, she told me how I should have treated her—oh dear, I'm so sorry I romped on her."

Atticus chuckled. "She earned it, so don't feel too remorseful."

I waited, on tenterhooks, for Uncle Jack to tell Atticus my side of it. But he didn't. He simply murmured, "Her use of bathroom invective leaves nothing to the imagination. But she doesn't know the meaning of half she says —she asked me what a whore-lady was . . ."

"Did you tell her?"

"No, I told her about Lord Melbourne."

"Jack! When a child asks you something, answer him, for goodness' sake. But don't make a production of it. Children are children, but they can spot an evasion quicker than adults, and evasion simply muddles 'em. No," my father mused, "you had the right answer this afternoon, but the wrong reasons. Bad language is a stage all children go through, and it dies with time when they learn they're not attracting attention with it. Hotheadedness isn't. Scout's got to learn to keep her head and learn soon, with what's in store for her these next few months. She's coming along, though. Jem's getting older and she follows his example a good bit now. All she needs is assistance sometimes."

"Atticus, you've never laid a hand on her."

"I admit that. So far I've been able to get by with threats. Jack, she minds me as well as she can. Doesn't come up to scratch half the time, but she tries."

"That's not the answer," said Uncle Jack.

"No, the answer is she knows I know she tries. That's what makes the difference. What bothers me is that she and Jem will have to absorb some ugly things pretty soon. I'm not worried about Jem keeping his head, but Scout'd just as soon jump on someone as look at him if her pride's at stake. . . ."

I waited for Uncle Jack to break his promise. He still didn't.

"Atticus, how bad is this going to be? You haven't had too much chance to discuss it."

"It couldn't be worse, Jack. The only thing we've got is a black man's word against the Ewells'. The evidence boils down to you-did—I-didn't. The jury couldn't possibly be expected to take Tom Robinson's word against the Ewells'—are you acquainted with the Ewells?"

Uncle Jack said yes, he remembered them. He described them to Atticus, but Atticus said, "You're a generation off. The present ones are the same, though."

"What are you going to do, then?"

"Before I'm through, I intend to jar the jury a bit—I

think we'll have a reasonable chance on appeal, though. I really can't tell at this stage, Jack. You know, I'd hoped to get through life without a case of this kind, but John Taylor pointed at me and said, 'You're It.' "

"Let this cup pass from you, eh?"

"Right. But do you think I could face my children otherwise? You know what's going to happen as well as I do, Jack, and I hope and pray I can get Jem and Scout through it without bitterness, and most of all, without catching Maycomb's usual disease. Why reasonable people go stark raving mad when anything involving a Negro comes up, is something I don't pretend to understand . . . I just hope that Jem and Scout come to me for their answers instead of listening to the town. I hope they trust me enough. . . . Jean Louise?"

My scalp jumped. I stuck my head around the corner. "Sir?"

"Go to bed."

I scurried to my room and went to bed. Uncle Jack was a prince of a fellow not to let me down. But I never figured out how Atticus knew I was listening, and it was not until many years later that I realized he wanted me to hear every word he said.

10.

Atticus was feeble: he was nearly fifty. When Jem and I asked him why he was so old, he said he got started late, which we felt reflected upon his abilities and manliness. He was much older than the parents of our school contemporaries, and there was nothing Jem or I could say about him when our classmates said, "*My* father—"

Jem was football crazy. Atticus was never too tired to play keep-away, but when Jem wanted to tackle him Atticus would say, "I'm too old for that, son."

Our father didn't do anything. He worked in an office, not in a drugstore. Atticus did not drive a dump-truck for the county, he was not the sheriff, he did not farm, work in a garage, or do anything that could possibly arouse the admiration of anyone.

Besides that, he wore glasses. He was nearly blind in his left eye, and said left eyes were the tribal curse of the Finches. Whenever he wanted to see something well, he turned his head and looked from his right eye.

He did not do the things our schoolmates' fathers did: he never went hunting, he did not play poker or fish or drink or smoke. He sat in the livingroom and read.

With these attributes, however, he would not remain as inconspicuous as we wished him to: that year, the school buzzed with talk about him defending Tom Robinson, none of which was complimentary. After my bout with Cecil Jacobs when I committed myself to a policy of cowardice, word got around that Scout Finch wouldn't fight any more, her daddy wouldn't let her. This was not entirely correct: I wouldn't fight publicly for Atticus, but the family was private ground. I would fight anyone from a third cousin upwards tooth and nail. Francis Hancock, for example, knew that.

When he gave us our air-rifles Atticus wouldn't teach us to shoot. Uncle Jack instructed us in the rudiments thereof; he said Atticus wasn't interested in guns. Atticus said to Jem one day, "I'd rather you shot at tin cans in the back yard, but I know you'll go after birds. Shoot all the bluejays you want, if you can hit 'em, but remember it's a sin to kill a mockingbird."

That was the only time I ever heard Atticus say it was a sin to do something, and I asked Miss Maudie about it.

"Your father's right," she said. "Mockingbirds don't do one thing but make music for us to enjoy. They don't eat up people's gardens, don't nest in corncribs, they don't do one thing but sing their hearts out for us. That's why it's a sin to kill a mockingbird."

"Miss Maudie, this is an old neighborhood, ain't it?"

"Been here longer than the town."

"Nome, I mean the folks on our street are all old. Jem and me's the only children around here. Mrs. Dubose is close on to a hundred and Miss Rachel's old and so are you and Atticus."

"I don't call fifty very old," said Miss Maudie tartly. "Not being wheeled around yet, am I? Neither's your father. But I must say Providence was kind enough to burn down that old mausoleum of mine, I'm too old to keep it up—maybe you're right, Jean Louise, this is a settled neighborhood. You've never been around young folks much, have you?"

"Yessum, at school."

"I mean young grown-ups. You're lucky, you know. You and Jem have the benefit of your father's age. If your father was thirty you'd find life quite different."

"I sure would. Atticus can't do anything. . . ."

"You'd be surprised," said Miss Maudie. "There's life in him yet."

"What can he do?"

"Well, he can make somebody's will so airtight can't anybody meddle with it."

"Shoot . . ."

"Well, did you know he's the best checker-player in this town? Why, down at the Landing when we were coming up, Atticus Finch could beat everybody on both sides of the river."

"Good Lord, Miss Maudie, Jem and me beat him all the time."

"It's about time you found out it's because he lets you. Did you know he can play a Jew's Harp?"

This modest accomplishment served to make me even more ashamed of him.

"*Well* . . ." she said.

"Well, what, Miss Maudie?"

"Well nothing. Nothing—it seems with all that you'd be proud of him. Can't everybody play a Jew's Harp. Now keep out of the way of the carpenters. You'd better go home, I'll be in my azaleas and can't watch you. Plank might hit you."

I went to the back yard and found Jem plugging away at a tin can, which seemed stupid with all the bluejays around. I returned to the front yard and busied myself for two hours erecting a complicated breastworks at the side of the porch, consisting of a tire, an orange crate, the laundry hamper, the porch chairs, and a small U.S. flag Jem gave me from a popcorn box.

When Atticus came home to dinner he found me crouched down aiming across the street. "What are you shooting at?"

"Miss Maudie's rear end."

Atticus turned and saw my generous target bending over her bushes. He pushed his hat to the back of his head and crossed the street. "Maudie," he called, "I thought I'd better warn you. You're in considerable peril."

Miss Maudie straightened up and looked toward me. She said, "Atticus, you are a devil from hell."

When Atticus returned he told me to break camp. "Don't you ever let me catch you pointing that gun at anybody again," he said.

I wished my father was a devil from hell. I sounded out Calpurnia on the subject. "Mr. Finch? Why, he can do lots of things."

"Like what?" I asked.

Calpurnia scratched her head. "Well, I don't rightly know," she said.

Jem underlined it when he asked Atticus if he was going out for the Methodists and Atticus said he'd break his neck if he did, he was just too old for that sort of thing. The Methodists were trying to pay off their church mortgage, and had challenged the Baptists to a game of touch football. Everybody in town's father was playing, it seemed, except Atticus. Jem said he didn't even want to go, but he was unable to resist football in any form, and he stood gloomily on the sidelines with Atticus and me watching Cecil Jacobs's father make touchdowns for the Baptists.

One Saturday Jem and I decided to go exploring with our air-rifles to see if we could find a rabbit or a squirrel. We had gone about five hundred yards beyond the Radley Place when I noticed Jem squinting at something down the street. He had turned his head to one side and was looking out of the corners of his eyes.

"Whatcha looking at?"

"That old dog down yonder," he said.

"That's old Tim Johnson, ain't it?"

"Yeah."

Tim Johnson was the property of Mr. Harry Johnson who drove the Mobile bus and lived on the southern edge of town. Tim was a liver-colored bird dog, the pet of Maycomb.

"What's he doing?"

"I don't know, Scout. We better go home."

"Aw Jem, it's February."

"I don't care, I'm gonna tell Cal."

We raced home and ran to the kitchen.

"Cal," said Jem, "can you come down the sidewalk a minute?"

"What for, Jem? I can't come down the sidewalk every time you want me."

"There's somethin' wrong with an old dog down yonder."

Calpurnia sighed. "I can't wrap up any dog's foot now. There's some gauze in the bathroom, go get it and do it yourself."

Jem shook his head. "He's sick, Cal. Something's wrong with him."

"What's he doin', trying to catch his tail?"

"No, he's doin' like this."

Jem gulped like a goldfish, hunched his shoulders and twitched his torso. "He's goin' like that, only not like he means to."

"Are you telling me a story, Jem Finch?" Calpurnia's voice hardened.

"No Cal, I swear I'm not."

"Was he runnin'?"

"No, he's just moseyin' along, so slow you can't hardly tell it. He's comin' this way."

Calpurnia rinsed her hands and followed Jem into the yard. "I don't see any dog," she said.

She followed us beyond the Radley Place and looked where Jem pointed. Tim Johnson was not much more than a speck in the distance, but he was closer to us. He walked erratically, as if his right legs were shorter than his left legs. He reminded me of a car stuck in a sandbed.

"He's gone lopsided," said Jem.

Calpurnia stared, then grabbed us by the shoulders and ran us home. She shut the wood door behind us, went to the telephone and shouted, "Gimme Mr. Finch's office!"

"Mr. Finch!" she shouted. "This is Cal. I swear to God there's a mad dog down the street a piece—he's comin' this way, yes sir, he's—Mr. Finch, I declare he is —old Tim Johnson, yes sir . . . yessir . . . yes—"

She hung up and shook her head when we tried to ask

her what Atticus had said. She rattled the telephone hook and said, "Miss Eula May—now ma'am, I'm through talkin' to Mr. Finch, please don't connect me no more— listen, Miss Eula May, can you call Miss Rachel and Miss Stephanie Crawford and whoever's got a phone on this street and tell 'em a mad dog's comin'? Please ma'am!"

Calpurnia listened. "I know it's February, Miss Eula May, but I know a mad dog when I see one. Please ma'am hurry!"

Calpurnia asked Jem, "Radleys got a phone?"

Jem looked in the book and said no. "They won't come out anyway, Cal."

"I don't care, I'm gonna tell 'em."

She ran to the front porch, Jem and I at her heels. "You stay in that house!" she yelled.

Calpurnia's message had been received by the neighborhood. Every wood door within our range of vision was closed tight. We saw no trace of Tim Johnson. We watched Calpurnia running toward the Radley Place, holding her skirt and apron above her knees. She went up to the front steps and banged on the door. She got no answer, and she shouted, "Mr. Nathan, Mr. Arthur, mad dog's comin'! Mad dog's comin'!"

"She's supposed to go around in back," I said.

Jem shook his head. "Don't make any difference now," he said.

Calpurnia pounded on the door in vain. No one acknowledged her warning; no one seemed to have heard it.

As Calpurnia sprinted to the back porch a black Ford swung into the driveway. Atticus and Mr. Heck Tate got out.

Mr. Heck Tate was the sheriff of Maycomb County. He was as tall as Atticus, but thinner. He was long-nosed, wore boots with shiny metal eye-holes, boot pants and a lumber jacket. His belt had a row of bullets sticking in it. He carried a heavy rifle. When he and Atticus reached the porch, Jem opened the door.

"Stay inside, son," said Atticus. "Where is he, Cal?"

"He oughta be here by now," said Calpurnia, pointing down the street.

"Not runnin', is he?" asked Mr. Tate.

"Naw sir, he's in the twitchin' stage, Mr. Heck."

"Should we go after him, Heck?" asked Atticus.

"We better wait, Mr. Finch. They usually go in a straight line, but you never can tell. He might follow the curve—hope he does or he'll go straight in the Radley back yard. Let's wait a minute."

"Don't think he'll get in the Radley yard," said Atticus. "Fence'll stop him. He'll probably follow the road. . . ."

I thought mad dogs foamed at the mouth, galloped, leaped and lunged at throats, and I thought they did it in August. Had Tim Johnson behaved thus, I would have been less frightened.

Nothing is more deadly than a deserted, waiting street. The trees were still, the mockingbirds were silent, the carpenters at Miss Maudie's house had vanished. I heard Mr. Tate sniff, then blow his nose. I saw him shift his gun to the crook of his arm. I saw Miss Stephanie Crawford's face framed in the glass window of her front door. Miss Maudie appeared and stood beside her. Atticus put his foot on the rung of a chair and rubbed his hand slowly down the side of his thigh.

"There he is," he said softly.

Tim Johnson came into sight, walking dazedly in the inner rim of the curve parallel to the Radley house.

"Look at him," whispered Jem. "Mr. Heck said they walked in a straight line. He can't even stay in the road."

"He looks more sick than anything," I said.

"Let anything get in front of him and he'll come straight at it."

Mr. Tate put his hand to his forehead and leaned forward. "He's got it all right, Mr. Finch."

Tim Johnson was advancing at a snail's pace, but he was not playing or sniffing at foliage: he seemed dedicated to one course and motivated by an invisible force that was inching him toward us. We could see him shiver like a horse shedding flies; his jaw opened and shut; he was alist, but he was being pulled gradually toward us.

"He's lookin' for a place to die," said Jem.

Mr. Tate turned around. "He's far from dead, Jem, he hasn't got started yet."

Tim Johnson reached the side street that ran in front of the Radley Place, and what remained of his poor mind made him pause and seem to consider which road he would take. He made a few hesitant steps and stopped in front of the Radley gate; then he tried to turn around, but was having difficulty.

Atticus said, "He's within range, Heck. You better get him before he goes down the side street—Lord knows who's around the corner. Go inside, Cal."

Calpurnia opened the screen door, latched it behind her, then unlatched it and held onto the hook. She tried to block Jem and me with her body, but we looked out from beneath her arms.

"Take him, Mr. Finch." Mr. Tate handed the rifle to Atticus; Jem and I nearly fainted.

"Don't waste time, Heck," said Atticus. "Go on."

"Mr. Finch, this is a one-shot job."

Atticus shook his head vehemently: "Don't just stand there, Heck! He won't wait all day for you—"

"For God's sake, Mr. Finch, look where he is! Miss and you'll go straight into the Radley house! I can't shoot that well and you know it!"

"I haven't shot a gun in thirty years—"

Mr. Tate almost threw the rifle at Atticus. "I'd feel mighty comfortable if you did now," he said.

In a fog, Jem and I watched our father take the gun and walk out into the middle of the street. He walked quickly, but I thought he moved like an underwater swimmer: time had slowed to a nauseating crawl.

When Atticus raised his glasses Calpurnia murmured, "Sweet Jesus help him," and put her hands to her cheeks.

Atticus pushed his glasses to his forehead; they slipped down, and he dropped them in the street. In the silence, I heard them crack. Atticus rubbed his eyes and chin; we saw him blink hard.

In front of the Radley gate, Tim Johnson had made up what was left of his mind. He had finally turned himself around, to pursue his original course up our street. He made two steps forward, then stopped and raised his head. We saw his body go rigid.

With movements so swift they seemed simultaneous, Atticus's hand yanked a ball-tipped lever as he brought the gun to his shoulder.

The rifle cracked. Tim Johnson leaped, flopped over and crumpled on the sidewalk in a brown-and-white heap. He didn't know what hit him.

Mr. Tate jumped off the porch and ran to the Radley

Place. He stopped in front of the dog, squatted, turned around and tapped his finger on his forehead above his left eye. "You were a little to the right, Mr. Finch," he called.

"Always was," answered Atticus. "If I had my 'druthers I'd take a shotgun."

He stooped and picked up his glasses, ground the broken lenses to powder under his heel, and went to Mr. Tate and stood looking down at Tim Johnson.

Doors opened one by one, and the neighborhood slowly came alive. Miss Maudie walked down the steps with Miss Stephanie Crawford.

Jem was paralyzed. I pinched him to get him moving, but when Atticus saw us coming he called, "Stay where you are."

When Mr. Tate and Atticus returned to the yard, Mr. Tate was smiling. "I'll have Zeebo collect him," he said. "You haven't forgot much, Mr. Finch. They say it never leaves you."

Atticus was silent.

"Atticus?" said Jem.

"Yes?"

"Nothin'."

"I saw that, One-Shot Finch!"

Atticus wheeled around and faced Miss Maudie. They looked at one another without saying anything, and Atticus got into the sheriff's car. "Come here," he said to Jem. "Don't you go near that dog, you understand? Don't go near him, he's just as dangerous dead as alive."

"Yes sir," said Jem. "Atticus—"

"What, son?"

"Nothing."

"What's the matter with you, boy, can't you talk?" said Mr. Tate, grinning at Jem. "Didn't you know your daddy's—"

"Hush, Heck," said Atticus, "let's go back to town."

When they drove away, Jem and I went to Miss Stephanie's front steps. We sat waiting for Zeebo to arrive in the garbage truck.

Jem sat in numb confusion, and Miss Stephanie said, "Uh, uh, uh, who'da thought of a mad dog in February? Maybe he wadn't mad, maybe he was just crazy. I'd hate to see Harry Johnson's face when he gets in from the

Mobile run and finds Atticus Finch's shot his dog. Bet he was just full of fleas from somewhere—"

Miss Maudie said Miss Stephanie'd be singing a different tune if Tim Johnson was still coming up the street, that they'd find out soon enough, they'd send his head to Montgomery.

Jem became vaguely articulate: "'d you see him, Scout? 'd you see him just standin' there? . . . 'n' all of a sudden he just relaxed all over, an' it looked like that gun was a part of him . . . an' he did it so quick, like . . . I hafta aim for ten minutes 'fore I can hit somethin'. . . ."

Miss Maudie grinned wickedly. "Well now, Miss Jean Louise," she said, "still think your father can't do anything? Still ashamed of him?"

"Nome," I said meekly.

"Forgot to tell you the other day that besides playing the Jew's Harp, Atticus Finch was the deadest shot in Maycomb County in his time."

"Dead shot . . ." echoed Jem.

"That's what I said, Jem Finch. Guess you'll change *your* tune now. The very idea, didn't you know his nickname was Ol' One-Shot when he was a boy? Why, down at the Landing when he was coming up, if he shot fifteen times and hit fourteen doves he'd complain about wasting ammunition."

"He never said anything about that," Jem muttered.

"Never said anything about it, did he?"

"No ma'am."

"Wonder why he never goes huntin' now," I said.

"Maybe I can tell you," said Miss Maudie. "If your father's anything, he's civilized in his heart. Marksmanship's a gift of God, a talent—oh, you have to practice to make it perfect, but shootin's different from playing the piano or the like. I think maybe he put his gun down when he realized that God had given him an unfair advantage over most living things. I guess he decided he wouldn't shoot till he had to, and he had to today."

"Looks like he'd be proud of it," I said.

"People in their right minds never take pride in their talents," said Miss Maudie.

We saw Zeebo drive up. He took a pitchfork from the back of the garbage truck and gingerly lifted Tim Johnson. He pitched the dog onto the truck, then poured something from a gallon jug on and around the spot where Tim fell. "Don't yawl come over here for a while," he called.

When we went home I told Jem we'd really have something to talk about at school on Monday. Jem turned on me.

"Don't say anything about it, Scout," he said.

"What? I certainly am. Ain't everybody's daddy the deadest shot in Maycomb County."

Jem said, "I reckon if he'd wanted us to know it, he'da told us. If he was proud of it, he'da told us."

"Maybe it just slipped his mind," I said.

"Naw, Scout, it's something you wouldn't understand. Atticus is real old, but I wouldn't care if he couldn't do anything—I wouldn't care if he couldn't do a blessed thing."

Jem picked up a rock and threw it jubilantly at the carhouse. Running after it, he called back: "Atticus is a gentleman, just like me!"

11.

When we were small, Jem and I confined our activities to the southern neighborhood, but when I was well into the second grade at school and tormenting Boo Radley became passé, the business section of Maycomb drew us frequently up the street past the real property of Mrs. Henry Lafayette Dubose. It was impossible to go to town without passing her house unless we wished to walk a mile out of the way. Previous minor encounters with her left me with no desire for more, but Jem said I had to grow up some time.

Mrs. Dubose lived alone except for a Negro girl in constant attendance, two doors up the street from us in a house with steep front steps and a dog-trot hall. She was very old; she spent most of each day in bed and the rest of it in a wheelchair. It was rumored that she kept a

CSA pistol concealed among her numerous shawls and wraps.

Jem and I hated her. If she was on the porch when we passed, we would be raked by her wrathful gaze, subjected to ruthless interrogation regarding our behavior, and given a melancholy prediction on what we would amount to when we grew up, which was always nothing. We had long ago given up the idea of walking past her house on the opposite side of the street; that only made her raise her voice and let the whole neighborhood in on it.

We could do nothing to please her. If I said as sunnily as I could, "Hey, Mrs. Dubose," I would receive for an answer, "Don't you say hey to me, you ugly girl! You say good afternoon, Mrs. Dubose!"

She was vicious. Once she heard Jem refer to our father as "Atticus" and her reaction was apoplectic. Besides being the sassiest, most disrespectful mutts who ever passed her way, we were told that it was quite a pity our father had not remarried after our mother's death. A lovelier lady than our mother never lived, she said, and it was heartbreaking the way Atticus Finch let her children run wild. I did not remember our mother, but Jem did—he would tell me about her sometimes—and he went livid when Mrs. Dubose shot us this message.

Jem, having survived Boo Radley, a mad dog and other terrors, had concluded that it was cowardly to stop at Miss Rachel's front steps and wait, and had decreed that we must run as far as the post office corner each evening to meet Atticus coming from work. Countless evenings Atticus would find Jem furious at something Mrs. Dubose had said when we went by.

"Easy does it, son," Atticus would say. "She's an old lady and she's ill. You just hold your head high and be a gentleman Whatever she says to you, it's your job not to let her make you mad."

Jem would say she must not be very sick, she hollered so. When the three of us came to her house, Atticus would sweep off his hat, wave gallantly to her and say, "Good evening, Mrs. Dubose! You look like a picture this evening."

I never heard Atticus say like a picture of what. He would tell her the courthouse news, and would say he hoped with all his heart she'd have a good day tomorrow. He would return his hat to his head, swing me to his shoulders in her very presence, and we would go home in the twilight. It was times like these when I thought my father, who hated guns and had never been to any wars, was the bravest man who ever lived.

The day after Jem's twelfth birthday his money was burning up his pockets, so we headed for town in the early afternoon. Jem thought he had enough to buy a miniature steam engine for himself and a twirling baton for me.

I had long had my eye on that baton: it was at V. J. Elmore's, it was bedecked with sequins and tinsel, it cost seventeen cents. It was then my burning ambition to grow up and twirl with the Maycomb County High School band. Having developed my talent to where I could throw up a stick and almost catch it coming down, I had caused Calpurnia to deny me entrance to the house every time she saw me with a stick in my hand. I felt that I could overcome this defect with a real baton, and I thought it generous of Jem to buy one for me.

Mrs. Dubose was stationed on her porch when we went by.

"Where are you two going at this time of day?" she shouted. "Playing hooky, I suppose. I'll just call up the principal and tell him!" She put her hands on the wheels of her chair and executed a perfect right face.

"Aw, it's Saturday, Mrs. Dubose," said Jem.

"Makes no difference if it's Saturday," she said obscurely. "I wonder if your father knows where you are?"

"Mrs. Dubose, we've been goin' to town by ourselves since we were this high." Jem placed his hand palm down about two feet above the sidewalk.

"Don't you lie to me!" she yelled. "Jeremy Finch, Maudie Atkinson told me you broke down her scuppernong arbor this morning. She's going to tell your father and then you'll wish you never saw the light of day! If you aren't sent to the reform school before next week, my name's not Dubose!"

Jem, who hadn't been near Miss Maudie's scuppernong arbor since last summer, and who knew Miss Maudie wouldn't tell Atticus if he had, issued a general denial.

"Don't you contradict me!" Mrs. Dubose bawled. "And

105

you—" she pointed an arthritic finger at me—"what are you doing in those overalls? You should be in a dress and camisole, young lady! You'll grow up waiting on tables if somebody doesn't change your ways—a Finch waiting on tables at the O.K. Café—hah!"

I was terrified. The O.K. Café was a dim organization on the north side of the square. I grabbed Jem's hand but he shook me loose.

"Come on, Scout," he whispered. "Don't pay any attention to her, just hold your head high and be a gentleman."

But Mrs. Dubose held us: "Not only a Finch waiting on tables but one in the courthouse lawing for niggers!"

Jem stiffened. Mrs. Dubose's shot had gone home and she knew it:

"Yes indeed, what has this world come to when a Finch goes against his raising? I'll tell you!" She put her hand to her mouth. When she drew it away, it trailed a long silver thread of saliva. "Your father's no better than the niggers and trash he works for!"

Jem was scarlet. I pulled at his sleeve, and we were followed up the sidewalk by a philippic on our family's moral degeneration, the major premise of which was that half the Finches were in the asylum anyway, but if our mother were living we would not have come to such a state.

I wasn't sure what Jem resented most, but I took umbrage at Mrs. Dubose's assessment of the family's mental hygiene. I had become almost accustomed to hearing insults aimed at Atticus. But this was the first one coming from an adult. Except for her remarks about Atticus, Mrs. Dubose's attack was only routine. There was a hint of summer in the air—in the shadows it was cool, but the sun was warm, which meant good times coming: no school and Dill.

Jem bought his steam engine and we went by Elmore's for my baton. Jem took no pleasure in his acquisition; he jammed it in his pocket and walked silently beside me toward home. On the way home I nearly hit Mr. Link Deas, who said, "Look out now, Scout!" when I missed a toss, and when we approached Mrs. Dubose's house my baton was grimy from having picked it up out of the dirt so many times.

She was not on the porch.

In later years, I sometimes wondered exactly what made Jem do it, what made him break the bonds of "You just be a gentleman, son," and the phase of self-conscious rectitude he had recently entered. Jem had probably stood as much guff about Atticus lawing for niggers as had I, and I took it for granted that he kept his temper—he had a naturally tranquil disposition and a slow fuse. At the time, however, I thought the only explanation for what he did was that for a few minutes he simply went mad.

What Jem did was something I'd do as a matter of course had I not been under Atticus's interdict, which I assumed included not fighting horrible old ladies. We had just come to her gate when Jem snatched my baton and ran flailing wildly up the steps into Mrs. Dubose's front yard, forgetting everything Atticus had said, forgetting that she packed a pistol under her shawls, forgetting that if Mrs. Dubose missed, her girl Jessie probably wouldn't.

He did not begin to calm down until he had cut the tops off every camellia bush Mrs. Dubose owned, until the ground was littered with green buds and leaves. He bent my baton against his knee, snapped it in two and threw it down.

By that time I was shrieking. Jem yanked my hair, said he didn't care, he'd do it again if he got a chance, and if I didn't shut up he'd pull every hair out of my head. I didn't shut up and he kicked me. I lost my balance and fell on my face. Jem picked me up roughly but looked like he was sorry. There was nothing to say.

We did not choose to meet Atticus coming home that evening. We skulked around the kitchen until Calpurnia threw us out. By some voo-doo system Calpurnia seemed to know all about it. She was a less than satisfactory source of palliation, but she did give Jem a hot biscuit-and-butter which he tore in half and shared with me. It tasted like cotton.

We went to the livingroom. I picked up a football magazine, found a picture of Dixie Howell, showed it to Jem and said, "This looks like you." That was the nicest thing I could think to say to him, but it was no help. He sat by the windows, hunched down in a rocking chair, scowling, waiting. Daylight faded.

Two geological ages later, we heard the soles of Atticus's shoes scrape the front steps. The screen door slammed, there was a pause—Atticus was at the hat rack in the hall—and we heard him call, "Jem!" His voice was like the winter wind.

Atticus switched on the ceiling light in the livingroom and found us there, frozen still. He carried my baton in one hand; its filthy yellow tassel trailed on the rug. He held out his other hand; it contained fat camellia buds.

"Jem," he said, "are you responsible for this?"

"Yes sir."

"Why'd you do it?"

Jem said softly, "She said you lawed for niggers and trash."

"You did this because she said that?"

Jem's lips moved, but his, "Yes sir," was inaudible.

"Son, I have no doubt that you've been annoyed by your contemporaries about me lawing for niggers, as you say, but to do something like this to a sick old lady is inexcusable. I strongly advise you to go down and have a talk with Mrs. Dubose," said Atticus. "Come straight home afterward."

Jem did not move.

"Go on, I said."

I followed Jem out of the livingroom. "Come back here," Atticus said to me. I came back.

Atticus picked up the *Mobile Press* and sat down in the rocking chair Jem had vacated. For the life of me, I did not understand how he could sit there in cold blood and read a newspaper when his only son stood an excellent chance of being murdered with a Confederate Army relic. Of course Jem antagonized me sometimes until I could kill him, but when it came down to it he was all I had. Atticus did not seem to realize this, or if he did he didn't care.

I hated him for that, but when you are in trouble you become easily tired: soon I was hiding in his lap and his arms were around me.

"You're mighty big to be rocked," he said.

"You don't care what happens to him," I said. "You just send him on to get shot at when all he was doin' was standin' up for you."

Atticus pushed my head under his chin. "It's not time

108

to worry yet," he said. "I never thought Jem'd be the one to lose his head over this—thought I'd have more trouble with you."

I said I didn't see why we had to keep our heads anyway, that nobody I knew at school had to keep his head about anything.

"Scout," said Atticus, "when summer comes you'll have to keep your head about far worse things . . . it's not fair for you and Jem, I know that, but sometimes we have to make the best of things, and the way we conduct ourselves when the chips are down—well, all I can say is, when you and Jem are grown, maybe you'll look back on this with some compassion and some feeling that I didn't let you down. This case, Tom Robinson's case, is something that goes to the essence of a man's conscience — Scout, I couldn't go to church and worship God if I didn't try to help that man."

"Atticus, you must be wrong. . . ."

"How's that?"

"Well, most folks seem to think they're right and you're wrong. . . ."

"They're certainly entitled to think that, and they're entitled to full respect for their opinions," said Atticus, "but before I can live with other folks I've got to live with myself. The one thing that doesn't abide by majority rule is a person's conscience."

When Jem returned, he found me still in Atticus's lap. "Well, son?" said Atticus. He set me on my feet, and I made a secret reconnaissance of Jem. He seemed to be all in one piece, but he had a queer look on his face. Perhaps she had given him a dose of calomel.

"I cleaned it up for her and said I was sorry, but I ain't, and that I'd work on 'em ever Saturday and try to make 'em grow back out."

"There was no point in saying you were sorry if you aren't," said Atticus. "Jem, she's old and ill. You can't hold her responsible for what she says and does. Of course, I'd rather she'd have said it to me than to either of you, but we can't always have our 'druthers."

Jem seemed fascinated by a rose in the carpet. "Atticus," he said, "she wants me to read to her."

"Read to her?"

"Yes sir. She wants me to come every afternoon after

109

school and Saturdays and read to her out loud for two hours. Atticus, do I have to?"

"Certainly."

"But she wants me to do it for a month."

"Then you'll do it for a month."

Jem planted his big toe delicately in the center of the rose and pressed it in. Finally he said, "Atticus, it's all right on the sidewalk but inside it's—it's all dark and creepy. There's shadows and things on the ceiling. . . ."

Atticus smiled grimly. "That should appeal to your imagination. Just pretend you're inside the Radley house."

The following Monday afternoon Jem and I climbed the steep front steps to Mrs. Dubose's house and padded down the open hallway. Jem, armed with *Ivanhoe* and full of superior knowledge, knocked at the second door on the left.

"Mrs. Dubose?" he called.

Jessie opened the wood door and unlatched the screen door.

"Is that you, Jem Finch?" she said. "You got your sister with you. I don't know—"

"Let 'em both in, Jessie," said Mrs. Dubose. Jessie admitted us and went off to the kitchen.

An oppressive odor met us when we crossed the threshold, an odor I had met many times in rain-rotted gray houses where there are coal-oil lamps, water dippers, and unbleached domestic sheets. It always made me afraid, expectant, watchful.

In the corner of the room was a brass bed, and in the bed was Mrs. Dubose. I wondered if Jem's activities had put her there, and for a moment I felt sorry for her. She was lying under a pile of quilts and looked almost friendly.

There was a marble-topped washstand by her bed; on it were a glass with a teaspoon in it, a red ear syringe, a box of absorbent cotton, and a steel alarm clock standing on three tiny legs.

"So you brought that dirty little sister of yours, did you?" was her greeting.

Jem said quietly, "My sister ain't dirty and I ain't scared of you," although I noticed his knees shaking.

110

I was expecting a tirade, but all she said was, "You may commence reading, Jeremy."

Jem sat down in a cane-bottom chair and opened *Ivanhoe*. I pulled up another one and sat beside him.

"Come closer," said Mrs. Dubose. "Come to the side of the bed."

We moved our chairs forward. This was the nearest I had ever been to her, and the thing I wanted most to do was move my chair back again.

She was horrible. Her face was the color of a dirty pillowcase, and the corners of her mouth glistened with wet, which inched like a glacier down the deep grooves enclosing her chin. Old-age liver spots dotted her cheeks, and her pale eyes had black pinpoint pupils. Her hands were knobby, and the cuticles were grown up over her fingernails. Her bottom plate was not in, and her upper lip protruded; from time to time she would draw her nether lip to her upper plate and carry her chin with it. This made the wet move faster.

I didn't look any more than I had to. Jem reopened *Ivanhoe* and began reading. I tried to keep up with him, but he read too fast. When Jem came to a word he didn't know, he skipped it, but Mrs. Dubose would catch him and make him spell it out. Jem read for perhaps twenty minutes, during which time I looked at the soot-stained mantelpiece, out the window, anywhere to keep from looking at her. As he read along, I noticed that Mrs. Dubose's corrections grew fewer and farther between, that Jem had even left one sentence dangling in mid-air. She was not listening.

I looked toward the bed.

Something had happened to her. She lay on her back, with the quilts up to her chin. Only her head and shoulders were visible. Her head moved slowly from side to side. From time to time she would open her mouth wide, and I could see her tongue undulate faintly. Cords of saliva would collect on her lips; she would draw them in, then open her mouth again. Her mouth seemed to have a private existence of its own. It worked separate and apart from the rest of her, out and in, like a clam hole at low tide. Occasionally it would say, "Pt," like some viscous substance coming to a boil.

I pulled Jem's sleeve.

He looked at me, then at the bed. Her head made its regular sweep toward us, and Jem said, "Mrs. Dubose, are you all right?" She did not hear him.

The alarm clock went off and scared us stiff. A minute later, nerves still tingling, Jem and I were on the side-walk headed for home. We did not run away, Jessie sent us: before the clock wound down she was in the room pushing Jem and me out of it.

"Shoo," she said, "you all go home."

Jem hesitated at the door.

"It's time for her medicine," Jessie said. As the door swung shut behind us I saw Jessie walking quickly toward Mrs. Dubose's bed.

It was only three forty-five when we got home, so Jem and I drop-kicked in the back yard until it was time to meet Atticus. Atticus had two yellow pencils for me and a football magazine for Jem, which I suppose was a silent reward for our first day's session with Mrs. Dubose. Jem told him what happened.

"Did she frighten you?" asked Atticus.

"No sir," said Jem, "but she's so nasty. She has fits or somethin'. She spits a lot."

"She can't help that. When people are sick they don't look nice sometimes."

"She scared me," I said.

Atticus looked at me over his glasses. "You don't have to go with Jem, you know."

The next afternoon at Mrs. Dubose's was the same as the first, and so was the next, until gradually a pattern emerged: everything would begin normally- -that is, Mrs. Dubose would hound Jem for a while on her favorite subjects, her camellias and our father's nigger-loving propensities; she would grow increasingly silent, then go away from us. The alarm clock would ring, Jessie would shoo us out, and the rest of the day was ours.

"Atticus," I said one evening, "what exactly is a nigger-lover?"

Atticus's face was grave. "Has somebody been calling you that?"

"No sir, Mrs. Dubose calls you that. She warms up every afternoon calling you that. Francis called me that last Christmas, that's where I first heard it."

"Is that the reason you jumped on him?" asked Atticus.

"Yes sir . . ."

"Then why are you asking me what it means?"

I tried to explain to Atticus that it wasn't so much what Francis said that had infuriated me as the way he had said it. "It was like he'd said snot-nose or somethin'."

"Scout," said Atticus, "nigger-lover is just one of those terms that don't mean anything—like snot-nose. It's hard to explain—ignorant, trashy people use it when they think somebody's favoring Negroes over and above themselves. It's slipped into usage with some people like ourselves, when they want a common, ugly term to label somebody."

"You aren't really a nigger-lover, then, are you?"

"I certainly am. I do my best to love everybody . . . I'm hard put, sometimes—baby, it's never an insult to be called what somebody thinks is a bad name. It just shows you how poor that person is, it doesn't hurt you. So don't let Mrs. Dubose get you down. She has enough troubles of her own."

One afternoon a month later Jem was ploughing his way through Sir Walter Scout, as Jem called him, and Mrs. Dubose was correcting him at every turn, when there was a knock on the door. "Come in!" she screamed.

Atticus came in. He went to the bed and took Mrs. Dubose's hand. "I was coming from the office and didn't see the children," he said. "I thought they might still be here."

Mrs. Dubose smiled at him. For the life of me I could not figure out how she could bring herself to speak to him when she seemed to hate him so. "Do you know what time it is, Atticus?" she said. "Exactly fourteen minutes past five. The alarm clock's set for five-thirty. I want you to know that."

It suddenly came to me that each day we had been staying a little longer at Mrs. Dubose's, that the alarm clock went off a few minutes later every day, and that she was well into one of her fits by the time it sounded. Today she had antagonized Jem for nearly two hours with no intention of having a fit, and I felt hopelessly trapped. The alarm clock was the signal for our release; if one day it did not ring, what would we do?

113

"I have a feeling that Jem's reading days are numbered," said Atticus.

"Only a week longer, I think," she said, "just to make sure . . ."

Jem rose. "But—"

Atticus put out his hand and Jem was silent. On the way home, Jem said he had to do it just for a month and the month was up and it wasn't fair.

"Just one more week, son," said Atticus.

"No," said Jem.

"Yes," said Atticus.

The following week found us back at Mrs. Dubose's. The alarm clock had ceased sounding, but Mrs. Dubose would release us with, "That'll do," so late in the afternoon Atticus would be home reading the paper when we returned. Although her fits had passed off, she was in every other way her old self: when Sir Walter Scott became involved in lengthy descriptions of moats and castles, Mrs. Dubose would become bored and pick on us:

"Jeremy Finch, I told you you'd live to regret tearing up my camellias. You regret it now, don't you?"

Jem would say he certainly did.

"Thought you could kill my Snow-on-the-Mountain, did you? Well, Jessie says the top's growing back out. Next time you'll know how to do it right, won't you? You'll pull it up by the roots, won't you?"

Jem would say he certainly would.

"Don't you mutter at me, boy! You hold up your head and say yes ma'am. Don't guess you feel like holding it up, though, with your father what he is."

Jem's chin would come up, and he would gaze at Mrs. Dubose with a face devoid of resentment. Through the weeks he had cultivated an expression of polite and detached interest, which he would present to her in answer to her most blood-curdling inventions.

At last the day came. When Mrs. Dubose said, "That'll do," one afternoon, she added, "And that's all. Good-day to you."

It was over. We bounded down the sidewalk on a spree of sheer relief, leaping and howling.

That spring was a good one: the days grew longer and gave us more playing time. Jem's mind was occupied mostly with the vital statistics of every college football player in the nation. Every night Atticus would read us the sports pages of the newspapers. Alabama might go to the Rose Bowl again this year, judging from its prospects, not one of whose names we could pronounce. Atticus was in the middle of Windy Seaton's column one evening when the telephone rang.

He answered it, then went to the hat rack in the hall. "I'm going down to Mrs. Dubose's for a while," he said. "I won't be long."

But Atticus stayed away until long past my bedtime. When he returned he was carrying a candy box. Atticus sat down in the livingroom and put the box on the floor beside his chair.

"What'd she want?" asked Jem.

We had not seen Mrs. Dubose for over a month. She was never on the porch any more when we passed.

"She's dead, son," said Atticus. "She died a few minutes ago."

"Oh," said Jem. "Well."

"Well is right," said Atticus. "She's not suffering any more. She was sick for a long time. Son, didn't you know what her fits were?"

Jem shook his head.

"Mrs. Dubose was a morphine addict," said Atticus. "She took it as a pain-killer for years. The doctor put her on it. She'd have spent the rest of her life on it and died without so much agony, but she was too contrary—"

"Sir?" said Jem.

Atticus said, "Just before your escapade she called me to make her will. Dr. Reynolds told her she had only a few months left. Her business affairs were in perfect order but she said, 'There's still one thing out of order.'"

"What was that?" Jem was perplexed.

"She said she was going to leave this world beholden to nothing and nobody. Jem, when you're sick as she was, it's all right to take anything to make it easier, but it wasn't all right for her. She said she meant to break herself of it before she died, and that's what she did."

Jem said, "You mean that's what her fits were?"

"Yes, that's what they were. Most of the time you were reading to her I doubt if she heard a word you said. Her whole mind and body were concentrated on that alarm clock. If you hadn't fallen into her hands, I'd have made you go read to her anyway. It may have been some distraction. There was another reason—"

"Did she die free?" asked Jem.

"As the mountain air," said Atticus. "She was conscious to the last, almost. Conscious," he smiled, "and cantankerous. She still disapproved heartily of my doings, and said I'd probably spend the rest of my life bailing you out of jail. She had Jessie fix you this box—"

Atticus reached down and picked up the candy box. He handed it to Jem.

Jem opened the box. Inside, surrounded by wads of damp cotton, was a white, waxy, perfect camellia. It was a Snow-on-the-Mountain.

Jem's eyes nearly popped out of his head. "Old hell-devil, old hell-devil!" he screamed, flinging it down. "Why can't she leave me alone?"

In a flash Atticus was up and standing over him. Jem buried his face in Atticus's shirt front. "Sh-h," he said. "I think that was her way of telling you—everything's all right now, Jem, everything's all right. You know, she was a great lady."

"A lady?" Jem raised his head. His face was scarlet. "After all those things she said about you, a lady?"

"She was. She had her own views about things, a lot different from mine, maybe . . . son, I told you that if you hadn't lost your head I'd have made you go read to her. I wanted you to see something about her—I wanted you to see what real courage is, instead of getting the idea that courage is a man with a gun in his hand. It's when you know you're licked before you begin but you begin anyway and you see it through no matter what. You rarely win, but sometimes you do. Mrs. Dubose won, all ninety-eight pounds of her. According to her views, she died beholden to nothing and nobody. She was the bravest person I ever knew."

Jem picked up the candy box and threw it in the fire. He picked up the camellia, and when I went off to bed I saw him fingering the wide petals. Atticus was reading the paper.

PART TWO

12.

Jem was twelve. He was difficult to live with, inconsistent, moody. His appetite was appalling, and he told me so many times to stop pestering him I consulted Atticus: "Reckon he's got a tapeworm?" Atticus said no, Jem was growing. I must be patient with him and disturb him as little as possible.

This change in Jem had come about in a matter of weeks. Mrs. Dubose was not cold in her grave—Jem had seemed grateful enough for my company when he went to read to her. Overnight, it seemed, Jem had acquired an alien set of values and was trying to impose them on me: several times he went so far as to tell me what to do. After one altercation when Jem hollered, "It's time you started bein' a girl and acting right!" I burst into tears and fled to Calpurnia.

"Don't you fret too much over Mister Jem—" she began.

"Mis-ter Jem?"

"Yeah, he's just about Mister Jem now."

"He ain't that old," I said. "All he needs is somebody to beat him up, and I ain't big enough."

"Baby," said Calpurnia, "I just can't help it if Mister Jem's growin' up. He's gonna want to be off to himself a lot now, doin' whatever boys do, so you just come right on in the kitchen when you feel lonesome. We'll find lots of things to do in here."

The beginning of that summer boded well: Jem could do as he pleased; Calpurnia would do until Dill came. She seemed glad to see me when I appeared in the kitchen, and by watching her I began to think there was some skill involved in being a girl.

But summer came and Dill was not there. I received a letter and a snapshot from him. The letter said he had a new father whose picture was enclosed, and he would have to stay in Meridian because they planned to build a fishing boat. His father was a lawyer like Atticus, only much younger. Dill's new father had a pleasant face, which made me glad Dill had captured him, but I was crushed. Dill concluded by saying he would love me forever and not to worry, he would come get me and marry me as soon as he got enough money together, so please write.

The fact that I had a permanent fiancé was little compensation for his absence: I had never thought about it, but summer was Dill by the fishpool smoking string, Dill's eyes alive with complicated plans to make Boo Radley emerge; summer was the swiftness with which Dill would reach up and kiss me when Jem was not looking, the longings we sometimes felt each other feel. With him, life was routine; without him, life was unbearable. I stayed miserable for two days.

As if that were not enough, the state legislature was called into emergency session and Atticus left us for two weeks. The Governor was eager to scrape a few barnacles off the ship of state; there were sit-down strikes in Birmingham; bread lines in the cities grew longer, people in the country grew poorer. But these were events remote from the world of Jem and me.

We were surprised one morning to see a cartoon in the *Montgomery Advertiser* above the caption, "Maycomb's

Finch." It showed Atticus barefooted and in short pants, chained to a desk: he was diligently writing on a slate while some frivolous-looking girls yelled, "Yoo-hoo!" at him.

"That's a compliment," explained Jem. "He spends his time doin' things that wouldn't get done if nobody did 'em."

"Huh?"

In addition to Jem's newly developed characteristics, he had acquired a maddening air of wisdom.

"Oh, Scout, it's like reorganizing the tax systems of the counties and things. That kind of thing's pretty dry to most men."

"How do you know?"

"Oh, go on and leave me alone. I'm readin' the paper."

Jem got his wish. I departed for the kitchen.

While she was shelling peas, Calpurnia suddenly said, "What am I gonna do about you all's church this Sunday?"

"Nothing, I reckon. Atticus left us collection."

Calpurnia's eyes narrowed and I could tell what was going through her mind. "Cal," I said, "you know we'll behave. We haven't done anything in church in years."

Calpurnia evidently remembered a rainy Sunday when we were both fatherless and teacherless. Left to its own devices, the class tied Eunice Ann Simpson to a chair and placed her in the furnace room. We forgot her, trooped upstairs to church, and were listening quietly to the sermon when a dreadful banging issued from the radiator pipes, persisting until someone investigated and brought forth Eunice Ann saying she didn't want to play Shadrach any more—Jem Finch said she wouldn't get burnt if she had enough faith, but it was hot down there.

"Besides, Cal, this isn't the first time Atticus has left us," I protested.

"Yeah, but he makes certain your teacher's gonna be there. I didn't hear him say this time—reckon he forgot it." Calpurnia scratched her head. Suddenly she smiled. "How'd you and Mister Jem like to come to church with me tomorrow?"

"Really?"

"How 'bout it?" grinned Calpurnia.

If Calpurnia had ever bathed me roughly before, it was nothing compared to her supervision of that Saturday night's routine. She made me soap all over twice, drew fresh water in the tub for each rinse; she stuck my head in the basin and washed it with Octagon soap and castile. She had trusted Jem for years, but that night she invaded his privacy and provoked an outburst: "Can't anybody take a bath in this house without the whole family lookin'?"

Next morning she began earlier than usual, to "go over our clothes." When Calpurnia stayed overnight with us she slept on a folding cot in the kitchen; that morning it was covered with our Sunday habiliments. She had put so much starch in my dress it came up like a tent when I sat down. She made me wear a petticoat and she wrapped a pink sash tightly around my waist. She went over my patent-leather shoes with a cold biscuit until she saw her face in them.

"It's like we were goin' to Mardi Gras," said Jem. "What's all this for, Cal?"

"I don't want anybody sayin' I don't look after my children," she muttered. "Mister Jem, you absolutely can't wear that tie with that suit. It's green."

"'smatter with that?"

"Suit's blue. Can't you tell?"

"Hee hee," I howled, "Jem's color blind."

His face flushed angrily, but Calpurnia said, "Now you all quit that. You're gonna go to First Purchase with smiles on your faces."

First Purchase African M.E. Church was in the Quarters outside the southern town limits, across the old sawmill tracks. It was an ancient paint-peeled frame building, the only church in Maycomb with a steeple and bell, called First Purchase because it was paid for from the first earnings of freed slaves. Negroes worshiped in it on Sundays and white men gambled in it on weekdays.

The churchyard was brick-hard clay, as was the cemetery beside it. If someone died during a dry spell, the body was covered with chunks of ice until rain softened the earth. A few graves in the cemetery were marked with crumbling tombstones; newer ones were outlined with brightly colored glass and broken Coca-Cola bottles.

120

Lightning rods guarding some graves denoted dead who rested uneasily; stumps of burned-out candles stood at the heads of infant graves. It was a happy cemetery.

The warm bittersweet smell of clean Negro welcomed us as we entered the churchyard—Hearts of Love hairdressing mingled with asafoetida, snuff, Hoyt's Cologne, Brown's Mule, peppermint, and lilac talcum.

When they saw Jem and me with Calpurnia, the men stepped back and took off their hats; the women crossed their arms at their waists, weekday gestures of respectful attention. They parted and made a small pathway to the church door for us. Calpurnia walked between Jem and me, responding to the greetings of her brightly clad neighbors.

"What you up to, Miss Cal?" said a voice behind us.

Calpurnia's hands went to our shoulders and we stopped and looked around: standing in the path behind us was a tall Negro woman. Her weight was on one leg; she rested her left elbow in the curve of her hip, pointing at us with upturned palm. She was bullet-headed with strange almond-shaped eyes, straight nose, and an Indian-bow mouth. She seemed seven feet high.

I felt Calpurnia's hand dig into my shoulder. "What you want, Lula?" she asked, in tones I had never heard her use. She spoke quietly, contemptuously.

"I wants to know why you bringin' white chillun to nigger church."

"They's my comp'ny," said Calpurnia. Again I thought her voice strange: she was talking like the rest of them.

"Yeah, an' I reckon you's comp'ny at the Finch house durin' the week."

A murmur ran through the crowd. "Don't you fret," Calpurnia whispered to me, but the roses on her hat trembled indignantly.

When Lula came up the pathway toward us Calpurnia said, "Stop right there, nigger."

Lula stopped, but she said, "You ain't got no business bringin' white chillun here—they got their church, we got our'n. It is our church, ain't it, Miss Cal?"

Calpurnia said, "It's the same God, ain't it?"

Jem said, "Let's go home, Cal, they don't want us here—"

I agreed: they did not want us here. I sensed, rather than saw, that we were being advanced upon. They seemed to be drawing closer to us, but when I looked up at Calpurnia there was amusement in her eyes. When I looked down the pathway again, Lula was gone. In her place was a solid mass of colored people.

One of them stepped from the crowd. It was Zeebo, the garbage collector. "Mister Jem," he said, "we're mighty glad to have you all here. Don't pay no 'tention to Lula, she's contentious because Reverend Sykes threatened to church her. She's a troublemaker from way back, got fancy ideas an' haughty ways—we're mighty glad to have you all."

With that, Calpurnia led us to the church door where we were greeted by Reverend Sykes, who led us to the front pew.

First Purchase was unceiled and unpainted within. Along its walls unlighted kerosene lamps hung on brass brackets; pine benches served as pews. Behind the rough oak pulpit a faded pink silk banner proclaimed God Is Love, the church's only decoration except a rotogravure print of Hunt's *The Light of the World*. There was no sign of piano, organ, hymn-books, church programs—the familiar ecclesiastical impedimenta we saw every Sunday. It was dim inside, with a damp coolness slowly dispelled by the gathering congregation. At each seat was a cheap cardboard fan bearing a garish Garden of Gethsemane, courtesy Tyndal's Hardware Co. (You-Name-It-We-Sell-It).

Calpurnia motioned Jem and me to the end of the row and placed herself between us. She fished in her purse, drew out her handkerchief, and untied the hard wad of change in its corner. She gave a dime to me and a dime to Jem. "We've got ours," he whispered. "You keep it," Calpurnia said, "you're my company." Jem's face showed brief indecision on the ethics of withholding his own dime, but his innate courtesy won and he shifted his dime to his pocket. I did likewise with no qualms.

"Cal," I whispered, "where are the hymn-books?"

"We don't have any," she said.

"Well how—?"

"Sh-h," she said. Reverend Sykes was standing behind the pulpit staring the congregation to silence. He was a short, stocky man in a black suit, black tie, white shirt, and a gold watch-chain that glinted in the light from the frosted windows.

He said, "Brethren and sisters, we are particularly glad to have company with us this morning. Mister and Miss Finch. You all know their father. Before I begin I will read some announcements."

Reverend Sykes shuffled some papers, chose one and held it at arm's length. "The Missionary Society meets in the home of Sister Annette Reeves next Tuesday. Bring your sewing."

He read from another paper. "You all know of Brother Tom Robinson's trouble. He has been a faithful member of First Purchase since he was a boy. The collection taken up today and for the next three Sundays will go to Helen—his wife, to help her out at home."

I punched Jem. "That's the Tom Atticus's de—"
"Sh-h!"

I turned to Calpurnia but was hushed before I opened my mouth. Subdued, I fixed my attention upon Reverend Sykes, who seemed to be waiting for me to settle down. "Will the music superintendent lead us in the first hymn," he said.

Zeebo rose from his pew and walked down the center aisle, stopping in front of us and facing the congregation. He was carrying a battered hymn-book. He opened it and said, "We'll sing number two seventy-three."

This was too much for me. "How're we gonna sing it if there ain't any hymn-books?"

Calpurnia smiled. "Hush baby," she whispered, "you'll see in a minute."

Zeebo cleared his throat and read in a voice like the rumble of distant artillery:

"There's a land beyond the river."

Miraculously on pitch, a hundred voices sang out Zeebo's words. The last syllable, held to a husky hum, was followed by Zeebo saying,

"That we call the sweet forever."

Music again swelled around us; the last note lingered and Zeebo met it with the next line: "And we only reach that shore by faith's decree."

The congregation hesitated, Zeebo repeated the line carefully, and it was sung. At the chorus Zeebo closed the book, a signal for the congregation to proceed without his help.

On the dying notes of "Jubilee," Zeebo said, "In that far-off sweet forever, just beyond the shining river."

Line for line, voices followed in simple harmony until the hymn ended in a melancholy murmur.

I looked at Jem, who was looking at Zeebo from the corners of his eyes. I didn't believe it either, but we had both heard it.

Reverend Sykes then called on the Lord to bless the sick and the suffering, a procedure no different from our church practice, except Reverend Sykes directed the Deity's attention to several specific cases.

His sermon was a forthright denunciation of sin, an austere declaration of the motto on the wall behind him: he warned his flock against the evils of heady brews, gambling, and strange women. Bootleggers caused enough trouble in the Quarters, but women were worse. Again, as I had often met it in my own church, I was confronted with the Impurity of Women doctrine that seemed to preoccupy all clergymen.

Jem and I had heard the same sermon Sunday after Sunday, with only one exception. Reverend Sykes used his pulpit more freely to express his views on individual lapses from grace: Jim Hardy had been absent from church for five Sundays and he wasn't sick; Constance Jackson had better watch her ways--she was in grave danger for quarreling with her neighbors; she had erected the only spite fence in the history of the Quarters.

Reverend Sykes closed his sermon. He stood beside a table in front of the pulpit and requested the morning offering, a proceeding that was strange to Jem and me. One by one, the congregation came forward and dropped nickels and dimes into a black enameled coffee can. Jem and I followed suit, and received a soft, "Thank you, thank you," as our dimes clinked.

To our amazement, Reverend Sykes emptied the can onto the table and raked the coins into his hand. He straightened up and said, "This is not enough, we must have ten dollars."

The congregation stirred. "You all know what it's for —Helen can't leave those children to work while Tom's in jail. If everybody gives one more dime, we'll have it—" Reverend Sykes waved his hand and called to someone in the back of the church. "Alec, shut the doors. Nobody leaves here till we have ten dollars."

Calpurnia scratched in her handbag and brought forth a battered leather coin purse. "Naw Cal," Jem whispered, when she handed him a shiny quarter, "we can put ours in. Gimme your dime, Scout."

The church was becoming stuffy, and it occurred to me that Reverend Sykes intended to sweat the amount due out of his flock. Fans crackled, feet shuffled, tobacco-chewers were in agony.

Reverend Sykes startled me by saying sternly, "Carlow Richardson, I haven't seen you up this aisle yet."

A thin man in khaki pants came up the aisle and deposited a coin. The congregation murmured approval.

Reverend Sykes then said, "I want all of you with no children to make a sacrifice and give one more dime apiece. Then we'll have it."

Slowly, painfully, the ten dollars was collected. The door was opened, and the gust of warm air revived us. Zeebo lined *On Jordan's Stormy Banks*, and church was over.

I wanted to stay and explore, but Calpurnia propelled me up the aisle ahead of her. At the church door, while she paused to talk with Zeebo and his family, Jem and I chatted with Reverend Sykes. I was bursting with questions, but decided I would wait and let Calpurnia answer them.

"We were 'specially glad to have you all here," said Reverend Sykes. "This church has no better friend than your daddy."

My curiosity burst: "Why were you all takin' up collection for Tom Robinson's wife?"

"Didn't you hear why?" asked Reverend Sykes. "Helen's got three little'uns and she can't go out to work—"

"Why can't she take 'em with her, Reverend?" I asked. It was customary for field Negroes with tiny children to deposit them in whatever shade there was while their parents worked—usually the babies sat in the shade between two rows of cotton. Those unable to sit were strapped papoose-style on their mothers' backs, or resided in extra cotton bags.

Reverend Sykes hesitated. "To tell you the truth, Miss Jean Louise, Helen's finding it hard to get work these days . . . when it's picking time, I think Mr. Link Deas'll take her."

"Why not, Reverend?"

Before he could answer, I felt Calpurnia's hand on my shoulder. At its pressure I said, "We thank you for lettin' us come." Jem echoed me, and we made our way homeward.

"Cal, I know Tom Robinson's in jail an' he's done somethin' awful, but why won't folks hire Helen?" I asked.

Calpurnia, in her navy voile dress and tub of a hat, walked between Jem and me. "It's because of what folks say Tom's done," she said. "Folks aren't anxious to—to have anything to do with any of his family."

"Just what did he do, Cal?"

Calpurnia sighed. "Old Mr. Bob Ewell accused him of rapin' his girl an' had him arrested an' put in jail—"

"Mr. Ewell?" My memory stirred. "Does he have anything to do with those Ewells that come every first day of school an' then go home? Why, Atticus said they were absolute trash—I never heard Atticus talk about folks the way he talked about the Ewells. He said—"

"Yeah, those are the ones."

"Well, if everybody in Maycomb knows what kind of folks the Ewells are they'd be glad to hire Helen . . . what's rape, Cal?"

"It's somethin' you'll have to ask Mr. Finch about," she said. "He can explain it better than I can. You all hungry? The Reverend took a long time unwindin' this morning, he's not usually so tedious."

"He's just like our preacher," said Jem, "but why do you all sing hymns that way?"

"Linin'?" she asked.

"Is that what it is?"

"Yeah, it's called linin'. They've done it that way as long as I can remember."

Jem said it looked like they could save the collection money for a year and get some hymn-books.

Calpurnia laughed. "Wouldn't do any good," she said. "They can't read."

126

"Can't read?" I asked. "All those folks?"

"That's right," Calpurnia nodded. "Can't but about four folks in First Purchase read . . . I'm one of 'em."

"Where'd you go to school, Cal?" asked Jem.

"Nowhere. Let's see now, who taught me my letters? It was Miss Maudie Atkinson's aunt, old Miss Buford—"

"Are you *that* old?"

"I'm older than Mr. Finch, even." Calpurnia grinned. "Not sure how much, though. We started rememberin' one time, trying to figure out how old I was—I can remember back just a few years more'n he can, so I'm not much older, when you take off the fact that men can't remember as well as women."

"What's your birthday, Cal?"

"I just have it on Christmas, it's easier to remember that way—I don't have a real birthday."

"But Cal," Jem protested, "you don't look even near as old as Atticus."

"Colored folks don't show their ages so fast," she said.

"Maybe because they can't read. Cal, did you teach Zeebo?"

"Yeah, Mister Jem. There wasn't a school even when he was a boy. I made him learn, though."

Zeebo was Calpurnia's eldest son. If I had ever thought about it, I would have known that Calpurnia was of mature years—Zeebo had half-grown children—but then I had never thought about it.

"Did you teach him out of a primer, like us?" I asked.

"No, I made him get a page of the Bible every day, and there was a book Miss Buford taught me out of—bet you don't know where I got it," she said.

We didn't know.

Calpurnia said, "Your Granddaddy Finch gave it to me."

"Were you from the Landing?" Jem asked. "You never told us that."

"I certainly am, Mister Jem. Grew up down there between the Buford Place and the Landin'. I've spent all my days workin' for the Finches or the Bufords, an' I moved to Maycomb when your daddy and your mamma married."

"What was the book, Cal?" I asked.

"Blackstone's *Commentaries*."

Jem was thunderstruck. "You mean you taught Zeebo outa *that*?"

"Why yes sir, Mister Jem." Calpurnia timidly put her fingers to her mouth. "They were the only books I had. Your grandaddy said Mr. Blackstone wrote fine English—"

"That's why you don't talk like the rest of 'em," said Jem.

"The rest of who?"

"Rest of the colored folks. Cal, but you talked like they did in church. . . ."

That Calpurnia led a modest double life never dawned on me. The idea that she had a separate existence outside our household was a novel one, to say nothing of her having command of two languages.

"Cal," I asked, "why do you talk nigger-talk to the— to your folks when you know it's not right?"

"Well, in the first place I'm black—"

"That doesn't mean you hafta talk that way when you know better," said Jem.

Calpurnia tilted her hat and scratched her head, then pressed her hat down carefully over her ears. "It's right hard to say," she said. "Suppose you and Scout talked colored-folks' talk at home—it'd be out of place, wouldn't it? Now what if I talked white-folks' talk at church, and with my neighbors? They'd think I was puttin' on airs to beat Moses."

"But Cal, you know better," I said.

"It's not necessary to tell all you know. It's not lady-like—in the second place, folks don't like to have somebody around knowin' more than they do. It aggravates 'em. You're not gonna change any of them by talkin' right, they've got to want to learn themselves, and when they don't want to learn there's nothing you can do but keep your mouth shut or talk their language."

"Cal, can I come to see you sometimes?"

She looked down at me. "See me, honey? You see me every day."

"Out to your house," I said. "Sometimes after work? Atticus can get me."

"Any time you want to," she said. "We'd be glad to have you."

128

We were on the sidewalk by the Radley Place.

"Look on the porch yonder," Jem said.

I looked over to the Radley Place, expecting to see its phantom occupant sunning himself in the swing. The swing was empty.

"I mean our porch," said Jem.

I looked down the street. Enarmored, upright, uncompromising, Aunt Alexandra was sitting in a rocking chair exactly as if she had sat there every day of her life.

13.

Put my bag in the front bedroom, Calpurnia," was the first thing Aunt Alexandra said. "Jean Louise, stop scratching your head," was the second thing she said.

Calpurnia picked up Aunty's heavy suitcase and opened the door. "I'll take it," said Jem, and took it. I heard the suitcase hit the bedroom floor with a thump. The sound had a dull permanence about it.

"Have you come for a visit, Aunty?" I asked. Aunt Alexandra's visits from the Landing were rare, and she traveled in state. She owned a bright green square Buick and a black chauffeur, both kept in an unhealthy state of tidiness, but today they were nowhere to be seen.

"Didn't your father tell you?" she asked.

Jem and I shook our heads.

"Probably he forgot. He's not in yet, is he?"

"Nome, he doesn't usually get back till late afternoon," said Jem.

"Well, your father and I decided it was time I came to stay with you for a while."

"For a while" in Maycomb meant anything from three days to thirty years. Jem and I exchanged glances.

"Jem's growing up now and you are too," she said to me. "We decided that it would be best for you to have some feminine influence. It won't be many years, Jean

Louise, before you become interested in clothes and boys—"

I could have made several answers to this: Cal's a girl, it would be many years before I would be interested in boys, I would never be interested in clothes . . . but I kept quiet.

"What about Uncle Jimmy?" asked Jem. "Is he comin', too?"

"Oh no, he's staying at the Landing. He'll keep the place going."

The moment I said, "Won't you miss him?" I realized that this was not a tactful question. Uncle Jimmy present or Uncle Jimmy absent made not much difference, he never said anything. Aunt Alexandra ignored my question.

I could think of nothing else to say to her. In fact I could never think of anything to say to her, and I sat thinking of past painful conversations between us: How are you, Jean Louise? Fine, thank you ma'am, how are you? Very well, thank you; what have you been doing with yourself? Nothin'. Don't you do anything? Nome. Certainly you have friends? Yessum. Well what do you all do? Nothin'.

It was plain that Aunty thought me dull in the extreme, because I once heard her tell Atticus that I was sluggish.

There was a story behind all this, but I had no desire to extract it from her then: today was Sunday, and Aunt Alexandra was positively irritable on the Lord's Day. I guess it was her Sunday corset. She was not fat, but solid, and she chose protective garments that drew up her bosom to giddy heights, pinched in her waist, flared out her rear, and managed to suggest that Aunt Alexandra's was once an hour-glass figure. From any angle, it was formidable.

The remainder of the afternoon went by in the gentle gloom that descends when relatives appear, but was dispelled when we heard a car turn in the driveway. It was Atticus, home from Montgomery. Jem, forgetting his dignity, ran with me to meet him. Jem seized his brief-case and bag, I jumped into his arms, felt his vague dry kiss and said, "'d you bring me a book? 'd you know Aunty's here?"

Atticus answered both questions in the affirmative. "How'd you like for her to come live with us?"

I said I would like it very much, which was a lie, but one must lie under certain circumstances and at all times when one can't do anything about them.

"We felt it was time you children needed—well, it's like this, Scout," Atticus said. "Your aunt's doing me a favor as well as you all. I can't stay here all day with you, and the summer's going to be a hot one."

"Yes sir," I said, not understanding a word he said. I had an idea, however, that Aunt Alexandra's appearance on the scene was not so much Atticus's doing as hers. Aunty had a way of declaring What Is Best For The Family, and I suppose her coming to live with us was in that category.

Maycomb welcomed her. Miss Maudie Atkinson baked a Lane cake so loaded with shinny it made me tight; Miss Stephanie Crawford had long visits with Aunt Alexandra, consisting mostly of Miss Stephanie shaking her head and saying, "Uh,uh,uh." Miss Rachel next door had Aunty over for coffee in the afternoons, and Mr. Nathan Radley went so far as to come up in the front yard and say he was glad to see her.

When she settled in with us and life resumed its daily pace, Aunt Alexandra seemed as if she had always lived with us. Her Missionary Society refreshments added to her reputation as a hostess (she did not permit Calpurnia to make the delicacies required to sustain the Society through long reports on Rice Christians); she joined and became Secretary of the Maycomb Amanuensis Club. To all parties present and participating in the life of the county, Aunt Alexandra was one of the last of her kind: she had river-boat, boarding-school manners; let any moral come along and she would uphold it; she was born in the objective case; she was an incurable gossip. When Aunt Alexandra went to school, self-doubt could not be found in any textbook, so she knew not its meaning. She was never bored, and given the slightest chance she would exercise her royal prerogative: she would arrange, advise, caution, and warn.

She never let a chance escape her to point out the shortcomings of other tribal groups to the greater glory of our own, a habit that amused Jem rather than annoyed

131

him: "Aunty better watch how she talks—scratch most folks in Maycomb and they're kin to us."

Aunt Alexandra, in underlining the moral of young Sam Merriweather's suicide, said it was caused by a morbid streak in the family. Let a sixteen-year-old girl giggle in the choir and Aunty would say, "It just goes to show you, all the Penfield women are flighty." Everybody in Maycomb, it seemed, had a Streak: a Drinking Streak, a Gambling Streak, a Mean Streak, a Funny Streak.

Once, when Aunty assured us that Miss Stephanie Crawford's tendency to mind other people's business was hereditary, Atticus said, "Sister, when you stop to think about it, our generation's practically the first in the Finch family not to marry its cousins. Would you say the Finches have an Incestuous Streak?"

Aunty said no, that's where we got our small hands and feet.

I never understood her preoccupation with heredity. Somewhere, I had received the impression that Fine Folks were people who did the best they could with the sense they had, but Aunt Alexandra was of the opinion, obliquely expressed, that the longer a family had been squatting on one patch of land the finer it was.

"That makes the Ewells fine folks, then," said Jem. The tribe of which Burris Ewell and his brethren consisted had lived on the same plot of earth behind the Maycomb dump, and had thrived on county welfare money for three generations.

Aunt Alexandra's theory had something behind it, though. Maycomb was an ancient town. It was twenty miles east of Finch's Landing, awkwardly inland for such an old town. But Maycomb would have been closer to the river had it not been for the nimble-wittedness of one Sinkfield, who in the dawn of history operated an inn where two pig-trails met, the only tavern in the territory. Sinkfield, no patriot, served and supplied ammunition to Indians and settlers alike, neither knowing or caring whether he was a part of the Alabama Territory or the Creek Nation so long as business was good. Business was excellent when Governor William Wyatt Bibb, with a view to promoting the newly created county's domestic tranquility, dispatched a team of surveyors to locate its exact center and there establish its seat of government. The surveyors, Sinkfield's guests, told their host that he was in the territorial confines of Maycomb County, and showed him the probable spot where the county seat would be built. Had not Sinkfield made a bold stroke to preserve his holdings, Maycomb would have sat in the middle of Winston Swamp, a place totally devoid of interest. Instead, Maycomb grew and sprawled out from its hub, Sinkfield's Tavern, because Sinkfield reduced his guests to myopic drunkenness one evening, induced them to bring forward their maps and charts, lop off a little here, add a bit there, and adjust the center of the county to meet his requirements. He sent them packing next day armed with their charts and five quarts of shinny in their saddlebags—two apiece and one for the Governor.

Because its primary reason for existence was government, Maycomb was spared the grubbiness that distinguished most Alabama towns its size. In the beginning its buildings were solid, its courthouse proud, its streets graciously wide. Maycomb's proportion of professional people ran high: one went there to have his teeth pulled, his wagon fixed, his heart listened to, his money deposited, his soul saved, his mules vetted. But the ultimate wisdom of Sinkfield's maneuver is open to question. He placed the young town too far away from the only kind of public transportation in those days— river-boat—and it took a man from the north end of the county two days to travel to Maycomb for store-bought goods. As a result the town remained the same size for a hundred years, an island in a patchwork sea of cotton-fields and timberland.

Although Maycomb was ignored during the War Between the States, Reconstruction rule and economic ruin forced the town to grow. It grew inward. New people so rarely settled there, the same families married the same families until the members of the community looked faintly alike. Occasionally someone would return from Montgomery or Mobile with an outsider, but the result caused only a ripple in the quiet stream of family resemblance. Things were more or less the same during my early years.

There was indeed a caste system in Maycomb, but to

my mind it worked this way: the older citizens, the present generation of people who had lived side by side for years and years, were utterly predictable to one another: they took for granted attitudes, character shadings, even gestures, as having been repeated in each generation and refined by time. Thus the dicta No Crawford Minds His Own Business, Every Third Merriweather Is Morbid, The Truth Is Not in the Delafields, All the Bufords Walk Like That, were simply guides to daily living: never take a check from a Delafield without a discreet call to the bank; Miss Maudie Atkinson's shoulder stoops because she was a Buford; if Mrs. Grace Merriweather sips gin out of Lydia E. Pinkham bottles it's nothing unusual—her mother did the same.

Aunt Alexandra fitted into the world of Maycomb like a hand into a glove, but never into the world of Jem and me. I so often wondered how she could be Atticus's and Uncle Jack's sister that I revived half-remembered tales of changelings and mandrake roots that Jem had spun long ago.

These were abstract speculations for the first month of her stay, as she had little to say to Jem or me, and we saw her only at mealtimes and at night before we went to bed. It was summer and we were outdoors. Of course some afternoons when I would run inside for a drink of water, I would find the livingroom overrun with Maycomb ladies, sipping, whispering, fanning, and I would be called: "Jean Louise, come speak to these ladies."

When I appeared in the doorway, Aunty would look as if she regretted her request; I was usually mud-splashed or covered with sand.

"Speak to your Cousin Lily," she said one afternoon, when she had trapped me in the hall.

"Who?" I said.

"Your Cousin Lily Brooke," said Aunt Alexandra.

"She our cousin? I didn't know that."

Aunt Alexandra managed to smile in a way that conveyed a gentle apology to Cousin Lily and firm disapproval to me. When Cousin Lily Brooke left I knew I was in for it.

It was a sad thing that my father had neglected to tell me about the Finch Family, or to install any pride into

134

his children. She summoned Jem, who sat warily on the sofa beside me. She left the room and returned with a purple-covered book on which *Meditations of Joshua S. St. Clair* was stamped in gold.

"Your cousin wrote this," said Aunt Alexandra. "He was a beautiful character."

Jem examined the small volume. "Is this the Cousin Joshua who was locked up for so long?"

Aunt Alexandra said, "How did you know that?"

"Why, Atticus said he went round the bend at the University. Said he tried to shoot the president. Said Cousin Joshua said he wasn't anything but a sewer-inspector and tried to shoot him with an old flintlock pistol, only it just blew up in his hand. Atticus said it cost the family five hundred dollars to get him out of that one—"

Aunt Alexandra was standing stiff as a stork. "That's all," she said. "We'll see about this."

Before bedtime I was in Jem's room trying to borrow a book, when Atticus knocked and entered. He sat on the side of Jem's bed, looked at us soberly, then he grinned.

"Er—h'rm," he said. He was beginning to preface some things he said with a throaty noise, and I thought he must at last be getting old, but he looked the same. "I don't exactly know how to say this," he began.

"Well, just say it," said Jem. "Have we done something?"

Our father was actually fidgeting. "No, I just want to explain to you that—your Aunt Alexandra asked me . . . son, you know you're a Finch, don't you?"

"That's what I've been told." Jem looked out of the corners of his eyes. His voice rose uncontrollably, "Atticus, what's the matter?"

Atticus crossed his knees and folded his arms. "I'm trying to tell you the facts of life."

Jem's disgust deepened. "I know all that stuff," he said.

Atticus suddenly grew serious. In his lawyer's voice, without a shade of inflection, he said: "Your aunt has asked me to try and impress upon you and Jean Louise that you are not from run-of-the-mill people, that you are the product of several generations' gentle breeding—" Atticus paused, watching me locate an elusive red-bug on my leg.

"Gentle breeding," he continued, when I had found and scratched it, "and that you should try to live up to your name—" Atticus persevered in spite of us: "She asked me to tell you you must try to behave like the little lady and gentleman that you are. She wants to talk to you about the family and what it's meant to Maycomb County through the years, so you'll have some idea of who you are, so you might be moved to behave accordingly," he concluded at a gallop.

Stunned, Jem and I looked at each other, then at Atticus, whose collar seemed to worry him. We did not speak to him.

Presently I picked up a comb from Jem's dresser and ran its teeth along the edge.

"Stop that noise," Atticus said.

His curtness stung me. The comb was midway in its journey, and I banged it down. For no reason I felt myself beginning to cry, but I could not stop. This was not my father. My father never thought these thoughts. My father never spoke so. Aunt Alexandra had put him up to this, somehow. Through my tears I saw Jem standing in a similar pool of isolation, his head cocked to one side.

There was nowhere to go, but I turned to go and met Atticus's vest front. I buried my head in it and listened to the small internal noises that went on behind the light blue cloth: his watch ticking, the faint crackle of his starched shirt, the soft sound of his breathing.

"Your stomach's growling," I said.

"I know it," he said.

"You better take some soda."

"I will," he said.

"Atticus, is all this behavin' an' stuff gonna make things different? I mean are you—?"

I felt his hand on the back of my head. "Don't you worry about anything," he said. "It's not time to worry."

When I heard that, I knew he had come back to us. The blood in my legs began to flow again, and I raised my head. "You really want us to do all that? I can't remember everything Finches are supposed to do. . . ."

"I don't want you to remember it. Forget it."

He went to the door and out of the room, shutting the

136

door behind him. He nearly slammed it, but caught himself at the last minute and closed it softly. As Jem and I stared, the door opened again and Atticus peered around. His eyebrows were raised, his glasses had slipped. "Get more like Cousin Joshua every day, don't I? Do you think I'll end up costing the family five hundred dollars?"

I know now what he was trying to do, but Atticus was only a man. It takes a woman to do that kind of work.

14.

Although we heard no more about the Finch family from Aunt Alexandra, we heard plenty from the town. On Saturdays, armed with our nickels, when Jem permitted me to accompany him (he was now positively allergic to my presence when in public), we would squirm our way through sweating sidewalk crowds and sometimes hear, "There's his chillun," or, "Yonder's some Finches." Turning to face our accusers, we would see only a couple of farmers studying the enema bags in the Mayco Drugstore window. Or two dumpy countrywomen in straw hats sitting in a Hoover cart.

"They c'n go loose and rape up the countryside for all of 'em who run this county care," was one obscure observation we met head on from a skinny gentleman when he passed us. Which reminded me that I had a question to ask Atticus.

"What's rape?" I asked him that night.

Atticus looked around from behind his paper. He was in his chair by the window. As we grew older, Jem and I thought it generous to allow Atticus thirty minutes to himself after supper.

He sighed, and said rape was carnal knowledge of a female by force and without consent.

"Well if that's all it is why did Calpurnia dry me up when I asked her what it was?"

Atticus looked pensive. "What's that again?"

"Well, I asked Calpurnia comin' from church that day what it was and she said ask you but I forgot to and now I'm askin' you."

His paper was now in his lap. "Again, please," he said.

I told him in detail about our trip to church with Calpurnia. Atticus seemed to enjoy it, but Aunt Alexandra, who was sitting in a corner quietly sewing, put down her embroidery and stared at us.

"You all were coming back from Calpurnia's church that Sunday?"

Jem said, "Yessum, she took us."

I remembered something. "Yessum, and she promised me I could come out to her house some afternoon. Atticus, I'll go next Sunday if it's all right, can I? Cal said she'd come get me if you were off in the car."

"You may *not*."

Aunt Alexandra said it. I wheeled around, startled, then turned back to Atticus in time to catch his swift glance at her, but it was too late. I said, "I didn't ask you!"

For a big man, Atticus could get up and down from a chair faster than anyone I ever knew. He was on his feet. "Apologize to your aunt," he said.

"I didn't ask her, I asked you—"

Atticus turned his head and pinned me to the wall with his good eye. His voice was deadly: "First, apologize to your aunt."

"I'm sorry, Aunty," I muttered.

"Now then," he said. "Let's get this clear: you do as Calpurnia tells you, you do as I tell you, and as long as your aunt's in this house, you will do as she tells you. Understand?"

I understood, pondered a while, and concluded that the only way I could retire with a shred of dignity was to go to the bathroom, where I stayed long enough to make them think I had to go. Returning, I lingered in the hall to hear a fierce discussion going on in the living-room. Through the door I could see Jem on the sofa with a football magazine in front of his face, his head turning as if its pages contained a live tennis match.

". . . you've got to do something about her," Aunty

138

was saying. "You've let things go on too long, Atticus, too long."

"I don't see any harm in letting her go out there. Cal'd look after her there as well as she does here."

Who was the "her" they were talking about? My heart sank: me. I felt the starched walls of a pink cotton penitentiary closing in on me, and for the second time in my life I thought of running away. Immediately.

"Atticus, it's all right to be soft-hearted, you're an easy man, but you have a daughter to think of. A daughter who's growing up."

"That's what I am thinking of."

"And don't try to get around it. You've got to face it sooner or later and it might as well be tonight. We don't need her now."

Atticus's voice was even: "Alexandra, Calpurnia's not leaving this house until she wants to. You may think otherwise, but I couldn't have got along without her all these years. She's a faithful member of this family and you'll simply have to accept things the way they are. Besides, sister, I don't want you working your head off for us—you've no reason to do that. We still need Cal as much as we ever did."

"But Atticus—"

"Besides, I don't think the children've suffered one bit from her having brought them up. If anything, she's been harder on them in some ways than a mother would have been . . . she's never let them get away with anything, she's never indulged them the way most colored nurses do. She tried to bring them up according to her lights, and Cal's lights are pretty good—and another thing, the children love her."

I breathed again. It wasn't me, it was only Calpurnia they were talking about. Revived, I entered the living-room. Atticus had retreated behind his newspaper and Aunt Alexandra was worrying her embroidery. Punk, punk, punk, her needle broke the taut circle. She stopped, and pulled the cloth tighter: punk-punk-punk. She was furious.

Jem got up and padded across the rug. He motioned me to follow. He led me to his room and closed the door. His face was grave.

"They've been fussing, Scout."

Jem and I fussed a great deal these days, but I had never heard of or seen anyone quarrel with Atticus. It was not a comfortable sight.

"Scout, try not to antagonize Aunty, hear?"

Atticus's remarks were still rankling, which made me miss the request in Jem's question. My feathers rose again. "You tryin' to tell me what to do?"

"Naw, it's—he's got a lot on his mind now, without us worrying him."

"Like what?" Atticus didn't appear to have anything especially on his mind.

"It's this Tom Robinson case that's worryin' him to death—"

I said Atticus didn't worry about anything. Besides, the case never bothered us except about once a week and then it didn't last.

"That's because you can't hold something in your mind but a little while," said Jem. "It's different with grown folks, we—"

His maddening superiority was unbearable these days. He didn't want to do anything but read and go off by himself. Still, everything he read he passed along to me, but with this difference: formerly, because he thought I'd like it; now, for my edification and instruction.

"Jee crawling hova, Jem! Who do you think you are?"

"Now I mean it, Scout, you antagonize Aunty and I'll —I'll spank you."

With that, I was gone. "You damn morphodite, I'll kill you!" He was sitting on the bed, and it was easy to grab his front hair and land one on his mouth. He slapped me and I tried another left, but a punch in the stomach sent me sprawling on the floor. It nearly knocked the breath out of me, but it didn't matter because I knew he was fighting, he was fighting me back. We were still equals.

"Ain't so high and mighty now, are you!" I screamed, sailing in again. He was still on the bed and I couldn't get a firm stance, so I threw myself at him as hard as I could, hitting, pulling, pinching, gouging. What had begun as a fist-fight became a brawl. We were still struggling when Atticus separated us.

"That's all," he said. "Both of you go to bed right now."

"Taah!" I said at Jem. He was being sent to bed at my bedtime.

"Who started it?" asked Atticus, in resignation.

"Jem did. He was tryin' to tell me what to do. I don't have to mind *him* now, do I?"

Atticus smiled. "Let's leave it at this: you mind Jem whenever he can make you. Fair enough?"

Aunt Alexandra was present but silent, and when she went down the hall with Atticus we heard her say, ". . . just one of the things I've been telling you about," a phrase that united us again.

Ours were adjoining rooms; as I shut the door between them Jem said, "Night, Scout."

"Night," I murmured, picking my way across the room to turn on the light. As I passed the bed I stepped on something warm, resilient, and rather smooth. It was not quite like hard rubber, and I had the sensation that it was alive. I also heard it move.

I switched on the light and looked at the floor by the bed. Whatever I had stepped on was gone. I tapped on Jem's door.

"What," he said.

"How does a snake feel?"

"Sort of rough. Cold. Dusty. Why?"

"I think there's one under my bed. Can you come look?"

"Are you bein' funny?" Jem opened the door. He was in his pajama bottoms. I noticed not without satisfaction that the mark of my knuckles was still on his mouth. When he saw I meant what I said, he said, "If you think I'm gonna put my face down to a snake you've got another think comin'. Hold on a minute."

He went to the kitchen and fetched the broom. "You better get up on the bed," he said.

"You reckon it's really one?" I asked. This was an occasion. Our houses had no cellars; they were built on stone blocks a few feet above the ground, and the entry of reptiles was not unknown but was not commonplace. Miss Rachel Haverford's excuse for a glass of neat whiskey every morning was that she never got over the fright of finding a rattler coiled in her bedroom closet, on her washing, when she went to hang up her negligee.

Jem made a tentative swipe under the bed. I looked

over the foot to see if a snake would come out. None did. Jem made a deeper swipe.

"Do snakes grunt?"

"It ain't a snake," Jem said. "It's somebody."

Suddenly a filthy brown package shot from under the bed. Jem raised the broom and missed Dill's head by an inch when it appeared.

"God Almighty." Jem's voice was reverent.

We watched Dill emerge by degrees. He was a tight fit. He stood up and eased his shoulders, turned his feet in their ankle sockets, rubbed the back of his neck. His circulation restored, he said, "Hey."

Jem petitioned God again. I was speechless.

"I'm 'bout to perish," said Dill. "Got anything to eat?"

In a dream, I went to the kitchen. I brought him back some milk and half a pan of corn bread left over from supper. Dill devoured it, chewing with his front teeth, as was his custom.

I finally found my voice. "How'd you get here?"

By an involved route. Refreshed by food, Dill recited this narrative: having been bound in chains and left to die in the basement (there were basements in Meridian) by his new father, who disliked him, and secretly kept alive on raw field peas by a passing farmer who heard his cries for help (the good man poked a bushel pod by pod through the ventilator), Dill worked himself free by pulling the chains from the wall. Still in wrist manacles, he wandered two miles out of Meridian where he discovered a small animal show and was immediately engaged to wash the camel. He traveled with the show all over Mississippi until his infallible sense of direction told him he was in Abbott County, Alabama, just across the river from Maycomb. He walked the rest of the way.

"How'd you get here?" asked Jem.

He had taken thirteen dollars from his mother's purse, caught the nine o'clock from Meridian and got off at Maycomb Junction. He had walked ten or eleven of the fourteen miles to Maycomb, off the highway in the scrub bushes lest the authorities be seeking him, and had ridden the remainder of the way clinging to the backboard of a cotton wagon. He had been under the bed for two hours, he thought; he had heard us in the diningroom, and the clink of forks on plates nearly drove him crazy.

He thought Jem and I would never go to bed; he had considered emerging and helping me beat Jem, as Jem had grown far taller, but he knew Mr. Finch would break it up soon, so he thought it best to stay where he was. He was worn out, dirty beyond belief, and home.

"They must not know you're here," said Jem. "We'd know if they were lookin' for you. . . ."

"Think they're still searchin' all the picture shows in Meridian." Dill grinned.

"You oughta let your mother know where you are," said Jem. "You oughta let her know you're here. . . ."

Dill's eyes flickered at Jem, and Jem looked at the floor. Then he rose and broke the remaining code of our childhood. He went out of the room and down the hall. "Atticus," his voice was distant, "can you come here a minute, sir?"

Beneath its sweat-streaked dirt Dill's face went white. I felt sick. Atticus was in the doorway.

He came to the middle of the room and stood with his hands in his pockets, looking down at Dill.

I finally found my voice: "It's okay, Dill. When he wants you to know somethin', he tells you."

Dill looked at me. "I mean it's all right," I said. "You know he wouldn't bother you, you know you ain't scared of Atticus."

"I'm not scared . . ." Dill muttered.

"Just hungry, I'll bet." Atticus's voice had its usual pleasant dryness. "Scout, we can do better than a pan of cold corn bread, can't we? You fill this fellow up and when I get back we'll see what we can see."

"Mr. Finch, don't tell Aunt Rachel, don't make me go back, *please* sir! I'll run off again—!"

"Whoa, son," said Atticus. "Nobody's about to make you go anywhere but to bed pretty soon. I'm just going over to tell Miss Rachel you're here and ask her if you could spend the night with us—you'd like that, wouldn't you? And for goodness' sake put some of the county back where it belongs, the soil erosion's bad enough as it is."

Dill stared at my father's retreating figure.

"He's tryin' to be funny," I said. "He means take a bath. See there, I told you he wouldn't bother you."

Jem was standing in a corner of the room, looking like the traitor he was. "Dill, I had to tell him," he said. "You

143

can't run three hundred miles off without your mother knowin'.'"

We left him without a word.

Dill ate, and ate, and ate. He hadn't eaten since last night. He used all his money for a ticket, boarded the train as he had done many times, coolly chatted with the conductor, to whom Dill was a familiar sight, but he had not the nerve to invoke the rule on small children traveling a distance alone: if you've lost your money the conductor will lend you enough for dinner and your father will pay him back at the end of the line.

Dill made his way through the leftovers and was reaching for a can of pork and beans in the pantry when Miss Rachel's Do-oo Je-sus went off in the hall. He shivered like a rabbit.

He bore with fortitude her Wait Till I Get You Home, Your Folks Are Out of Their Minds Worryin', was quite calm during That's All the Harris in You Coming Out, smiled at her Reckon You Can Stay One Night, and returned the hug at long last bestowed upon him.

Atticus pushed up his glasses and rubbed his face.

"Your father's tired," said Aunt Alexandra, her first words in hours, it seemed. She had been there, but I suppose struck dumb most of the time. "You children get to bed now."

We left them in the diningroom, Atticus still mopping his face. "From rape to riot to runaways," we heard him chuckle. "I wonder what the next two hours will bring."

Since things appeared to have worked out pretty well, Dill and I decided to be civil to Jem. Besides, Dill had to sleep with him so we might as well speak to him.

I put on my pajamas, read for a while and found myself suddenly unable to keep my eyes open. Dill and Jem were quiet; when I turned off my reading lamp there was no strip of light under the door to Jem's room.

I must have slept a long time, for when I was punched awake the room was dim with the light of the setting moon.

"Move over, Scout."

"He thought he had to," I mumbled. "Don't stay mad with him."

Dill got in bed beside me. "I ain't," he said. "I just wanted to sleep with you. Are you waked up?"

144

By this time I was, but lazily so. "Why'd you do it?"

No answer. "I said why'd you run off? Was he really hateful like you said?"

"Naw . . ."

"Didn't you all build that boat like you wrote you were gonna?"

"He just said we would. We never did."

I raised up on my elbow, facing Dill's outline. "It's no reason to run off. They don't get around to doin' what they say they're gonna do half the time. . . ."

"That wasn't it, he—they just wasn't interested in me."

This was the weirdest reason for flight I had ever heard. "How come?"

"Well, they stayed gone all the time, and when they were home, even, they'd get off in a room by themselves."

"What'd they do in there?"

"Nothin', just sittin' and readin'—but they didn't want me with 'em."

I pushed the pillow to the headboard and sat up. "You know something? I was fixin' to run off tonight because there they all were. You don't want 'em around you all the time, Dill—"

Dill breathed his patient breath, a half-sigh.

"—good night, Atticus's gone all day and sometimes half the night and off in the legislature and I don't know what—you don't want 'em around all the time, Dill, you couldn't do anything if they were."

"That's not it."

As Dill explained, I found myself wondering what life would be if Jem were different, even from what he was now; what I would do if Atticus did not feel the necessity of my presence, help and advice. Why, he couldn't get along a day without me. Even Calpurnia couldn't get along unless I was there. They needed me.

"Dill, you ain't telling me right—your folks couldn't do without you. They must be just mean to you. Tell you what to do about that—"

Dill's voice went on steadily in the darkness: "The thing is, what I'm tryin' to say is—they *do* get on a lot better without me, I can't help them any. They ain't mean. They buy me everything I want, but it's now-you've-got-it-go-play-with-it. You've got a roomful of things. I-got-you-that-book-so-go-read-it." Dill tried to deepen his voice. "You're not a boy. Boys get out and play baseball with other boys, they don't hang around the house worryin' their folks."

Dill's voice was his own again: "Oh, they ain't mean. They kiss you and hug you good night and good mornin' and good-bye and tell you they love you— Scout, let's get us a baby."

"Where?"

There was a man Dill had heard of who had a boat that he rowed across to a foggy island where all these babies were; you could order one—

"That's a lie. Aunty said God drops 'em down the chimney. At least that's what I think she said." For once, Aunty's diction had not been too clear.

"Well that ain't so. You get babies from each other. But there's this man, too—he has all these babies just waitin' to wake up, he breathes life into 'em. . . ."

Dill was off again. Beautiful things floated around in his dreamy head. He could read two books to my one, but he preferred the magic of his own inventions. He could add and subtract faster than lightning, but he preferred his own twilight world, a world where babies slept, waiting to be gathered like morning lilies. He was slowly talking himself to sleep and taking me with him, but in the quietness of his foggy island there rose the faded image of a gray house with sad brown doors.

"Dill?"

"Mm?"

"Why do you reckon Boo Radley's never run off?"

Dill sighed a long sigh and turned away from me.

"Maybe he doesn't have anywhere to run off to. . . ."

15.

After many telephone calls, much pleading on behalf of the defendant, and a long forgiving letter from his mother, it was decided that Dill could stay. We had a week of peace together. After that, little, it seemed. A nightmare was upon us.

It began one evening after supper. Dill was over; Aunt Alexandra was in her chair in the corner, Atticus was in his; Jem and I were on the floor reading. It had been a placid week: I had minded Aunty; Jem had outgrown the treehouse, but helped Dill and me construct a new rope ladder for it; Dill had hit upon a foolproof plan to make Boo Radley come out at no cost to ourselves (place a trail of lemon drops from the back door to the front yard and he'd follow it, like an ant). There was a knock on the front door, Jem answered it and said it was Mr. Heck Tate.

"Well, ask him to come in," said Atticus.

"I already did. There's some men outside in the yard, they want you to come out."

In Maycomb, grown men stood outside in the front yard for only two reasons: death and politics. I wondered who had died. Jem and I went to the front door, but Atticus called, "Go back in the house."

Jem turned out the livingroom lights and pressed his nose to a window screen. Aunt Alexandra protested. "Just for a second, Aunty, let's see who it is," he said.

Dill and I took another window. A crowd of men was standing around Atticus. They all seemed to be talking at once.

". . . movin' him to the county jail tomorrow," Mr. Tate was saying, "I don't look for any trouble, but I can't guarantee there won't be any. . . ."

"Don't be foolish, Heck," Atticus said. "This is Maycomb."

". . . said I was just uneasy."

"Heck, we've gotten one postponement of this case just to make sure there's nothing to be uneasy about. This is Saturday," Atticus said. "Trial'll probably be Monday. You can keep him one night, can't you? I don't think anybody in Maycomb'll begrudge me a client, with times this hard."

There was a murmur of glee that died suddenly when Mr. Link Deas said, "Nobody around here's up to anything, it's that Old Sarum bunch I'm worried about . . . can't you get a—what is it, Heck?"

"Change of venue," said Mr. Tate. "Not much point in that, now is it?"

Atticus said something inaudible. I turned to Jem, who waved me to silence.

"—besides," Atticus was saying, "you're not scared of that crowd, are you?"

". . . know how they do when they get shinnied up."

"They don't usually drink on Sunday, they go to church most of the day . . ." Atticus said.

"This is a special occasion, though. . . ." someone said.

They murmured and buzzed until Aunty said if Jem didn't turn on the livingroom lights he would disgrace the family. Jem didn't hear her.

"—don't see why you touched it in the first place," Mr. Link Deas was saying. "You've got everything to lose from this, Atticus. I mean everything."

"Do you really think so?"

This was Atticus's dangerous question. "Do you really think you want to move there, Scout?" Bam, bam, bam, and the checkerboard was swept clean of my men. "Do you really think that, son? Then read this." Jem would struggle the rest of an evening through the speeches of Henry W. Grady.

"Link, that boy might go to the chair, but he's not going till the truth's told." Atticus's voice was even. "And you know what the truth is."

There was a murmur among the group of men, made more ominous when Atticus moved back to the bottom front step and the men drew nearer to him.

Suddenly Jem screamed, "Atticus, the telephone's ringing!"

The men jumped a little and scattered; they were people we saw every day: merchants, in-town farmers; Dr. Reynolds was there; so was Mr. Avery.

"Well, answer it, son," called Atticus.

Laughter broke them up. When Atticus switched on the overhead light in the livingroom he found Jem at the window, pale except for the vivid mark of the screen on his nose.

"Why on earth are you all sitting in the dark?" he asked.

Jem watched him go to his chair and pick up the evening paper. I sometimes think Atticus subjected every crisis of his life to tranquil evaluation behind *The Mobile*

Register, The Birmingham News and *The Montgomery Advertiser.*

"They were after you, weren't they?" Jem went to him. "They wanted to get you, didn't they?"

Atticus lowered the paper and gazed at Jem. "What have you been reading?" he asked. Then he said gently, "No son, those were our friends."

"It wasn't a—a gang?" Jem was looking from the corners of his eyes.

Atticus tried to stifle a smile but didn't make it. "No, we don't have mobs and that nonsense in Maycomb. I've never heard of a gang in Maycomb."

"Ku Klux got after some Catholics one time."

"Never heard of any Catholics in Maycomb either," said Atticus, "you're confusing that with something else. Way back about nineteen-twenty there was a Klan, but it was a political organization more than anything. Besides, they couldn't find anybody to scare. They paraded by Mr. Sam Levy's house one night, but Sam just stood on his porch and told 'em things had come to a pretty pass, he'd sold 'em the very sheets on their backs. Sam made 'em so ashamed of themselves they went away."

The Levy family met all criteria for being Fine Folks: they did the best they could with the sense they had, and they had been living on the same plot of ground in Maycomb for five generations.

"The Ku Klux's gone," said Atticus. "It'll never come back."

I walked home with Dill and returned in time to overhear Atticus saying to Aunty, ". . . in favor of Southern womanhood as much as anybody, but not for preserving polite fiction at the expense of human life," a pronouncement that made me suspect they had been fussing again.

I sought Jem and found him in his room, on the bed deep in thought. "Have they been at it?" I asked.

"Sort of. She won't let him alone about Tom Robinson. She almost said Atticus was disgracin' the family. Scout . . . I'm scared."

"Scared'a what?"

"Scared about Atticus. Somebody might hurt him." Jem preferred to remain mysterious; all he would say to

149

my questions was go on and leave him alone.

Next day was Sunday. In the interval between Sunday School and Church when the congregation stretched its legs, I saw Atticus standing in the yard with another knot of men. Mr. Heck Tate was present, and I wondered if he had seen the light. He never went to church. Even Mr. Underwood was there. Mr. Underwood had no use for any organization but *The Maycomb Tribune,* of which he was the sole owner, editor, and printer. His days were spent at his linotype, where he refreshed himself occasionally from an ever-present gallon jug of cherry wine. He rarely gathered news; people brought it to him. It was said that he made up every edition of *The Maycomb Tribune* out of his own head and wrote it down on the linotype. This was believable. Something must have been up to haul Mr. Underwood out.

I caught Atticus coming in the door, and he said that they'd moved Tom Robinson to the Maycomb jail. He also said, more to himself than to me, that if they'd kept him there in the first place there wouldn't have been any fuss. I watched him take his seat on the third row from the front, and I heard him rumble, "Nearer my God to thee," some notes behind the rest of us. He never sat with Aunty, Jem and me. He liked to be by himself in church.

The fake peace that prevailed on Sundays was made more irritating by Aunt Alexandra's presence. Atticus would flee to his office directly after dinner, where if we sometimes looked in on him, we would find him sitting back in his swivel chair reading. Aunt Alexandra composed herself for a two-hour nap and dared us to make any noise in the yard, the neighborhood was resting. Jem in his old age had taken to his room with a stack of football magazines. So Dill and I spent our Sundays creeping around in Deer's Pasture.

Shooting on Sundays was prohibited, so Dill and I kicked Jem's football around the pasture for a while, which was no fun. Dill asked if I'd like to have a poke at Boo Radley. I said I didn't think it'd be nice to bother him, and spent the rest of the afternoon filling Dill in on last winter's events. He was considerably impressed.

We parted at suppertime, and after our meal Jem and I were settling down to a routine evening, when Atticus did something that interested us: he came into the livingroom carrying a long electrical extension cord. There was a light bulb on the end.

"I'm going out for a while," he said. "You folks'll be in bed when I come back, so I'll say good night now."

With that, he put his hat on and went out the back door.

"He's takin' the car," said Jem.

Our father had a few peculiarities: one was, he never ate desserts; another was that he liked to walk. As far back as I could remember, there was always a Chevrolet in excellent condition in the carhouse, and Atticus put many miles on it in business trips, but in Maycomb he walked to and from his office four times a day, covering about two miles. He said his only exercise was walking. In Maycomb, if one went for a walk with no definite purpose in mind, it was correct to believe one's mind incapable of definite purpose.

Later on, I bade my aunt and brother good night and was well into a book when I heard Jem rattling around in his room. His go-to-bed noises were so familiar to me that I knocked on his door: "Why ain't you going to bed?"

"I'm goin' downtown for a while." He was changing his pants.

"Why? It's almost ten o'clock, Jem."

He knew it, but he was going anyway.

"Then I'm goin' with you. If you say no you're not, I'm goin' anyway, hear?"

Jem saw that he would have to fight me to keep me home, and I suppose he thought a fight would antagonize Aunty, so he gave in with little grace.

I dressed quickly. We waited until Aunty's light went out, and we walked quietly down the back steps. There was no moon tonight.

"Dill'll wanta come," I whispered.

"So he will," said Jem gloomily.

We leaped over the driveway wall, cut through Miss Rachel's side yard and went to Dill's window. Jem whistled bob-white. Dill's face appeared at the screen, disappeared, and five minutes later he unhooked the screen and crawled out. An old campaigner, he did not speak until we were on the sidewalk. "What's up?"

"Jem's got the look-arounds," an affliction Calpurnia said all boys caught at his age.

"I've just got this feeling," Jem said, "just this feeling."

We went by Mrs. Dubose's house, standing empty and shuttered, her camellias grown up in weeds and johnson grass. There were eight more houses to the post office corner.

The south side of the square was deserted. Giant monkey-puzzle bushes bristled on each corner, and between them an iron hitching rail glistened under the street lights. A light shone in the county toilet, otherwise that side of the courthouse was dark. A larger square of stores surrounded the courthouse square; dim lights burned from deep within them.

Atticus's office was in the courthouse when he began his law practice, but after several years of it he moved to quieter quarters in the Maycomb Bank building. When we rounded the corner of the square, we saw the car parked in front of the bank. "He's in there," said Jem.

But he wasn't. His office was reached by a long hallway. Looking down the hall, we should have seen *Atticus Finch, Attorney-at-Law* in small sober letters against the light from behind his door. It was dark.

Jem peered in the bank door to make sure. He turned the knob. The door was locked. "Let's go up the street. Maybe he's visitin' Mr. Underwood."

Mr. Underwood not only ran *The Maycomb Tribune* office, he lived in it. That is, above it. He covered the courthouse and jailhouse news simply by looking out his upstairs window. The office building was on the northwest corner of the square, and to reach it we had to pass the jail.

The Maycomb jail was the most venerable and hideous of the county's buildings. Atticus said it was like something Cousin Joshua St. Clair might have designed. It was certainly someone's dream. Starkly out of place in a town of square-faced stores and steep-roofed houses, the Maycomb jail was a miniature Gothic joke one cell wide and two cells high, complete with tiny battlements and flying buttresses. Its fantasy was heightened by its red brick façade and the thick steel bars at its ecclesiastical windows. It stood on no lonely hill, but was wedged between Tyndal's Hardware Store and *The Maycomb Tribune* office. The jail was Maycomb's only conversation

152

piece: its detractors said it looked like a Victorian privy; its supporters said it gave the town a good solid respectable look, and no stranger would ever suspect that it was full of niggers.

As we walked up the sidewalk, we saw a solitary light burning in the distance. "That's funny," said Jem, "jail doesn't have an outside light."

"Looks like it's over the door," said Dill.

A long extension cord ran between the bars of a second-floor window and down the side of the building. In the light from its bare bulb, Atticus was sitting propped against the front door. He was sitting in one of his office chairs, and he was reading, oblivious of the nightbugs dancing over his head.

I made to run, but Jem caught me. "Don't go to him," he said, "he might not like it. He's all right, let's go home. I just wanted to see where he was."

We were taking a short cut across the square when four dusty cars came in from the Meridian highway, moving slowly in a line. They went around the square, passed the bank building, and stopped in front of the jail.

Nobody got out. We saw Atticus look up from his newspaper. He closed it, folded it deliberately, dropped it in his lap, and pushed his hat to the back of his head. He seemed to be expecting them.

"Come on," whispered Jem. We streaked across the square, across the street, until we were in the shelter of the Jitney Jungle door. Jem peeked up the sidewalk. "We can get closer," he said. We ran to Tyndal's Hardware door—near enough, at the same time discreet.

In ones and twos, men got out of the cars. Shadows became substance as lights revealed solid shapes moving toward the jail door. Atticus remained where he was. The men hid him from view.

"He in there, Mr. Finch?" a man said.

"He is," we heard Atticus answer, "and he's asleep. Don't wake him up."

In obedience to my father, there followed what I later realized was a sickeningly comic aspect of an unfunny situation: the men talked in near-whispers.

"You know what we want," another man said. "Get aside from the door, Mr. Finch."

"You can turn around and go home again, Walter," At-

153

ticus said pleasantly. "Heck Tate's around somewhere."

"The hell he is," said another man. "Heck's bunch's so deep in the woods they won't get out till mornin'."

"Indeed? Why so?"

"Called 'em off on a snipe hunt," was the succinct answer. "Didn't you think a'that, Mr. Finch?"

"Thought about it, but didn't believe it. Well then," my father's voice was still the same, "that changes things, doesn't it?"

"It do," another deep voice said. Its owner was a shadow.

"Do you really think so?"

This was the second time I heard Atticus ask that question in two days, and it meant somebody's man would get jumped. This was too good to miss. I broke away from Jem and ran as fast as I could to Atticus.

Jem shrieked and tried to catch me, but I had a lead on him and Dill. I pushed my way through dark smelly bodies and burst into the circle of light.

"H-ey, Atticus!"

I thought he would have a fine surprise, but his face killed my joy. A flash of plain fear was going out of his eyes, but returned when Dill and Jem wriggled into the light.

There was a smell of stale whiskey and pigpen about, and when I glanced around I discovered that these men were strangers. They were not the people I saw last night. Hot embarrassment shot through me: I had leaped triumphantly into a ring of people I had never seen before.

Atticus got up from his chair, but he was moving slowly, like an old man. He put the newspaper down very carefully, adjusting its creases with lingering fingers. They were trembling a little.

"Go home, Jem," he said. "Take Scout and Dill home."

We were accustomed to prompt, if not always cheerful acquiescence to Atticus's instructions, but from the way he stood Jem was not thinking of budging.

"Go home, I said."

Jem shook his head. As Atticus's fists went to his hips, so did Jem's, and as they faced each other I could see little resemblance between them: Jem's soft brown hair and eyes, his oval face and snug-fitting ears were our mother's, contrasting oddly with Atticus's graying

154

black hair and square-cut features, but they were some-how alike. Mutual defiance made them alike.

"Son, I said go home."

Jem shook his head.

"I'll send him home," a burly man said, and grabbed Jem roughly by the collar. He yanked Jem nearly off his feet.

"Don't you touch him!" I kicked the man swiftly. Bare-footed, I was surprised to see him fall back in real pain. I intended to kick his shin, but aimed too high.

"That'll do, Scout." Atticus put his hand on my shoulder. "Don't kick folks. No—" he said, as I was pleading justification.

"Ain't nobody gonna do Jem that way," I said.

"All right, Mr. Finch, get 'em outa here," someone growled. "You got fifteen seconds to get 'em outa here."

In the midst of this strange assembly, Atticus stood trying to make Jem mind him. "I ain't going," was his steady answer to Atticus's threats, requests, and finally, "Please Jem, take them home."

I was getting a bit tired of that, but felt Jem had his own reasons for doing as he did, in view of his prospects once Atticus did get him home. I looked around the crowd. It was a summer's night, but the men were dressed, most of them, in overalls and denim shirts buttoned up to the collars. I thought they must be cold-natured, as their sleeves were unrolled and buttoned at the cuffs. Some wore hats pulled firmly down over their ears. They were sullen-looking, sleepy-eyed men who seemed unused to late hours. I sought once more for a familiar face, and at the center of the semi-circle I found one.

"Hey, Mr. Cunningham."

The man did not hear me, it seemed.

"Hey, Mr. Cunningham. How's your entailment get-tin' along?"

Mr. Walter Cunningham's legal affairs were well known to me; Atticus had once described them at length. The big man blinked and hooked his thumbs in his overall straps. He seemed uncomfortable; he cleared his throat and looked away. My friendly overture had fallen flat.

Mr. Cunningham wore no hat, and the top half of his forehead was white in contrast to his sunscorched face, which led me to believe that he wore one most days. He shifted his feet, clad in heavy work shoes.

"Don't you remember me, Mr. Cunningham? I'm Jean Louise Finch. You brought us some hickory nuts one time, remember?" I began to sense the futility one feels when unacknowledged by a chance acquaintance.

"I go to school with Walter," I began again. "He's your boy, ain't he? Ain't he, sir?"

Mr. Cunningham was moved to a faint nod. He did know me, after all.

"He's in my grade," I said, "and he does right well. He's a good boy," I added, "a real nice boy. We brought him home for dinner one time. Maybe he told you about me, I beat him up one time but he was real nice about it. Tell him hey for me, won't you?"

Atticus had said it was the polite thing to talk to people about what they were interested in, not about what you were interested in. Mr. Cunningham displayed no interest in his son, so I tackled his entailment once more in a last-ditch effort to make him feel at home.

"Entailments are bad," I was advising him, when I slowly awoke to the fact that I was addressing the entire aggregation. The men were all looking at me, some had their mouths half-open. Atticus had stopped poking at Jem: they were standing together beside Dill. Their attention amounted to fascination. Atticus's mouth, even, was half-open, an attitude he had once described as uncouth. Our eyes met and he shut it.

"Well, Atticus, I was just sayin' to Mr. Cunningham that entailments are bad an' all that, but you said not to worry, it takes a long time sometimes . . . that you all'd ride it out together . . ." I was slowly drying up, wondering what idiocy I had committed. Entailments seemed all right enough for livingroom talk.

I began to feel sweat gathering at the edges of my hair; I could stand anything but a bunch of people looking at me. They were quite still.

"What's the matter?" I asked.

Atticus said nothing. I looked around and up at Mr. Cunningham, whose face was equally impassive. Then he did a peculiar thing. He squatted down and took me by both shoulders.

"I'll tell him you said hey, little lady," he said.

Then he straightened up and waved a big paw. "Let's

clear out," he called. "Let's get going, boys."

As they had come, in ones and twos the men shuffled back to their ramshackle cars. Doors slammed, engines coughed, and they were gone.

I turned to Atticus, but Atticus had gone to the jail and was leaning against it with his face to the wall. I went to him and pulled his sleeve. "Can we go home now?" He nodded, produced his handkerchief, gave his face a going-over and blew his nose violently.

"Mr. Finch?"

A soft husky voice came from the darkness above: "They gone?"

Atticus stepped back and looked up. "They've gone," he said. "Get some sleep, Tom. They won't bother you any more."

From a different direction, another voice cut crisply through the night: "You're damn tootin' they won't. Had you covered all the time, Atticus."

Mr. Underwood and a double-barreled shotgun were leaning out his window above *The Maycomb Tribune* office.

It was long past my bedtime and I was growing quite tired; it seemed that Atticus and Mr. Underwood would talk for the rest of the night, Mr. Underwood out the window and Atticus up at him. Finally Atticus returned, switched off the light above the jail door, and picked up his chair.

"Can I carry it for you, Mr. Finch?" asked Dill. He had not said a word the whole time.

"Why, thank you, son."

Walking toward the office, Dill and I fell into step behind Atticus and Jem. Dill was encumbered by the chair, and his pace was slower. Atticus and Jem were well ahead of us, and I assumed that Atticus was giving him hell for not going home, but I was wrong. As they passed under a streetlight, Atticus reached out and massaged Jem's hair, his one gesture of affection.

16.

Jem heard me. He thrust his head around the connecting door. As he came to my bed Atticus's light flashed on. We stayed where we were until it went off; we heard him turn over, and we waited until he was still again.

Jem took me to his room and put me in bed beside him. "Try to go to sleep," he said. "It'll be all over after tomorrow, maybe."

We had come in quietly, so as not to wake Aunty. Atticus killed the engine in the driveway and coasted to the carhouse; we went in the back door and to our rooms without a word. I was very tired, and was drifting into sleep when the memory of Atticus calmly folding his newspaper and pushing back his hat became Atticus standing in the middle of an empty waiting street, pushing up his glasses. The full meaning of the night's events hit me and I began crying. Jem was awfully nice about it: for once he didn't remind me that people nearly nine years old didn't do things like that.

Everybody's appetite was delicate this morning, except Jem's: he ate his way through three eggs. Atticus watched in frank admiration; Aunt Alexandra sipped coffee and radiated waves of disapproval. Children who slipped out at night were a disgrace to the family. Atticus said he was right glad his disgraces had come along, but Aunty said, "Nonsense, Mr. Underwood was there all the time."

"You know, it's a funny thing about Braxton," said Atticus. "He despises Negroes, won't have one near him."

Local opinion held Mr. Underwood to be an intense, profane little man, whose father in a fey fit of humor christened Braxton Bragg, a name Mr. Underwood had done his best to live down. Atticus said naming people after Confederate generals made slow steady drinkers.

158

Calpurnia was serving Aunt Alexandra more coffee, and she shook her head at what I thought was a pleading winning look. "You're still too little," she said. "I'll tell you when you ain't." I said it might help my stomach. "All right," she said, and got a cup from the sideboard. She poured one tablespoonful of coffee into it and filled the cup to the brim with milk. I thanked her by sticking out my tongue at it, and looked up to catch Aunty's warning frown. But she was frowning at Atticus.

She waited until Calpurnia was in the kitchen, then she said, "Don't talk like that in front of them."

"Talk like what in front of whom?" he asked.

"Like that in front of Calpurnia. You said Braxton Underwood despises Negroes right in front of her."

"Well, I'm sure Cal knows it. Everybody in Maycomb knows it."

I was beginning to notice a subtle change in my father these days, that came out when he talked with Aunt Alexandra. It was a quiet digging in, never outright irritation. There was a faint starchiness in his voice when he said, "Anything fit to say at the table's fit to say in front of Calpurnia. She knows what she means to this family."

"I don't think it's a good habit, Atticus. It encourages them. You know how they talk among themselves. Everything that happens in this town's out to the Quarters before sundown."

My father put down his knife. "I don't know of any law that says they can't talk. Maybe if we didn't give them so much to talk about they'd be quiet. Why don't you drink your coffee, Scout?"

I was playing in it with the spoon. "I thought Mr. Cunningham was a friend of ours. You told me a long time ago he was."

"He still is."

"But last night he wanted to hurt you."

Atticus placed his fork beside his knife and pushed his plate aside. "Mr. Cunningham's basically a good man," he said, "he just has his blind spots along with the rest of us."

Jem spoke. "Don't call that a blind spot. He'da killed you last night when he first went there."

"He might have hurt me a little," Atticus conceded, "but son, you'll understand folks a little better when

159

you're older. A mob's always made up of people, no matter what. Mr. Cunningham was part of a mob last night, but he was still a man. Every mob in every little Southern town is always made up of people you know—doesn't say much for them, does it?"

"I'll say not," said Jem.

"So it took an eight-year-old child to bring 'em to their senses, didn't it?" said Atticus. "That proves something —that a gang of wild animals *can* be stopped, simply because they're still human. Hmp, maybe we need a police force of children . . . you children last night made Walter Cunningham stand in my shoes for a minute. That was enough."

Well, I hoped Jem would understand folks a little better when he was older; I wouldn't. "First day Walter comes back to school'll be his last," I affirmed.

"You will not touch him," Atticus said flatly. "I don't want either of you bearing a grudge about this thing, no matter what happens."

"You see, don't you," said Aunt Alexandra, "what comes of things like this. Don't say I haven't told you."

Atticus said he'd never say that, pushed out his chair and got up. "There's a day ahead, so excuse me. Jem, I don't want you and Scout downtown today, please."

As Atticus departed, Dill came bounding down the hall into the diningroom. "It's all over town this morning," he announced, "all about how we held off a hundred folks with our bare hands. . . ."

Aunt Alexandra stared him to silence. "It was not a hundred folks," she said, "and nobody held anybody off. It was just a nest of those Cunninghams, drunk and disorderly."

"Aw, Aunty, that's just Dill's way," said Jem. He signaled us to follow him.

"You all stay in the yard today," she said, as we made our way to the front porch.

It was like Saturday. People from the south end of the county passed our house in a leisurely but steady stream.

Mr. Dolphus Raymond lurched by on his thoroughbred. "Don't see how he stays in the saddle," murmured Jem. "How c'n you stand to get drunk 'fore eight in the morning?"

A wagonload of ladies rattled past us. They wore cotton sunbonnets and dresses with long sleeves. A bearded man in a wool hat drove them. "Yonder's some Mennonites," Jem said to Dill. "They don't have buttons." They lived deep in the woods, did most of their trading across the river, and rarely came to Maycomb. Dill was interested. "They've all got blue eyes," Jem explained, "and the men can't shave after they marry. Their wives like for 'em to tickle 'em with their beards."

Mr. X Billups rode by on a mule and waved to us. "He's a funny man," said Jem. "X's his name, not his initial. He was in court one time and they asked him his name. He said X Billups. Clerk asked him to spell it and he said X. Asked him again and he said X. They kept at it till he wrote X on a sheet of paper and held it up for everybody to see. They asked him where he got his name and he said that's the way his folks signed him up when he was born."

As the county went by us, Jem gave Dill the histories and general attitudes of the more prominent figures: Mr. Tensaw Jones voted the straight Prohibition ticket; Miss Emily Davis dipped snuff in private; Mr. Byron Waller could play the violin; Mr. Jake Slade was cutting his third set of teeth.

A wagonload of unusually stern-faced citizens appeared. When they pointed to Miss Maudie Atkinson's yard, ablaze with summer flowers, Miss Maudie herself came out on the porch. There was an odd thing about Miss Maudie—on her porch she was too far away for us to see her features clearly, but we could always catch her mood by the way she stood. She was now standing arms akimbo, her shoulders drooping a little, her head cocked to one side, her glasses winking in the sunlight. We knew she wore a grin of the uttermost wickedness.

The driver of the wagon slowed down his mules, and a shrill-voiced woman called out: "He that cometh in vanity departeth in darkness!"

Miss Maudie answered: "A merry heart maketh a cheerful countenance!"

I guess that the foot-washers thought that the Devil was quoting Scripture for his own purposes, as the driver speeded his mules. Why they objected to Miss Maudie's yard was a mystery, heightened in my mind because for someone who spent all the daylight hours outdoors, Miss Maudie's command of Scripture was formidable.

"You goin' to court this morning?" asked Jem. We had strolled over.

"I am not," she said. "I have no business with the court this morning."

"Aren't you goin' down to watch?" asked Dill.

"I am not. 't's morbid, watching a poor devil on trial for his life. Look at all those folks, it's like a Roman carnival."

"They hafta try him in public, Miss Maudie," I said. "Wouldn't be right if they didn't."

"I'm quite aware of that," she said. "Just because it's public, I don't have to go, do I?"

Miss Stephanie Crawford came by. She wore a hat and gloves. "Um, um, um," she said. "Look at all those folks— you'd think William Jennings Bryan was speakin'."

"And where are you going, Stephanie?" inquired Miss Maudie.

"To the Jitney Jungle."

Miss Maudie said she'd never seen Miss Stephanie go to the Jitney Jungle in a hat in her life.

"Well," said Miss Stephanie, "I thought I might just look in at the courthouse, to see what Atticus's up to."

"Better be careful he doesn't hand you a subpoena."

We asked Miss Maudie to elucidate: she said Miss Stephanie seemed to know so much about the case she might as well be called on to testify.

We held off until noon, when Atticus came home to dinner and said they'd spent the morning picking the jury. After dinner, we stopped by for Dill and went to town.

It was a gala occasion. There was no room at the public hitching rail for another animal, mules and wagons were parked under every available tree. The courthouse square was covered with picnic parties sitting on newspapers, washing down biscuit and syrup with warm milk from fruit jars. Some people were gnawing on cold chicken and cold fried pork chops. The more affluent chased their food with drugstore Coca-Cola in bulb-shaped soda glasses. Greasy-faced children popped-the-whip through the crowd, and babies lunched at their mothers' breasts.

In a far corner of the square, the Negroes sat quietly in the sun, dining on sardines, crackers, and the more vivid flavors of Nehi Cola. Mr. Dolphus Raymond sat with them.

"Jem," said Dill, "he's drinkin' out of a sack."

Mr. Dolphus Raymond seemed to be so doing: two yellow drugstore straws ran from his mouth to the depths of a brown paper bag.

"Ain't ever seen anybody do that," murmured Dill. "How does he keep what's in it in it?"

Jem giggled. "He's got a Co-Cola bottle full of whiskey in there. That's so's not to upset the ladies. You'll see him sip it all afternoon, he'll step out for a while and fill it back up."

"Why's he sittin' with the colored folks?"

"Always does. He likes 'em better'n he likes us, I reckon. Lives by himself way down near the county line. He's got a colored woman and all sorts of mixed chillun. Show you some of 'em if we see 'em."

"He doesn't look like trash," said Dill.

"He's not, he owns all one side of the riverbank down there, and he's from a real old family to boot."

"Then why does he do like that?"

"That's just his way," said Jem. "They say he never got over his weddin'. He was supposed to marry one of the—the Spender ladies, I think. They were gonna have a huge weddin', but they didn't—after the rehearsal the bride went upstairs and blew her head off. Shotgun. She pulled the trigger with her toes."

"Did they ever know why?"

"No," said Jem, "nobody ever knew quite why but Mr. Dolphus. They said it was because she found out about his colored woman, he reckoned he could keep her and get married too. He's been sorta drunk ever since. You know, though, he's real good to those chillun—"

"Jem," I asked, "what's a mixed child?"

"Half white, half colored. You've seen 'em, Scout. You know that red-kinky-headed one that delivers for the drugstore. He's half white. They're real sad."

"Sad, how come?"

"They don't belong anywhere. Colored folks won't have 'em because they're half white; white folks won't have 'em 'cause they're colored, so they're just in-betweens, don't belong anywhere. But Mr. Dolphus, now, they say he's shipped two of his up north. They don't mind 'em up

163

north. Yonder's one of 'em."

A small boy clutching a Negro woman's hand walked toward us. He looked all Negro to me: he was rich chocolate with flaring nostrils and beautiful teeth. Sometimes he would skip happily, and the Negro woman tugged his hand to make him stop.

Jem waited until they passed us. "That's one of the little ones," he said.

"How can you tell?" asked Dill. "He looked black to me."

"You can't sometimes, not unless you know who they are. But he's half Raymond, all right."

"But how can you *tell*?" I asked.

"I told you, Scout, you just hafta know who they are."

"Well how do you know we ain't Negroes?"

"Uncle Jack Finch says we really don't know. He says as far as he can trace back the Finches we ain't, but for all he knows we mighta come straight out of Ethiopia durin' the Old Testament."

"Well if we came out durin' the Old Testament it's too long ago to matter."

"That's what I thought," said Jem, "but around here once you have a drop of Negro blood, that makes you all black. Hey, look—"

Some invisible signal had made the lunchers on the square rise and scatter bits of newspaper, cellophane, and wrapping paper. Children came to mothers, babies were cradled on hips as men in sweat-stained hats collected their families and herded them through the courthouse doors. In the far corner of the square the Negroes and Mr. Dolphus Raymond stood up and dusted their breeches. There were few women and children among them, which seemed to dispel the holiday mood. They waited patiently at the doors behind the white families.

"Let's go in," said Dill.

"Naw, we better wait till they get in, Atticus might not like it if he sees us," said Jem.

The Maycomb County courthouse was faintly reminiscent of Arlington in one respect: the concrete pillars supporting its south roof were too heavy for their light burden. The pillars were all that remained standing when the original courthouse burned in 1856. Another courthouse was built around them. It is better to say, built in spite of them. But for the south porch, the Maycomb County courthouse was early Victorian, presenting an unoffensive vista when seen from the north. From the other side, however, Greek revival columns clashed with a big nineteenth-century clock tower housing a rusty unreliable instrument, a view indicating a people determined to preserve every physical scrap of the past.

To reach the courtroom, on the second floor, one passed sundry sunless county cubbyholes: the tax assessor, the tax collector, the county clerk, the county solicitor, the circuit clerk, the judge of probate lived in cool dim hutches that smelled of decaying record books mingled with old damp cement and stale urine. It was necessary to turn on the lights in the daytime; there was always a film of dust on the rough floorboards. The inhabitants of these offices were creatures of their environment: little gray-faced men, they seemed untouched by wind or sun.

We knew there was a crowd, but we had not bargained for the multitudes in the first-floor hallway. I got separated from Jem and Dill, but made my way toward the wall by the stairwell, knowing Jem would come for me eventually. I found myself in the middle of the Idlers' Club and made myself as unobtrusive as possible. This was a group of white-shirted, khaki-trousered, suspendered old men who had spent their lives doing nothing and passed their twilight days doing same on pine benches under the live oaks on the square. Attentive critics of courthouse business, Atticus said they knew as much law as the Chief Justice, from long years of observation. Normally, they were the court's only spectators, and today they seemed resentful of the interruption of their comfortable routine. When they spoke, their voices sounded casually important. The conversation was about my father.

". . . thinks he knows what he's doing," one said.

"Oh-h now, I wouldn't say that," said another. "Atticus Finch's a deep reader, a mighty deep reader."

"He reads all right, that's all he does." The club snickered.

"Lemme tell you somethin' now, Billy," a third said, "you know the court appointed him to defend this nigger."

"Yeah, but Atticus aims to defend him. That's what I

don't like about it."

This was news, news that put a different light on things: Atticus had to, whether he wanted to or not. I thought it odd that he hadn't said anything to us about it—we could have used it many times in defending him and ourselves. He had to, that's why he was doing it, equaled fewer fights and less fussing. But did that explain the town's attitude? The court appointed Atticus to defend him. Atticus aimed to defend him. That's what they didn't like about it. It was confusing.

The Negroes, having waited for the white people to go upstairs, began to come in. "Whoa now, just a minute," said a club member, holding up his walking stick. "Just don't start up them there stairs yet awhile."

The club began its stiff-jointed climb and ran into Dill and Jem on their way down looking for me. They squeezed past and Jem called, "Scout, come on, there ain't a seat left. We'll hafta stand up."

"Looka there, now," he said irritably, as the black people surged upstairs. The old men ahead of them would take most of the standing room. We were out of luck and it was my fault, Jem informed me. We stood miserably by the wall.

"Can't you all get in?"

Reverend Sykes was looking down at us, black hat in hand.

"Hey, Reverend," said Jem. "Naw, Scout here messed us up."

"Well, let's see what we can do."

Reverend Sykes edged his way upstairs. In a few moments he was back. "There's not a seat downstairs. Do you all reckon it'll be all right if you all came to the balcony with me?"

"Gosh yes," said Jem. Happily, we sped ahead of Reverend Sykes to the courtroom floor. There, we went up a covered staircase and waited at the door. Reverend Sykes came puffing behind us, and steered us gently through the black people in the balcony. Four Negroes rose and gave us their front-row seats.

The Colored balcony ran along three walls of the courtroom like a second-story veranda, and from it we could see everything.

The jury sat to the left, under long windows. Sunburned, lanky, they seemed to be all farmers, but this was natural: townfolk rarely sat on juries, they were either struck or excused. One or two of the jury looked vaguely like dressed-up Cunninghams. At this stage they sat straight and alert.

The circuit solicitor and another man, Atticus and Tom Robinson sat at tables with their backs to us. There was a brown book and some yellow tablets on the solicitor's table; Atticus's was bare.

Just inside the railing that divided the spectators from the court, the witnesses sat on cowhide-bottomed chairs. Their backs were to us.

Judge Taylor was on the bench, looking like a sleepy old shark, his pilot fish writing rapidly below in front of him. Judge Taylor looked like most judges I had ever seen: amiable, white-haired, slightly ruddy-faced, he was a man who ran his court with an alarming informality— he sometimes propped his feet up, he often cleaned his fingernails with his pocket knife. In long equity hearings, especially after dinner, he gave the impression of dozing, an impression dispelled forever when a lawyer once deliberately pushed a pile of books to the floor in a desperate effort to wake him up. Without opening his eyes, Judge Taylor murmured, "Mr. Whitley, do that again and it'll cost you one hundred dollars."

He was a man learned in the law, and although he seemed to take his job casually, in reality he kept a firm grip on any proceedings that came before him. Only once was Judge Taylor ever seen at a dead standstill in open court, and the Cunninghams stopped him. Old Sarum, their stamping grounds, was populated by two families separate and apart in the beginning, but unfortunately bearing the same name. The Cunninghams married the Coninghams until the spelling of the names was academic —academic until a Cunningham disputed a Coningham over land titles and took to the law. During a controversy of this character, Jeems Cunningham testified that his mother spelled it Cunningham on deeds and things, but she was really a Coningham, she was an uncertain speller, a seldom reader, and was given to looking far away sometimes when she sat on the front gallery in the evening. After nine hours of listening to the eccentricities of Old Sarum's inhabitants, Judge Taylor threw the case out

167

of court. When asked upon what grounds, Judge Taylor said, "Champertous connivance," and declared he hoped to God the litigants were satisfied by each having had their public say. They were. That was all they had wanted in the first place.

Judge Taylor had one interesting habit. He permitted smoking in his courtroom but did not himself indulge: sometimes, if one was lucky, one had the privilege of watching him put a long dry cigar into his mouth and munch it slowly up. Bit by bit the dead cigar would disappear, to reappear some hours later as a flat slick mess, its essence extracted and mingling with Judge Taylor's digestive juices. I once asked Atticus how Mrs. Taylor stood to kiss him, but Atticus said they didn't kiss much.

The witness stand was to the right of Judge Taylor, and when we got to our seats Mr. Heck Tate was already on it.

17.

Jem," I said, "are those the Ewells sittin' down yonder?"

"Hush," said Jem, "Mr. Heck Tate's testifyin'."

Mr. Tate had dressed for the occasion. He wore an ordinary business suit, which made him look somehow like every other man: gone were his high boots, lumber jacket, and bullet-studded belt. From that moment he ceased to terrify me. He was sitting forward in the witness chair, his hands clasped between his knees, listening attentively to the circuit solicitor.

The solicitor, a Mr. Gilmer, was not well known to us. He was from Abbottsville; we saw him only when court convened, and that rarely, for court was of no special interest to Jem and me. A balding, smooth-faced man, he could have been anywhere between forty and sixty. Although his back was to us, we knew he had a slight cast in one of his eyes which he used to his advantage: he seemed to be looking at a person when he was actually doing nothing of the kind, thus he was hell on juries and witnesses. The jury, thinking themselves under close scrutiny, paid attention; so did the witnesses, thinking likewise.

". . . in your own words, Mr. Tate," Mr. Gilmer was saying.

"Well," said Mr. Tate, touching his glasses and speaking to his knees, "I was called—"

"Could you say it to the jury, Mr. Tate? Thank you. Who called you?"

Mr. Tate said, "I was fetched by Bob—by Mr. Bob Ewell yonder, one night—"

"What night, sir?"

Mr. Tate said, "It was the night of November twenty-first. I was just leaving my office to go home when B— Mr. Ewell came in, very excited he was, and said get out to his house quick, some nigger'd raped his girl."

"Did you go?"

"Certainly. Got in the car and went out as fast as I could."

"And what did you find?"

"Found her lying on the floor in the middle of the front room, one on the right as you go in. She was pretty well beat up, but I heaved her to her feet and she washed her face in a bucket in the corner and said she was all right. I asked her who hurt her and she said it was Tom Robinson—"

Judge Taylor, who had been concentrating on his fingernails, looked up as if he were expecting an objection, but Atticus was quiet.

"—asked her if he beat her like that, she said yes he had. Asked her if he took advantage of her and she said yes he did. So I went down to Robinson's house and brought him back. She identified him as the one, so I took him in. That's all there was to it."

"Thank you," said Mr. Gilmer.

Judge Taylor said, "Any questions, Atticus?"

"Yes," said my father. He was sitting behind his table; his chair was skewed to one side, his legs were crossed and one arm was resting on the back of his chair.

"Did you call a doctor, Sheriff? Did anybody call a doctor?" asked Atticus.

"No sir," said Mr. Tate.

"Didn't call a doctor?"

"No sir," repeated Mr. Tate.

"Why not?" There was an edge to Atticus's voice.

"Well I can tell you why I didn't. It wasn't necessary, Mr. Finch. She was mighty banged up. Something sho' happened, it was obvious."

"But you didn't call a doctor? While you were there did anyone send for one, fetch one, carry her to one?"

"No sir—"

Judge Taylor broke in. "He's answered the question three times, Atticus. He didn't call a doctor."

Atticus said, "I just wanted to make sure, Judge," and the judge smiled.

Jem's hand, which was resting on the balcony rail, tightened around it. He drew in his breath suddenly. Glancing below, I saw no corresponding reaction, and wondered if Jem was trying to be dramatic. Dill was watching peacefully, and so was Reverend Sykes beside him. "What is it?" I whispered, and got a terse, "Sh-h!"

"Sheriff," Atticus was saying, "you say she was mighty banged up. In what way?"

"Well—"

"Just describe her injuries, Heck."

"Well, she was beaten around the head. There was already bruises comin' on her arms, and it happened about thirty minutes before—"

"How do you know?"

Mr. Tate grinned. "Sorry, that's what they said. Anyway, she was pretty bruised up when I got there, and she had a black eye comin'."

"Which eye?"

Mr. Tate blinked and ran his hands through his hair. "Let's see," he said softly, then he looked at Atticus as if he considered the question childish. "Can't you remember?" Atticus asked.

Mr. Tate pointed to an invisible person five inches in front of him and said, "Her left."

"Wait a minute, Sheriff," said Atticus. "Was it her left facing you or her left looking the same way you were?"

Mr. Tate said, "Oh yes, that'd make it her right. It was her right eye, Mr. Finch. I remember now, she was bunged up on that side of her face. . . ."

Mr. Tate blinked again, as if something had suddenly

170

been made plain to him. Then he turned his head and looked around at Tom Robinson. As if by instinct, Tom Robinson raised his head.

Something had been made plain to Atticus also, and it brought him to his feet. "Sheriff, please repeat what you said."

"It was her right eye, I said."

"No . . ." Atticus walked to the court reporter's desk and bent down to the furiously scribbling hand. It stopped, flipped back the shorthand pad, and the court reporter said, " 'Mr. Finch. I remember now she was bunged up on that side of the face.' "

Atticus looked up at Mr. Tate. "Which side again, Heck?"

"The right side, Mr. Finch, but she had more bruises—you wanta hear about 'em?"

Atticus seemed to be bordering on another question, but he thought better of it and said, "Yes, what were her other injuries?" As Mr. Tate answered, Atticus turned and looked at Tom Robinson as if to say this was something they hadn't bargained for.

". . . her arms were bruised, and she showed me her neck. There were definite finger marks on her gullet—"

"All around her throat? At the back of her neck?"

"I'd say they were all around, Mr. Finch."

"You would?"

"Yes sir, she had a small throat, anybody could'a reached around it with—"

"Just answer the question yes or no, please, Sheriff," said Atticus dryly, and Mr. Tate fell silent.

Atticus sat down and nodded to the circuit solicitor, who shook his head at the judge, who nodded to Mr. Tate, who rose stiffly and stepped down from the witness stand.

Below us, heads turned, feet scraped the floor, babies were shifted to shoulders, and a few children scampered out of the courtroom. The Negroes behind us whispered softly among themselves; Dill was asking Reverend Sykes what it was all about, but Reverend Sykes said he didn't know. So far, things were utterly dull: nobody had thundered, there were no arguments between opposing counsel, there was no drama; a grave disappointment to all present, it seemed. Atticus was proceeding amiably, as if he were involved in a title dispute. With his infinite capac-

171

ity for calming turbulent seas, he could make a rape case as dry as a sermon. Gone was the terror in my mind of stale whiskey and barnyard smells, of sleepy-eyed sullen men, of a husky voice calling in the night, "Mr. Finch? They gone?" Our nightmare had gone with daylight, everything would come out all right.

All the spectators were as relaxed as Judge Taylor, except Jem. His mouth was twisted into a purposeful half-grin, and his eyes happy about, and he said something about corroborating evidence, which made me sure he was showing off.

". . . Robert E. Lee Ewell!"

In answer to the clerk's booming voice, a little bantam cock of a man rose and strutted to the stand, the back of his neck reddening at the sound of his name. When he turned around to take the oath, we saw that his face was as red as his neck. We also saw no resemblance to his namesake. A shock of wispy new-washed hair stood up from his forehead; his nose was thin, pointed, and shiny; he had no chin to speak of—it seemed to be part of his crepey neck.

"—so help me God," he crowed.

Every town the size of Maycomb had families like the Ewells. No economic fluctuations changed their status—people like the Ewells lived as guests of the county in prosperity as well as in the depths of a depression. No truant officers could keep their numerous offspring in school; no public health officer could free them from congenital defects, various worms, and the diseases indigenous to filthy surroundings.

Maycomb's Ewells lived behind the town garbage dump in what was once a Negro cabin. The cabin's plank walls were supplemented with sheets of corrugated iron, its roof shingled with tin cans hammered flat, so only its general shape suggested its original design: square, with four tiny rooms opening onto a shotgun hall, the cabin rested uneasily upon four irregular lumps of limestone. Its windows were merely open spaces in the walls, which in the summertime were covered with greasy strips of cheesecloth to keep out the varmints that feasted on Maycomb's refuse.

The varmints had a lean time of it, for the Ewells gave the dump a thorough gleaning every day, and the fruits of their industry (those that were not eaten) made the plot of ground around the cabin look like the playhouse of an insane child: what passed for a fence was bits of tree-limbs, broomsticks and tool shafts, all tipped with rusty hammer-heads, snaggle-toothed rake heads, shovels, axes and grubbing hoes, held on with pieces of barbed wire. Enclosed by this barricade was a dirty yard containing the remains of a Model-T Ford (on blocks), a discarded dentist's chair, an ancient icebox, plus lesser items: old shoes, worn-out table radios, picture frames, and fruit jars, under which scrawny orange chickens pecked hopefully.

One corner of the yard, though, bewildered Maycomb. Against the fence, in a line, were six chipped-enamel slop jars holding brilliant red geraniums, cared for as tenderly as if they belonged to Miss Maudie Atkinson, had Miss Maudie deigned to permit a geranium on her premises. People said they were Mayella Ewell's.

Nobody was quite sure how many children were on the place. Some people said six, others said nine; there were always several dirty-faced ones at the windows when anyone passed by. Nobody had occasion to pass by except at Christmas, when the churches delivered baskets, and when the mayor of Maycomb asked us to please help the garbage collector by dumping our own trees and trash.

Atticus took us with him last Christmas when he complied with the mayor's request. A dirt road ran from the highway past the dump, down to a small Negro settlement some five hundred yards beyond the Ewells'. It was necessary either to back out to the highway or go the full length of the road and turn around; most people turned around in the Negroes' front yards. In the frosty December dusk, their cabins looked neat and snug with pale blue smoke rising from the chimneys and doorways glowing amber from the fires inside. There were delicious smells about: chicken, bacon frying crisp as the twilight air. Jem and I detected squirrel cooking, but it took an old countryman like Atticus to identify possum and rabbit, aromas that vanished when we rode back past the Ewell residence.

All the little man on the witness stand had that made him any better than his nearest neighbors was, that if

173

scrubbed with lye soap in very hot water, his skin was white.

"Mr. Robert Ewell?" asked Mr. Gilmer.

"That's m'name, cap'n," said the witness.

Mr. Gilmer's back stiffened a little, and I felt sorry for him. Perhaps I'd better explain something now. I've heard that lawyers' children, on seeing their parents in court in the heat of argument, get the wrong idea: they think opposing counsel to be the personal enemies of their parents, they suffer agonies, and are surprised to see them often go out arm-in-arm with their tormenters during the first recess. This was not true of Jem and me. We acquired no traumas from watching our father win or lose. I'm sorry that I can't provide any drama in this respect; if I did, it would not be true. We could tell, however, when debate became more acrimonious than professional, but this was from watching lawyers other than our father. I never heard Atticus raise his voice in my life, except to a deaf witness. Mr. Gilmer was doing his job, as Atticus was doing his. Besides, Mr. Ewell was Mr. Gilmer's witness, and he had no business being rude to him of all people.

"Are you the father of Mayella Ewell?" was the next question.

"Well, if I ain't I can't do nothing about it now, her ma's dead," was the answer.

Judge Taylor stirred. He turned slowly in his swivel chair and looked benignly at the witness. "Are you the father of Mayella Ewell?" he asked, in a way that made the laughter below us stop suddenly.

"Yes sir," Mr. Ewell said meekly.

Judge Taylor went on in tones of good will: "This the first time you've ever been in court? I don't recall ever seeing you here." At the witness's affirmative nod he continued, "Well, let's get something straight. There will be no more audibly obscene speculations on any subject from anybody in this courtroom as long as I'm sitting here. Do you understand?"

Mr. Ewell nodded, but I don't think he did. Judge Taylor sighed and said, "All right, Mr. Gilmer?"

"Thank you, sir. Mr. Ewell, would you tell us in your own words what happened on the evening of November twenty-first, please?"

174

Jem grinned and pushed his hair back. Just-in-your-own words was Mr. Gilmer's trademark. We often wondered who else's words Mr. Gilmer was afraid his witness might employ.

"Well, the night of November twenty-one I was comin' in from the woods with a load o'kindlin' and just as I got to the fence I heard Mayella screamin' like a stuck hog inside the house—"

Here Judge Taylor glanced sharply at the witness and must have decided his speculations devoid of evil intent, for he subsided sleepily.

"What time was it, Mr. Ewell?"

"Just 'fore sundown. Well, I was sayin' Mayella was screamin' fit to beat Jesus—" another glance from the bench silenced Mr. Ewell.

"Yes? She was screaming?" said Mr. Gilmer.

Mr. Ewell looked confusedly at the judge. "Well, Mayella was raisin' this holy racket so I dropped m'load and run as fast as I could but I run into th' fence, but when I got distangled I run up to th' window and I seen—" Mr. Ewell's face grew scarlet. He stood up and pointed his finger at Tom Robinson. "—I seen that black nigger yonder ruttin' on my Mayella!"

So serene was Judge Taylor's court, that he had few occasions to use his gavel, but he hammered fully five minutes. Atticus was on his feet at the bench saying something to him, Mr. Heck Tate as first officer of the county stood in the middle aisle quelling the packed courtroom. Behind us, there was an angry muffled groan from the colored people.

Reverend Sykes leaned across Dill and me, pulling at Jem's elbow. "Mr. Jem," he said, "you better take Miss Jean Louise home. Mr. Jem, you hear me?"

Jem turned his head. "Scout, go home. Dill, you'n'Scout go home."

"You gotta make me first," I said, remembering Atticus's blessed dictum.

Jem scowled furiously at me, then said to Reverend Sykes, "I think it's okay, Reverend, she doesn't understand it."

I was mortally offended. "I most certainly do, I c'n understand anything you can."

"Aw hush. She doesn't understand it, Reverend, she ain't nine yet."

Reverend Sykes's black eyes were anxious. "Mr. Finch know you all are here? This ain't fit for Miss Jean Louise or you boys either."

Jem shook his head. "He can't see us this far away. It's all right, Reverend."

I knew Jem would win, because I knew nothing could make him leave now. Dill and I were safe, for a while: Atticus could see us from where he was, if he looked.

As Judge Taylor banged his gavel, Mr. Ewell was sitting smugly in the witness chair, surveying his handiwork. With one phrase he had turned happy picknickers into a sulky, tense, murmuring crowd, being slowly hypnotized by gavel taps lessening in intensity until the only sound in the courtroom was a dim pink-pink-pink: the judge might have been rapping the bench with a pencil.

In possession of his court once more, Judge Taylor leaned back in his chair. He looked suddenly weary; his age was showing, and I thought about what Atticus had said—he and Mrs. Taylor didn't kiss much—he must have been nearly seventy.

"There has been a request," Judge Taylor said, "that this courtroom be cleared of spectators, or at least of women and children, a request that will be denied for the time being. People generally see what they look for, and hear what they listen for, and they have the right to subject their children to it, but I can assure you of one thing: you will receive what you see and hear in silence or you will leave this courtroom, but you won't leave it until the whole boiling of you come before me on contempt charges. Mr. Ewell, you will keep your testimony within the confines of Christian English usage, if that is possible. Proceed, Mr. Gilmer."

Mr. Ewell reminded me of a deaf-mute. I was sure he had never heard the words Judge Taylor directed at him —his mouth struggled silently with them—but their import registered on his face. Smugness faded from it, replaced by a dogged earnestness that fooled Judge Taylor not at all: as long as Mr. Ewell was on the stand, the judge kept his eyes on him, as if daring him to make a false move.

Mr. Gilmer and Atticus exchanged glances. Atticus was sitting down again, his fist rested on his cheek and we could not see his face. Mr. Gilmer looked rather desperate. A question from Judge Taylor made him relax: "Mr. Ewell, did you see the defendant having sexual intercourse with your daughter?"

"Yes, I did."

The spectators were quiet, but the defendant said something. Atticus whispered to him, and Tom Robinson was silent.

"You say you were at the window?" asked Mr. Gilmer.

"Yes sir."

"How far is it from the ground?"

"'bout three foot."

"Did you have a clear view of the room?"

"Yes sir."

"How did the room look?"

"Well, it was all slung about, like there was a fight."

"What did you do when you saw the defendant?"

"Well, I run around the house to get in, but he run out the front door just ahead of me. I sawed who he was, all right. I was too distracted about Mayella to run after'im. I run in the house and she was lyin' on the floor squallin'—"

"Then what did you do?"

"Why, I run for Tate quick as I could. I knowed who it was, all right, lived down yonder in that nigger-nest, passed the house every day. Jedge, I've asked this county for fifteen years to clean out that nest down yonder, they're dangerous to live around 'sides devaluin' my property—"

"Thank you, Mr. Ewell," said Mr. Gilmer hurriedly.

The witness made a hasty descent from the stand and ran smack into Atticus, who had risen to question him. Judge Taylor permitted the court to laugh.

"Just a minute, sir," said Atticus genially. "Could I ask you a question or two?"

Mr. Ewell backed up into the witness chair, settled himself, and regarded Atticus with haughty suspicion, an expression common to Maycomb County witnesses when confronted by opposing counsel.

"Mr. Ewell," Atticus began, "folks were doing a lot of running that night. Let's. see, you say you ran to the house, you ran to the window, you ran inside, you ran to Mayella, you ran for Mr. Tate. Did you, during all this running, run for a doctor?"

"Wadn't no need to. I seen what happened."

"But there's one thing I don't understand," said Atticus. "Weren't you concerned with Mayella's condition?"

"I most positively was," said Mr. Ewell. "I seen who done it."

"No, I mean her physical condition. Did you not think the nature of her injuries warranted immediate medical attention?"

"What?"

"Didn't you think she should have had a doctor, immediately?"

The witness said he never thought of it, he had never called a doctor to any of his'n in his life, and if he had it would have cost him five dollars. "That all?" he asked.

"Not quite," said Atticus casually. "Mr. Ewell, you heard the sheriff's testimony, didn't you?"

"How's that?"

"You were in the courtroom when Mr. Heck Tate was on the stand, weren't you? You heard everything he said, didn't you?"

Mr. Ewell considered the matter carefully, and seemed to decide that the question was safe.

"Yes," he said.

"Do you agree with his description of Mayella's injuries?"

"How's that?"

Atticus looked around at Mr. Gilmer and smiled. Mr. Ewell seemed determined not to give the defense the time of day.

"Mr. Tate testified that her right eye was blackened, that she was beaten around the—"

"Oh yeah," said the witness. "I hold with everything Tate said."

"You do?" asked Atticus mildly. "I just want to make sure." He went to the court reporter, said something, and the reporter entertained us for some minutes by reading Mr. Tate's testimony as if it were stock-market quotations: ". . . which eye her left oh yes that'd make it her right it was her right eye Mr. Finch I remember now she was bunged." He flipped the page. "Up on that

178

side of the face Sheriff please repeat what you said it was her right eye I said—"

"Thank you, Bert," said Atticus. "You heard it again, Mr. Ewell. Do you have anything to add to it? Do you agree with the sheriff?"

"I holds with Tate. Her eye was blacked and she was mighty beat up."

The little man seemed to have forgotten his previous humiliation from the bench. It was becoming evident that he thought Atticus an easy match. He seemed to grow ruddy again: his chest swelled, and once more he was a red little rooster. I thought he'd burst his shirt at Atticus's next question:

"Mr. Ewell, can you read and write?"

Mr. Gilmer interrupted. "Objection," he said. "Can't see what witness's literacy has to do with the case, irrelevant'n'immaterial."

Judge Taylor was about to speak but Atticus said, "Judge, if you'll allow the question plus another one you'll soon see."

"All right, let's see," said Judge Taylor, "but make sure we see, Atticus. Overruled."

Mr. Gilmer seemed as curious as the rest of us as to what bearing the state of Mr. Ewell's education had on the case.

"I'll repeat the question," said Atticus. "Can you read and write?"

"I most positively can."

"Will you write your name and show us?"

"I most positively will. How do you think I sign my relief checks?"

Mr. Ewell was endearing himself to his fellow citizens. The whispers and chuckles below us probably had to do with what a card he was.

I was becoming nervous. Atticus seemed to know what he was doing- -but it seemed to me that he'd gone frog-sticking without a light. Never, never, never, on cross-examination ask a witness a question you don't already know the answer to, was a tenet I absorbed with my baby-food. Do it, and you'll often get an answer you don't want, an answer that might wreck your case.

Atticus was reaching into the inside pocket of his coat. He drew out an envelope, then reached into his vest pocket and unclipped his fountain pen. He moved leisurely, and had turned so that he was in full view of the jury. He unscrewed the fountain-pen cap and placed it gently on his table. He shook the pen a little, then handed it with the envelope to the witness. "Would you write your name for us?" he asked. "Clearly now, so the jury can see you do it."

Mr. Ewell wrote on the back of the envelope and looked up complacently to see Judge Taylor staring at him as if he were some fragrant gardenia in full bloom on the witness stand, to see Mr. Gilmer half-sitting, half-standing at his table. The jury was watching him, one man was leaning forward with his hands over the railing.

"What's so interestin'?" he asked.

"You're left-handed, Mr. Ewell," said Judge Taylor.

Mr. Ewell turned angrily to the judge and said he didn't see what his being left-handed had to do with it, that he was a Christ-fearing man and Atticus Finch was taking advantage of him. Tricking lawyers like Atticus Finch took advantage of him all the time with their tricking ways. He had told them what happened, he'd say it again and again—which he did. Nothing Atticus asked him after that shook his story, that he'd looked through the window, then ran the nigger off, then ran for the sheriff. Atticus finally dismissed him.

Mr. Gilmer asked him one more question. "About your writing with your left hand, are you ambidextrous, Mr. Ewell?"

"I most positively am not, I can use one hand good as the other. One hand good as the other," he added, glaring at the defense table.

Jem seemed to be having a quiet fit. He was pounding the balcony rail softly, and once he whispered, "We've got him."

I didn't think so: Atticus was trying to show, it seemed to me, that Mr. Ewell could have beaten up Mayella. That much I could follow. If her right eye was blacked and she was beaten mostly on the right side of the face, it would tend to show that a left-handed person did it. Sherlock Holmes and Jem Finch would agree. But Tom Robinson could easily be left-handed, too. Like Mr. Heck Tate, I imagined a person facing me, went through a swift mental pantomime, and concluded that he might have held

180

her with his right hand and pounded her with his left. I looked down at him. His back was to us, but I could see his broad shoulders and bull-thick neck. He could easily have done it. I thought Jem was counting his chickens.

18.

But someone was booming again. "Mayella Violet Ewell—!"

A young girl walked to the witness stand. As she raised her hand and swore that the evidence she gave would be the truth, the whole truth, and nothing but the truth so help her God, she seemed somehow fragile-looking, but when she sat facing us in the witness chair she became what she was, a thick-bodied girl accustomed to strenuous labor.

In Maycomb County, it was easy to tell when someone bathed regularly, as opposed to yearly lavations: Mr. Ewell had a scalded look; as if an overnight soaking had deprived him of protective layers of dirt, his skin appeared to be sensitive to the elements. Mayella looked as if she tried to keep clean, and I was reminded of the row of red geraniums in the Ewell yard.

Mr. Gilmer asked Mayella to tell the jury in her own words what happened on the evening of November twenty-first of last year, just in her own words, please.

Mayella sat silently.

"Where were you at dusk on that evening?" began Mr. Gilmer patiently.

"On the porch."

"Which porch?"

"Ain't but one, the front porch."

"What were you doing on the porch?"

"Nothin'."

Judge Taylor said, "Just tell us what happened. You can do that, can't you?"

Mayella stared at him and burst into tears. She covered her mouth with her hands and sobbed. Judge Taylor let her cry for a while, then he said, "That's enough now. Don't be 'fraid of anybody here, as long as you tell the truth. All this is strange to you, I know, but you've nothing to be ashamed of and nothing to fear. What are you scared of?"

Mayella said something behind her hands. "What was that?" asked the judge.

"Him," she sobbed, pointing at Atticus.

"Mr. Finch?"

She nodded vigorously, saying, "Don't want him doin' me like he done Papa, tryin' to make him out left-handed . . ."

Judge Taylor scratched his thick white hair. It was plain that he had never been confronted with a problem of this kind. "How old are you?" he asked.

"Nineteen-and-a-half," Mayella said.

Judge Taylor cleared his throat and tried unsuccessfully to speak in soothing tones. "Mr. Finch has no idea of scaring you," he growled, "and if he did, I'm here to stop him. That's one thing I'm sitting up here for. Now you're a big girl, so you just sit up straight and tell the—tell us what happened to you. You can do that, can't you?"

I whispered to Jem, "Has she got good sense?"

Jem was squinting down at the witness stand. "Can't tell yet," he said. "She's got enough sense to get the judge sorry for her, but she might be just—oh, I don't know."

Mollified, Mayella gave Atticus a final terrified glance and said to Mr. Gilmer, "Well sir, I was on the porch and —and he came along and, you see, there was this old chiffarobe in the yard Papa'd brought in to chop up for kindlin'—Papa told me to do it while he was off in the woods but I wadn't feelin' strong enough then, so he came by—"

"Who is 'he'?"

Mayella pointed to Tom Robinson. "I'll have to ask you to be more specific, please," said Mr. Gilmer. "The reporter can't put down gestures very well."

"That'n yonder," she said. "Robinson."

"Then what happened?"

"I said come here, nigger, and bust up this chiffarobe for me, I gotta nickel for you. He coulda done it easy enough, he could. So he come in the yard an' I went in the house to get him the nickel and I turned around an 'fore I knew it he was on me. Just run up behind me, he did. He got me round the neck, cussin' me an' sayin' dirt —I fought'n'hollered, but he had me round the neck. He hit me agin an' agin—"

Mr. Gilmer waited for Mayella to collect herself: she had twisted her handkerchief into a sweaty rope; when she opened it to wipe her face it was a mass of creases from her hot hands. She waited for Mr. Gilmer to ask another question, but when he didn't, she said, "—he chunked me on the floor an' choked me'n took advantage of me."

"Did you scream?" asked Mr. Gilmer. "Did you scream and fight back?"

"Reckon I did, hollered for all I was worth, kicked and hollered loud as I could."

"Then what happened?"

"I don't remember too good, but next thing I knew Papa was in the room a'standin' over me hollerin' who done it, who done it? Then I sorta fainted an' the next thing I knew Mr. Tate was pullin' me up offa the floor and leadin' me to the water bucket."

Apparently Mayella's recital had given her confidence, but it was not her father's brash kind: there was something stealthy about hers, like a steady-eyed cat with a twitchy tail.

"You say you fought him off as hard as you could? Fought him tooth and nail?" asked Mr. Gilmer.

"I positively did," Mayella echoed her father.

"You are positive that he took full advantage of you?"

Mayella's face contorted, and I was afraid that she would cry again. Instead, she said, "He done what he was after."

Mr. Gilmer called attention to the hot day by wiping his head with his hand. "That's all for the time being," he said pleasantly, "but you stay there. I expect big bad Mr. Finch has some questions to ask you."

"State will not prejudice the witness against counsel for the defense," murmured Judge Taylor primly, "at least not at this time."

Atticus got up grinning but instead of walking to the witness stand, he opened his coat and hooked his thumbs in his vest, then he walked slowly across the room to the windows. He looked out, but didn't seem especially interested in what he saw, then he turned and strolled back to the witness stand. From long years of experience, I could tell he was trying to come to a decision about something.

"Miss Mayella," he said, smiling, "I won't try to scare you for a while, not yet. Let's just get acquainted. How old are you?"

"Said I was nineteen, said it to the judge yonder." Mayella jerked her head resentfully at the bench.

"So you did, so you did, ma'am. You'll have to bear with me, Miss Mayella, I'm getting along and can't remember as well as I used to. I might ask you things you've already said before, but you'll give me an answer, won't you? Good."

I could see nothing in Mayella's expression to justify Atticus's assumption that he had secured her wholehearted cooperation. She was looking at him furiously.

"Won't answer a word you say long as you keep on mockin' me," she said.

"Ma'am?" asked Atticus, startled.

"Long's you keep on makin' fun o'me."

Judge Taylor said, "Mr. Finch is not making fun of you. What's the matter with you?"

Mayella looked from under lowered eyelids at Atticus, but she said to the judge: "Long's he keeps on callin' me ma'am an sayin' Miss Mayella. I don't hafta take his sass, I ain't called upon to take it."

Atticus resumed his stroll to the windows and let Judge Taylor handle this one. Judge Taylor was not the kind of figure that ever evoked pity, but I did feel a pang for him as he tried to explain. "That's just Mr. Finch's way," he told Mayella. "We've done business in this court for years and years, and Mr. Finch is always courteous to everybody. He's not trying to mock you, he's trying to be polite. That's just his way."

The judge leaned back. "Atticus, let's get on with these proceedings, and let the record show that the witness has not been sassed, her views to the contrary."

I wondered if anybody had ever called her "ma'am" or "Miss Mayella" in her life; probably not, as she took offense to routine courtesy. What on earth was her life like? I soon found out.

"You say you're nineteen," Atticus resumed. "How

many sisters and brothers have you?" He walked from the windows back to the stand.

"Seb'm," she said, and I wondered if they were all like the specimen I had seen the first day I started to school.

"You the eldest? The oldest?"

"Yes."

"How long has your mother been dead?"

"Don't know—long time."

"Did you ever go to school?"

"Read'n'write good as Papa yonder."

Mayella sounded like a Mr. Jingle in a book I had been reading.

"How long did you go to school?"

"Two year—three year—dunno."

Slowly but surely I began to see the pattern of Atticus's questions: from questions that Mr. Gilmer did not deem sufficiently irrelevant or immaterial to object to, Atticus was quietly building up before the jury a picture of the Ewells' home life. The jury learned the following things: their relief check was far from enough to feed the family, and there was strong suspicion that Papa drank it up anyway—he sometimes went off in the swamp for days and came home sick; the weather was seldom cold enough to require shoes, but when it was, you could make dandy ones from strips of old tires; the family hauled its water in buckets from a spring that ran out at one end of the dump—they kept the surrounding area clear of trash—and it was everybody for himself as far as keeping clean went: if you wanted to wash you hauled your own water; the younger children had perpetual colds and suffered from chronic ground-itch; there was a lady who came around sometimes and asked Mayella why she didn't stay in school—she wrote down the answer; with two members of the family reading and writing, there was no need for the rest of them to learn—Papa needed them at home.

"Miss Mayella," said Atticus, in spite of himself, "a nineteen-year-old girl like you must have friends. Who are your friends?"

The witness frowned as if puzzled. "Friends?"

"Yes, don't you know anyone near your age, or older, or younger? Boys and girls? Just ordinary friends?"

Mayella's hostility, which had subsided to grudging

185

neutrality, flared again. "You makin' fun o'me agin, Mr. Finch?"

Atticus let her question answer his.

"Do you love your father, Miss Mayella?" was his next.

"Love him, whatcha mean?"

"I mean, is he good to you, is he easy to get along with?"

"He does tollable, 'cept when—"

"Except when?"

Mayella looked at her father, who was sitting with his chair tipped against the railing. He sat up straight and waited for her to answer.

"Except when nothin'," said Mayella. "I said he does tollable."

Mr. Ewell leaned back again.

"Except when he's drinking?" asked Atticus so gently that Mayella nodded.

"Does he ever go after you?"

"How you mean?"

"When he's—riled, has he ever beaten you?"

Mayella looked around, down at the court reporter, up at the judge. "Answer the question, Miss Mayella," said Judge Taylor.

"My paw's never touched a hair o' my head in my life," she declared firmly. "He never touched me."

Atticus's glasses had slipped a little, and he pushed them up on his nose. "We've had a good visit, Miss Mayella, and now I guess we'd better get to the case. You say you asked Tom Robinson to come chop up a—what was it?"

"A chiffarobe, a old dresser full of drawers on one side."

"Was Tom Robinson well known to you?"

"Whaddya mean?"

"I mean did you know who he was, where he lived?"

Mayella nodded. "I knowed who he was, he passed the house every day."

"Was this the first time you asked him to come inside the fence?"

Mayella jumped slightly at the question. Atticus was making his slow pilgrimage to the windows, as he had been doing: he would ask a question, then look out, waiting for an answer. He did not see her involuntary jump, but it seemed to me that he knew she had moved. He

186

turned around and raised his eyebrows. "Was—" he began again.

"Yes it was."

"Didn't you ever ask him to come inside the fence before?"

She was prepared now. "I did not, I certainly did not."

"One did not's enough," said Atticus serenely. "You never asked him to do odd jobs for you before?"

"I mighta," conceded Mayella. "There was several niggers around."

"Can you remember any other occasions?"

"No."

"All right, now to what happened. You said Tom Robinson was behind you in the room when you turned around, that right?"

"Yes."

"You said he 'got you around the neck cussing and saying dirt'—is that right?"

"'t's right."

Atticus's memory had suddenly become accurate. "You say 'he caught me and choked me and took advantage of me'—is that right?"

"That's what I said."

"Do you remember him beating you about the face?"

The witness hesitated.

"You seem sure enough that he choked you. All this time you were fighting back, remember? You 'kicked and hollered as loud as you could.' Do you remember him beating you about the face?"

Mayella was silent. She seemed to be trying to get something clear to herself. I thought for a moment she was doing Mr. Heck Tate's and my trick of pretending there was a person in front of us. She glanced at Mr. Gilmer.

"It's an easy question, Miss Mayella, so I'll try again. Do you remember him beating you about the face?" Atticus's voice had lost its comfortableness; he was speaking in his arid, detached professional voice. "Do you remember him beating you about the face?"

"No, I don't recollect if he hit me. I mean yes I do, he hit me."

"Was your last sentence your answer?"

"Huh? Yes, he hit—I just don't remember, I just don't

remember . . . it all happened so quick."

Judge Taylor looked sternly at Mayella. "Don't you cry, young woman—" he began, but Atticus said, "Let her cry if she wants to, Judge. We've got all the time in the world."

Mayella sniffed wrathfully and looked at Atticus. "I'll answer any question you got—get me up here an' mock me, will you? I'll answer any question you got—"

"That's fine," said Atticus. "There're only a few more. Miss Mayella, not to be tedious, you've testified that the defendant hit you, grabbed you around the neck, choked you, and took advantage of you. I want you to be sure you have the right man. Will you identify the man who raped you?"

"I will, that's him right yonder."

Atticus turned to the defendant. "Tom, stand up. Let Miss Mayella have a good long look at you. Is this the man, Miss Mayella?"

Tom Robinson's powerful shoulders rippled under his thin shirt. He rose to his feet and stood with his right hand on the back of his chair. He looked oddly off balance, but it was not from the way he was standing. His left arm was fully twelve inches shorter than his right, and hung dead at his side. It ended in a small shriveled hand, and from as far away as the balcony I could see that it was no use to him.

"Scout," breathed Jem. "Scout, look! Reverend, he's crippled!"

Reverend Sykes leaned across me and whispered to Jem. "He got it caught in a cotton gin, caught it in Mr. Dolphus Raymond's cotton gin when he was a boy . . . like to bled to death . . . tore all the muscles loose from his bones—"

Atticus said, "Is this the man who raped you?"

"It most certainly is."

Atticus's next question was one word long. "How?"

Mayella was raging. "I don't know how he done it, but he done it—I said it all happened so fast I—"

"Now let's consider this calmly—" began Atticus, but Mr. Gilmer interrupted with an objection: he was not irrelevant or immaterial, but Atticus was browbeating the witness.

Judge Taylor laughed outright. "Oh sit down, Horace,

he's doing nothing of the sort. If anything, the witness's browbeating Atticus."

Judge Taylor was the only person in the courtroom who laughed. Even the babies were still, and I suddenly wondered if they had been smothered at their mothers' breasts.

"Now," said Atticus, "Miss Mayella, you've testified that the defendant choked and beat you—you didn't say that he sneaked up behind you and knocked you cold, but you turned around and there he was—" Atticus was back behind his table, and he emphasized his words by tapping his knuckles on it. "—do you wish to reconsider any of your testimony?"

"You want me to say something that didn't happen?"

"No ma'am, I want you to say something that did happen. Tell us once more, please, what happened?"

"I told'ja what happened."

"You testified that you turned around and there he was. He choked you then?"

"Yes."

"Then he released your throat and hit you?"

"I said he did."

"He blacked your left eye with his right fist?"

"I ducked and it—it glanced, that's what it did. I ducked and it glanced off." Mayella had finally seen the light.

"You're becoming suddenly clear on this point. A while ago you couldn't remember too well, could you?"

"I said he hit me."

"All right. He choked you, he hit you, then he raped you, that right?"

"It most certainly is."

"You're a strong girl, what were you doing all the time, just standing there?"

"I told'ja I hollered'n'kicked'n'fought—"

Atticus reached up and took off his glasses, turned his good right eye to the witness, and rained questions on her. Judge Taylor said, "One question at a time, Atticus. Give the witness a chance to answer."

"All right, why didn't you run?"

"I tried to . . ."

"Tried to? What kept you from it?"

"I—he slung me down. That's what he did, he slung

189

me down'n got on top of me."

"You were screaming all this time?"

"I certainly was."

"Then why didn't the other children hear you? Where were they? At the dump?"

No answer.

"Where were they?"

"Why didn't your screams make them come running? The dump's closer than the woods, isn't it?"

No answer.

"Or didn't you scream until you saw your father in the window? You didn't think to scream until then, did you?"

No answer.

"Did you scream first at your father instead of at Tom Robinson? Was that it?"

No answer.

"Who beat you up? Tom Robinson or your father?"

No answer.

"What did your father see in the window, the crime of rape or the best defense to it? Why don't you tell the truth, child, didn't Bob Ewell beat you up?"

When Atticus turned away from Mayella he looked like his stomach hurt, but Mayella's face was a mixture of terror and fury. Atticus sat down wearily and polished his glasses with his handkerchief.

Suddenly Mayella became articulate. "I got somethin' to say," she said.

Atticus raised his head. "Do you want to tell us what happened?"

But she did not hear the compassion in his invitation. "I got somethin' to say an' then I ain't gonna say no more. That nigger yonder took advantage of me an' if you fine fancy gentlemen don't wanta do nothin' about it then you're all yellow stinkin' cowards, stinkin' cowards, the lot of you. Your fancy airs don't come to nothin'—your ma'amin' and Miss Mayellerin' don't come to nothin', Mr. Finch—"

Then she burst into real tears. Her shoulders shook with angry sobs. She was as good as her word. She answered no more questions, even when Mr. Gilmer tried to get her back on the track. I guess if she hadn't been so poor and ignorant, Judge Taylor would have put her under the jail for the contempt she had shown everybody in the courtroom. Somehow, Atticus had hit her hard in a way that was not clear to me, but it gave him no pleasure to do so. He sat with his head down, and I never saw anybody glare at anyone with the hatred Mayella showed when she left the stand and walked by Atticus's table.

When Mr. Gilmer told Judge Taylor that the state rested, Judge Taylor said, "It's time we all did. We'll take ten minutes."

Atticus and Mr. Gilmer met in front of the bench and whispered, then they left the courtroom by a door behind the witness stand, which was a signal for us all to stretch. I discovered that I had been sitting on the edge of the long bench, and I was somewhat numb. Jem got up and yawned, Dill did likewise, and Reverend Sykes wiped his face on his hat. The temperature was an easy ninety, he said.

Mr. Braxton Underwood, who had been sitting quietly in a chair reserved for the Press, soaking up testimony with his sponge of a brain, allowed his bitter eyes to rove over the Colored balcony, and they met mine. He gave a snort and looked away.

"Jem," I said, "Mr. Underwood's seen us."

"That's okay. He won't tell Atticus, he'll just put it on the social side of the *Tribune*." Jem turned back to Dill, explaining, I suppose, the finer points of the trial to him, but I wondered what they were. There had been no lengthy debates between Atticus and Mr. Gilmer on any points; Mr. Gilmer seemed to be prosecuting almost reluctantly; witnesses had been led by the nose as asses are, with few objections. But Atticus had once told us that in Judge Taylor's court any lawyer who was a strict constructionist on evidence usually wound up receiving strict instructions from the bench. He distilled this for me to mean that Judge Taylor might look lazy and operate in his sleep, but he was seldom reversed, and that was the proof of the pudding. Atticus said he was a good judge.

Presently Judge Taylor returned and climbed into his swivel chair. He took a cigar from his vest pocket and examined it thoughtfully. I punched Dill. Having passed the judge's inspection, the cigar suffered a vicious bite. "We come down sometimes to watch him," I explained. "It's gonna take him the rest of the afternoon, now. You watch." Unaware of public scrutiny from above, Judge Taylor disposed of the severed end by propelling it expertly to his lips and saying, "Fhluck!" He hit a spittoon so squarely we could hear it slosh. "Bet he was hell with a spitball," murmured Dill.

As a rule, a recess meant a general exodus, but today people weren't moving. Even the Idlers who had failed to shame younger men from their seats had remained standing along the walls. I guess Mr. Heck Tate had reserved the county toilet for court officials.

Atticus and Mr. Gilmer returned, and Judge Taylor looked at his watch. "It's gettin' on to four," he said, which was intriguing, as the courthouse clock must have struck the hour at least twice. I had not heard it or felt its vibrations.

"Shall we try to wind up this afternoon?" asked Judge Taylor. "How 'bout it, Atticus?"

"I think we can," said Atticus.

"How many witnesses you got?"

"One."

"Well, call him."

19.

Thomas Robinson reached around, ran his fingers under his left arm and lifted it. He guided his arm to the Bible and his rubber-like left hand sought contact with the black binding. As he raised his right hand, the useless one slipped off the Bible and hit the clerk's table. He was trying again when Judge Taylor growled, "That'll do, Tom." Tom took the oath and stepped into the witness chair. Atticus very quickly induced him to tell us:

Tom was twenty-five years of age; he was married with three children; he had been in trouble with the law before: he once received thirty days for disorderly conduct.

"It must have been disorderly," said Atticus. "What did it consist of?"

"Got in a fight with another man, he tried to cut me."

"Did he succeed?"

"Yes suh, a little, not enough to hurt. You see, I—" Tom moved his left shoulder.

"Yes," said Atticus. "You were both convicted?"

"Yes suh, I had to serve 'cause I couldn't pay the fine. Other fellow paid his'n."

Dill leaned across me and asked Jem what Atticus was doing. Jem said Atticus was showing the jury that Tom had nothing to hide.

"Were you acquainted with Mayella Violet Ewell?" asked Atticus.

"Yes suh, I had to pass her place goin' to and from the field every day."

"Whose field?"

"I picks for Mr. Link Deas."

"Were you picking cotton in November?"

"No suh, I works in his yard fall an' wintertime. I works pretty steady for him all year round, he's got a lot of pecan trees'n things."

"You say you had to pass the Ewell place to get to and from work. Is there any other way to go?"

"No suh, none's I know of."

"Tom, did she ever speak to you?"

"Why, yes suh, I'd tip m'hat when I'd go by, and one day she asked me to come inside the fence and bust up a chiffarobe for her."

"When did she ask you to chop up the—the chiffarobe?"

"Mr. Finch, it was way last spring. I remember it because it was choppin' time and I had my hoe with me. I said I didn't have nothin' but this hoe, but she said she had a hatchet. She give me the hatchet and I broke up the chiffarobe. She said, 'I reckon I'll hafta give you a nickel, won't I?' an' I said, 'No ma'am, there ain't no charge.' Then I went home. Mr. Finch, that was way last spring, way over a year ago."

"Did you ever go on the place again?"

"Yes suh."

"When?"

"Well, I went lots of times."

Judge Taylor instinctively reached for his gavel, but let his hand fall. The murmur below us died without his help.

"Under what circumstances?"

"Please, suh?"

"Why did you go inside the fence lots of times?"

Tom Robinson's forehead relaxed. "She'd call me in, suh. Seemed like every time I passed by yonder she'd have some little somethin' for me to do—choppin' kindlin', totin' water for her. She watered them red flowers every day—"

"Were you paid for your services?"

"No suh, not after she offered me a nickel the first time. I was glad to do it, Mr. Ewell didn't seem to help her none, and neither did the chillun, and I knowed she didn't have no nickels to spare."

"Where were the other children?"

"They was always around, all over the place. They'd watch me work, some of 'em, some of 'em'd set in the window."

"Would Miss Mayella talk to you?"

"Yes sir, she talked to me."

As Tom Robinson gave his testimony, it came to me that Mayella Ewell must have been the loneliest person in the world. She was even lonelier than Boo Radley, who had not been out of the house in twenty-five years. When Atticus asked had she any friends, she seemed not to know what he meant, then she thought he was making fun of her. She was as sad, I thought, as what Jem called a mixed child: white people wouldn't have anything to do with her because she lived among pigs; Negroes wouldn't have anything to do with her because she was white. She couldn't live like Mr. Dolphus Raymond, who preferred the company of Negroes, because she didn't own a riverbank and she wasn't from a fine old family. Nobody said, "That's just their way," about the Ewells. Maycomb gave them Christmas baskets, welfare money, and the back of its hand. Tom Robinson was probably the only person who was ever decent to her. But she said he took advantage of her, and when she stood up she looked at him as if he were dirt beneath her feet.

"Did you ever," Atticus interrupted my meditations, "at any time, go on the Ewell property—did you ever set foot on the Ewell property without an express invitation from one of them?"

"No suh, Mr. Finch, I never did. I wouldn't do that, suh."

Atticus sometimes said that one way to tell whether a witness was lying or telling the truth was to listen rather than watch: I applied his test—Tom denied it three times in one breath, but quietly, with no hint of whining in his voice, and I found myself believing him in spite of his protesting too much. He seemed to be a respectable Negro, and a respectable Negro would never go up into somebody's yard of his own volition.

"Tom, what happened to you on the evening of November twenty-first of last year?"

Below us, the spectators drew a collective breath and leaned forward. Behind us, the Negroes did the same.

Tom was a black-velvet Negro, not shiny, but soft black velvet. The whites of his eyes shone in his face, and when he spoke we saw flashes of his teeth. If he had been whole, he would have been a fine specimen of a man.

"Mr. Finch," he said, "I was goin' home as usual that evenin', an' when I passed the Ewell place Miss Mayella were on the porch, like she said she were. It seemed real quiet like, an' I didn't quite know why. I was studyin' why, just passin' by, when she says for me to come there and help her a minute. Well, I went inside the fence an' looked around for some kindlin' to work on, but I didn't see none, and she says, 'Naw, I got somethin' for you to do in the house. Th' old door's off its hinges an' fall's comin' on pretty fast.' I said you got a screwdriver, Miss Mayella? She said she sho' had. Well, I went up the steps an' she motioned me to come inside, and I went in the front room an' looked at the door. I said Miss Mayella, this door look all right. I pulled it back'n forth and those hinges was all right. Then she shet the door in my face. Mr. Finch, I was wonderin' why it was so quiet like, an' it come to me that there weren't a chile on the place, not a one of 'em, and I said Miss Mayella, where the chillun?"

Tom's black velvet skin had begun to shine, and he ran his hand over his face.

"I say where the chillun?" he continued, "an' she says —she was laughin', sort of—she says they all gone to

195

town to get ice creams. She says, 'Took me a slap year to save seb'm nickels, but I done it. They all gone to town.' "

Tom's discomfort was not from the humidity. "What did you say then, Tom?" asked Atticus.

"I said somethin' like, why Miss Mayella, that's right smart o'you to treat 'em. An' she said, 'You think so?' I don't think she understood what I was thinkin'—I meant it was smart of her to save like that, an' nice of her to treat 'em."

"I understand you, Tom. Go on," said Atticus.

"Well, I said I best be goin', I couldn't do nothin' for her, an' she says oh yes I could, an' I ask her what, and she says to just step on that chair yonder an' git that box down from on top of the chiffarobe."

"Not the same chiffarobe you busted up?" asked Atticus.

The witness smiled. "Naw suh, another one. Most as tall as the room. So I done what she told me, an' I was just reachin' when the next thing I knows she—she'd grabbed me round the legs, grabbed me round th' legs, Mr. Finch. She scared me so bad I hopped down an' turned the chair over—that was the only thing, only furniture, 'sturbed in that room, Mr. Finch, when I left it. I swear 'fore God."

"What happened after you turned the chair over?"

Tom Robinson had come to a dead stop. He glanced at Atticus, then at the jury, then at Mr. Underwood sitting across the room.

"Tom, you're sworn to tell the whole truth. Will you tell it?"

Tom ran his hand nervously over his mouth.

"What happened after that?"

"Answer the question," said Judge Taylor. One-third of his cigar had vanished.

"Mr. Finch, I got down offa that chair an' turned around an' she sorta jumped on me."

"Jumped on you? Violently?"

"No suh, she—she hugged me. She hugged me round the waist."

This time Judge Taylor's gavel came down with a bang, and as it did the overhead lights went on in the courtroom. Darkness had not come, but the afternoon sun had left the windows. Judge Taylor quickly restored order.

"Then what did she do?"

The witness swallowed hard. "She reached up an' kissed me 'side of th' face. She says she never kissed a grown man before an' she might as well kiss a nigger. She says what her papa do to her don't count. She says, 'Kiss me back, nigger.' I say Miss Mayella lemme outa here an' tried to run but she got her back to the door an' I'da had to push her. I didn't wanta harm her, Mr. Finch, an' I say lemme pass, but just when I say it Mr. Ewell yonder hollered through th' window."

"What did he say?"

Tom Robinson swallowed again, and his eyes widened. "Somethin' not fittin' to say—not fittin' for these folks'n chillun to hear—"

"What did he say, Tom? You *must* tell the jury what he said."

Tom Robinson shut his eyes tight. "He says you goddamn whore, I'll kill ya."

"Then what happened?"

"Mr. Finch, I was runnin' so fast I didn't know what happened."

"Tom, did you ràpe Mayella Ewell?"

"I did not, suh."

"Did you harm her in any way?"

"I did not, suh."

"Did you resist her advances?"

"Mr. Finch, I tried. I tried to 'thout bein' ugly to her. I didn't wanta be ugly, I didn't wanta push her or nothin'."

It occurred to me that in their own way, Tom Robinson's manners were as good as Atticus's. Until my father explained it to me later, I did not understand the subtlety of Tom's predicament: he would not have dared strike a white woman under any circumstances and expect to live long, so he took the first opportunity to run—a sure sign of guilt.

"Tom, go back once more to Mr. Ewell," said Atticus. "Did he say anything to you?"

"Not anything, suh. He mighta said somethin', but I weren't there—"

"That'll do," Atticus cut in sharply. "What you did

hear, who was he talking to?"

"Mr. Finch, he were talkin' and lookin' at Miss Mayella."

"Then you ran?"

"I sho' did, suh."

"Why did you run?"

"I was scared, suh."

"Why were you scared?"

"Mr. Finch, if you was a nigger like me, you'd be scared, too."

Atticus sat down. Mr. Gilmer was making his way to the witness stand, but before he got there Mr. Link Deas rose from the audience and announced:

"I just want the whole lot of you to know one thing right now. That boy's worked for me eight years an' I ain't had a speck o'trouble outa him. Not a speck."

"*Shut your mouth, sir!*" Judge Taylor was wide awake and roaring. He was also pink in the face. His speech was miraculously unimpaired by his cigar. "Link Deas," he yelled, "if you have anything you want to say you can say it under oath and at the proper time, but until then you get out of this room, you hear me? Get out of this room, sir, you hear me? I'll be damned if I'll listen to this case again!"

Judge Taylor looked daggers at Atticus, as if daring him to speak, but Atticus had ducked his head and was laughing into his lap. I remembered something he had said about Judge Taylor's ex cathedra remarks sometimes exceeding his duty, but that few lawyers ever did anything about them. I looked at Jem, but Jem shook his head. "It ain't like one of the jurymen got up and started talking," he said. "I think it'd be different then. Mr. Link was just disturbin' the peace or something."

Judge Taylor told the reporter to expunge anything he happened to have written down after Mr. Finch if you were a nigger like me you'd be scared too, and told the jury to disregard the interruption. He looked suspiciously down the middle aisle and waited, I suppose, for Mr. Link Deas to effect total departure. Then he said, "Go ahead, Mr. Gilmer."

"You were given thirty days once for disorderly conduct, Robinson?" asked Mr. Gilmer.

"Yes suh."

"What'd the nigger look like when you got through with him?"

"He beat me, Mr. Gilmer."

"Yes, but you were convicted, weren't you?"

Atticus raised his head. "It was a misdemeanor and it's in the record, Judge." I thought he sounded tired.

"Witness'll answer, though," said Judge Taylor, just as wearily.

"Yes suh, I got thirty days."

I knew that Mr. Gilmer would sincerely tell the jury that anyone who was convicted of disorderly conduct could easily have had it in his heart to take advantage of Mayella Ewell, that was the only reason he cared. Reasons like that helped.

"Robinson, you're pretty good at busting up chiffa-robes and kindling with one hand, aren't you?"

"Yes suh, I reckon so."

"Strong enough to choke the breath out of a woman and sling her to the floor?"

"I never done that, suh."

"But you are strong enough to?"

"I reckon so, suh."

"Had your eye on her a long time, hadn't you, boy?"

"No suh, I never looked at her."

"Then you were mighty polite to do all that chopping and hauling for her, weren't you, boy?"

"I was just tryin' to help her out, suh."

"That was mighty generous of you, you had chores at home after your regular work, didn't you?"

"Yes suh."

"Why didn't you do them instead of Miss Ewell's?"

"I done 'em both, suh."

"You must have been pretty busy. Why?"

"Why what, suh?"

"Why were you so anxious to do that woman's chores?"

Tom Robinson hesitated, searching for an answer. "Looked like she didn't have nobody to help her, like I says—"

"With Mr. Ewell and seven children on the place, boy?"

"Well, I says it looked like they never help her none—"

"You did all this chopping and work from sheer goodness, boy?"

"Tried to help her, I says."

Mr. Gilmer smiled grimly at the jury. "You're a mighty good fellow, it seems—did all this for not one penny?"

"Yes suh. I felt right sorry for her, she seemed to try more'n the rest of 'em—"

"*You* felt sorry for *her*, you felt *sorry* for her?" Mr. Gilmer seemed ready to rise to the ceiling.

The witness realized his mistake and shifted uncomfortably in the chair. But the damage was done. Below us, nobody liked Tom Robinson's answer. Mr. Gilmer paused a long time to let it sink in.

"Now you went by the house as usual, last November twenty-first," he said, "and she asked you to come in and bust up a chiffarobe?"

"No suh."

"Do you deny that you went by the house?"

"No suh—she said she had somethin' for me to do inside the house—"

"She says she asked you to bust up a chiffarobe, is that right?"

"No suh, it ain't."

"Then you say she's lying, boy?"

Atticus was on his feet, but Tom Robinson didn't need him. "I don't say she's lyin', Mr. Gilmer, I say she's mistaken in her mind."

To the next ten questions, as Mr. Gilmer reviewed Mayella's version of events, the witness's steady answer was that she was mistaken in her mind.

"Didn't Mr. Ewell run you off the place, boy?"

"No suh, I don't think he did."

"Don't think, what do you mean?"

"I mean I didn't stay long enough for him to run me off."

"You're very candid about this, why did you run so fast?"

"I says I was scared, suh."

"If you had a clear conscience, why were you scared?"

"Like I says before, it weren't safe for any nigger to be in a—fix like that."

"But you weren't in a fix—you testified that you were

resisting Miss Ewell. Were you so scared that she'd hurt you, you ran, a big buck like you?"

"No suh, I's scared I'd be in court, just like I am now."

"Scared of arrest, scared you'd have to face up to what you did?"

"No suh, scared I'd hafta face up to what I didn't do."

"Are you being impudent to me, boy?"

"No suh, I didn't go to be."

This was as much as I heard of Mr. Gilmer's cross-examination, because Jem made me take Dill out. For some reason Dill had started crying and couldn't stop; quietly at first, then his sobs were heard by several people in the balcony. Jem said if I didn't go with him he'd make me, and Reverend Sykes said I'd better go, so I went. Dill had seemed to be all right that day, nothing wrong with him, but I guessed he hadn't fully recovered from running away.

"Ain't you feeling good?" I asked, when we reached the bottom of the stairs.

Dill tried to pull himself together as we ran down the south steps. Mr. Link Deas was a lonely figure on the top step. "Anything happenin', Scout?" he asked as we went by. "No sir," I answered over my shoulder. "Dill here, he's sick."

"Come on out under the trees," I said. "Heat got you, I expect." We chose the fattest live oak and we sat under it.

"It was just him I couldn't stand," Dill said.

"Who, Tom?"

"That old Mr. Gilmer doin' him thataway, talking so hateful to him—"

"Dill, that's his job. Why, if we didn't have prosecutors—well, we couldn't have defense attorneys, I reckon."

Dill exhaled patiently. "I know all that, Scout. It was the way he said it made me sick, plain sick."

"He's supposed to act that way, Dill, he was cross—"

"He didn't act that way when—"

"Dill, those were his own witnesses."

"Well, Mr. Finch didn't act that way to Mayella and old man Ewell when he cross-examined them. The way that man called him 'boy' all the time and sneered at him, an' looked around at the jury every time he answered—"

"Well, Dill, after all he's just a Negro."

"I don't care one speck. It ain't right, somehow it ain't right to do 'em that way. Hasn't anybody got any business talkin' like that—it just makes me sick."

"That's just Mr. Gilmer's way, Dill, he does 'em all that way. You've never seen him get good'n down on one yet. Why, when—well, today Mr. Gilmer seemed to me like he wasn't half trying. They do 'em all that way, most lawyers, I mean."

"Mr. Finch doesn't."

"He's not an example, Dill, he's—" I was trying to grope in my memory for a sharp phrase of Miss Maudie Atkinson's. I had it: "He's the same in the courtroom as he is on the public streets."

"That's not what I mean," said Dill.

"I know what you mean, boy," said a voice behind us. We thought it came from the tree-trunk, but it belonged to Mr. Dolphus Raymond. He peered around the trunk at us. "You aren't thin-hided, it just makes you sick, doesn't it?"

20.

Come on round here, son, I got something that'll settle your stomach."

As Mr. Dolphus Raymond was an evil man I accepted his invitation reluctantly, but I followed Dill. Somehow, I didn't think Atticus would like it if we became friendly with Mr. Raymond, and I knew Aunt Alexandra wouldn't.

"Here," he said, offering Dill his paper sack with straws in it. "Take a good sip, it'll quieten you."

Dill sucked on the straws, smiled, and pulled at length.

"Hee hee," said Mr. Raymond, evidently taking delight in corrupting a child.

"Dill, you watch out, now," I warned.

Dill released the straws and grinned. "Scout, it's nothing but Coca-Cola."

Mr. Raymond sat up against the tree-trunk. He had been lying on the grass. "You little folks won't tell on me now, will you? It'd ruin my reputation if you did."

"You mean all you drink in that sack's Coca-Cola? Just plain Coca-Cola?"

"Yes ma'am," Mr. Raymond nodded. I liked his smell: it was of leather, horses, cottonseed. He wore the only English riding boots I had ever seen. "That's all I drink, most of the time."

"Then you just pretend you're half—? I beg your pardon, sir," I caught myself. "I didn't mean to be—"

Mr. Raymond chuckled, not at all offended, and I tried to frame a discreet question: "Why do you do like you do?"

"Wh—oh yes, you mean why do I pretend? Well, it's very simple," he said. "Some folks don't—like the way I live. Now I could say the hell with 'em, I don't care if they don't like it. I do say I don't care if they don't like it, right enough—but I don't say the hell with 'em, see?"

Dill and I said, "No sir."

"I try to give 'em a reason, you see. It helps folks if they can latch onto a reason. When I come to town, which is seldom, if I weave a little and drink out of this sack, folks can say Dolphus Raymond's in the clutches of whiskey—that's why he won't change his ways. He can't help himself, that's why he lives the way he does."

"That ain't honest, Mr. Raymond, making yourself out badder'n you are already—"

"It ain't honest but it's mighty helpful to folks. Secretly, Miss Finch, I'm not much of a drinker, but you see they could never, never understand that I live like I do because that's the way I want to live."

I had a feeling that I shouldn't be here listening to this sinful man who had mixed children and didn't care who knew it, but he was fascinating. I had never encountered a being who deliberately perpetrated fraud against himself. But why had he entrusted us with his deepest secret? I asked him why.

"Because you're children and you can understand it," he said, "and because I heard that one—"

He jerked his head at Dill: "Things haven't caught up with that one's instinct yet. Let him get a little older and he won't get sick and cry. Maybe things'll strike him as being—not quite right, say, but he won't cry, not when he gets a few years on him."

"Cry about what, Mr. Raymond?" Dill's maleness was beginning to assert itself.

"Cry about the simple hell people give other people— without even thinking. Cry about the hell white people give colored folks, without even stopping to think that they're people, too."

"Atticus says cheatin' a colored man is ten times worse than cheatin' a white man," I muttered. "Says it's the worst thing you can do."

Mr. Raymond said, "I don't reckon it's— Miss Jean Louise, you don't know your pa's not a run-of-the-mill man, it'll take a few years for that to sink in—you haven't seen enough of the world yet. You haven't even seen this town, but all you gotta do is step back inside the courthouse."

Which reminded me that we were missing nearly all of Mr. Gilmer's cross-examination. I looked at the sun, and it was dropping fast behind the store-tops on the west side of the square. Between two fires, I could not decide which I wanted to jump into: Mr. Raymond or the 5th Judicial Circuit Court. "C'mon, Dill," I said. "You all right, now?"

"Yeah. Glad t've metcha, Mr. Raymond, and thanks for the drink, it was mighty settlin'."

We raced back to the courthouse, up the steps, up two flights of stairs, and edged our way along the balcony rail. Reverend Sykes had saved our seats.

The courtroom was still, and again I wondered where the babies were. Judge Taylor's cigar was a brown speck in the center of his mouth; Mr. Gilmer was writing on one of the yellow pads on his table, trying to outdo the court reporter, whose hand was jerking rapidly. "Shoot," I muttered, "we missed it."

Atticus was halfway through his speech to the jury. He had evidently pulled some papers from his briefcase that rested beside his chair, because they were on his table. Tom Robinson was toying with them.

". . . absence of any corroborative evidence, this man was indicted on a capital charge and is now on trial for his life. . . ."

I punched Jem. "How long's he been at it?"

"He's just gone over the evidence," Jem whispered, "and we're gonna win, Scout. I don't see how we can't.

He's been at it 'bout five minutes. He made it as plain and easy as—well, as I'da explained it to you. You could've understood it, even."

"Did Mr. Gilmer—?"

"Sh-h. Nothing new, just the usual. Hush now."

We looked down again. Atticus was speaking easily, with the kind of detachment he used when he dictated a letter. He walked slowly up and down in front of the jury, and the jury seemed to be attentive: their heads were up, and they followed Atticus's route with what seemed to be appreciation. I guess it was because Atticus wasn't a thunderer.

Atticus paused, then he did something he didn't ordinarily do. He unhitched his watch and chain and placed them on the table, saying, "With the court's permission—"

Judge Taylor nodded, and then Atticus did something I never saw him do before or since, in public or in private: he unbuttoned his vest, unbuttoned his collar, loosened his tie, and took off his coat. He never loosened a scrap of his clothing until he undressed at bedtime, and to Jem and me, this was the equivalent of him standing before us stark naked. We exchanged horrified glances.

Atticus put his hands in his pockets, and as he returned to the jury, I saw his gold collar button and the tips of his pen and pencil winking in the light.

"Gentlemen," he said. Jem and I again looked at each other: Atticus might have said, "Scout." His voice had lost its aridity, its detachment, and he was talking to the jury as if they were folks on the post office corner.

"Gentlemen," he was saying, "I shall be brief, but I would like to use my remaining time with you to remind you that this case is not a difficult one, it requires no minute sifting of complicated facts, but it does require you to be sure beyond all reasonable doubt as to the guilt of the defendant. To begin with, this case should never have come to trial. This case is as simple as black and white.

"The state has not produced one iota of medical evidence to the effect that the crime Tom Robinson is charged with ever took place. It has relied instead upon the testimony of two witnesses whose evidence has not only been called into serious question on cross-examination, but has been flatly contradicted by the defendant. The defendant is not guilty, but somebody in this courtroom is.

"I have nothing but pity in my heart for the chief witness for the state, but my pity does not extend so far as to her putting a man's life at stake, which she has done in an effort to get rid of her own guilt.

"I say guilt, gentlemen, because it was guilt that motivated her. She has committed no crime, she has merely broken a rigid and time-honored code of our society, a code so severe that whoever breaks it is hounded from our midst as unfit to live with. She is the victim of cruel poverty and ignorance, but I cannot pity her: she is white. She knew full well the enormity of her offense, but because her desires were stronger than the code she was breaking, she persisted in breaking it. She persisted, and her subsequent reaction is something that all of us have known at one time or another. She did something every child has done—she tried to put the evidence of her offense away from her. But in this case she was no child hiding stolen contraband: she struck out at her victim—of necessity she must put him away from her—he must be removed from her presence, from this world. She must destroy the evidence of her offense.

"What was the evidence of her offense? Tom Robinson, a human being. She must put Tom Robinson away from her. Tom Robinson was her daily reminder of what she did. What did she do? She tempted a Negro.

"She was white, and she tempted a Negro. She did something that in our society is unspeakable: she kissed a black man. Not an old Uncle, but a strong young Negro man. No code mattered to her before she broke it, but it came crashing down on her afterwards.

"Her father saw it, and the defendant has testified as to his remarks. What did her father do? We don't know, but there is circumstantial evidence to indicate that Mayella Ewell was beaten savagely by someone who led almost exclusively with his left. We do know in part what Mr. Ewell did: he did what any God-fearing, persevering, respectable white man would do under the circumstances —he swore out a warrant, no doubt signing it with his left hand, and Tom Robinson now sits before you, having taken the oath with the only good hand he possesses—his right hand.

"And so a quiet, respectable, humble Negro who had the unmitigated temerity to 'feel sorry' for a white woman has had to put his word against two white people's. I need not remind you of their appearance and conduct on the stand—you saw them for yourselves. The witnesses for the state, with the exeception of the sheriff of Maycomb County, have presented themselves to you gentlemen, to this court, in the cynical confidence that their testimony would not be doubted, confident that you gentlemen would go along with them on the assumption—the evil assumption—that *all* Negroes lie, that *all* Negroes are basically immoral beings, that *all* Negro men are not to be trusted around our women, an assumption one associates with minds of their caliber.

"Which, gentlemen, we know is in itself a lie as black as Tom Robinson's skin, a lie I do not have to point out to you. You know the truth, and the truth is this: some Negroes lie, some Negroes are immoral, some Negro men are not to be trusted around women—black or white. But this is a truth that applies to the human race and to no particular race of men. There is not a person in this courtroom who has never told a lie, who has never done an immoral thing, and there is no man living who has never looked upon a woman without desire."

Atticus paused and took out his handkerchief. Then he took off his glasses and wiped them, and we saw another "first": we had never seen him sweat—he was one of those men whose faces never perspired, but now it was shining tan.

"One more thing, gentlemen, before I quit. Thomas Jefferson once said that all men are created equal, a phrase that the Yankees and the distaff side of the Executive branch in Washington are fond of hurling at us. There is a tendency in this year of grace, 1935, for certain people to use this phrase out of context, to satisfy all conditions. The most ridiculous example I can think of is that the people who run public education promote the stupid and idle along with the industrious—because all men are created equal, educators will gravely tell you, the children left behind suffer terrible feelings of inferiority. We know all men are not created equal in the

207

sense some people would have us believe—some people are smarter than others, some people have more opportunity because they're born with it, some men make more money than others, some ladies make better cakes than others—some people are born gifted beyond the normal scope of most men.

"But there is one way in this country in which all men are created equal—there is one human institution that makes a pauper the equal of a Rockefeller, the stupid man the equal of an Einstein, and the ignorant man the equal of any college president. That institution, gentlemen, is a court. It can be the Supreme Court of the United States or the humblest J.P. court in the land, or this honorable court which you serve. Our courts have their faults, as does any human institution, but in this country our courts are the great levelers, and in our courts all men are created equal.

"I'm no idealist to believe firmly in the integrity of our courts and in the jury system—that is no ideal to me, it is a living, working reality. Gentlemen, a court is no better than each man of you sitting before me on this jury. A court is only as sound as its jury, and a jury is only as sound as the men who make it up. I am confident that you gentlemen will review without passion the evidence you have heard, come to a decision, and restore this defendant to his family. In the name of God, do your duty."

Atticus's voice had dropped, and as he turned away from the jury he said something I did not catch. He said it more to himself than to the court. I punched Jem. "What'd he say?"

" 'In the name of God, believe him,' I think that's what he said."

Dill suddenly reached over me and tugged at Jem. "Looka yonder!"

We followed his finger with sinking hearts. Calpurnia was making her way up the middle aisle, walking straight toward Atticus.

21.

She stopped shyly at the railing and waited to get Judge Taylor's attention. She was in a fresh apron and she carried an envelope in her hand.

Judge Taylor saw her and said, "It's Calpurnia, isn't it?"

"Yes sir," she said. "Could I just pass this note to Mr. Finch, please sir? It hasn't got anything to do with—with the trial."

Judge Taylor nodded and Atticus took the envelope from Calpurnia. He opened it, read its contents and said, "Judge, I—this note is from my sister. She says my children are missing, haven't turned up since noon . . . I . . . could you—"

"I know where they are, Atticus." Mr. Underwood spoke up. "They're right up yonder in the colored balcony —been there since precisely one-eighteen P.M."

Our father turned around and looked up. "Jem, come down from there," he called. Then he said something to the Judge we didn't hear. We climbed across Reverend Sykes and made our way to the staircase.

Atticus and Calpurnia met us downstairs. Calpurnia looked peeved, but Atticus looked exhausted.

Jem was jumping in excitement. "We've won, haven't we?"

"I've no idea," said Atticus shortly. "You've been here all afternoon? Go home with Calpurnia and get your supper—and stay home."

"Aw, Atticus, let us come back," pleaded Jem. "Please let us hear the verdict, *please* sir."

"The jury might be out and back in a minute, we don't know—" but we could tell Atticus was relenting. "Well, you've heard it all, so you might as well hear the rest. Tell you what, you all can come back when you've eaten your supper—eat slowly, now, you won't miss anything important—and if the jury's still out, you can wait with us. But I expect it'll be over before you get back."

"You think they'll acquit him that fast?" asked Jem.

Atticus opened his mouth to answer, but shut it and left us.

I prayed that Reverend Sykes would save our seats for us, but stopped praying when I remembered that people got up and left in droves when the jury was out—tonight, they'd overrun the drugstore, the O.K. Café and the hotel, that is, unless they had brought their suppers too.

Calpurnia marched us home: "—skin every one of you alive, the very idea, you children listenin' to all that! Mister Jem, don't you know better'n to take your little sister to that trial? Miss Alexandra'll absolutely have a stroke of paralysis when she finds out! Ain't fittin' for children to hear. . . ."

The streetlights were on, and we glimpsed Calpurnia's indignant profile as we passed beneath them. "Mister Jem, I thought you was gettin' some kinda head on your shoulders—the very idea, she's your little sister! The very *idea*, sir! You oughta be perfectly ashamed of yourself—ain't you got any sense at all?"

I was exhilarated. So many things had happened so fast I felt it would take years to sort them out, and now here was Calpurnia giving her precious Jem down the country—what new marvels would the evening bring?

Jem was chuckling. "Don't you want to hear about it, Cal?"

"Hush your mouth, sir! When you oughta be hangin' your head in shame you go along laughin'—" Calpurnia revived a series of rusty threats that moved Jem to little remorse, and she sailed up the front steps with her classic, "If Mr. Finch don't wear you out, I will—get in that house, sir!"

Jem went in grinning, and Calpurnia nodded tacit consent to having Dill in to supper. "You all call Miss Rachel right now and tell her where you are," she told him. "She's run distracted lookin' for you—you watch out she don't ship you back to Meridian first thing in the mornin'."

Aunt Alexandra met us and nearly fainted when Calpurnia told her where we were. I guess it hurt her when we told her Atticus said we could go back, because she didn't say a word during supper. She just rearranged food on her plate, looking at it sadly while Calpurnia served Jem, Dill and me with a vengeance. Calpurnia poured milk, dished out potato salad and ham, muttering, "'shamed of yourselves," in varying degrees of intensity. "Now you all eat slow," was her final command.

Reverend Sykes had saved our places. We were surprised to find that we had been gone nearly an hour, and were equally surprised to find the courtroom exactly as we had left it, with minor changes: the jury box was empty, the defendant was gone; Judge Taylor had been gone, but he reappeared as we were seating ourselves.

"Nobody's moved, hardly," said Jem.

"They moved around some when the jury went out," said Reverend Sykes. "The menfolk down there got the womenfolk their suppers, and they fed their babies."

"How long have they been out?" asked Jem.

"'bout thirty minutes. Mr. Finch and Mr. Gilmer did some more talkin', and Judge Taylor charged the jury."

"How was he?" asked Jem.

"What say? Oh, he did right well. I ain't complainin' one bit—he was mighty fair-minded. He sorta said if you believe this, then you'll have to return one verdict, but if you believe this, you'll have to return another one. I thought he was leanin' a little to our side—" Reverend Sykes scratched his head.

Jem smiled. "He's not supposed to lean, Reverend, but don't fret, we've won it," he said wisely. "Don't see how any jury could convict on what we heard—"

"Now don't you be so confident, Mr. Jem, I ain't ever seen any jury decide in favor of a colored man over a white man. . ." But Jem took exception to Reverend Sykes, and we were subjected to a lengthy review of the evidence with Jem's ideas on the law regarding rape: it wasn't rape if she let you, but she had to be eighteen—in Alabama, that is—and Mayella was nineteen. Apparently you had to kick and holler, you had to be overpowered and stomped on, preferably knocked stone cold. If you were under eighteen, you didn't have to go through all this.

"Mr. Jem," Reverend Sykes demurred, "this ain't a polite thing for little ladies to hear . . ."

"Aw, she doesn't know what we're talkin' about," said Jem. "Scout, this is too old for you, ain't it?"

211

"It most certainly is not, I know every word you're saying." Perhaps I was too convincing, because Jem hushed and never discussed the subject again.

"What time is it, Reverend?" he asked.

"Gettin' on toward eight."

I looked down and saw Atticus strolling around with his hands in his pockets: he made a tour of the windows, then walked by the railing over to the jury box. He looked in it, inspected Judge Taylor on his throne, then went back to where he started. I caught his eye and waved to him. He acknowledged my salute with a nod, and resumed his tour.

Mr. Gilmer was standing at the windows talking to Mr. Underwood. Bert, the court reporter, was chain-smoking: he sat back with his feet on the table.

But the officers of the court, the ones present—Atticus, Mr. Gilmer, Judge Taylor sound asleep, and Bert, were the only ones whose behavior seemed normal. I had never seen a packed courtroom so still. Sometimes a baby would cry out fretfully, and a child would scurry out, but the grown people sat as if they were in church. In the balcony, the Negroes sat and stood around us with biblical patience.

The old courthouse clock suffered its preliminary strain and struck the hour, eight deafening bongs that shook our bones.

When it bonged eleven times I was past feeling: tired from fighting sleep, I allowed myself a short nap against Reverend Sykes's comfortable arm and shoulder. I jerked awake and made an honest effort to remain so, by looking down and concentrating on the heads below: there were sixteen bald ones, fourteen men that could pass for redheads, forty heads varying between brown and black, and—I remembered something Jem had once explained to me when he went through a brief period of psychical research: he said if enough people—a stadium full, maybe—were to concentrate on one thing, such as setting a tree afire in the woods, that the tree would ignite of its own accord. I toyed with the idea of asking everyone below to concentrate on setting Tom Robinson free, but thought if they were as tired as I, it wouldn't work.

212

Dill was sound asleep, his head on Jem's shoulder, and Jem was quiet.

"Ain't it a long time?" I asked him.

"Sure is, Scout," he said happily.

"Well, from the way you put it, it'd just take five minutes."

Jem raised his eyebrows. "There are things you don't understand," he said, and I was too weary to argue.

But I must have been reasonably awake, or I would not have received the impression that was creeping into me. It was not unlike one I had last winter, and I shivered, though the night was hot. The feeling grew until the atmosphere in the courtroom was exactly the same as a cold February morning, when the mockingbirds were still, and the carpenters had stopped hammering on Miss Maudie's new house, and every wood door in the neighborhood was shut as tight as the doors of the Radley Place. A deserted, waiting, empty street, and the courtroom was packed with people. A steaming summer night was no different from a winter morning. Mr. Heck Tate, who had entered the courtroom and was talking to Atticus, might have been wearing his high boots and lumber jacket. Atticus had stopped his tranquil journey and had put his foot onto the bottom rung of a chair; as he listened to what Mr. Tate was saying, he ran his hand slowly up and down his thigh. I expected Mr. Tate to say any minute, "Take him, Mr. Finch. . . ."

But Mr. Tate said, "This court will come to order," in a voice that rang with authority, and the heads below us jerked up. Mr. Tate left the room and returned with Tom Robinson. He steered Tom to his place beside Atticus, and stood there. Judge Taylor had roused himself to sudden alertness and was sitting up straight, looking at the empty jury box.

What happened after that had a dreamlike quality: in a dream I saw the jury return, moving like underwater swimmers, and Judge Taylor's voice came from far away and was tiny. I saw something only a lawyer's child could be expected to see, could be expected to watch for, and it was like watching Atticus walk into the street, raise a rifle to his shoulder and pull the trigger, but watching all the time knowing that the gun was empty.

A jury never looks at a defendant it has convicted,

and when this jury came in, not one of them looked at Tom Robinson. The foreman handed a piece of paper to Mr. Tate who handed it to the clerk who handed it to the judge. . . .

I shut my eyes. Judge Taylor was polling the jury: "Guilty . . . guilty . . . guilty . . . guilty . . ." I peeked at Jem: his hands were white from gripping the balcony rail, and his shoulders jerked as if each "guilty" was a separate stab between them.

Judge Taylor was saying something. His gavel was in his fist, but he wasn't using it. Dimly, I saw Atticus pushing papers from the table into his briefcase. He snapped it shut, went to the court reporter and said something, nodded to Mr. Gilmer, and then went to Tom Robinson and whispered something to him. Atticus put his hand on Tom's shoulder as he whispered. Atticus took his coat off the back of his chair and pulled it over his shoulder. Then he left the courtroom, but not by his usual exit. He must have wanted to go home the short way, because he walked quickly down the middle aisle toward the south exit. I followed the top of his head as he made his way to the door. He did not look up.

Someone was punching me, but I was reluctant to take my eyes from the people below us, and from the image of Atticus's lonely walk down the aisle.

"Miss Jean Louise?"

I looked around. They were standing. All around us and in the balcony on the opposite wall, the Negroes were getting to their feet. Reverend Sykes's voice was as distant as Judge Taylor's:

"Miss Jean Louise, stand up. Your father's passin'."

22.

It was Jem's turn to cry. His face was streaked with angry tears as we made our way through the cheerful crowd. "It ain't right," he muttered, all the way to the corner of the square where we found Atticus waiting. Atticus was standing under the street light looking as though nothing had happened: his vest was buttoned, his collar and tie were neatly in place, his watch-chain glistened, he was his impassive self again.

"It ain't right, Atticus," said Jem.

"No son, it's not right."

We walked home.

Aunt Alexandra was waiting up. She was in her dressing gown, and I could have sworn she had on her corset underneath it. "I'm sorry, brother," she murmured. Having never heard her call Atticus "brother" before, I stole a glance at Jem, but he was not listening. He would look up at Atticus, then down at the floor, and I wondered if he thought Atticus somehow responsible for Tom Robinson's conviction.

"Is he all right?" Aunty asked, indicating Jem.

"He'll be so presently," said Atticus. "It was a little too strong for him." Our father sighed. "I'm going to bed," he said. "If I don't wake up in the morning, don't call me."

"I didn't think it wise in the first place to let them—"

"This is their home, sister," said Atticus. "We've made it this way for them, they might as well learn to cope with it."

"But they don't have to go to the courthouse and wallow in it—"

"It's just as much Maycomb County as missionary teas."

"Atticus—" Aunt Alexandra's eyes were anxious. "You are the last person I thought would turn bitter over this."

"I'm not bitter, just tired. I'm going to bed."

"Atticus—" said Jem bleakly.

He turned in the doorway. "What, son?"

"How could they do it, how could they?"

"I don't know, but they did it. They've done it before and they did it tonight and they'll do it again and when they do it—seems that only children weep. Good night."

But things are always better in the morning. Atticus rose at his usual ungodly hour and was in the livingroom behind the *Mobile Register* when we stumbled in. Jem's morning face posed the question his sleepy lips struggled to ask.

"It's not time to worry yet," Atticus reassured him, as we went to the diningroom. "We're not through yet. There'll be an appeal, you can count on that. Gracious alive, Cal, what's all this?" He was staring at his breakfast plate.

Calpurnia said, "Tom Robinson's daddy sent you along this chicken this morning. I fixed it."

"You tell him I'm proud to get it—bet they don't have chicken for breakfast at the White House. What are these?"

"Rolls," said Calpurnia. "Estelle down at the hotel sent 'em."

Atticus looked up at her, puzzled, and she said, "You better step out here and see what's in the kitchen, Mr. Finch."

We followed him. The kitchen table was loaded with enough food to bury the family: hunks of salt pork, tomatoes, beans, even scuppernongs. Atticus grinned when he found a jar of pickled pigs' knuckles. "Reckon Aunty'll let me eat these in the diningroom?"

Calpurnia said, "This was all 'round the back steps when I got here this morning. They—they 'preciate what you did, Mr. Finch. They—they aren't oversteppin' themselves, are they?"

Atticus's eyes filled with tears. He did not speak for a moment. "Tell them I'm very grateful," he said. "Tell them—tell them they must never do this again. Times are too hard. . . ."

He left the kitchen, went in the diningroom and excused himself to Aunt Alexandra, put on his hat and went to town.

We heard Dill's step in the hall, so Calpurnia left Atticus's uneaten breakfast on the table. Between rabbit-bites Dill told us of Miss Rachel's reaction to last night, which was: if a man like Atticus Finch wants to butt his head against a stone wall it's his head.

"I'da got her told," growled Dill, gnawing a chicken leg, "but she didn't look much like tellin' this morning. Said she was up half the night wonderin' where I was, said she'da had the sheriff after me but he was at the hearing."

"Dill, you've got to stop goin' off without tellin' her," said Jem. "It just aggravates her."

Dill sighed patiently. "I told her till I was blue in the face where I was goin'—she's just seein' too many snakes in the closet. Bet that woman drinks a pint for breakfast every morning—know she drinks two glasses full. Seen her."

"Don't talk like that, Dill," said Aunt Alexandra. "It's not becoming to a child. It's—cynical."

"I ain't cynical, Miss Alexandra. Tellin' the truth's not cynical, is it?"

"The way you tell it, it is."

Jem's eyes flashed at her, but he said to Dill, "Let's go. You can take that runner with you."

When we went to the front porch, Miss Stephanie Crawford was busy telling it to Miss Maudie Atkinson and Mr. Avery. They looked around at us and went on talking. Jem made a feral noise in his throat. I wished for a weapon.

"I hate grown folks lookin' at you," said Dill. "Makes you feel like you've done something."

Miss Maudie yelled for Jem Finch to come there.

Jem groaned and heaved himself up from the swing. "We'll go with you," Dill said.

Miss Stephanie's nose quivered with curiosity. She wanted to know who all gave us permission to go to court —she didn't see us but it was all over town this morning that we were in the Colored balcony. Did Atticus put us up there as a sort of—? Wasn't it right close up there with all those—? Did Scout understand all the—? Didn't it make us mad to see our daddy beat?

"Hush, Stephanie." Miss Maudie's diction was deadly. "I've not got all the morning to pass on the porch—Jem Finch, I called to find out if you and your colleagues can eat some cake. Got up at five to make it, so you better say yes. Excuse us, Stephanie. Good morning, Mr. Avery."

There was a big cake and two little ones on Miss Maudie's kitchen table. There should have been three little ones. It was not like Miss Maudie to forget Dill, and we must have shown it. But we understood when she cut from the big cake and gave the slice to Jem.

As we ate, we sensed that this was Miss Maudie's way of saying that as far as she was concerned, nothing had changed. She sat quietly in a kitchen chair, watching us.

Suddenly she spoke: "Don't fret, Jem. Things are never as bad as they seem."

Indoors, when Miss Maudie wanted to say something lengthy she spread her fingers on her knees and settled her bridgework. This she did, and we waited.

"I simply want to tell you that there are some men in this world who were born to do our unpleasant jobs for us. Your father's one of them."

"Oh," said Jem. "Well."

"Don't you oh well me, sir," Miss Maudie replied, recognizing Jem's fatalistic noises, "you are not old enough to appreciate what I said."

Jem was staring at his half-eaten cake. "It's like bein' a caterpillar in a cocoon, that's what it is," he said. "Like somethin' asleep wrapped up in a warm place. I always thought Maycomb folks were the best folks in the world, least that's what they seemed like."

"We're the safest folks in the world," said Miss Maudie. "We're so rarely called on to be Christians, but when we are, we've got men like Atticus to go for us."

Jem grinned ruefully. "Wish the rest of the county thought that."

"You'd be surprised how many of us do."

"Who?" Jem's voice rose. "Who in this town did one thing to help Tom Robinson, just who?"

"His colored friends for one thing, and people like us. People like Judge Taylor. People like Mr. Heck Tate. Stop eating and start thinking, Jem. Did it ever strike you that Judge Taylor naming Atticus to defend that boy was no accident? That Judge Taylor might have had his reasons for naming him?"

This was a thought. Court-appointed defenses were usually given to Maxwell Green, Maycomb's latest addition to the bar, who needed the experience. Maxwell Green should have had Tom Robinson's case.

"You think about that," Miss Maudie was saying. "It was no accident. I was sittin' there on the porch last night, waiting. I waited and waited to see you all come down the sidewalk, and as I waited I thought, Atticus Finch won't win, he can't win, but he's the only man in these parts who can keep a jury out so long in a case like that. And I thought to myself, well, we're making a step

—it's just a baby-step, but it's a step."

" 't's all right to talk like that—can't any Christian judges an' lawyers make up for heathen juries," Jem muttered. "Soon's I get grown—"

"That's something you'll have to take up with your father," Miss Maudie said.

We went down Miss Maudie's cool new steps into the sunshine and found Mr. Avery and Miss Stephanie Crawford still at it. They had moved down the sidewalk and were standing in front of Miss Stephanie's house. Miss Rachel was walking toward them.

"I think I'll be a clown when I get grown," said Dill.

Jem and I stopped in our tracks.

"Yes sir, a clown," he said. "There ain't one thing in this world I can do about folks except laugh, so I'm gonna join the circus and laugh my head off."

"You got it backwards, Dill," said Jem. "Clowns are sad, it's folks that laugh at them."

"Well I'm gonna be a new kind of clown. I'm gonna stand in the middle of the ring and laugh at the folks. Just looka yonder," he pointed. "Every one of 'em oughta be ridin' broomsticks. Aunt Rachel already does."

Miss Stephanie and Miss Rachel were waving wildly at us, in a way that did not give the lie to Dill's observation.

"Oh gosh," breathed Jem. "I reckon it'd be ugly not to see 'em."

Something was wrong. Mr. Avery was red in the face from a sneezing spell and nearly blew us off the sidewalk when we came up. Miss Stephanie was trembling with excitement, and Miss Rachel caught Dill's shoulder. "You get on in the back yard and stay there," she said. "There's danger a'comin'."

" 's matter?" I asked.

"Ain't you heard yet? It's all over town—"

At that moment Aunt Alexandra came to the door and called us, but she was too late. It was Miss Stephanie's pleasure to tell us: this morning Mr. Bob Ewell stopped Atticus on the post office corner, spat in his face, and told him he'd get him if it took the rest of his life.

23.

          I wish Bob Ewell wouldn't chew tobacco," was all Atticus said about it.

According to Miss Stephanie Crawford, however, Atticus was leaving the post office when Mr. Ewell approached him, cursed him, spat on him, and threatened to kill him. Miss Stephanie (who, by the time she had told it twice was there and had seen it all—passing by from the Jitney Jungle, she was)—Miss Stephanie said Atticus didn't bat an eye, just took out his handkerchief and wiped his face and stood there and let Mr. Ewell call him names wild horses could not bring her to repeat. Mr. Ewell was a veteran of an obscure war; that plus Atticus's peaceful reaction probably prompted him to inquire, "Too proud to fight, you nigger-lovin' bastard?" Miss Stephanie said Atticus said, "No, too old," put his hands in his pockets and strolled on. Miss Stephanie said you had to hand it to Atticus Finch, he could be right dry sometimes.

Jem and I didn't think it entertaining.

"After all, though," I said, "he was the deadest shot in the county one time. He could—"

"You know he wouldn't carry a gun, Scout. He ain't even got one—" said Jem. "You know he didn't even have one down at the jail that night. He told me havin' a gun around's an invitation to somebody to shoot you."

"This is different," I said. "We can ask him to borrow one."

We did, and he said, "Nonsense."

Dill was of the opinion that an appeal to Atticus's better nature might work: after all, we would starve if Mr. Ewell killed him, besides be raised exclusively by Aunt Alexandra, and we all knew the first thing she'd do before Atticus was under the ground good would be to fire Calpurnia. Jem said it might work if I cried and flung a fit, being young and a girl. That didn't work either.

But when he noticed us dragging around the neighborhood, not eating, taking little interest in our normal pursuits, Atticus discovered how deeply frightened we were. He tempted Jem with a new football magazine one night; when he saw Jem flip the pages and toss it aside, he said, "What's bothering you, son?"

Jem came to the point: "Mr. Ewell."

"What has happened?"

"Nothing's happened. We're scared for you, and we think you oughta do something about him."

Atticus smiled wryly. "Do what? Put him under a peace bond?"

"When a man says he's gonna get you, looks like he means it."

"He meant it when he said it," said Atticus. "Jem, see if you can stand in Bob Ewell's shoes a minute. I destroyed his last shred of credibility at that trial, if he had any to begin with. The man had to have some kind of comeback, his kind always does. So if spitting in my face and threatening me saved Mayella Ewell one extra beating, that's something I'll gladly take. He had to take it out on somebody and I'd rather it be me than that houseful of children out there. You understand?"

Jem nodded.

Aunt Alexandra entered the room as Atticus was saying, "We don't have anything to fear from Bob Ewell, he got it all out of his system that morning."

"I wouldn't be so sure of that, Atticus," she said. "His kind'd do anything to pay off a grudge. You know how those people are."

"What on earth could Ewell do to me, sister?"

"Something furtive," Aunt Alexandra said. "You may count on that."

"Nobody has much chance to be furtive in Maycomb," Atticus answered.

After that, we were not afraid. Summer was melting away, and we made the most of it. Atticus assured us that nothing would happen to Tom Robinson until the higher court reviewed his case, and that Tom had a good chance of going free, or at least of having a new trial. He was at Enfield Prison Farm, seventy miles away in Chester County. I asked Atticus if Tom's wife and children were allowed to visit him, but Atticus said no.

"If he loses his appeal," I asked one evening, "what'll happen to him?"

"He'll go to the chair," said Atticus, "unless the Governor commutes his sentence. Not time to worry yet, Scout. We've got a good chance."

Jem was sprawled on the sofa reading *Popular Mechanics*. He looked up. "It ain't right. He didn't kill anybody even if he was guilty. He didn't take anybody's life."

"You know rape's a capital offense in Alabama," said Atticus.

"Yessir, but the jury didn't have to give him death— if they wanted to they could've gave him twenty years."

"Given," said Atticus. "Tom Robinson's a colored man, Jem. No jury in this part of the world's going to say, 'We think you're guilty, but not very,' on a charge like that. It was either a straight acquittal or nothing."

Jem was shaking his head. "I know it's not right, but I can't figure out what's wrong—maybe rape shouldn't be a capital offense. . . ."

Atticus dropped his newspaper beside his chair. He said he didn't have any quarrel with the rape statute, none whatever, but he did have deep misgivings when the state asked for and the jury gave a death penalty on purely circumstantial evidence. He glanced at me, saw I was listening, and made it easier. "—I mean, before a man is sentenced to death for murder, say, there should be one or two eye-witnesses. Someone should be able to say, 'Yes, I was there and saw him pull the trigger.'"

"But lots of folks have been hung—hanged—on circumstantial evidence," said Jem.

"I know, and lots of 'em probably deserved it, too— but in the absence of eye-witnesses there's always a doubt, sometimes only the shadow of a doubt. The law says 'reasonable doubt,' but I think a defendant's entitled to the shadow of a doubt. There's always the possibility, no matter how improbable, that he's innocent."

"Then it all goes back to the jury, then. We oughta do away with juries." Jem was adamant.

Atticus tried hard not to smile but couldn't help it. "You're rather hard on us, son. I think maybe there might be a better way. Change the law. Change it so that only judges have the power of fixing the penalty in capital cases."

"Then go up to Montgomery and change the law."

"You'd be surprised how hard that'd be. I won't live to see the law changed, and if you live to see it you'll be an old man."

This was not good enough for Jem. "No sir, they oughta do away with juries. He wasn't guilty in the first place and they said he was."

"If you had been on that jury, son, and eleven other boys like you, Tom would be a free man," said Atticus. "So far nothing in your life has interfered with your reasoning process. Those are twelve reasonable men in everyday life, Tom's jury, but you saw something come between them and reason. You saw the same thing that night in front of the jail. When that crew went away, they didn't go as reasonable men, they went because we were there. There's something in our world that makes men lose their heads—they couldn't be fair if they tried. In our courts, when it's a white man's word against a black man's, the white man always wins. They're ugly, but those are the facts of life."

"Doesn't make it right," said Jem stolidly. He beat his fist softly on his knee. "You just can't convict a man on evidence like that—you can't."

"You couldn't, but they could and did. The older you grow the more of it you'll see. The one place where a man ought to get a square deal is in a courtroom, be he any color of the rainbow, but people have a way of carrying their resentments right into a jury box. As you grow older, you'll see white men cheat black men every day of your life, but let me tell you something and don't you forget it—whenever a white man does that to a black man, no matter who he is, how rich he is, or how fine a family he comes from, that white man is trash."

Atticus was speaking so quietly his last word crashed on our ears. I looked up, and his face was vehement. "There's nothing more sickening to me than a low-grade white man who'll take advantage of a Negro's ignorance. Don't fool yourselves—it's all adding up and one of these days we're going to pay the bill for it. I hope it's not in you children's time."

Jem was scratching his head. Suddenly his eyes widened. "Atticus," he said, "why don't people like us and Miss Maudie ever sit on juries? You never see anybody from Maycomb on a jury—they all come from out in the woods."

Atticus leaned back in his rocking-chair. For some reason he looked pleased with Jem. "I was wondering when that'd occur to you," he said. "There are lots of reasons. For one thing, Miss Maudie can't serve on a jury because she's a woman—"

"You mean women in Alabama can't—?" I was indignant.

"I do. I guess it's to protect our frail ladies from sordid cases like Tom's. Besides," Atticus grinned, "I doubt if we'd ever get a complete case tried—the ladies'd be interrupting to ask questions."

Jem and I laughed. Miss Maudie on a jury would be impressive. I thought of old Mrs. Dubose in her wheelchair—"Stop that rapping, John Taylor, I want to ask this man something." Perhaps our forefathers were wise.

Atticus was saying, "With people like us—that's our share of the bill. We generally get the juries we deserve. Our stout Maycomb citizens aren't interested, in the first place. In the second place, they're afraid. Then, they're—"

"Afraid, why?" asked Jem.

"Well, what if—say, Mr. Link Deas had to decide the amount of damages to award, say, Miss Maudie, when Miss Rachel ran over her with a car. Link wouldn't like the thought of losing either lady's business at his store, would he? So he tells Judge Taylor that he can't serve on the jury because he doesn't have anybody to keep store for him while he's gone. So Judge Taylor excuses him. Sometimes he excuses him wrathfully."

"What'd make him think either one of 'em'd stop trading with him?" I asked.

Jem said, "Miss Rachel would, Miss Maudie wouldn't. But a jury's vote's secret, Atticus."

Our father chuckled. "You've many more miles to go, son. A jury's vote's supposed to be secret. Serving on a jury forces a man to make up his mind and declare himself about something. Men don't like to do that. Sometimes it's unpleasant."

"Tom's jury sho' made up its mind in a hurry," Jem muttered.

Atticus's fingers went to his watchpocket. "No it didn't," he said, more to himself than to us. "That was the one thing that made me think, well, this may be the shadow of a beginning. That jury took a few hours. An inevitable verdict, maybe, but usually it takes 'em just a few minutes. This time—" he broke off and looked at us. "You might like to know that there was one fellow who took considerable wearing down—in the beginning he was rarin' for an outright acquittal."

"Who?" Jem was astonished.

Atticus's eyes twinkled. "It's not for me to say, but I'll tell you this much. He was one of your Old Sarum friends . . ."

"One of the Cunninghams?" Jem yelped. "One of—I didn't recognize any of 'em . . . you're jokin'." He looked at Atticus from the corners of his eyes.

"One of their connections. On a hunch, I didn't strike him. Just on a hunch. Could've, but I didn't."

"Golly Moses," Jem said reverently. "One minute they're tryin' to kill him and the next they're tryin' to turn him loose . . . I'll never understand those folks as long as I live."

Atticus said you just had to know 'em. He said the Cunninghams hadn't taken anything from or off of anybody since they migrated to the New World. He said the other thing about them was, once you earned their respect they were for you tooth and nail. Atticus said he had a feeling, nothing more than a suspicion, that they left the jail that night with considerable respect for the Finches. Then too, he said, it took a thunderbolt plus another Cunningham to make one of them change his mind. "If we'd had two of that crowd, we'd've had a hung jury."

Jem said slowly, "You mean you actually put on the jury a man who wanted to kill you the night before? How could you take such a risk, Atticus, how could you?"

"When you analyze it, there was little risk. There's no difference between one man who's going to convict and another man who's going to convict, is there? There's a faint difference between a man who's going to convict and a man who's a little disturbed in his mind, isn't there? He was the only uncertainty on the whole list."

"What kin was that man to Mr. Walter Cunningham?" I asked.

Atticus rose, stretched and yawned. It was not even our bedtime, but we knew he wanted a chance to read his newspaper. He picked it up, folded it, and tapped my head. "Let's see now," he droned to himself. "I've got it. Double first cousin."

"How can that be?"

"Two sisters married two brothers. That's all I'll tell you—you figure it out."

I tortured myself and decided that if I married Jem and Dill had a sister whom he married our children would be double first cousins. "Gee minetti, Jem," I said, when Atticus had gone, "they're funny folks. 'd you hear that, Aunty?"

Aunt Alexandra was hooking a rug and not watching us, but she was listening. She sat in her chair with her workbasket beside it, her rug spread across her lap. Why ladies hooked woolen rugs on boiling nights never became clear to me.

"I heard it," she said.

I remembered the distant disastrous occasion when I rushed to young Walter Cunningham's defense. Now I was glad I'd done it. "Soon's school starts I'm gonna ask Walter home to dinner," I planned, having forgotten my private resolve to beat him up the next time I saw him. "He can stay over sometimes after school, too. Atticus could drive him back to Old Sarum. Maybe he could spend the night with us sometime, okay, Jem?"

"We'll see about that," Aunt Alexandra said, a declaration that with her was always a threat, never a promise. Surprised, I turned to her. "Why not, Aunty? They're good folks."

She looked at me over her sewing glasses. "Jean Louise, there is no doubt in my mind that they're good folks. But they're not our kind of folks."

Jem says, "She means they're yappy, Scout."

"What's a yap?"

"Aw, tacky. They like fiddlin' and things like that."

"Well I do too—"

"Don't be silly, Jean Louise," said Aunt Alexandra. "The thing is, you can scrub Walter Cunningham till he shines, you can put him in shoes and a new suit, but he'll never be like Jem. Besides, there's a drinking streak in that family a mile wide. Finch women aren't interested in that sort of people."

"Aun-ty," said Jem, "she ain't nine yet."

"She may as well learn it now."

Aunt Alexandra had spoken. I was reminded vividly of the last time she had put her foot down. I never knew why. It was when I was absorbed with plans to visit Calpurnia's house—I was curious, interested; I wanted to be her "company," to see how she lived, who her friends were. I might as well have wanted to see the other side of the moon. This time the tactics were different, but Aunt Alexandra's aim was the same. Perhaps this was why she had come to live with us—to help us choose our friends. I would hold her off as long as I could: "If they're good folks, then why can't I be nice to Walter?"

"I didn't say not to be nice to him. You should be friendly and polite to him, you should be gracious to everybody, dear. But you don't have to invite him home."

"What if he was kin to us, Aunty?"

"The fact is that he is not kin to us, but if he were, my answer would be the same."

"Aunty," Jem spoke up, "Atticus says you can choose your friends but you sho' can't choose your family, an' they're still kin to you no matter whether you acknowledge 'em or not, and it makes you look right silly when you don't."

"That's your father all over again," said Aunt Alexandra, "and I still say that Jean Louise will not invite Walter Cunningham to this house. If he were her double first cousin once removed he would still not be received in this house unless he comes to see Atticus on business. Now that is that."

She had said Indeed Not, but this time she would give her reasons: "But I want to play with Walter, Aunty, why can't I?"

She took off her glasses and stared at me. "I'll tell you why," she said. "Because—he—is—trash, that's why you can't play with him. I'll not have you around him, picking up his habits and learning Lord-knows-what. You're enough of a problem to your father as it is."

I don't know what I would have done, but Jem stopped me. He caught me by the shoulders, put his arm around me, and led me sobbing in fury to his bedroom. Atticus heard us and poked his head around the door. "'s all right, sir," Jem said gruffly, "'s not anything." Atticus went away.

"Have a chew, Scout." Jem dug into his pocket and extracted a Tootsie Roll. It took a few minutes to work the candy into a comfortable wad inside my jaw.

Jem was rearranging the objects on his dresser. His hair stuck up behind and down in front, and I wondered if it would ever look like a man's—maybe if he shaved it off and started over, his hair would grow back neatly in place. His eyebrows were becoming heavier, and I noticed a new slimness about his body. He was growing taller.

When he looked around, he must have thought I would start crying again, for he said, "Show you something if you won't tell anybody." I said what. He unbuttoned his shirt, grinning shyly.

"Well what?"

"Well can't you see it?"

"Well no."

"Well it's hair."

"Where?"

"There. Right there."

He had been a comfort to me, so I said it looked lovely, but I didn't see anything. "It's real nice, Jem."

"Under my arms, too," he said. "Goin' out for football next year. Scout, don't let Aunty aggravate you."

It seemed only yesterday that he was telling me not to aggravate Aunty.

"You know she's not used to girls," said Jem, "leastways, not girls like you. She's trying to make you a lady. Can't you take up sewin' or somethin'?"

"Hell no. She doesn't like me, that's all there is to it, and I don't care. It was her callin' Walter Cunningham trash that got me goin', Jem, not what she said about being a problem to Atticus. We got that all straight one time, I asked him if I was a problem and he said not much of one, at most one that he could always figure out, and not to worry my head a second about botherin' him. Naw, it was Walter—that boy's not trash, Jem. He ain't like the Ewells."

Jem kicked off his shoes and swung his feet to the

bed. He propped himself against a pillow and switched on the reading light. "You know something, Scout? I've got it all figured out, now. I've thought about it a lot lately and I've got it figured out. There's four kinds of folks in the world. There's the ordinary kind like us and the neighbors, there's the kind like the Cunninghams out in the woods, the kind like the Ewells down at the dump, and the Negroes."

"What about the Chinese, and the Cajuns down yonder in Baldwin County?"

"I mean in Maycomb County. The thing about it is, our kind of folks don't like the Cunninghams, the Cunninghams don't like the Ewells, and the Ewells hate and despise the colored folks."

I told Jem if that was so, then why didn't Tom's jury, made up of folks like the Cunninghams, acquit Tom to spite the Ewells?

Jem waved my question away as being infantile.

"You know," he said, "I've seen Atticus pat his foot when there's fiddlin' on the radio, and he loves pot liquor better'n any man I ever saw—"

"Then that makes us like the Cunninghams," I said. "I can't see why Aunty—"

"No, lemme finish—it does, but we're still different somehow. Atticus said one time the reason Aunty's so hipped on the family is because all we've got's background and not a dime to our names."

"Well Jem, I don't know—Atticus told me one time that most of this Old Family stuff's foolishness because everybody's family's just as old as everybody else's. I said did that include the colored folks and Englishmen and he said yes."

"Background doesn't mean Old Family," said Jem. "I think it's how long your family's been readin' and writin'. Scout, I've studied this real hard and that's the only reason I can think of. Somewhere along when the Finches were in Egypt one of 'em must have learned a hieroglyphic or two and he taught his boy." Jem laughed. "Imagine Aunty being proud her great-grandaddy could read an' write—ladies pick funny things to be proud of."

"Well I'm glad he could, or who'da taught Atticus and them, and if Atticus couldn't read, you and me'd be in a fix. I don't think that's what background is, Jem."

"Well then, how do you explain why the Cunninghams are different? Mr. Walter can hardly sign his name, I've seen him. We've just been readin' and writin' longer'n they have."

"No, everybody's gotta learn, nobody's born knowin'. That Walter's as smart as he can be, he just gets held back sometimes because he has to stay out and help his daddy. Nothin's wrong with him. Naw, Jem, I think there's just one kind of folks. Folks."

Jem turned around and punched his pillow. When he settled back his face was cloudy. He was going into one of his declines, and I grew wary. His brows came together; his mouth became a thin line. He was silent for a while.

"That's what I thought, too," he said at last, "when I was your age. If there's just one kind of folks, why can't they get along with each other? If they're all alike, why do they go out of their way to despise each other? Scout, I think I'm beginning to understand something. I think I'm beginning to understand why Boo Radley's stayed shut up in the house all this time . . . it's because he *wants* to stay inside."

24.

Calpurnia wore her stiffest starched apron. She carried a tray of charlotte. She backed up to the swinging door and pressed gently. I admired the ease and grace with which she handled heavy loads of dainty things. So did Aunt Alexandra, I guess, because she had let Calpurnia serve today.

August was on the brink of September. Dill would be leaving for Meridian tomorrow; today he was off with Jem at Barker's Eddy. Jem had discovered with angry amazement that nobody had ever bothered to teach Dill how to swim, a skill Jem considered necessary as walking. They had spent two afternoons at the creek, they said they were going in naked and I couldn't come, so I divided

230

the lonely hours between Calpurnia and Miss Maudie.

Today Aunt Alexandra and her missionary circle were fighting the good fight all over the house. From the kitchen, I heard Mrs. Grace Merriweather giving a report in the livingroom on the squalid lives of the Mrunas, it sounded like to me. They put the women out in huts when their time came, whatever that was; they had no sense of family—I knew that'd distress Aunty—they subjected children to terrible ordeals when they were thirteen; they were crawling with yaws and earworms, they chewed up and spat out the bark of a tree into a communal pot and then got drunk on it.

Immediately thereafter, the ladies adjourned for refreshments.

I didn't know whether to go into the diningroom or stay out. Aunt Alexandra told me to join them for refreshments; it was not necessary that I attend the business part of the meeting, she said it'd bore me. I was wearing my pink Sunday dress, shoes, and a petticoat, and reflected that if I spilled anything Calpurnia would have to wash my dress again for tomorrow. This had been a busy day for her. I decided to stay out.

"Can I help you, Cal?" I asked, wishing to be of some service.

Calpurnia paused in the doorway. "You be still as a mouse in that corner," she said, "an' you can help me load up the trays when I come back."

The gentle hum of ladies' voices grew louder as she opened the door: "Why, Alexandra, I never saw such charlotte . . . just lovely . . . I never can get my crust like this, never can . . . who'd've thought of little dewberry tarts . . . Calpurnia? . . . who'da thought it . . . anybody tell you that the preacher's wife's . . . no-oo, well she is, and that other one not walkin' yet. . . ."

They became quiet, and I knew they had all been served. Calpurnia returned and put my mother's heavy silver pitcher on a tray. "This coffee pitcher's a curiosity," she murmured, "they don't make 'em these days."

"Can I carry it in?"

"If you be careful and don't drop it. Set it down at the end of the table by Miss Alexandra. Down there by the cups'n things. She's gonna pour."

I tried pressing my behind against the door as Calpurnia had done, but the door didn't budge. Grinning, she held it open for me. "Careful now, it's heavy. Don't look at it and you won't spill it."

My journey was successful: Aunt Alexandra smiled brilliantly. "Stay with us, Jean Louise," she said. This was a part of her campaign to teach me to be a lady.

It was customary for every circle hostess to invite her neighbors in for refreshments, be they Baptists or Presbyterians, which accounted for the presence of Miss Rachel (sober as a judge), Miss Maudie and Miss Stephanie Crawford. Rather nervous, I took a seat beside Miss Maudie and wondered why ladies put on their hats to go across the street. Ladies in bunches always filled me with vague apprehension and a firm desire to be elsewhere, but this feeling was what Aunt Alexandra called being "spoiled."

The ladies were cool in fragile pastel prints: most of them were heavily powdered but unrouged; the only lipstick in the room was Tangee Natural. Cutex Natural sparkled on their fingernails, but some of the younger ladies wore Rose. They smelled heavenly. I sat quietly, having conquered my hands by tightly gripping the arms of the chair, and waited for someone to speak to me.

Miss Maudie's gold bridgework twinkled. "You're mighty dressed up, Miss Jean Louise," she said. "Where are your britches today?"

"Under my dress."

I hadn't meant to be funny, but the ladies laughed. My cheeks grew hot as I realized my mistake, but Miss Maudie looked gravely down at me. She never laughed at me unless I meant to be funny.

In the sudden silence that followed, Miss Stephanie Crawford called from across the room, "Whatcha going to be when you grow up, Jean Louise? A lawyer?"

"Nome, I hadn't thought about it . . ." I answered, grateful that Miss Stephanie was kind enough to change the subject. Hurriedly I began choosing my vocation. Nurse? Aviator? "Well . . ."

"Why shoot, I thought you wanted to be a lawyer, you've already commenced going to court."

The ladies laughed again. "That Stephanie's a card," somebody said. Miss Stephanie was encouraged to pursue the subject: "Don't you want to grow up to be a lawyer?"

Miss Maudie's hand touched mine and I answered mildly enough, "Nome, just a lady."

Miss Stephanie eyed me suspiciously, decided that I meant no impertinence, and contented herself with, "Well, you won't get very far until you start wearing dresses more often."

Miss Maudie's hand closed tightly on mine, and I said nothing. Its warmth was enough.

Mrs. Grace Merriweather sat on my left, and I felt it would be polite to talk to her. Mr. Merriweather, a faithful Methodist under duress, apparently saw nothing personal in singing, "Amazing Grace, how sweet the sound, that saved a wretch like me . . ." It was the general opinion of Maycomb, however, that Mrs. Merriweather had sobered him up and made a reasonably useful citizen of him. For certainly Mrs. Merriweather was the most devout lady in Maycomb. I searched for a topic of interest to her. "What did you all study this afternoon?" I asked.

"Oh child, those poor Mrunas," she said, and was off. Few other questions would be necessary.

Mrs. Merriweather's large brown eyes always filled with tears when she considered the oppressed. "Living in that jungle with nobody but J. Grimes Everett," she said. "Not a white person'll go near 'em but that saintly J. Grimes Everett."

Mrs. Merriweather played her voice like an organ; every word she said received its full measure: "The poverty . . . the darkness . . . the immorality—nobody but J. Grimes Everett knows. You know, when the church gave me that trip to the camp grounds J. Grimes Everett said to me—"

"Was he there, ma'am? I thought—"

"Home on leave. J. Grimes Everett said to me, he said, 'Mrs. Merriweather, you have no conception, no *conception* of what we are fighting over there.' That's what he said to me."

"Yes ma'am."

"I said to him, 'Mr. Everett,' I said, 'the ladies of the Maycomb Alabama Methodist Episcopal Church South are behind you one hundred per cent.' That's what I said to him. And you know, right then and there I made a pledge in my heart. I said to myself, when I go home I'm

233

going to give a course on the Mrunas and bring J. Grimes Everett's message to Maycomb and that's just what I'm doing."

"Yes ma'am."

When Mrs. Merriweather shook her head, her black curls jiggled. "Jean Louise," she said, "you are a fortunate girl. You live in a Christian home with Christian folks in a Christian town. Out there in J. Grimes Everett's land there's nothing but sin and squalor."

"Yes ma'am."

"Sin and squalor—what was that, Gertrude?" Mrs. Merriweather turned on her chimes for the lady sitting beside her. "Oh that. Well, I always say forgive and forget, forgive and forget. Thing that church ought to do is help her lead a Christian life for those children from here on out. Some of the men ought to go out there and tell that preacher to encourage her."

"Excuse me, Mrs. Merriweather," I interrupted, "are you all talking about Mayella Ewell?"

"May—? No, child. That darky's wife. Tom's wife, Tom—"

"Robinson, ma'am."

Mrs. Merriweather turned back to her neighbor. "There's one thing I truly believe, Gertrude," she continued, "but some people just don't see it my way. If we just let them know wc forgive 'em, that we've forgotten it, then this whole thing'll blow over."

"Ah—Mrs. Merriweather," I interrupted once more, "what'll blow over?"

Again, she turned to me. Mrs. Merriweather was one of those childless adults who find it necessary to assume a different tone of voice when speaking to children. "Nothing, Jean Louise," she said, in stately largo, "the cooks and field hands are just dissatisfied, but they're settling down now—they grumbled all next day after that trial."

Mrs. Merriweather faced Mrs. Farrow: "Gertrude, I tell you there's nothing more distracting than a sulky darky. Their mouths go down to here. Just ruins your day to have one of 'em in the kitchen. You know what I said to my Sophy, Gertrude? I said, 'Sophy,' I said, 'you simply are not being a Christian today. Jesus Christ never went around grumbling and complaining,' and you

234

know, it did her good. She took her eyes off that floor and said, 'Nome, Miz Merriweather, Jesus never went around grumblin'.' I tell you, Gertrude, you never ought to let an opportunity go by to witness for the Lord."

I was reminded of the ancient little organ in the chapel at Finch's Landing. When I was very small, and if I had been very good during the day, Atticus would let me pump its bellows while he picked out a tune with one finger. The last note would linger as long as there was air to sustain it. Mrs. Merriweather had run out of air, I judged, and was replenishing her supply while Mrs. Farrow composed herself to speak.

Mrs. Farrow was a splendidly built woman with pale eyes and narrow feet. She had a fresh permanent wave, and her hair was a mass of tight gray ringlets. She was the second most devout lady in Maycomb. She had a curious habit of prefacing everything she said with a soft sibilant sound.

"S-s-s Grace," she said, "it's just like I was telling Brother Hutson the other day. 'S-s-s Brother Hutson,' I said, 'looks like we're fighting a losing battle, a losing battle.' I said, 'S-s-s it doesn't matter to 'em one bit. We can educate 'em till we're blue in the face, we can try till we drop to make Christians out of 'em, but there's no lady safe in her bed these nights.' He said to me, 'Mrs. Farrow, I don't know what we're coming to down here.' S-s-s I told him that was certainly a fact."

Mrs. Merriweather nodded wisely. Her voice soared over the clink of coffee cups and the soft bovine sounds of the ladies munching their dainties. "Gertrude," she said, "I tell you there are some good but misguided people in this town. Good, but misguided. Folks in this town who think they're doing right, I mean. Now far be it from me to say who, but some of 'em in this town thought they were doing the right thing a while back, but all they did was stir 'em up. That's all they did. Might've looked like the right thing to do at the time, I'm sure I don't know, I'm not read in that field, but sulky . . . dissatisfied . . . I tell you if my Sophy'd kept it up another day I'd have let her go. It's never entered that wool of hers that the only reason I keep her is because this depression's on and she needs her dollar and a quarter every week she can get it."

235

"His food doesn't stick going down, does it?"

Miss Maudie said it. Two tight lines had appeared at the corners of her mouth. She had been sitting silently beside me, her coffee cup balanced on one knee. I had lost the thread of conversation long ago, when they quit talking about Tom Robinson's wife, and had contented myself with thinking of Finch's Landing and the river. Aunt Alexandra had got it backwards: the business part of the meeting was blood-curdling, the social hour was dreary.

"Maudie, I'm sure I don't know what you mean," said Mrs. Merriweather.

"I'm sure you do," Miss Maudie said shortly.

She said no more. When Miss Maudie was angry her brevity was icy. Something had made her deeply angry, and her gray eyes were as cold as her voice. Mrs. Merriweather reddened, glanced at me, and looked away. I could not see Mrs. Farrow.

Aunt Alexandra got up from the table and swiftly passed more refreshments, neatly engaging Mrs. Merriweather and Mrs. Gates in brisk conversation. When she had them well on the road with Mrs. Perkins, Aunt Alexandra stepped back. She gave Miss Maudie a look of pure gratitude, and I wondered at the world of women. Miss Maudie and Aunt Alexandra had never been especially close, and here was Aunty silently thanking her for something. For what, I knew not. I was content to learn that Aunt Alexandra could be pierced sufficiently to feel gratitude for help given. There was no doubt about it, I must soon enter this world, where on its surface fragrant ladies rocked slowly, fanned gently, and drank cool water.

But I was more at home in my father's world. People like Mr. Heck Tate did not trap you with innocent questions to make fun of you; even Jem was not highly critical unless you said something stupid. Ladies seemed to live in faint horror of men, seemed unwilling to approve wholeheartedly of them. But I liked them. There was something about them, no matter how much they cussed and drank and gambled and chewed; no matter how undelectable they were, there was something about them that I instinctively liked . . . they weren't—

"Hypocrites, Mrs. Perkins, born hypocrites," Mrs. Merriweather was saying. "At least we don't have that sin on our shoulders down here. People up there set 'em free, but you don't see 'em settin' at the table with 'em. At least we don't have the deceit to say to 'em yes you're as good as we are but stay away from us. Down here we just say you live your way and we'll live ours. I think that woman, that Mrs. Roosevelt's lost her mind—just plain lost her mind coming down to Birmingham and tryin' to sit with 'em. If I was the Mayor of Birmingham I'd—"

Well, neither of us was the Mayor of Birmingham, but I wished I was the Governor of Alabama for one day: I'd let Tom Robinson go so quick the Missionary Society wouldn't have time to catch its breath. Calpurnia was telling Miss Rachel's cook the other day how bad Tom was taking things and she didn't stop talking when I came into the kitchen. She said there wasn't a thing Atticus could do to make being shut up easier for him, that the last thing he said to Atticus before they took him down to the prison camp was, "Good-bye, Mr. Finch, there ain't nothin' you can do now, so there ain't no use tryin'." Calpurnia said Atticus told her that the day they took Tom to prison he just gave up hope. She said Atticus tried to explain things to him, and that he must do his best not to lose hope because Atticus was doing his best to get him free. Miss Rachel's cook asked Calpurnia why didn't Atticus just say yes, you'll go free, and leave it at that—seemed like that'd be a big comfort to Tom. Calpurnia said, "Because you ain't familiar with the law. First thing you learn when you're in a lawin' family is that there ain't any definite answers to anything. Mr. Finch couldn't say somethin's so when he doesn't know for sure it's so."

The front door slammed and I heard Atticus's footsteps in the hall. Automatically I wondered what time it was. Not nearly time for him to be home, and on Missionary Society days he usually stayed down town until black dark.

He stopped in the doorway. His hat was in his hand, and his face was white.

"Excuse me, ladies," he said. "Go right ahead with your meeting, don't let me disturb you. Alexandra, could you come to the kitchen a minute? I want to borrow Calpurnia for a while."

He didn't go through the diningroom, but went down

237

the back hallway and entered the kitchen from the rear door. Aunt Alexandra and I met him. The diningroom door opened again and Miss Maudie joined us. Calpurnia had half risen from her chair.

"Cal," Atticus said, "I want you to go with me out to Helen Robinson's house—"

"What's the matter?" Aunt Alexandra asked, alarmed by the look on my father's face.

"Tom's dead."

Aunt Alexandra put her hands to her mouth.

"They shot him," said Atticus. "He was running. It was during their exercise period. They said he just broke into a blind raving charge at the fence and started climbing over. Right in front of them—"

"Didn't they try to stop him? Didn't they give him any warning?" Aunt Alexandra's voice shook.

"Oh yes, the guards called to him to stop. They fired a few shots in the air, then to kill. They got him just as he went over the fence. They said if he'd had two good arms he'd have made it, he was moving that fast. Seventeen bullet holes in him. They didn't have to shoot him that much. Cal, I want you to come out with me and help me tell Helen."

"Yes sir," she murmured, fumbling at her apron. Miss Maudie went to Calpurnia and untied it.

"This is the last straw, Atticus," Aunt Alexandra said.

"Depends on how you look at it," he said. "What was one Negro, more or less, among two hundred of 'em? He wasn't Tom to them, he was an escaping prisoner."

Atticus leaned against the refrigerator, pushed up his glasses, and rubbed his eyes. "We had such a good chance," he said. "I told him what I thought, but I couldn't in truth say that we had more than a good chance. I guess Tom was tired of white men's chances and preferred to take his own. Ready, Cal?"

"Yessir, Mr. Finch."

"Then let's go."

Aunt Alexandra sat down in Calpurnia's chair and put her hands to her face. She sat quite still; she was so quiet I wondered if she would faint. I heard Miss Maudie breathing as if she had just climbed the steps, and in the diningroom the ladies chattered happily.

I thought Aunt Alexandra was crying, but when she

took her hands away from her face, she was not. She looked weary. She spoke, and her voice was flat.

"I can't say I approve of everything he does, Maudie, but he's my brother, and I just want to know when this will ever end." Her voice rose: "It tears him to pieces. He doesn't show it much, but it tears him to pieces. I've seen him when—what else do they want from him, Maudie, what else?"

"What does who want, Alexandra?" Miss Maudie asked.

"I mean this town. They're perfectly willing to let him do what they're too afraid to do themselves—it might lose 'em a nickel. They're perfectly willing to let him wreck his health doing what they're afraid to do, they're—"

"Be quiet, they'll hear you," said Miss Maudie. "Have you ever thought of it this way, Alexandra? Whether Maycomb knows it or not, we're paying the highest tribute we can pay a man. We trust him to do right. It's that simple."

"Who?" Aunt Alexandra never knew she was echoing her twelve-year-old nephew.

"The handful of people in this town who say that fair play is not marked White Only; the handful of people who say a fair trial is for everybody, not just us; the handful of people with enough humility to think, when they look at a Negro, there but for the Lord's kindness am I." Miss Maudie's old crispness was returning: "The handful of people in this town with background, that's who they are."

Had I been attentive, I would have had another scrap to add to Jem's definition of background, but I found myself shaking and couldn't stop. I had seen Enfield Prison Farm, and Atticus had pointed out the exercise yard to me. It was the size of a football field.

"Stop that shaking," commanded Miss Maudie, and I stopped. "Get up, Alexandra, we've left 'em long enough."

Aunt Alexandra rose and smoothed the various whale-bone ridges along her hips. She took her handkerchief from her belt and wiped her nose. She patted her hair and said, "Do I show it?"

"Not a sign," said Miss Maudie. "Are you together again, Jean Louise?"

"Yes ma'am."

"Then let's join the ladies," she said grimly.

Their voices swelled when Miss Maudie opened the door to the diningroom. Aunt Alexandra was ahead of me, and I saw her head go up as she went through the door.

"Oh, Mrs. Perkins," she said, "you need some more coffee. Let me get it."

"Calpurnia's on an errand for a few minutes, Grace," said Miss Maudie. "Let me pass you some more of those dewberry tarts. 'dyou hear what that cousin of mine did the other day, the one who likes to go fishing? . . ."

And so they went, down the row of laughing women, around the diningroom, refilling coffee cups, dishing out goodies as though their only regret was the temporary domestic disaster of losing Calpurnia.

The gentle hum began again: "Yes sir, Mrs. Perkins, that J. Grimes Everett is a martyred saint, he . . . needed to get married so they ran . . . to the beauty parlor every Saturday afternoon . . . soon as the sun goes down. He goes to bed with the . . . chickens, a crate full of sick chickens, Fred says that's what started it all. Fred says . . ."

Aunt Alexandra looked across the room at me and smiled. She looked at a tray of cookies on the table and nodded at them. I carefully picked up the tray and watched myself walk to Mrs. Merriweather. With my best company manners, I asked her if she would have some. After all, if Aunty could be a lady at a time like this, so could I.

25.

Don't do that, Scout. Set him out on the back steps."

"Jem, are you crazy? . . ."

"I said set him out on the back steps."

Sighing, I scooped up the small creature, placed him

240

on the bottom step and went back to my cot. September had come, but not a trace of cool weather with it, and we were still sleeping on the back screen porch. Lightning bugs were still about, the night crawlers and flying insects that beat against the screen the summer long had not gone wherever they go when autumn comes.

A roly-poly had found his way inside the house; I reasoned that the tiny varmint had crawled up the steps and under the door. I was putting my book on the floor beside my cot when I saw him. The creatures are no more than an inch long, and when you touch them they roll themselves into a tight gray ball.

I lay on my stomach, reached down and poked him. He rolled up. Then, feeling safe, I suppose, he slowly unrolled. He traveled a few inches on his hundred legs and I touched him again. He rolled up. Feeling sleepy, I decided to end things. My hand was going down on him when Jem spoke.

Jem was scowling. It was probably a part of the stage he was going through, and I wished he would hurry up and get through it. He was certainly never cruel to animals, but I had never known his charity to embrace the insect world.

"Why couldn't I mash him?" I asked.

"Because they don't bother you," Jem answered in the darkness. He had turned out his reading light.

"Reckon you're at the stage now where you don't kill flies and mosquitoes now, I reckon," I said. "Lemme know when you change your mind. Tell you one thing, though, I ain't gonna sit around and not scratch a redbug."

"Aw dry up," he answered drowsily.

Jem was the one who was getting more like a girl every day, not I. Comfortable, I lay on my back and waited for sleep, and while waiting I thought of Dill. He had left us the first of the month with firm assurances that he would return the minute school was out—he guessed his folks had got the general idea that he liked to spend his summers in Maycomb. Miss Rachel took us with them in the taxi to Maycomb Junction, and Dill waved to us from the train window until he was out of sight. He was not out of mind: I missed him. The last two days of his time with us, Jem had taught him to swim—

Taught him to swim. I was wide awake, remembering what Dill had told me.

Barker's Eddy is at the end of a dirt road off the Meridian highway about a mile from town. It is easy to catch a ride down the highway on a cotton wagon or from a passing motorist, and the short walk to the creek is easy, but the prospect of walking all the way back home at dusk, when the traffic is light, is tiresome, and swimmers are careful not to stay too late.

According to Dill, he and Jem had just come to the highway when they saw Atticus driving toward them. He looked like he had not seen them, so they both waved. Atticus finally slowed down; when they caught up with him he said, "You'd better catch a ride back. I won't be going home for a while." Calpurnia was in the back seat.

Jem protested, then pleaded, and Atticus said, "All right, you can come with us if you stay in the car."

On the way to Tom Robinson's, Atticus told them what had happened.

They turned off the highway, rode slowly by the dump and past the Ewell residence, down the narrow lane to the Negro cabins. Dill said a crowd of black children were playing marbles in Tom's front yard. Atticus parked the car and got out. Calpurnia followed him through the front gate.

Dill heard him ask one of the children, "Where's your mother, Sam?" and heard Sam say, "She down at Sis Stevens's, Mr. Finch. Want me run fetch her?"

Dill said Atticus looked uncertain, then he said yes, and Sam scampered off. "Go on with your game, boys," Atticus said to the children.

A little girl came to the cabin door and stood looking at Atticus. Dill said her hair was a wad of tiny stiff pigtails, each ending in a bright bow. She grinned from ear to ear and walked toward our father, but she was too small to navigate the steps. Dill said Atticus went to her, took off his hat, and offered her his finger. She grabbed it and he eased her down the steps. Then he gave her to Calpurnia.

Sam was trotting behind his mother when they came up. Dill said Helen said, " 'evenin', Mr. Finch, won't you have a seat?" But she didn't say any more. Neither did Atticus.

"Scout," said Dill, "she just fell down in the dirt. Just fell down in the dirt, like a giant with a big foot just came along and stepped on her. Just ump—" Dill's fat foot hit the ground. "Like you'd step on an ant."

Dill said Calpurnia and Atticus lifted Helen to her feet and half carried, half walked her to the cabin. They stayed inside a long time, and Atticus came out alone. When they drove back by the dump, some of the Ewells hollered at them, but Dill didn't catch what they said.

Maycomb was interested by the news of Tom's death for perhaps two days; two days was enough for the information to spread through the county. "Did you hear about? . . . No? Well, they say he was runnin' fit to beat lightnin' . . ." To Maycomb, Tom's death was typical. Typical of a nigger to cut and run. Typical of a nigger's mentality to have no plan, no thought for the future, just run blind first chance he saw. Funny thing, Atticus Finch might've got him off scot free, but wait—? Hell no. You know how they are. Easy come, easy go. Just shows you, that Robinson boy was legally married, they say he kept himself clean, went to church and all that, but when it comes down to the line the veneer's mighty thin. Nigger always comes out in 'em.

A few more details, enabling the listener to repeat his version in turn, then nothing to talk about until *The Maycomb Tribune* appeared the following Thursday. There was a brief obituary in the Colored News, but there was also an editorial.

Mr. B. B. Underwood was at his most bitter, and he couldn't have cared less who canceled advertising and subscriptions. (But Maycomb didn't play that way: Mr. Underwood could holler till he sweated and write whatever he wanted to, he'd still get his advertising and subscriptions. If he wanted to make a fool of himself in his paper that was his business.) Mr. Underwood didn't talk about miscarriages of justice, he was writing so children could understand. Mr. Underwood simply figured it was a sin to kill cripples, be they standing, sitting, or escaping. He likened Tom's death to the senseless slaughter of songbirds by hunters and children, and Maycomb thought he was trying to write an editorial poetical enough to be reprinted in *The Montgomery Advertiser*.

How could this be so, I wondered, as I read Mr. Underwood's editorial. Senseless killing—Tom had been given due process of law to the day of his death; he had been tried openly and convicted by twelve good men and true; my father had fought for him all the way. Then Mr. Underwood's meaning became clear: Atticus had used every tool available to free men to save Tom Robinson, but in the secret courts of men's hearts Atticus had no case. Tom was a dead man the minute Mayella Ewell opened her mouth and screamed.

The name Ewell gave me a queasy feeling. Maycomb had lost no time in getting Mr. Ewell's views on Tom's demise and passing them along through that English Channel of gossip, Miss Stephanie Crawford. Miss Stephanie told Aunt Alexandra in Jem's presence ("Oh foot, he's old enough to listen,") that Mr. Ewell said it made one down and about two more to go. Jem told me not to be afraid, Mr. Ewell was more hot gas than anything. Jem also told me that if I breathed a word to Atticus, if in any way I let Atticus know I knew, Jem would personally never speak to me again.

26.

School started, and so did our daily trips past the Radley Place. Jem was in the seventh grade and went to high school, beyond the grammar-school building; I was now in the third grade, and our routines were so different I only walked to school with Jem in the mornings and saw him at mealtimes. He went out for football, but was too slender and too young yet to do anything but carry the team water buckets. This he did with enthusiasm; most afternoons he was seldom home before dark.

The Radley Place had ceased to terrify me, but it was no less gloomy, no less chilly under its great oaks, and no less uninviting. Mr. Nathan Radley could still be seen on a clear day, walking to and from town; we knew Boo was there, for the same old reason—nobody'd seen him carried out yet. I sometimes felt a twinge of remorse, when passing by the old place, at ever having taken part in what must have been sheer torment to Arthur Radley—what reasonable recluse wants children peeping through his shutters, delivering greetings on the end of a fishing-pole, wandering in his collards at night?

And yet I remembered. Two Indian-head pennies, chewing gum, soap dolls, a rusty medal, a broken watch and chain. Jem must have put them away somewhere. I stopped and looked at the tree one afternoon: the trunk was swelling around its cement patch. The patch itself was turning yellow.

We had almost seen him a couple of times, a good enough score for anybody.

But I still looked for him each time I went by. Maybe someday we would see him. I imagined how it would be: when it happened, he'd just be sitting in the swing when I came along. "Hidy do, Mr. Arthur," I would say, as if I had said it every afternoon of my life. "Evening, Jean Louise," he would say, as if he had said it every afternoon of my life, "right pretty spell we're having, isn't it?" "Yes sir, right pretty," I would say, and go on.

It was only a fantasy. We would never see him. He probably did go out when the moon was down and gaze upon Miss Stephanie Crawford. I'd have picked somebody else to look at, but that was his business. He would never gaze at us.

"You aren't starting that again, are you?" said Atticus one night, when I expressed a stray desire just to have one good look at Boo Radley before I died. "If you are, I'll tell you right now: stop it. I'm too old to go chasing you off the Radley property. Besides, it's dangerous. You might get shot. You know Mr. Nathan shoots at every shadow he sees, even shadows that leave size-four bare footprints. You were lucky not to be killed."

I hushed then and there. At the same time I marveled at Atticus. This was the first he had let us know he knew a lot more about something than we thought he knew. And it had happened years ago. No, only last summer— no, summer before last, when . . . time was playing tricks on me. I must remember to ask Jem.

So many things had happened to us, Boo Radley was the least of our fears. Atticus said he didn't see how anything else could happen, that things had a way of settling down, and after enough time passed people would forget that Tom Robinson's existence was ever brought to their attention.

Perhaps Atticus was right, but the events of the summer hung over us like smoke in a closed room. The adults in Maycomb never discussed the case with Jem and me; it seemed that they discussed it with their children, and their attitude must have been that neither of us could help having Atticus for a parent, so their children must be nice to us in spite of him. The children would never have thought that up for themselves: had our classmates been left to their own devices, Jem and I would have had several swift, satisfying fist-fights apiece and ended the matter for good. As it was, we were compelled to hold our heads high and be, respectively, a gentleman and a lady. In a way, it was like the era of Mrs. Henry Lafayette Dubose, without all her yelling. There was one odd thing, though, that I never understood: in spite of Atticus's shortcomings as a parent, people were content to re-elect him to the state legislature that year, as usual, without opposition. I came to the conclusion that people were just peculiar, I withdrew from them, and never thought about them until I was forced to.

I was forced to one day in school. Once a week, we had a Current Events period. Each child was supposed to clip an item from a newspaper, absorb its contents, and reveal them to the class. This practice allegedly overcame a variety of evils: standing in front of his fellows encouraged good posture and gave a child poise; delivering a short talk made him word-conscious; learning his current event strengthened his memory; being singled out made him more than ever anxious to return to the Group.

The idea was profound, but as usual, in Maycomb it didn't work very well. In the first place, few rural children had access to newspapers, so the burden of Current Events was borne by the town children, convincing the bus children more deeply that the town children got all the attention anyway. The rural children who could, usually brought clippings from what they called The Grit Paper, a publication spurious in the eyes of Miss Gates, our teacher. Why she frowned when a child recited from The Grit Paper I never knew, but in some way it was associated with liking fiddling, eating syrupy biscuits for lunch, being a holy-roller, singing *Sweetly Sings the Donkey* and pronouncing it dunkey, all of which the state paid teachers to discourage.

Even so, not many of the children knew what a Current Event was. Little Chuck Little, a hundred years old in his knowledge of cows and their habits, was halfway through an Uncle Natchell story when Miss Gates stopped him: "Charles, that is not a current event. That is an advertisement."

Cecil Jacobs knew what one was, though. When his turn came, he went to the front of the room and began, "Old Hitler—"

"Adolf Hitler, Cecil," said Miss Gates. "One never begins with Old anybody."

"Yes ma'am," he said. "Old Adolf Hitler has been prosecutin' the—"

"Persecuting, Cecil . . ."

"Nome, Miss Gates, it says here—well anyway, old Adolf Hitler has been after the Jews and he's puttin' 'em in prisons and he's taking away all their property and he won't let any of 'em out of the country and he's washin' all the feeble-minded and—"

"Washing the feeble-minded?"

"Yes ma'am, Miss Gates, I reckon they don't have sense enough to wash themselves, I don't reckon an idiot could keep hisself clean. Well anyway, Hitler's started a program to round up all the half-Jews too and he wants to register 'em in case they might wanta cause him any trouble and I think this is a bad thing and that's my current event."

"Very good, Cecil," said Miss Gates. Puffing, Cecil returned to his seat.

A hand went up in the back of the room. "How can he do that?"

"Who do what?" asked Miss Gates patiently.

"I mean how can Hitler just put a lot of folks in a pen like that, looks like the govamint'd stop him," said the owner of the hand.

"Hitler is the government," said Miss Gates, and seizing an opportunity to make education dynamic, she went to the blackboard. She printed DEMOCRACY in large

247

letters. "Democracy," she said. "Does anybody have a definition?"

"Us," somebody said.

I raised my hand, remembering an old campaign slogan Atticus had once told me about.

"What do you think it means, Jean Louise?"

" 'Equal rights for all, special privileges for none'," I quoted.

"Very good, Jean Louise, very good," Miss Gates smiled. In front of DEMOCRACY, she printed WE ARE A. "Now class, say it all together, 'We are a democracy'."

We said it. Then Miss Gates said, "That's the difference between America and Germany. We are a democracy and Germany is a dictatorship. Dictator-ship," she said. "Over here we don't believe in persecuting anybody. Persecution comes from people who are prejudiced. Pre-judice," she enunciated carefully. "There are no better people in the world than the Jews, and why Hitler doesn't think so is a mystery to me."

An inquiring soul in the middle of the room said, "Why don't they like the Jews, you reckon, Miss Gates?"

"I don't know, Henry. They contribute to every society they live in, and most of all, they are a deeply religious people. Hitler's trying to do away with religion, so maybe he doesn't like them for that reason."

Cecil spoke up. "Well I don't know for certain," he said, "they're supposed to change money or somethin', but that ain't no cause to persecute 'em. They're white, ain't they?"

Miss Gates said, "When you get to high school, Cecil, you'll learn that the Jews have been persecuted since the beginning of history, even driven out of their own country. It's one of the most terrible stories in history. Time for arithmetic, children."

As I had never liked arithmetic, I spent the period looking out the window. The only time I ever saw Atticus scowl was when Elmer Davis would give us the latest on Hitler. Atticus would snap off the radio and say, "Hmp!" I asked him once why he was impatient with Hitler and Atticus said, "Because he's a maniac."

This would not do, I mused, as the class proceeded with its sums. One maniac and millions of German folks. Looked to me like they'd shut Hitler in a pen instead of letting him shut them up. There was something else wrong—I would ask my father about it.

I did, and he said he could not possibly answer my question because he didn't know the answer.

"But it's okay to hate Hitler?"

"It is not," he said. "It's not okay to hate anybody."

"Atticus," I said, "there's somethin' I don't understand. Miss Gates said it was awful, Hitler doin' like he does, she got real red in the face about it—"

"I should think she would."

"But—"

"Yes?"

"Nothing, sir." I went away, not sure that I could explain to Atticus what was on my mind, not sure that I could clarify what was only a feeling. Perhaps Jem could provide the answer. Jem understood school things better than Atticus.

Jem was worn out from a day's water-carrying. There were at least twelve banana peels on the floor by his bed, surrounding an empty milk bottle. "Whatcha stuffin' for?" I asked.

"Coach says if I can gain twenty-five pounds by year after next I can play," he said. "This is the quickest way."

"If you don't throw it all up. Jem," I said, "I wanta ask you somethin'."

"Shoot." He put down his book and stretched his legs.

"Miss Gates is a nice lady, ain't she?"

"Why sure," said Jem. "I liked her when I was in her room."

"She hates Hitler a lot . . ."

"What's wrong with that?"

"Well, she went on today about how bad it was him treatin' the Jews like that. Jem, it's not right to persecute anybody, is it? I mean have mean thoughts about anybody, even, is it?"

"Gracious no, Scout. What's eatin' you?"

"Well, coming out of the courthouse that night Miss Gates was—she was goin' down the steps in front of us, you musta not seen her—she was talking with Miss Stephanie Crawford. I heard her say it's time somebody taught 'em a lesson, they were gettin' way above themselves, an' the next thing they think they can do is marry us. Jem, how can you hate Hitler so bad an' then turn around and be ugly about folks right at home—"

Jem was suddenly furious. He leaped off the bed, grabbed me by the collar and shook me. "I never wanta hear about that courthouse again, ever, ever, you hear me? You hear me? Don't you ever say one word to me about it again, you hear? Now go on!"

I was too surprised to cry. I crept from Jem's room and shut the door softly, lest undue noise set him off again. Suddenly tired, I wanted Atticus. He was in the living-room, and I went to him and tried to get in his lap.

Atticus smiled. "You're getting so big now, I'll just have to hold a part of you." He held me close. "Scout," he said softly, "don't let Jem get you down. He's having a rough time these days. I heard you back there."

Atticus said that Jem was trying hard to forget something, but what he was really doing was storing it away for a while, until enough time passed. Then he would be able to think about it and sort things out. When he was able to think about it, Jem would be himself again.

27.

Things did settle down, after a fashion, as Atticus said they would. By the middle of October, only two small things out of the ordinary happened to two Maycomb citizens. No, there were three things, and they did not directly concern us—the Finches —but in a way they did.

The first thing was that Mr. Bob Ewell acquired and lost a job in a matter of days and probably made himself unique in the annals of the nineteen-thirties: he was the only man I ever heard of who was fired from the WPA for laziness. I suppose his brief burst of fame brought on a briefer burst of industry, but his job lasted only as long as his notoriety: Mr. Ewell found himself as forgotten as Tom Robinson. Thereafter, he resumed his regular weekly appearances at the welfare office for his check, and received it with no grace amid obscure mutterings that the bastards who thought they ran this town wouldn't permit an honest man to make a living. Ruth Jones, the welfare lady, said Mr. Ewell openly accused Atticus of getting his job. She was upset enough to walk down to Atticus's office and tell him about it. Atticus told Miss Ruth not to fret, that if Bob Ewell wanted to discuss Atticus's "getting" his job, he knew the way to the office.

The second thing happened to Judge Taylor. Judge Taylor was not a Sunday-night churchgoer; Mrs. Taylor was. Judge Taylor savored his Sunday night hour alone in his big house, and churchtime found him holed up in his study reading the writings of Bob Taylor (no kin, but the judge would have been proud to claim it). One Sunday night, lost in fruity metaphors and florid diction, Judge Taylor's attention was wrenched from the page by an irritating scratching noise. "Hush," he said to Ann Taylor, his fat nondescript dog. Then he realized he was speaking to an empty room; the scratching noise was coming from the rear of the house. Judge Taylor clumped to the back porch to let Ann out and found the screen door swinging open. A shadow on the corner of the house caught his eye, and that was all he saw of his visitor. Mrs. Taylor came home from church to find her husband in his chair, lost in the writings of Bob Taylor, with a shotgun across his lap.

The third thing happened to Helen Robinson, Tom's widow. If Mr. Ewell was as forgotten as Tom Robinson, Tom Robinson was as forgotten as Boo Radley. But Tom was not forgotten by his employer, Mr. Link Deas. Mr. Link Deas made a job for Helen. He didn't really need her, but he said he felt right bad about the way things turned out. I never knew who took care of her children while Helen was away. Calpurnia said it was hard on Helen, because she had to walk nearly a mile out of her way to avoid the Ewells, who, according to Helen, "chunked at her" the first time she tried to use the public road. Mr. Link Deas eventually received the impression that Helen was coming to work each morning from the wrong direction, and dragged the reason out of her. "Just let it be, Mr. Link, please suh," Helen begged. "The hell I will," said Mr. Link. He told her to come by his store that afternoon before she left. She did, and Mr. Link closed his store, put his hat firmly on his head, and

251

walked Helen home. He walked her the short way, by the Ewells'. On his way back, Mr. Link stopped at the crazy gate.

"Ewell?" he called. "I say Ewell!"

The windows, normally packed with children, were empty.

"I know every last one of you's in there a-layin' on the floor! Now hear me, Bob Ewell: if I hear one more peep outa my girl Helen about not bein' able to walk this road I'll have you in jail before sundown!" Mr. Link spat in the dust and walked home.

Helen went to work next morning and used the public road. Nobody chunked at her, but when she was a few yards beyond the Ewell house, she looked around and saw Mr. Ewell walking behind her. She turned and walked on, and Mr. Ewell kept the same distance behind her until she reached Mr. Link Deas's house. All the way to the house, Helen said, she heard a soft voice behind her, crooning foul words. Thoroughly frightened, she telephoned Mr. Link at his store, which was not too far from his house. As Mr. Link came out of his store he saw Mr. Ewell leaning on the fence. Mr. Ewell said, "Don't you look at me, Link Deas, like I was dirt. I ain't jumped your—"

"First thing you can do, Ewell, is get your stinkin' carcass off my property. You're leanin' on it an' I can't afford fresh paint for it. Second thing you can do is stay away from my cook or I'll have you up for assault—"

"I ain't touched her, Link Deas, and ain't about to go with no nigger!"

"You don't have to touch her, all you have to do is make her afraid, an' if assault ain't enough to keep you locked up awhile, I'll get you in on the Ladies' Law, so get outa my sight! If you don't think I mean it, just bother that girl again!"

Mr. Ewell evidently thought he meant it, for Helen reported no further trouble.

"I don't like it, Atticus, I don't like it at all," was Aunt Alexandra's assessment of these events. "That man seems to have a permanent running grudge against everybody connected with that case. I know how that kind are about paying off grudges, but I don't understand

252

why he should harbor one—he had his way in court, didn't he?"

"I think I understand," said Atticus. "It might be because he knows in his heart that very few people in Maycomb really believed his and Mayella's yarns. He thought he'd be a hero, but all he got for his pain was . . . was, okay, we'll convict this Negro but get back to your dump. He's had his fling with about everybody now, so he ought to be satisfied. He'll settle down when the weather changes."

"But why should he try to burgle John Taylor's house? He obviously didn't know John was home or he wouldn't've tried. Only lights John shows on Sunday nights are on the front porch and back in his den . . ."

"You don't know if Bob Ewell cut that screen, you don't know who did it," said Atticus. "But I can guess. I proved him a liar but John made him look like a fool. All the time Ewell was on the stand I couldn't dare look at John and keep a straight face. John looked at him as if he were a three-legged chicken or a square egg. Don't tell me judges don't try to prejudice juries," Atticus chuckled.

By the end of October, our lives had become the familiar routine of school, play, study. Jem seemed to have put out of his mind whatever it was he wanted to forget, and our classmates mercifully let us forget our father's eccentricities. Cecil Jacobs asked me one time if Atticus was a Radical. When I asked Atticus, Atticus was so amused I was rather annoyed, but he said he wasn't laughing at me. He said, "You tell Cecil I'm about as radical as Cotton Tom Heflin."

Aunt Alexandra was thriving. Miss Maudie must have silenced the whole missionary society at one blow, for Aunty again ruled that roost. Her refreshments grew even more delicious. I learned more about the poor Mrunas' social life from listening to Mrs. Merriweather: they had so little sense of family that the whole tribe was one big family. A child had as many fathers as there were men in the community, as many mothers as there were women. J. Grimes Everett was doing his utmost to change this state of affairs, and desperately needed our prayers.

Maycomb was itself again. Precisely the same as last year and the year before that, with only two minor changes. Firstly, people had removed from their store windows and automobiles the stickers that said NRA— WE DO OUR PART. I asked Atticus why, and he said it was because the National Recovery Act was dead. I asked who killed it; he said nine old men.

The second change in Maycomb since last year was not one of national significance. Until then, Halloween in Maycomb was a completely unorganized affair. Each child did what he wanted to do, with assistance from other children if there was anything to be moved, such as placing a light buggy on top of the livery stable. But parents thought things went too far last year, when the peace of Miss Tutti and Miss Frutti was shattered.

Misses Tutti and Frutti Barber were maiden ladies, sisters, who lived together in the only Maycomb residence boasting a cellar. The Barber ladies were rumored to be Republicans, having migrated from Clanton, Alabama, in 1911. Their ways were strange to us, and why they wanted a cellar nobody knew, but they wanted one, and they dug one, and they spent the rest of their lives chasing generations of children out of it.

Misses Tutti and Frutti (their names were Sarah and Frances), aside from their Yankee ways, were both deaf. Miss Tutti denied it and lived in a world of silence, but Miss Frutti, not about to miss anything, employed an ear trumpet so enormous that Jem declared it was a loudspeaker from one of those dog Victrolas.

With these facts in mind and Halloween at hand, some wicked children had waited until the Misses Barber were thoroughly asleep, slipped into their livingroom (nobody but the Radleys locked up at night), stealthily made away with every stick of furniture therein, and hid it in the cellar. I deny having taken part in such a thing.

"I heard 'em!" was the cry that awoke the Misses Barber's neighbors at dawn next morning. "Heard 'em drive a truck up to the door! Stomped around like horses. They're in New Orleans by now!"

Miss Tutti was sure those traveling fur sellers who came through town two days ago had purloined their furniture. "Da-rk they were," she said. "Syrians."

Mr. Heck Tate was summoned. He surveyed the area and said he thought it was a local job. Miss Frutti said she'd know a Maycomb voice anywhere, and there were no

Maycomb voices in that parlor last night—rolling their r's all over her premises, they were. Nothing less than the bloodhounds must be used to locate their furniture, Miss Tutti insisted, so Mr. Tate was obliged to go ten miles out the road, round up the county hounds, and put them on the trail.

Mr. Tate started them off at the Misses Barber's front steps, but all they did was run around to the back of the house and howl at the cellar door. When Mr. Tate set them in motion three times, he finally guessed the truth. By noontime that day, there was not a barefooted child to be seen in Maycomb and nobody took off his shoes until the hounds were returned.

So the Maycomb ladies said things would be different this year. The high-school auditorium would be open, there would be a pageant for the grown-ups; apple-bobbing, taffy-pulling, pinning the tail on the donkey for the children. There would also be a prize of twenty-five cents for the best Halloween costume, created by the wearer.

Jem and I both groaned. Not that we'd ever done anything, it was the principle of the thing. Jem considered himself too old for Halloween anyway; he said he wouldn't be caught anywhere near the high school at something like that. Oh well, I thought, Atticus would take me.

I soon learned, however, that my services would be required on stage that evening. Mrs. Grace Merriweather had composed an original pageant entitled *Maycomb County: Ad Astra Per Aspera*, and I was to be a ham. She thought it would be adorable if some of the children were costumed to represent the county's agricultural products: Cecil Jacobs would be dressed up to look like a cow; Agnes Boone would make a lovely butterbean, another child would be a peanut, and on down the line until Mrs. Merriweather's imagination and the supply of children were exhausted.

Our only duties, as far as I could gather from our two rehearsals, were to enter from stage left as Mrs. Merriweather (not only the author, but the narrator) identified us. When she called out, "Pork," that was my cue. Then the assembled company would sing, "Maycomb County, Maycomb County, we will aye be true to thee," as the grand finale, and Mrs. Merriweather would mount the stage with the state flag.

My costume was not much of a problem. Mrs. Crenshaw, the local seamstress, had as much imagination as Mrs. Merriweather. Mrs. Crenshaw took some chicken wire and bent it into the shape of a cured ham. This she covered with brown cloth, and painted it to resemble the original. I could duck under and someone would pull the contraption down over my head. It came almost to my knees. Mrs. Crenshaw thoughtfully left two peepholes for me. She did a fine job; Jem said I looked exactly like a ham with legs. There were several discomforts, though: it was hot, it was a close fit; if my nose itched I couldn't scratch, and once inside I could not get out of it alone.

When Halloween came, I assumed that the whole family would be present to watch me perform, but I was disappointed. Atticus said as tactfully as he could that he just didn't think he could stand a pageant tonight, he was all in. He had been in Montgomery for a week and had come home late that afternoon. He thought Jem might escort me if I asked him.

Aunt Alexandra said she just had to get to bed early, she'd been decorating the stage all afternoon and was worn out—she stopped short in the middle of her sentence. She closed her mouth, then opened it to say something, but no words came.

"'s matter, Aunty?" I asked.

"Oh nothing, nothing," she said, "somebody just walked over my grave." She put away from her whatever it was that gave her a pinprick of apprehension, and suggested that I give the family a preview in the livingroom. So Jem squeezed me into my costume, stood at the livingroom door, called out "Po-ork," exactly as Mrs. Merriweather would have done, and I marched in. Atticus and Aunt Alexandra were delighted.

I repeated my part for Calpurnia in the kitchen and she said I was wonderful. I wanted to go across the street to show Miss Maudie, but Jem said she'd probably be at the pageant anyway.

After that, it didn't matter whether they went or not. Jem said he would take me. Thus began our longest journey together.

28.

The weather was unusually warm for the last day of October. We didn't even need jackets. The wind was growing stronger, and Jem said it might be raining before we got home. There was no moon.

The street light on the corner cast sharp shadows on the Radley house. I heard Jem laugh softly. "Bet nobody bothers them tonight," he said. Jem was carrying my ham costume, rather awkwardly, as it was hard to hold. I thought it gallant of him to do so.

"It is a scary place though, ain't it?" I said. "Boo doesn't mean anybody any harm, but I'm right glad you're along."

"You know Atticus wouldn't let you go to the schoolhouse by yourself," Jem said.

"Don't see why, it's just around the corner and across the yard."

"That yard's a mighty long place for little girls to cross at night," Jem teased. "Ain't you scared of haints?"

We laughed. Haints, Hot Steams, incantations, secret signs, had vanished with our years as mist with sunrise. "What was that old thing," Jem said, "Angel bright, life-in-death; get off the road, don't suck my breath."

"Cut it out, now," I said. We were in front of the Radley Place.

Jem said, "Boo must not be at home. Listen."

High above us in the darkness a solitary mocker poured out his repertoire in blissful unawareness of whose tree he sat in, plunging from the shrill kee, kee of the sunflower bird to the irascible qua-ack of a bluejay, to the sad lament of Poor Will, Poor Will, Poor Will.

We turned the corner and I tripped on a root growing in the road. Jem tried to help me, but all he did was drop my costume in the dust. I didn't fall, though, and soon we were on our way again.

We turned off the road and entered the schoolyard. It was pitch black.

"How do you know where we're at, Jem?" I asked, when we had gone a few steps.

"I can tell we're under the big oak because we're passin' through a cool spot. Careful now, and don't fall again."

We had slowed to a cautious gait, and were feeling our way forward so as not to bump into the tree. The tree was a single and ancient oak; two children could not reach around its trunk and touch hands. It was far away from teachers, their spies, and curious neighbors: it was near the Radley lot, but the Radleys were not curious. A small patch of earth beneath its branches was packed hard from many fights and furtive crap games.

The lights in the high school auditorium were blazing in the distance, but they blinded us, if anything. "Don't look ahead, Scout," Jem said. "Look at the ground and you won't fall."

"You should have brought the flashlight, Jem."

"Didn't know it was this dark. Didn't look like it'd be this dark earlier in the evening. So cloudy, that's why. It'll hold off a while, though."

Someone leaped at us.

"God amighty!" Jem yelled.

A circle of light burst in our faces, and Cecil Jacobs jumped in glee behind it. "Ha-a-a, gotcha!" he shrieked. "Thought you'd be comin' along this way!"

"What are you doin' way out here by yourself, boy? Ain't you scared of Boo Radley?"

Cecil had ridden safely to the auditorium with his parents, hadn't seen us, then had ventured down this far because he knew good and well we'd be coming along. He thought Mr. Finch'd be with us, though.

"Shucks, ain't much but around the corner," said Jem. "Who's scared to go around the corner?" We had to admit that Cecil was pretty good, though. He *had* given us a fright, and he could tell it all over the schoolhouse, that was his privilege.

"Say," I said, "ain't you a cow tonight? Where's your costume?"

"It's up behind the stage," he said. "Mrs. Merriweather says the pageant ain't comin' on for a while. You can put yours back of the stage by mine, Scout, and we can go with the rest of 'em."

This was an excellent idea, Jem thought. He also thought it a good thing that Cecil and I would be together. This way, Jem would be left to go with people his own age.

When we reached the auditorium, the whole town was there except Atticus and the ladies worn out from decorating, and the usual outcasts and shut-ins. Most of the county, it seemed, was there: the hall was teeming with slicked-up country people. The high school building had a wide downstairs hallway; people milled around booths that had been installed along each side.

"Oh Jem, I forgot my money," I sighed, when I saw them.

"Atticus didn't," Jem said. "Here's thirty cents, you can do six things. See you later on."

"Okay," I said, quite content with thirty cents and Cecil. I went with Cecil down to the front of the auditorium, through a door on one side, and backstage. I got rid of my ham costume and departed in a hurry, for Mrs. Merriweather was standing at a lectern in front of the first row of seats making last-minute, frenzied changes in the script.

"How much money you got?" I asked Cecil. Cecil had thirty cents, too, which made us even. We squandered our first nickels on the House of Horrors, which scared us not at all; we entered the black seventh-grade room and were led around by the temporary ghoul in residence and were made to touch several objects alleged to be component parts of a human being. "Here's his eyes," we were told when we touched two peeled grapes on a saucer. "Here's his heart," which felt like raw liver. "These are his innards," and our hands were thrust into a plate of cold spaghetti.

Cecil and I visited several booths. We each bought a sack of Mrs. Judge Taylor's homemade divinity. I wanted to bob for apples, but Cecil said it wasn't sanitary. His mother said he might catch something from everybody's heads having been in the same tub. "Ain't anything around town now to catch," I protested. But Cecil said his mother said it was unsanitary to eat after folks. I later asked Aunt Alexandra about this, and she said people who held such views were usually climbers.

We were about to purchase a blob of taffy when Mrs. Merriweather's runners appeared and told us to go backstage, it was time to get ready. The auditorium was filling with people; the Maycomb County High School band had assembled in front below the stage; the stage footlights were on and the red velvet curtain rippled and billowed from the scurrying going on behind it.

Backstage, Cecil and I found the narrow hallway teeming with people: adults in homemade three-corner hats, Confederate caps, Spanish-American War hats, and World War helmets. Children dressed as various agricultural enterprises crowded around the one small window.

"Somebody's mashed my costume," I wailed in dismay. Mrs. Merriweather galloped to me, reshaped the chicken wire, and thrust me inside.

"You all right in there, Scout?" asked Cecil. "You sound so far off, like you was on the other side of a hill."

"You don't sound any nearer," I said.

The band played the national anthem, and we heard the audience rise. Then the bass drum sounded. Mrs. Merriweather, stationed behind her lectern beside the band, said: "Maycomb County: Ad Astra Per Aspera." The bass drum boomed again. "That means," said Mrs. Merriweather, translating for the rustic elements, "from the mud to the stars." She added, unnecessarily, it seemed to me, "A pageant."

"Reckon they wouldn't know what it was if she didn't tell 'em," whispered Cecil, who was immediately shushed.

"The whole town knows it," I breathed.

"But the country folks've come in," Cecil said.

"Be quiet back there," a man's voice ordered, and we were silent.

The bass drum went boom with every sentence Mrs. Merriweather uttered. She chanted mournfully about Maycomb County being older than the state, that it was a part of the Mississippi and Alabama Territories, that the first white man to set foot in the virgin forests was the Probate Judge's great-grandfather five times removed, who was never heard of again. Then came the fearless Colonel Maycomb, for whom the county was named.

Andrew Jackson appointed him to a position of author-

260

ity, and Colonel Maycomb's misplaced self-confidence and slender sense of direction brought disaster to all who rode with him in the Creek Indian Wars. Colonel Maycomb persevered in his efforts to make the region safe for democracy, but his first campaign was his last. His orders, relayed to him by a friendly Indian runner, were to move south. After consulting a tree to ascertain from its lichen which way was south, and taking no lip from the subordinates who ventured to correct him, Colonel Maycomb set out on a purposeful journey to rout the enemy and entangled his troops so far northwest in the forest primeval that they were eventually rescued by settlers moving inland.

Mrs. Merriweather gave a thirty-minute description of Colonel Maycomb's exploits. I discovered that if I bent my knees I could tuck them under my costume and more or less sit. I sat down, listened to Mrs. Merriweather's drone and the bass drum's boom and was soon fast asleep.

They said later that Mrs. Merriweather was putting her all into the grand finale, that she had crooned, "Po-ork," with a confidence born of pine trees and butterbeans entering on cue. She waited a few seconds, then called, "Po-ork?" When nothing materialized, she yelled, "Pork!"

I must have heard her in my sleep, or the band playing *Dixie* woke me, but it was when Mrs. Merriweather triumphantly mounted the stage with the state flag that I chose to make my entrance. Chose is incorrect: I thought I'd better catch up with the rest of them.

They told me later that Judge Taylor went out behind the auditorium and stood there slapping his knees so hard Mrs. Taylor brought him a glass of water and one of his pills.

Mrs. Merriweather seemed to have a hit, everybody was cheering so, but she caught me backstage and told me I had ruined her pageant. She made me feel awful, but when Jem came to fetch me he was sympathetic. He said he couldn't see my costume much from where he was sitting. How he could tell I was feeling bad under my costume I don't know, but he said I did all right, I just came in a little late, that was all. Jem was becoming almost as good as Atticus at making you feel right when things went wrong. Almost—not even Jem could make me go

261

through that crowd, and he consented to wait backstage with me until the audience left.

"You wanta take it off, Scout?" he asked.

"Naw, I'll just keep it on," I said. I could hide my mortification under it.

"You all want a ride home?" someone asked.

"No sir, thank you," I heard Jem say. "It's just a little walk."

"Be careful of haints," the voice said. "Better still, tell the haints to be careful of Scout."

"There aren't many folks left now," Jem told me. "Let's go."

We went through the auditorium to the hallway, then down the steps. It was still black dark. The remaining cars were parked on the other side of the building, and their headlights were little help. "If some of 'em were goin' in our direction we could see better," said Jem. "Here Scout, let me hold onto your—hock. You might lose your balance."

"I can see all right."

"Yeah, but you might lose your balance." I felt a slight pressure on my head, and assumed that Jem had grabbed that end of the ham. "You got me?"

"Uh huh."

We began crossing the black schoolyard, straining to see our feet. "Jem," I said, "I forgot my shoes, they're back behind the stage."

"Well let's go get 'em." But as we turned around the auditorium lights went off. "You can get 'em tomorrow," he said.

"But tomorrow's Sunday," I protested, as Jem turned me homeward.

"You can get the Janitor to let you in . . . Scout?"

"Hm?"

"Nothing."

Jem hadn't started that in a long time. I wondered what he was thinking. He'd tell me when he wanted to, probably when we got home. I felt his fingers press the top of my costume, too hard, it seemed. I shook my head. "Jem, you don't hafta—"

"Hush a minute, Scout," he said, pinching me.

We walked along silently. "Minute's up," I said. "Whatcha thinkin' about?" I turned to look at him, but his outline was barely visible.

"Thought I heard something," he said. "Stop a minute."

We stopped.

"Hear anything?" he asked.

"No."

We had not gone five paces before he made me stop again.

"Jem, are you tryin' to scare me? You know I'm too old—"

"Be quiet," he said, and I knew he was not joking.

The night was still. I could hear his breath coming easily beside me. Occasionally there was a sudden breeze that hit my bare legs, but it was all that remained of a promised windy night. This was the stillness before a thunderstorm. We listened.

"Heard an old dog just then," I said.

"It's not that," Jem answered. "I hear it when we're walkin' along, but when we stop I don't hear it."

"You hear my costume rustlin'. Aw, it's just Halloween got you. . . ."

I said it more to convince myself than Jem, for sure enough, as we began walking, I heard what he was talking about. It was not my costume.

"It's just old Cecil," said Jem presently. "He won't get us again. Let's don't let him think we're hurrying."

We slowed to a crawl. I asked Jem how Cecil could follow us in this dark, looked to me like he'd bump into us from behind.

"I can see you, Scout," Jem said.

"How? I can't see you."

"Your fat streaks are showin'. Mrs. Crenshaw painted 'em with some of that shiny stuff so they'd show up under the footlights. I can see you pretty well, an' I expect Cecil can see you well enough to keep his distance."

I would show Cecil that we knew he was behind us and we were ready for him. "Cecil Jacobs is a big wet he-en!" I yelled suddenly, turning around.

We stopped. There was no acknowledgement save he-en bouncing off the distant schoolhouse wall.

"I'll get him," said Jem. *"He-y!"*

Hay-e-hay-e-hay-ey, answered the schoolhouse wall. It was unlike Cecil to hold out for so long; once he pulled a joke he'd repeat it time and again. We should have been leapt at already. Jem signaled for me to stop again.

He said softly, "Scout, can you take that thing off?"

"I think so, but I ain't got anything on under it much."

"I've got your dress here."

"I can't get it on in the dark."

"Okay," he said, "never mind."

"Jem, are you afraid?"

"No. Think we're almost to the tree now. Few yards from that, an' we'll be to the road. We can see the street light then." Jem was talking in an unhurried, flat toneless voice. I wondered how long he would try to keep the Cecil myth going.

"You reckon we oughta sing, Jem?"

"No. Be real quiet again, Scout."

We had not increased our pace. Jem knew as well as I that it was difficult to walk fast without stumping a toe, tripping on stones, and other inconveniences, and I was barefooted. Maybe it was the wind rustling the trees. But there wasn't any wind and there weren't any trees except the big oak.

Our company shuffled and dragged his feet, as if wearing heavy shoes. Whoever it was wore thick cotton pants; what I thought were trees rustling was the soft swish of cotton on cotton, wheek, wheek, with every step.

I felt the sand go cold under my feet and I knew we were near the big oak. Jem pressed my head. We stopped and listened.

Shuffle-foot had not stopped with us this time. His trousers swished softly and steadily. Then they stopped. He was running, running toward us with no child's steps.

"Run, Scout! Run! Run!" Jem screamed.

I took one giant step and found myself reeling: my arms useless, in the dark, I could not keep my balance.

"Jem, Jem, help me, Jem!"

Something crushed the chicken wire around me. Metal ripped on metal and I fell to the ground and rolled as far as I could, floundering to escape my wire prison. From somewhere near by came scuffling, kicking sounds, sounds of shoes and flesh scraping dirt and roots. Someone rolled against me and I felt Jem. He was up like lightning and pulling me with him but, though my head and shoulders were free, I was so entangled we didn't get very far.

We were nearly to the road when I felt Jem's hand leave me, felt him jerk backwards to the ground. More scuffling, and there came a dull crunching sound and Jem screamed.

I ran in the direction of Jem's scream and sank into a flabby male stomach. Its owner said, "Uff!" and tried to catch my arms, but they were tightly pinioned. His stomach was soft but his arms were like steel. He slowly squeezed the breath out of me. I could not move. Suddenly he was jerked backwards and flung on the ground, almost carrying me with him. I thought, Jem's up.

One's mind works very slowly at times. Stunned, I stood there dumbly. The scuffling noises were dying; someone wheezed and the night was still again.

Still but for a man breathing heavily, breathing heavily and staggering. I thought he went to the tree and leaned against it. He coughed violently, a sobbing, bone-shaking cough.

"Jem?"

There was no answer but the man's heavy breathing.

"Jem?"

Jem didn't answer.

The man began moving around, as if searching for something. I heard him groan and pull something heavy along the ground. It was slowly coming to me that there were now four people under the tree.

"Atticus . . . ?"

The man was walking heavily and unsteadily toward the road.

I went to where I thought he had been and felt frantically along the ground, reaching out with my toes. Presently I touched someone.

"Jem?"

My toes touched trousers, a belt buckle, buttons, something I could not identify, a collar, and a face. A prickly stubble on the face told me it was not Jem's. I smelled stale whiskey.

I made my way along in what I thought was the direction of the road. I was not sure, because I had been turned around so many times. But I found it and looked down to the street light. A man was passing under it.

The man was walking with the staccato steps of someone carrying a load too heavy for him. He was going around the corner. He was carrying Jem. Jem's arm was dangling crazily in front of him.

By the time I reached the corner the man was crossing our front yard. Light from our front door framed Atticus for an instant; he ran down the steps, and together, he and the man took Jem inside.

I was at the front door when they were going down the hall. Aunt Alexandra was running to meet me. "Call Dr. Reynolds!" Atticus's voice came sharply from Jem's room. "Where's Scout?"

"Here she is," Aunt Alexandra called, pulling me along with her to the telephone. She tugged at me anxiously. "I'm all right, Aunty," I said, "you better call."

She pulled the receiver from the hook and said, "Eula May, get Dr. Reynolds, quick!"

"Agnes, is your father home? Oh God, where is he? Please tell him to come over here as soon as he comes in. Please, it's urgent!"

There was no need for Aunt Alexandra to identify herself; people in Maycomb knew each other's voices.

Atticus came out of Jem's room. The moment Aunt Alexandra broke the connection, Atticus took the receiver from her. He rattled the hook, then said, "Eula May, get me the sheriff, please."

"Heck? Atticus Finch. Someone's been after my children. Jem's hurt. Between here and the schoolhouse. I can't leave my boy. Run out there for me, please, and see if he's still around. Doubt if you'll find him now, but I'd like to see him if you do. Got to go now. Thanks, Heck."

"Atticus, is Jem dead?"

"No, Scout. Look after her, sister," he called, as he went down the hall.

Aunt Alexandra's fingers trembled as she unwound the crushed fabric and wire from around me. "Are you all right, darling?" she asked over and over as she worked me free.

It was a relief to be out. My arms were beginning to tingle, and they were red with small hexagonal marks. I rubbed them, and they felt better.

"Aunty, is Jem dead?"

"No—no, darling, he's unconscious. We won't know how badly he's hurt until Dr. Reynolds gets here. Jean Louise, what happened?"

"I don't know."

She left it at that. She brought me something to put on, and had I thought about it then, I would have never let her forget it: in her distraction, Aunty brought me my overalls. "Put these on, darling," she said, handing me the garments she most despised.

She rushed back to Jem's room, then came to me in the hall. She patted me vaguely, and went back to Jem's room.

A car stopped in front of the house. I knew Dr. Reynolds's step almost as well as my father's. He had brought Jem and me into the world, had led us through every childhood disease known to man including the time Jem fell out of the treehouse, and he had never lost our friendship. Dr. Reynolds said if we had been boil-prone things would have been different, but we doubted it.

He came in the door and said, "Good Lord." He walked toward me, said, "You're still standing," and changed his course. He knew every room in the house. He also knew that if I was in bad shape, so was Jem.

After ten forevers Dr. Reynolds returned. "Is Jem dead?" I asked.

"Far from it," he said, squatting down to me. "He's got a bump on the head just like yours, and a broken arm. Scout, look that way—no, don't turn your head, roll your eyes. Now look over yonder. He's got a bad break, so far as I can tell now it's in the elbow. Like somebody tried to wring his arm off . . . now look at me."

"Then he's not dead?"

"No-o!" Dr. Reynolds got to his feet. "We can't do much tonight," he said, "except try to make him as comfortable as we can. We'll have to X-ray his arm—looks like he'll be wearing his arm 'way out by his side for a while. Don't worry, though, he'll be as good as new. Boys his age bounce."

While he was talking, Dr. Reynolds had been looking keenly at me, lightly fingering the bump that was coming on my forehead. "You don't feel broke anywhere, do you?"

Dr. Reynolds's small joke made me smile. "Then you don't think he's dead, then?"

He put on his hat. "Now I may be wrong, of course, but I think he's very alive. Shows all the symptoms of it. Go have a look at him, and when I come back we'll get together and decide."

Dr. Reynolds's step was young and brisk. Mr. Heck Tate's was not. His heavy boots punished the porch and he opened the door awkwardly, but he said the same thing Dr. Reynolds said when he came in. "You all right, Scout?" he added.

"Yes sir, I'm goin' in to see Jem. Atticus'n'them's in there."

"I'll go with you," said Mr. Tate.

Aunt Alexandra had shaded Jem's reading light with a towel, and his room was dim. Jem was lying on his back. There was an ugly mark along one side of his face. His left arm lay out from his body; his elbow was bent slightly, but in the wrong direction. Jem was frowning.

"Jem . . . ?"

Atticus spoke. "He can't hear you, Scout, he's out like a light. He was coming around, but Dr. Reynolds put him out again."

"Yes sir." I retreated. Jem's room was large and square. Aunt Alexandra was sitting in a rocking-chair by the fireplace. The man who brought Jem in was standing in a corner, leaning against the wall. He was some countryman I did not know. He had probably been at the pageant, and was in the vicinity when it happened. He must have heard our screams and come running.

Atticus was standing by Jem's bed.

Mr. Heck Tate stood in the doorway. His hat was in his hand, and a flashlight bulged from his pants pocket. He was in his working clothes.

"Come in, Heck," said Atticus. "Did you find anything? I can't conceive of anyone low-down enough to do a thing like this, but I hope you found him."

Mr. Tate sniffed. He glanced sharply at the man in the corner, nodded to him, then looked around the room—at Jem, at Aunt Alexandra, then at Atticus.

"Sit down, Mr. Finch," he said pleasantly.

Atticus said, "Let's all sit down. Have that chair, Heck. I'll get another one from the livingroom."

Mr. Tate sat in Jem's desk chair. He waited until Atticus returned and settled himself. I wondered why

Atticus had not brought a chair for the man in the corner, but Atticus knew the ways of country people far better than I. Some of his rural clients would park their long-eared steeds under the chinaberry trees in the back yard, and Atticus would often keep appointments on the back steps. This one was probably more comfortable where he was.

"Mr. Finch," said Mr. Tate, "tell you what I found. I found a little girl's dress—it's out there in my car. That your dress, Scout?"

"Yes sir, if it's a pink one with smockin'," I said. Mr. Tate was behaving as if he were on the witness stand. He liked to tell things his own way, untrammeled by state or defense, and sometimes it took him a while.

"I found some funny-looking pieces of muddy-colored cloth—"

"That's m'costume, Mr. Tate."

Mr. Tate ran his hands down his thighs. He rubbed his left arm and investigated Jem's mantelpiece, then he seemed to be interested in the fireplace. His fingers sought his long nose.

"What is it, Heck?" said Atticus.

Mr. Tate found his neck and rubbed it. "Bob Ewell's lyin' on the ground under that tree down yonder with a kitchen knife stuck up under his ribs. He's dead, Mr. Finch."

29.

Aunt Alexandra got up and reached for the mantelpiece. Mr. Tate rose, but she declined assistance. For once in his life, Atticus's instinctive courtesy failed him: he sat where he was.

Somehow, I could think of nothing but Mr. Bob Ewell saying he'd get Atticus if it took him the rest of his life. Mr. Ewell almost got him, and it was the last thing he did.

"Are you sure?" Atticus said bleakly.

"He's dead all right," said Mr. Tate. "He's good and dead. He won't hurt these children again."

"I didn't mean that." Atticus seemed to be talking in his sleep. His age was beginning to show, his one sign of inner turmoil: the strong line of his jaw melted a little, one became aware of telltale creases forming under his ears, one noticed not his jet-black hair but the gray patches growing at his temples.

"Hadn't we better go to the livingroom?" Aunt Alexandra said at last.

"If you don't mind," said Mr. Tate, "I'd rather us stay in here if it won't hurt Jem any. I want to have a look at his injuries while Scout . . . tells us about it."

"Is it all right if I leave?" she asked. "I'm just one person too many in here. I'll be in my room if you want me, Atticus." Aunt Alexandra went to the door, but she stopped and turned. "Atticus, I had a feeling about this tonight—I—this is my fault," she began. "I should have—"

Mr. Tate held up his hand. "You go ahead, Miss Alexandra, I know it's been a shock to you. And don't you fret yourself about anything—why, if we followed our feelings all the time we'd be like cats chasin' their tails. Miss Scout, see if you can tell us what happened, while it's still fresh in your mind. You think you can? Did you see him following you?"

I went to Atticus and felt his arms go around me. I buried my head in his lap. "We started home. I said Jem, I've forgot m'shoes. Soon's we started back for 'em the lights went out. Jem said I could get 'em tomorrow. . . ."

"Scout, raise up so Mr. Tate can hear you," Atticus said. I crawled into his lap.

"Then Jem said hush a minute. I thought he was thinkin'—he always wants you to hush so he can think—then he said he heard somethin'. We thought it was Cecil."

"Cecil?"

"Cecil Jacobs. He scared us once tonight, an' we thought it was him again. He had on a sheet. They gave a quarter for the best costume, I don't know who won it—"

"Where were you when you thought it was Cecil?"

"Just a little piece from the schoolhouse. I yelled somethin' at him—"

"You yelled, what?"

"Cecil Jacobs is a big fat hen, I think. We didn't hear nothin'—then Jem yelled hello or somethin' loud enough to wake the dead—"

"Just a minute, Scout," said Mr. Tate. "Mr. Finch, did you hear them?"

Atticus said he didn't. He had the radio on. Aunt Alexandra had hers going in her bedroom. He remembered because she told him to turn his down a bit so she could hear hers. Atticus smiled. "I always play a radio too loud."

"I wonder if the neighbors heard anything. . . ." said Mr. Tate.

"I doubt it, Heck. Most of them listen to their radios or go to bed with the chickens. Maudie Atkinson may have been up, but I doubt it."

"Go ahead, Scout," Mr. Tate said.

"Well, after Jem yelled we walked on. Mr. Tate, I was shut up in my costume but I could hear it myself, then. Footsteps, I mean. They walked when we walked and stopped when we stopped. Jem said he could see me because Mrs. Crenshaw put some kind of shiny paint on my costume. I was a ham."

"How's that?" asked Mr. Tate, startled.

Atticus described my role to Mr. Tate, plus the construction of my garment. "You should have seen her when she came in," he said, "it was crushed to a pulp."

Mr. Tate rubbed his chin. "I wondered why he had those marks on him. His sleeves were perforated with little holes. There were one or two little puncture marks on his arms to match the holes. Let me see that thing if you will, sir."

Atticus fetched the remains of my costume. Mr. Tate turned it over and bent it around to get an idea of its former shape. "This thing probably saved her life," he said. "Look."

He pointed with a long forefinger. A shiny clean line stood out on the dull wire. "Bob Ewell meant business," Mr. Tate muttered.

"He was out of his mind," said Atticus.

"Don't like to contradict you, Mr. Finch—wasn't

crazy, mean as hell. Low-down skunk with enough liquor in him to make him brave enough to kill children. He'd never have met you face to face."

Atticus shook his head. "I can't conceive of a man who'd—"

"Mr. Finch, there's just some kind of men you have to shoot before you can say hidy to 'em. Even then, they ain't worth the bullet it takes to shoot 'em. Ewell 'as one of 'em."

Atticus said, "I thought he got it all out of him the day he threatened me. Even if he hadn't, I thought he'd come after me."

"He had guts enough to pester a poor colored woman, he had guts enough to pester Judge Taylor when he thought the house was empty, so do you think he'da met you to your face in daylight?" Mr. Tate sighed. "We'd better get on. Scout, you heard him behind you—"

"Yes sir. When we got under the tree—"

"How'd you know you were under the tree, you couldn't see thunder out there."

"I was barefooted, and Jem says the ground's always cooler under a tree."

"We'll have to make him a deputy, go ahead."

"Then all of a sudden somethin' grabbed me an' mashed my costume . . . think I ducked on the ground . . . heard a tusslin' under the tree sort of . . . they were bammin' against the trunk, sounded like. Jem found me and started pullin' me toward the road. Some —Mr. Ewell yanked him down, I reckon. They tussled some more and then there was this funny noise—Jem hollered . . ." I stopped. That was Jem's arm.

"Anyway, Jem hollered and I didn't hear him any more an' the next thing—Mr. Ewell was tryin' to squeeze me to death, I reckon . . . then somebody yanked Mr. Ewell down. Jem must have got up, I guess. That's all I know . . ."

"And then?" Mr. Tate was looking at me sharply.

"Somebody was staggerin' around and pantin' and— coughing fit to die. I thought it was Jem at first, but it didn't sound like him, so I went lookin' for Jem on the ground. I thought Atticus had come to help us and had got wore out—"

"Who was it?"

"Why there he is, Mr. Tate, he can tell you his name."

As I said it, I half pointed to the man in the corner, but brought my arm down quickly lest Atticus reprimand me for pointing. It was impolite to point.

He was still leaning against the wall. He had been leaning against the wall when I came into the room, his arms folded across his chest. As I pointed he brought his arms down and pressed the palms of his hands against the wall. They were white hands, sickly white hands that had never seen the sun, so white they stood out garishly against the dull cream wall in the dim light of Jem's room.

I looked from his hands to his sand-stained khaki pants; my eyes traveled up his thin frame to his torn denim shirt. His face was as white as his hands, but for a shadow on his jutting chin. His cheeks were thin to hollowness; his mouth was wide; there were shallow, almost delicate indentations at his temples, and his gray eyes were so colorless I thought he was blind. His hair was dead and thin, almost feathery on top of his head.

When I pointed to him his palms slipped slightly, leaving greasy sweat streaks on the wall, and he hooked his thumbs in his belt. A strange small spasm shook him, as if he heard fingernails scrape slate, but as I gazed at him in wonder the tension slowly drained from his face. His lips parted into a timid smile, and our neighbor's image blurred with my sudden tears.

"Hey, Boo," I said.

30.

Mr. Arthur, honey," said Atticus, gently correcting me. "Jean Louise, this is Mr. Arthur Radley. I believe he already knows you."

If Atticus could blandly introduce me to Boo Radley at a time like this, well—that was Atticus.

Boo saw me run instinctively to the bed where Jem was sleeping, for the same shy smile crept across his face.

Hot with embarrassment, I tried to cover up by covering Jem up.

"Ah-ah, don't touch him," Atticus said.

Mr. Heck Tate sat looking intently at Boo through his horn-rimmed glasses. He was about to speak when Dr. Reynolds came down the hall.

"Everybody out," he said, as he came in the door. "Evenin', Arthur, didn't notice you the first time I was here."

Dr. Reynolds's voice was as breezy as his step, as though he had said it every evening of his life, an announcement that astounded me even more than being in the same room with Boo Radley. Of course . . . even Boo Radley got sick sometimes, I thought. But on the other hand I wasn't sure.

Dr. Reynolds was carrying a big package wrapped in newspaper. He put it down on Jem's desk and took off his coat. "You're quite satisfied he's alive, now? Tell you how I knew. When I tried to examine him he kicked me. Had to put him out good and proper to touch him. So scat," he said to me.

"Er—" said Atticus, glancing at Boo. "Heck, let's go out on the front porch. There are plenty of chairs out there, and it's still warm enough."

I wondered why Atticus was inviting us to the front porch instead of the livingroom, then I understood. The livingroom lights were awfully strong.

We filed out, first Mr. Tate—Atticus was waiting at the door for him to go ahead of him. Then he changed his mind and followed Mr. Tate.

People have a habit of doing everyday things even under the oddest conditions. I was no exception: "Come along, Mr. Arthur," I heard myself saying, "you don't know the house real well. I'll just take you to the porch, sir."

He looked down at me and nodded.

I led him through the hall and past the livingroom.

"Won't you have a seat, Mr. Arthur? This rocking-chair's nice and comfortable."

My small fantasy about him was alive again: he would be sitting on the porch . . . right pretty spell we're having, isn't it, Mr. Arthur?

Yes, a right pretty spell. Feeling slightly unreal, I led

him to the chair farthest from Atticus and Mr. Tate. It was in deep shadow. Boo would feel more comfortable in the dark.

Atticus was sitting in the swing, and Mr. Tate was in a chair next to him. The light from the livingroom windows was strong on them. I sat beside Boo.

"Well, Heck," Atticus was saying, "I guess the thing to do—good Lord, I'm losing my memory . . ." Atticus pushed up his glasses and pressed his fingers to his eyes. "Jem's not quite thirteen . . . no, he's already thirteen —I can't remember. Anyway, it'll come before county court—"

"What will, Mr. Finch?" Mr. Tate uncrossed his legs and leaned forward.

"Of course it was clear-cut self defense, but I'll have to go to the office and hunt up—"

"Mr. Finch, do you think Jem killed Bob Ewell? Do you think that?"

"You heard what Scout said, there's no doubt about it. She said Jem got up and yanked him off her—he probably got hold of Ewell's knife somehow in the dark . . . we'll find out tomorrow."

"Mis-ter Finch, hold on," said Mr. Tate. "Jem never stabbed Bob Ewell."

Atticus was silent for a moment. He looked at Mr. Tate as if he appreciated what he said. But Atticus shook his head.

"Heck, it's mighty kind of you and I know you're doing it from that good heart of yours, but don't start anything like that."

Mr. Tate got up and went to the edge of the porch. He spat into the shrubbery, then thrust his hands into his hip pockets and faced Atticus. "Like what?" he said.

"I'm sorry if I spoke sharply, Heck," Atticus said simply, "but nobody's hushing this up. I don't live that way."

"Nobody's gonna hush anything up, Mr. Finch."

Mr. Tate's voice was quiet, but his boots were planted so solidly on the porch floorboards it seemed that they grew there. A curious contest, the nature of which eluded me, was developing between my father and the sheriff.

It was Atticus's turn to get up and go to the edge of the porch. He said, "H'rm," and spat dryly into the yard.

He put his hands in his pockets and faced Mr. Tate.

"Heck, you haven't said it, but I know what you're thinking. Thank you for it. Jean Louise—" he turned to me. "You said Jem yanked Mr. Ewell off you?"

"Yes sir, that's what I thought . . . I—"

"See there, Heck? Thank you from the bottom of my heart, but I don't want my boy starting out with something like this over his head. Best way to clear the air is to have it all out in the open. Let the county come and bring sandwiches. I don't want him growing up with a whisper about him, I don't want anybody saying, 'Jem Finch . . . his daddy paid a mint to get him out of that.' Sooner we get this over with the better."

"Mr. Finch," Mr. Tate said stolidly, "Bob Ewell fell on his knife. He killed himself."

Atticus walked to the corner of the porch. He looked at the wisteria vine. In his own way, I thought, each was as stubborn as the other. I wondered who would give in first. Atticus's stubbornness was quiet and rarely evident, but in some ways he was as set as the Cunninghams. Mr. Tate's was unschooled and blunt, but it was equal to my father's.

"Heck," Atticus's back was turned. "If this thing's hushed up it'll be a simple denial to Jem of the way I've tried to raise him. Sometimes I think I'm a total failure as a parent, but I'm all they've got. Before Jem looks at anyone else he looks at me, and I've tried to live so I can look squarely back at him . . . if I connived at something like this, frankly I couldn't meet his eye, and the day I can't do that I'll know I've lost him. I don't want to lose him and Scout, because they're all I've got."

"Mr. Finch." Mr. Tate was still planted to the floorboards. "Bob Ewell fell on his knife. I can prove it."

Atticus wheeled around. His hands dug into his pockets. "Heck, can't you even try to see it my way? You've got children of your own, but I'm older than you. When mine are grown I'll be an old man if I'm still around, but right now I'm—if they don't trust me they won't trust anybody. Jem and Scout know what happened. If they hear of me saying down town something different happened—Heck, I won't have them any more. I can't live one way in town and another way in my home."

Mr. Tate rocked on his heels and said patiently, "He'd flung Jem down, he stumbled over a root under that tree and—look, I can show you."

Mr. Tate reached in his side pocket and withdrew a long switchblade knife. As he did so, Dr. Reynolds came to the door. "The son—deceased's under that tree, doctor, just inside the schoolyard. Got a flashlight? Better have this one."

"I can ease around and turn my car lights on," said Dr. Reynolds, but he took Mr. Tate's flashlight. "Jem's all right. He won't wake up tonight, I hope, so don't worry. That the knife that killed him, Heck?"

"No sir, still in him. Looked like a kitchen knife from the handle. Ken oughta be there with the hearse by now, doctor, 'night."

Mr. Tate flicked open the knife. "It was like this," he said. He held the knife and pretended to stumble; as he leaned forward his left arm went down in front of him. "See there? Stabbed himself through that soft stuff between his ribs. His whole weight drove it in."

Mr. Tate closed the knife and jammed it back in his pocket. "Scout is eight years old," he said. "She was too scared to know exactly what went on."

"You'd be surprised," Atticus said grimly.

"I'm not sayin' she made it up, I'm sayin' she was too scared to know exactly what happened. It was mighty dark out there, black as ink. 'd take somebody mighty used to the dark to make a competent witness . . ."

"I won't have it," Atticus said softly.

"God damn it, I'm not thinking of Jem!"

Mr. Tate's boot hit the floorboards so hard the lights in Miss Maudie's bedroom went on. Miss Stephanie Crawford's lights went on. Atticus and Mr. Tate looked across the street, then at each other. They waited.

When Mr. Tate spoke again his voice was barely audible. "Mr. Finch, I hate to fight you when you're like this. You've been under a strain tonight no man should ever have to go through. Why you ain't in the bed from it I don't know, but I do know that for once you haven't been able to put two and two together, and we've got to settle this tonight because tomorrow'll be too late. Bob Ewell's got a kitchen knife in his craw."

Mr. Tate added that Atticus wasn't going to stand

277

there and maintain that any boy Jem's size with a busted arm had fight enough left in him to tackle and kill a grown man in the pitch dark.

"Heck," said Atticus abruptly, "that was a switch-blade you were waving. Where'd you get it?"

"Took it off a drunk man," Mr. Tate answered coolly.

I was trying to remember. Mr. Ewell was on me . . . then he went down. . . . Jem must have gotten up. At least I thought . . .

"Heck?"

"I said I took it off a drunk man downtown tonight. Ewell probably found that kitchen knife in the dump somewhere. Honed it down and bided his time . . . just bided his time."

Atticus made his way to the swing and sat down. His hands dangled limply between his knees. He was looking at the floor. He had moved with the same slowness that night in front of the jail, when I thought it took him forever to fold his newspaper and toss it in his chair.

Mr. Tate clumped softly around the porch. "It ain't your decision, Mr. Finch, it's all mine. It's my decision and my responsibility. For once, if you don't see it my way, there's not much you can do about it. If you wanta try, I'll call you a liar to your face. Your boy never stabbed Bob Ewell," he said slowly, "didn't come near a mile of it and now you know it. All he wanted to do was get him and his sister safely home."

Mr. Tate stopped pacing. He stopped in front of Atticus, and his back was to us. "I'm not a very good man, sir, but I am sheriff of Maycomb County. Lived in this town all my life an' I'm goin' on forty-three years old. Know everything that's happened here since before I was born. There's a black boy dead for no reason, and the man responsible for it's dead. Let the dead bury the dead this time, Mr. Finch. Let the dead bury the dead."

Mr. Tate went to the swing and picked up his hat. It was lying beside Atticus. Mr. Tate pushed back his hair and put his hat on.

"I never heard tell that it's against the law for a citizen to do his utmost to prevent a crime from being committed, which is exactly what he did, but maybe you'll say it's my duty to tell the town all about it and not hush it up. Know what'd happen then? All the ladies in Maycomb includin' my wife'd be knocking on his door bringing angel food cakes. To my way of thinkin', Mr. Finch, taking the one man who's done you and this town a great service an' draggin' him with his shy ways into the limelight—to me, that's a sin. It's a sin and I'm not about to have it on my head. If it was any other man it'd be different. But not this man, Mr. Finch."

Mr. Tate was trying to dig a hole in the floor with the toe of his boot. He pulled his nose, then he massaged his left arm. "I may not be much, Mr. Finch, but I'm still sheriff of Maycomb County and Bob Ewell fell on his knife. Good night, sir."

Mr. Tate stamped off the porch and strode across the front yard. His car door slammed and he drove away.

Atticus sat looking at the floor for a long time. Finally he raised his head. "Scout," he said, "Mr. Ewell fell on his knife. Can you possibly understand?"

Atticus looked like he needed cheering up. I ran to him and hugged him and kissed him with all my might. "Yes sir, I understand," I reassured him. "Mr. Tate was right."

Atticus disengaged himself and looked at me. "What do you mean?"

"Well, it'd be sort of like shootin' a mockingbird, wouldn't it?"

Atticus put his face in my hair and rubbed it. When he got up and walked across the porch into the shadows, his youthful step had returned. Before he went inside the house, he stopped in front of Boo Radley. "Thank you for my children, Arthur," he said.

31.

When Boo Radley shuffled to his feet, light from the livingroom windows glistened on his forehead. Every move he made was uncertain, as if he were not sure his hands and feet could make proper contact with the things he touched. He coughed his dreadful raling cough, and was so shaken he had to sit down again. His hand searched for his hip pocket, and he pulled out a handkerchief. He coughed into it, then he wiped his forehead.

Having been so accustomed to his absence, I found it incredible that he had been sitting beside me all this time, present. He had not made a sound.

Once more, he got to his feet. He turned to me and nodded toward the front door.

"You'd like to say good night to Jem, wouldn't you, Mr. Arthur? Come right in."

I led him down the hall. Aunt Alexandra was sitting by Jem's bed. "Come in, Arthur," she said. "He's still asleep. Dr. Reynolds gave him a heavy sedative. Jean Louise, is your father in the livingroom?"

"Yes ma'am, I think so."

"I'll just go speak to him a minute. Dr. Reynolds left some . . ." her voice trailed away.

Boo had drifted to a corner of the room, where he stood with his chin up, peering from a distance at Jem. I took him by the hand, a hand surprisingly warm for its whiteness. I tugged him a little, and he allowed me to lead him to Jem's bed.

Dr. Reynolds had made a tent-like arrangement over Jem's arm, to keep the cover off, I guess, and Boo leaned forward and looked over it. An expression of timid curiosity was on his face, as though he had never seen a boy before. His mouth was slightly open, and he looked at Jem from head to foot. Boo's hand came up, but he let it drop to his side.

"You can pet him, Mr. Arthur, he's asleep. You couldn't if he was awake, though, he wouldn't let you . . ." I found myself explaining. "Go ahead."

Boo's hand hovered over Jem's head.

"Go on, sir, he's asleep."

His hand came down lightly on Jem's hair.

I was beginning to learn his body English. His hand tightened on mine and he indicated that he wanted to leave.

I led him to the front porch, where his uneasy steps halted. He was still holding my hand and he gave no sign of letting me go.

"Will you take me home?"

He almost whispered it, in the voice of a child afraid of the dark.

I put my foot on the top step and stopped. I would lead him through our house, but I would never lead him home.

"Mr. Arthur, bend your arm down here, like that. That's right, sir."

I slipped my hand into the crook of his arm.

He had to stoop a little to accommodate me, but if Miss Stephanie Crawford was watching from her upstairs window, she would see Arthur Radley escorting me down the sidewalk, as any gentleman would do.

We came to the street light on the corner, and I wondered how many times Dill had stood there hugging the fat pole, watching, waiting, hoping. I wondered how many times Jem and I had made this journey, but I entered the Radley front gate for the second time in my life. Boo and I walked up the steps to the porch. His fingers found the front doorknob. He gently released my hand, opened the door, went inside, and shut the door behind him. I never saw him again.

Neighbors bring food with death and flowers with sickness and little things in between. Boo was our neighbor. He gave us two soap dolls, a broken watch and chain, a pair of good-luck pennies, and our lives. But neighbors give in return. We never put back into the tree what we took out of it: we had given him nothing, and it made me sad.

I turned to go home. Street lights winked down the street all the way to town. I had never seen our neighborhood from this angle. There were Miss Maudie's, Miss Stephanie's—there was our house, I could see the porch swing—Miss Rachel's house was beyond us, plainly visible. I could even see Mrs. Dubose's.

I looked behind me. To the left of the brown door was a long shuttered window. I walked to it, stood in front of it, and turned around. In daylight, I thought, you could see to the postoffice corner.

Daylight . . . in my mind, the night faded. It was daytime and the neighborhood was busy. Miss Stephanie Crawford crossed the street to tell the latest to Miss Rachel. Miss Maudie bent over her azaleas. It was summertime, and two children scampered down the sidewalk toward a man approaching in the distance. The man waved, and the children raced each other to him.

It was still summertime, and the children came closer. A boy trudged down the sidewalk dragging a fishing-pole behind him. A man stood waiting with his hands on his hips. Summertime, and his children played in the front yard with their friend, enacting a strange little drama of their own invention.

It was fall, and his children fought on the sidewalk in front of Mrs. Dubose's. The boy helped his sister to her feet, and they made their way home. Fall, and his children trotted to and fro around the corner, the day's woes and triumphs on their faces. They stopped at an oak tree, delighted, puzzled, apprehensive.

Winter, and his children shivered at the front gate, silhouetted against a blazing house. Winter, and a man walked into the street, dropped his glasses, and shot a dog.

Summer, and he watched his children's heart break. Autumn again, and Boo's children needed him.

Atticus was right. One time he said you never really know a man until you stand in his shoes and walk around in them. Just standing on the Radley porch was enough.

The street lights were fuzzy from the fine rain that was falling. As I made my way home, I felt very old, but when I looked at the tip of my nose I could see fine misty beads, but looking cross-eyed made me dizzy so I quit. As I made my way home, I thought what a thing to tell Jem tomorrow. He'd be so mad he missed it he wouldn't speak to me for days. As I made my way home, I thought Jem and I would get grown but there wasn't much else left for us to learn, except possibly algebra.

I ran up the steps and into the house. Aunt Alexandra had gone to bed, and Atticus's room was dark. I would see if Jem might be reviving. Atticus was in Jem's room, sitting by his bed. He was reading a book.

"Is Jem awake yet?"

"Sleeping peacefully. He won't be awake until morning."

"Oh. Are you sittin' up with him?"

"Just for an hour or so. Go to bed, Scout. You've had a long day."

"Well, I think I'll stay with you for a while."

"Suit yourself," said Atticus. It must have been after midnight, and I was puzzled by his amiable acquiescence. He was shrewder than I, however: the moment I sat down I began to feel sleepy.

"Whatcha readin'?" I asked.

Atticus turned the book over. "Something of Jem's. Called *The Gray Ghost.*"

I was suddenly awake. "Why'd you get that one?"

"Honey, I don't know. Just picked it up. One of the few things I haven't read," he said pointedly.

"Read it out loud, please, Atticus. It's real scary."

"No," he said. "You've had enough scaring for a while. This is too—"

"Atticus, I wasn't scared."

He raised his eyebrows, and I protested: "Leastways not till I started telling Mr. Tate about it. Jem wasn't scared. Asked him and he said he wasn't. Besides, nothin's real scary except in books."

Atticus opened his mouth to say something, but shut it again. He took his thumb from the middle of the book and turned back to the first page. I moved over and leaned my head against his knee. "H'rm," he said. "*The Gray Ghost,* by Seckatary Hawkins. Chapter One . . ."

I willed myself to stay awake, but the rain was so soft and the room was so warm and his voice was so deep and his knee was so snug that I slept.

Seconds later, it seemed, his shoe was gently nudging my ribs. He lifted me to my feet and walked me to my room. "Heard every word you said," I muttered. ". . . wasn't sleep at all, 's about a ship an' Three-Fingered Fred 'n' Stoner's Boy. . . ."

He unhooked my overalls, leaned me against him, and pulled them off. He held me up with one hand and reached for my pajamas with the other.

"Yeah, an' they all thought it was Stoner's Boy messin' up their clubhouse an' throwin' ink all over it an' . . ."

He guided me to the bed and sat me down. He lifted my legs and put me under the cover.

"An' they chased him 'n' never could catch him 'cause they didn't know what he looked like, an' Atticus, when

283

they finally saw him, why he hadn't done any of those things . . . Atticus, he was real nice. . . ."

His hands were under my chin, pulling up the cover, tucking it around me.

"Most people are, Scout, when you finally see them."

He turned out the light and went into Jem's room. He would be there all night, and he would be there when Jem waked up in the morning.